Haunted Illusions

Deborah J Hughes

Chapter 1

When my cell phone rang, a cold shiver raced along my spine, giving me a clear sign this was no ordinary call. Under usual circumstances I'd be intrigued, even eager to answer, but not today. Not now. Though my spirit was certainly willing, the timing couldn't be worse.

With just two weeks left in my pregnancy—maybe less, if the signs were anything to go by—my reasonable side told me not to get involved in anything unrelated to the baby. But another voice argued that if spirit was calling then I needed to answer it, and with that sentiment echoing in my mind, I answered the call. "Hello?"

"Hi, Tess! How are you doing?"

The cheerful voice sounded familiar, and as I was trying to place it, she solved the mystery for me.

"This is Janice, we met at Barb's a couple weeks ago during her séance. Do you remember?"

"Yes, of course. Hello, Janice." She'd spoken to me about a situation she was having, and I had told her to call if she needed help with it. I meant it when I told her that, but I didn't think she'd be calling so soon. Not with me about to have my baby.

As if on cue, a piercing pain began in my lower back, spreading to my abdomen and tightening my skin to uncomfortable proportions. After sucking in a gasp of surprise, I began the breathing techniques taught to me in Lamaze class. These Braxton Hicks contractions were becoming more frequent, even sending us to the hospital at one point because we thought it was time. Only it wasn't, and so now I knew to wait until the contractions came at regular intervals, and they lasted longer than a few seconds.

"I hate calling you this soon after our discussion, I know you are about to have your baby, but I promise it's nothing that would be taxing for you. And if you say no, then that's fine too. I will totally understand."

Her tone was apologetic, and I knew it was sincere. Given that, something recent must have occurred to have her call me. Though I was heartened by her reassurance that whatever she was about to ask wasn't anything taxing, and she would understand if I needed to refuse, I also knew I probably wouldn't do that. "It's fine, Janice. What's happened?"

Kade walked into the room and when he heard me say Janice's name, his expression hardened. He was going to be a problem if whatever she wanted from me was considered taxing by his definition, not hers.

"I have a buyer for the house. A cash buyer!" The excitement in her voice fell to a somber tone. "Before I can even think of accepting the offer, I need to know the house is okay. That it isn't, you know … haunted."

Janice told me at the séance that when her grandmother passed away a few months earlier, she'd left everything to her. Since she did not want her grandparents' house, she decided to sell it, after first using some of her inheritance to fund necessary renovations.

Not long after contractors began working on the house, however, they began reporting strange phenomena – noises, objects moving, and eerie feelings. The house, they claimed, was haunted. Janice couldn't shake the worry that it was her grandfather's spirit causing the disturbances. He never liked the house and insisted that it not be lived in once he and her

2

grandmother were gone. In fact, he'd even gone so far as to suggest that it be burned down! Such rambling, she believed, was a product of his Alzheimer's and since her grandmother, before her dementia advanced, had given her blessing for Janice to do whatever she felt best, she decided to go ahead with her plans to sell it. Only now she was worried her grandfather was upset with her for not carrying out his wishes.

"It's a nice property," Janice had insisted. "Too big and isolated for me, of course, and I told my grandparents back when they discussed signing everything over to me, that I didn't ever want to live there, which made grandpa really happy."

"They never said anything about it being haunted or having strange things happen there?" My initial feeling about it was that it could indeed be her grandfather causing the trouble, but I had to rule out there being a history of ghost activity first.

"No, never. My grandmother loved the house, and as I said, my grandfather hated it. I don't know why. As for it being haunted, I never felt anything like that. It's an old house, and ever since they moved out it makes me uncomfortable to be there, but that's because they aren't there anymore. As for the contractors, I don't know what to think, but they wouldn't stay once it started getting dark, and they have spread stories all over town that it's haunted."

It was her grandfather's feelings towards the house that had grabbed my interest, and I'd questioned her more about it. "I know you thought it was your grandfather's disease making him tell you to burn the house down, but did he have the same sentiment before he got sick?"

"Well sort of. He would joke about it sometimes and say he wished the old place would catch fire and burn down, and I know he tried to get grandma to sell it through the years, but she was adamant about staying there. It was a hard decision for her to move into the assisted living facility, but she couldn't take care of grandpa and herself and there was no one to stay at the house with them. I mean, I would have but I have a job and kids. I just couldn't do it."

It was then that I'd told her I'd try to help her out with it, though I was sure I'd implied that I wouldn't do so until after I'd had my baby.

"Tess?"

Janice jarred me from my thoughts, and I made an apologetic sound, but before I could speak, yet another pain pierced my lower back, wrapping around my abdomen and tightening hard enough that I sucked in a breath and let it out slowly. "Sorry, Janice, I am going through the Braxton Hicks pains and it's very distracting."

"Oh, I'm sorry! Are you sure you are not in labor?"

"I don't think so. I've been having these for a while, though not usually in my back, and they are not coming at regular intervals or lasting long enough to be concerned about." I saw Kade narrow his eyes as his gaze swept over me, and I waved a dismissive hand, letting him know he had nothing to be concerned about. "So how is it you have a buyer when you told me you weren't going to list it until the spring? I thought you wanted to wait until after I'd had a chance to check it out. Isn't it still being renovated?"

"They finished up a few days ago. As to how this buyer found out about it, I'm not sure, but you know how fast word gets out in a small town. It's not like I've been keeping it a secret. So anyways, this buyer asked me how much I wanted for it, and since I haven't discussed it other than casually with my realtor, I threw out a number we'd discussed on a best-case scenario, thinking it would be too high to interest him, and he said he had cash right now to purchase it!" She blew a small airy whistle.

4

"I wish I had that kind of money laying around ready to hand over just like that!"

A cash buyer offering an amount that had Janice all giddy was indeed a good reason to be calling me. "Are you sure your house isn't worth more than what you told him? It might be why he jumped on it so fast."

"I called my realtor, who happens to be a good friend of mine, and she said he was definitely buying over what she would expect the house to appraise at, and she said I should accept it before he changes his mind."

"Oh, good for you! So, what do you want me to do exactly?"

"If you could just go there … you don't even have to get out of your car … and tell me if you get any feelings about it being, you know, haunted. If you do, I will hold him off until you are okay to check into it a bit more. But if you don't get any weird feelings about it, I can at least entertain the idea of accepting his offer."

It was a reasonable, non-taxing request, and I saw no problem with it, despite those initial feelings that plagued me when she first called. Maybe anxiety caused it, what with me being super sensitive lately. "I can do that." Seeing that Kade was motioning for me to hold off, I again waved my hand to let him know it was fine.

Janice heaved a grateful sigh. "Thank you so much, Tess! I totally respect your gift, and I know, without any doubt, that if something is there, you will know. And if so, I will hold off selling it until all is well. I just hope it isn't grandpa."

Though I was more than willing to do this favor for her, I did get a sense that things were not going to go quite as well as she was hoping. But … what could go wrong? "I will go out there sometime this morning and get back with you later."

"That's great, Tess. Thank you so much. This really means a lot to me. I promise I will compensate you for your time."

"No, Janice, there's no compensation necessary. I am glad to do it as a favor to a friend."

After exchanging a few more pleasantries, I disconnected from the call then stood to face Kade, who was standing in front of the fireplace, feet planted slightly apart, arms folded, and an uncompromising look on his handsome face. "Before you start getting all worked up, I am just going to drive to the house, sit quietly in my car and see what I get. Then I will drive away, and that's the end of it."

"Nothing is ever that simple with you, Tess."

He had a point, but I'd already given my word. "It will take me no more than a half hour tops."

He threw up his hands in exasperation and gave me a look - one that said past experience contradicted my assumption on this matter. "When the spirit world is involved, things are always unpredictable, and you get pulled in so easily." He crossed over to me and gently placed a hand on my very rounded belly. "Our daughter is about to enter the world, and I don't want anything happening that might jeopardize that in any way." He kissed my temple, his lips lingering there as he spoke. "I just don't want you dealing with any stress."

After drawing far enough away to look at him, I placed both my hands over his and pressed them gently against me. "I promise I won't enter the house."

Kade stared into my eyes, and I stared right back, unblinking, letting him know he'd better be careful about questioning the validity of my promise.

6

After a few tense seconds, his unrelenting attitude softened, and he let out a sigh. "You won't even get out of the car?"

On that I hesitated. "Only if I feel the need to be out in the open to get a better feel for things." Again, I pressed my hands against his, giving reinforcement to my words. "But I will not, under any circumstances, enter the house." He couldn't come with me, and I knew that was his biggest concern. He didn't like me doing something without him being there to protect me.

"It's just an ice fishing derby, I don't need to go." The look in his eyes told me he was serious about rethinking his plans.

"Kade, really? I just told you … I am going to drive there on roads that are very clear, in weather that is equally clear, and I am not going to enter the house. Do you really want to cancel out on this fishing derby? I mean, you guys have been planning it for almost a month." The only reason he agreed to go was that the pond, where the derby was to be held, was not far from the hospital where we planned for our baby to be delivered. If I was to go into labor, then he'd be close enough to meet me at the hospital, and Robin had agreed to take me so I wouldn't have to drive. But since it was highly unlikely there would be a baby today, and what I planned to do wasn't anything taxing, it was silly for him to cancel his plans because of mine.

But how often do things go as planned, especially when the spirit world is involved?

That niggling thought I kept to myself, especially as I didn't feel any sense of danger, just maybe a need to be cautious and aware.

Kade pressed his forehead to mine and kissed the tip of my nose. "Okay. But stay in touch with me the whole time."

"The whole time?"

"When you get there and then when you leave and again when you are home."

"Okay. I can do that, and I love all your concern for me."

This time he leaned in for a kiss - one that started as a nibble then turned into something more satisfying. It ended when another piercing pain, once again localized in the lower middle of my back, made me pull away. Though I probably should have told him about it, I didn't say anything. I didn't want to get into another discussion on whether I should be going or not. Besides, they were just "practice" pains, for they were not happening at regular intervals—this one occurring much further apart than the first two.

An hour later, I was waving goodbye to Kade and blowing good luck kisses as he drove off. Once he was out of sight, I got into my nice toasty car - thanks to Kade starting it earlier - and headed off to the Wheeler farm—Janice's inherited, possibly haunted house.

As I passed Silver Lake, I saw several people ice fishing and a couple others ice skating. My interest, however, was directed at Rosemary's island. The conditions were perfect for walking out to it, and if I weren't so close to my due date, I would have suggested it to Kade. But that would have to wait for another time. Besides, there was some dispute going on as to who owned the island, though my dear friend Tara was certain she'd win out in the end. Until it was all figured out, it was probably best to stay away.

The Wheeler farm was at the end of a private road that also gave access to two other properties. The moment I turned onto it … okay, maybe even before then … I started sensing a disturbance in the atmosphere. As the feeling grew, unease fluttered in my gut, and I gripped

8

the steering wheel. Darn it. Just as Kade predicted, this wasn't going to be an easy- peasy little thing.

Chapter 2

I passed the first of two other houses sharing the road with the Wheeler farm, and I felt no spike in my psychic radar, which told me the cause for my unease wasn't coming from there. Besides, it looked unoccupied.

The second house was not visible from the road. I just knew of its location because of the driveway leading to it, the trees being too thick to see anything more. My inner alarm, though, was going off, and just as I wondered if the problem might be stemming from there, the Wheeler house came into view.

Given how close the two houses were to each other, I wasn't sure if it was the neighboring house or Janice's, but one of them was causing a sudden gripping sense of panic. Strangely, I didn't sense any spirits. That concerned me enough to ease off the gas, bringing my car to an idling halt. Spirits I could handle. Living people, however, were a whole different issue.

Although the house and yard showed no signs of recent activity, my unease remained. In fact, I was getting an increasing sense of urgency, like someone's life was on the line somehow. Dear God, was it my own? Was Kade right? Maybe I shouldn't have come here alone. A moment of panic consumed me, and I sought to get hold of it, calming myself with slow deep breaths and a steady stream of self-talk.

It's okay, Tess. You are in no danger. There's nothing here. Nothing that could harm you anyway. Besides, you have your wonderful spirit guide Sheila, your spiritual shield. And you aren't going into the house. No matter what.

It was my reminder of Sheila that calmed me more than anything else, and I shut my eyes to focus better on her. Within seconds, I felt the familiar tickle on my chin, like cobwebs brushing against my skin. It was her signature sign that she was with me, and it put me at ease. Giving thanks for her presence, I opened my eyes and took stock of my feelings, noting that I felt much better. Calmer. Everything was fine. At least for the moment.

After sitting for a few more minutes, soaking up the atmosphere and doing my best to keep distracting thoughts at bay, I sensed no presence of lurking ghosts. But I did sense something … some sort of unrest, though it could be nothing more than unsettled energy. Perhaps it was just the lingering effects from previous activity. Whatever had happened with the contracting crew, it was possible that ghostly shenanigans were involved, though all was quiet for the time being.

The panicky feelings that bombarded me earlier weren't all that surprising, and quite frankly, I should have expected it. My presence often triggered supernatural attention. Spirits seeking to communicate can sense my awareness of their world, and they often crowded my psychic space, hoping to get through.

Now that I was paying closer attention, I was fairly certain it was a girl causing the disturbance. The more I concentrated on her, the stronger my sense of her became. Given her energy, she might harass a construction crew—but why? And what did she want?

I started to reach out to her when a strong blast of emotion ripped through me, making me gasp, and a contraction began, hardening my abdomen like an over inflated basketball. I protectively wrapped my arms about myself and breathed slowly through the pain. It lasted longer than the others and oh what a relief it was when it began to ease up. Phew, that was a strong one! I rubbed my hands all over my massive belly (at least to me it seemed massive), and silently assured my sweet daughter that she would be okay.

This was my second big contraction in the past hour, the other occurring shortly before leaving the house. Not wanting to concern Kade, who was packing his SUV at the time, I didn't alert him or mention it. A glance at my watch told me this one was 30 minutes from that one. Do two contractions at 30 minutes apart count as regular? Not that it really mattered. Not yet. It was when they started getting closer that I needed to be concerned.

I glanced at my cell phone and considered telling Kade, for I really shouldn't be keeping this from him, but he wouldn't be able to concentrate on fishing or enjoy the company of his friends if I did that. No, there was no need to interrupt his day. Besides, he'd insist that I leave right this minute, and I needed to investigate that calling just a little more. Someone was sending out a cry for help. I just wasn't sure if it was coming from the living or the dead.

Before I did anything more, though, I sent Kade a quick text letting him know that I had arrived at the house.

His reply was quick. *Anything going on?*

I sense something. Going to sit here and see if I get anything more.

Let me know. I love you. Be careful.

I will. Love you too. Always.

After sitting for about ten minutes and getting nothing, I wondered if getting out of the car would help. I grabbed my purse, because it contained my digital notepad, an invaluable tool for jotting down notes, and opened the door.

The crisp winter air was very still, making it bearable to tolerate, and after some struggle—everything was more difficult at this stage of my pregnancy—I managed to exit the car. Since all the activity spurred a contraction, I had to wait until it passed before focusing my mind on the energies around me.

It didn't take long to hear her come through again.

Please, please help me!

The message was as clear as if it were shouted right next to me, and I swung about, turning from the house and instead scanning the trees to the left of where I was parked. I couldn't ignore that call and I wouldn't, but where was she?

I looked at the house again and took a step toward it, the snow crunching beneath my feet. We hadn't had any snowfall in several days so most of that accumulation was gone, but patches of it remained here and there. Given there were no footprints visible in the snow, I didn't believe anyone in the living, breathing world was around. More importantly, I sensed no immediate danger. So, I took another step then stopped.

She wasn't in the house. I can't explain how I knew that. I just did. So, I turned to do another slow scan of the surrounding area, coming up with nothing—no sense of an otherworldly presence or anyone in distress. Even so, she was out there somewhere. I did not imagine that plea for help,

14

and though a part of me wanted to call it a wrap and head home, I couldn't turn my back on her.

So, I scanned again, casting my feelers further afield. When my gaze reached the trees to my left, I knew she'd called from that direction. I felt quite certain of it. I knew enough at this point in my life to trust my spiritual instinct, and, though I probably should just get in the car and drive back home, I started walking, sending out my own message as I did so. *"Tell me where you are. Keep calling to me."*

A twinge of guilt tugged at my conscience because I'd promised Kade I would do nothing more than step out of my car, and only then if I felt it necessary to make a better connection. He wouldn't like me checking this out. But, I rationalized, I didn't tell him I wouldn't leave the proximity of the car, did I? I just promised I would not go into the house. So, technically I wasn't breaking my word to him.

Anyways, he'd understand. I couldn't just get in my car and drive away knowing that someone might need my help. Besides what harm could come to me? I felt no sense of danger, though there was something dark lurking just beyond the perimeter of my thoughts. The acknowledgment of it was immediately followed with a sense of foreboding, faltering my steps. I had my daughter to consider. Perhaps I should come back later with Kade. But I knew, even as I thought it, that he would not be on board with any such idea, and I couldn't blame him for it. Perhaps Tara would come.

Please someone help me! I need to get out of here!

That got me going again. I couldn't leave just yet, not after that desperate message, and Kade would understand. He would no more ignore this call than I would. Besides, I now knew it came from a young girl, maybe not as young as Anya, who was about to turn seventeen soon, but definitely young, early twenties? Late teens? An impression of short dark hair and deep blue eyes began to form in my mind, the image becoming clearer as I made my way through the trees, which were not so dense that I had to fight my way through them. That was a good thing because I would have had to abandon this possible rescue mission otherwise. Already I was panting from the excursion, my lung capacity hindered by the pressing of a baby on my diaphragm. The leaves didn't even crunch beneath my feet because the ground was frozen solid. It had been a long frigid winter. February was always the worst month in Maine. At least that was my experience in the two winters I'd lived here.

When I finally made it out into the open, I found myself just a few feet from a gravel driveway. It led to a house that was obviously occupied. Smoke rose from the chimney and an old red pickup truck was parked in front of a garage next to the house. I ducked back into the trees and took a moment to assess the situation. The scene before me looked innocent enough, but it was what might be happening inside the house that concerned me. Although the cries for help had stopped, what if it's because she'd passed out? Or worse.

The strongest need to flee passed through me and I even turned away, though my feet refused to move but a step or two. Could I live with myself if I found out someone died because I ignored those calls for help? The feelings swirling inside of me were coming from somewhere. I sensed heartache, confusion, sorrow … so many mixed emotions, but none of them screamed of danger. Even so, foreboding hung over me like an oppressive cloud, making me uneasy, but not to the point of making me flee back to my car, though that was probably the best thing to do.

"Sheila, what do I do?"

"Whatever you decide, that is what you should do."

I should have known my dear spirit guide would say something like that. At times it was frustrating to seek her advice, especially for guidance about situations like this. She couldn't interfere, and I knew that, making it useless to expect as much. My life was mine to live, and the choices mine to make. But she could at least give me some helpful advice!

"Trust in yourself, Tess."

That bolstered my confidence. She was right. I knew the drill at this point—the fact I had within me all the capabilities needed to get through every situation. So, I closed my eyes and focused on surrounding myself with spiritual protection. Nothing could harm me without my consent and that I would not give. I had my daughter to consider here, and as if to lend credence to that thought, another contraction began, though it wasn't as bad as the last one. A glance at my watch told me another thirty minutes had passed. That made three in a row at the same interval. Not that it was cause for alarm … not yet. The fact it could mean something as time went on, though, had me moving again. I needed to know everything was okay with whoever was in that house. Once I had my answer and dealt with it accordingly, I'd skedaddle back to my car and go home.

As I stepped onto the driveway and made my way toward the house, it suddenly occurred to me that I didn't have my cell phone on me. Once again, I stopped to think, wondering if I should go back to get it. But the idea of going all the way back to the car, traipsing through those trees again, and then driving here to the house - because there was no way I was going to make that trip on foot a third time - didn't sit well with me. How much time would that take? Surely too much, and besides, I was already here.

As indecision warred within me, I thought about that call for help and calmed my mind. Perhaps I'd try one more time to connect with her. But I got nothing, and my gaze settled on the house. She was in there. She had to be.

I'd only taken a few more steps, putting me about ten feet from the porch stairs, when the door opened and an elderly man stepped out. Slightly stooped, looking frailer than he probably was, he regarded me in silence. Then, after taking a couple of steps—maybe to get a better look at me—a light of joy lit up his eyes. That, more than anything else, relaxed my caution, and I took a few steps to be closer to him. If we were going to talk, I wanted to do it without having to raise our voices.

One thing I didn't get from him was any sign of worry. No hint that something troublesome was going on inside his home. As for that spark of joy in his eyes, I didn't think it came from relief that help had arrived. Maybe he was just glad for some company. Either way, it seemed I might be wrong about someone needing rescue. Either that or he was unaware of the situation.

Since I was pretty sure it was a young girl calling for help, maybe it was a daughter or his grandchild. As we studied each other, I tried to gauge his age. At a guess, I'd say perhaps late sixties or early seventies. It was hard to tell these days. Some people looked younger than their years and others looked older. Not that certain ages had a particular look, but over time one comes to notice that certain age groups often share common traits—like gray hair, which he had, and wrinkles, which he also had, and paper-thin skin, which he didn't seem to have.

Not wanting the silence between us to get awkward, I gave him a friendly smile. "Hello, I'm sorry to bother you."

The man glanced beyond me, as if looking for something that might explain how I got in his yard, then brought his gaze back to mine. "Where did you come from?"

I waved a hand in the general direction of the Wheeler farm. "Next door."

The man's bushy gray eyebrows (another common trait of older men) raised in surprise. "Next door? At the Wheeler place? No one lives there."

"No, I just stopped in to check it out."

He nodded in understanding, though it offered nothing in the way of an explanation for my being there in his yard.

"I decided to walk around the property…" Why was I lying? I started to just admit the truth when another contraction began building momentum. This one was stronger than the others, and I drew in a sharp breath, putting my hand on my belly as if that might calm things down. Hmm, this one was closer than the other three.

The man hobbled down the three stairs to the ground and took a cautious step towards me, his actions slow, as if taking care to not startle me. "Are you okay?"

Once the pain receded, I took a quick glance at my watch. Ten minutes. Was it common for pains to start coming that close after only three others at half hour increments? I thought it was a gradual process, the pains coming closer together over a longer period of time. "Yes, I'm fine." I patted my belly, which could not be hidden, not even beneath a thick woolen coat. "I've been having these pains all morning. Not sure if it's anything to worry about yet."

A concerned frown deepened the lines on his face. "You want to come in a minute and sit down?"

I hesitated for only a moment. Though foreboding thrummed through me, the concern on his face and tender care in his eyes convinced me to trust him, leading me to dismiss the fact that feelings of foreboding were often a warning sign.

If I wanted to get a clearer sense of that distress call, then I needed to be closer to her. If she was in the house, I'd know once I was inside. If she wasn't in there, I wasn't sure what I'd do next. I couldn't stay here much longer in any case. Something was definitely going on with my pregnancy. Our daughter might not be born today, but it was going to happen sooner rather than later.

The man touched my arm in a manner that did not make me feel threatened. His touch was gentle and fleeting then hovering. "You really should come in and sit a spell."

He was right, I did need to sit down. "I'm Tess, by the way." I don't know why I didn't give him my last name, but I felt a slight sense of preservation, the feeling that I shouldn't give him too much information.

He gave me an odd look then nodded slowly. "So, Tess, is it?"

I thought it an odd response, but the need to sit was outweighing any concerns to question it. "Yes, and you are?"

He looked at me as if trying to figure something out then gave what sounded like a resigned sigh. "Charlie."

"It's nice to meet you, Charlie. I appreciate your offer, and I think I'll take you up on it. But just for a little while."

Giving a satisfied nod and smiling broadly, he stood with his arms at his side, his posture slightly hunched and his eyes scanning me with concern. "May I give you a hand, my dear?"

Although I felt a little uncomfortable about accepting his offer to go into the house, I could see no reason to be worried, despite that sense of foreboding, which was likely just a response to being alone with a stranger. His concern seemed genuine, and that made me feel better about going into his house. Besides, I wasn't sure I had the strength to keep standing much longer.

Giving a nod that I would like his help, though he didn't look much stronger than me, I took his proffered arm. The walkway in front of the steps looked slippery, and the last thing I needed to do was fall. It was also the last thing he needed. We would support each other.

As we made our way across the slippery patch of ground and up the front steps, doubts about going into the house began to take hold, and I wondered if I'd just made a very bad decision. I knew nothing about Charlie, and considering it was a desperate plea for help that drew me here, I should have thought this through a little more. If he had any sort of role in her situation, it would not bode well for me to be in his care. I did, however, take comfort in Sheila's silence. Surely, she'd give me at least some small sense of warning if this was an unwise decision on my part. Not that she'd done any such thing in previous situations. But still.

A wise decision or not, I needed to be inside the house to determine if the call came from there, and I really, really needed to sit down. Besides, my instincts were telling me I was right where I needed to be. Despite the girl's current silence, I felt quite certain the call came from inside Charlie's house, and unsettling though it was, this kind gentleman, who was being very considerate and gentle with me, didn't come across as a threat.

A good thing too, because my back was aching to a nearly unbearable point and that had me concerned. Hopefully, a short rest would give me the strength I needed to make the trek through the woods back to my car. Or maybe Charlie would give me a lift there.

We entered a narrow hallway with an enclosed stairwell to the left of the door and a small mudroom—at least that's what it looked like to me— just beyond it. Charlie led me to the right, into a moderately sized living room. The sparse furniture looked old and worn, but everything was neat and tidy. A wood stove was giving off enough heat to make the room toasty warm, and the television—its flat screen looking out of place in an otherwise dated room—was on a cooking show, the sound turned down low.

The kitchen, which could pass as "retro" by today's standards, was open to the living room. A long counter with overhanging cupboards provided some separation between the two spaces. Dishes were drying beside the sink on the wall opposite the counter. The fact there was only one cup and a bowl—probably for cereal since a box of Cream of Wheat was beside the stove—strongly suggested this kind man lived alone. The fact that he was neat and tidy, for some odd reason, made me feel better.

"Sit down right here at the table and I will make some tea." He pulled out a chair and looked at my coat, his eyes coming up to meet mine, his look questioning. "Do you want to take your coat off for a minute?"

The fact he wanted to make some tea, of all things, made me relax even more. It was a friendly, comforting gesture, which put me in mind of Rosemary. Though I did not plan to stay long, I was feeling overheated and nodded that I would indeed like to remove my coat, which I set about unbuttoning after placing my purse on the table.

Charlie stood behind me and patiently waited to help me slip it off, then hung it on the back of the chair I was to sit on, his eyes taking in my belly as he did so. "You are due very soon then?"

"In two weeks but she could come at any time."

"She?" He seemed startled by that and glanced away, his expression thoughtful.

More than anything, I wished I could read his mind. What did it matter to him what I was having? And then I thought about the girl who sent out the plea for help. Maybe she wasn't alive after all. Maybe she was connected to his past in some way. I did sense grief in his soul. It hung

22

over him like the cloud of foreboding that hung over me. "Modern technology takes all the guess work out of pregnancy." Not that I'd needed it to know I was having a daughter. But Charlie didn't need to know that. I smiled at him, and he smiled back.

"Yes, it does, though some of that highfalutin fancy-dancy gadgetry doesn't help with everything."

Now what did he mean by that? It was true enough and could encompass many things, but I knew there was more weight to his words than just a broad context of meaning.

"Does tea sound okay to you?" He turned away and began filling a tea kettle with water. "We might get some freezing rain tonight, though it looks pretty clear right now. I hope you don't have far to travel today."

"No, not far." Once again, I found myself reluctant to give him any information, like the fact that I lived right here in Bucksport, not too far away from him.

While he got out tea supplies, I glanced around, noticing once again that he was a very clean and tidy man. The house lacked a woman's touch, though traces of one remained. There were signs of it in the faded doilies on the end tables next to the couch and on a threadbare pillow, covered with a hand-embroidered slipcover of flowers and birds, resting on a rocking chair that looked too delicate for someone like Charlie. It was placed near a semicircular table located under a window facing the garage. On the table sat a vase of dried roses, aged and brittle, with what I suspected to be an urn right beside it.

There were pictures on the wall, and since the only light in the living room came from the curtained windows, they were cast in shadow, making it impossible for me to see them clearly. Unfortunately, because I was too busy trying to sense the girl I'd come to rescue, I didn't take the time to look at them as I passed by. I was quite certain, however, that they included an older woman and a young girl. His wife and daughter? So where were they? Clearly, they no longer lived here.

"What do you have in your tea?"

Startled from my mindful wanderings, I returned my attention to Charlie, who stood with a steaming tea kettle in hand, the spout hovering over one of the cups. "Just one sugar and a splash of cream if you have it."

Charlie nodded and smiled. "Ah yes, that's right."

It was a strange response, one that sent a shiver of unease skittering through me. A sinking feeling in my gut took hold and I knew, in a blinding flash of understanding, that I shouldn't have entered Charlie's home.

Chapter 3

I was about to tell Charlie that I'd changed my mind about the tea, when a wave of sorrow swept through me, and it wasn't coming from Charlie. No, this was coming from elsewhere. But where and from whom?

As if he sensed my sudden unease, Charlie spoke over his shoulder as he stirred a spoon in one of the cups. "My wife loved tea. She had it the same way." He turned to look at me, a wretched expression clouding his face. "As did my daughter."

I don't know why that increased my anxiety, but it did. Perhaps because his daughter might be the source of those distress calls. "What happened to them?"

Charlie paused from our tea preparations to stare at me, and it was obvious to me that something was bothering him. He didn't like my questions, but then he might be a very private man. Perhaps I should ease off on prying for information.

"My wife died of cancer about fifteen years ago." He turned to set the tea kettle on the stove. "Doesn't seem like it was that long ago and yet it sometimes feels like it's been much longer." He shook his head, perhaps to clear the memories clouding it, and turned to smile at me, his expression still very sad. "Time is a weird thing."

"Yes, it is." *So, what happened to your daughter?* I wished I dared ask him, but I felt I was pushing his boundaries.

"Would you like something to eat with your tea? I have some ginger biscuits."

Those actually sounded like a great idea, and I relaxed a little more. That moment of panic I'd experienced earlier was no longer an issue. Charlie was a lonely, grieving widower who, I suspected, had also lost his daughter. There was nothing to worry about. Surely. "That sounds lovely, Charlie, thank you."

He set my cup and a teaspoon in front of me then added a small carton of creamer he fetched from the refrigerator—a rounded, blue pastel-colored model with chrome handles, looking like it had come straight from the 1960s. "You go ahead and fix your tea, and I'll get us a plate of biscuits."

I busied myself with the task set before me, using the time to give myself a silent pep talk. *Everything is fine, Tess. There's no girl here needing rescuing. At least, not anyone who is still living. It could be his wife or daughter you heard. Charlie is just a lonely old man grateful for some company.*

Charlie returned to the table with a plate of ginger biscuits and nodded for me to help myself. He sat down and stirred his tea then pulled out his tea bag, using his spoon to hold it, and lifted his cup to me in a silent toast.

We sat for a moment in silence, sipping our tea, which I found slightly odd in taste but continued to drink anyway so as not to offend him. Maybe the tea bags were old. Hopefully not fifteen years old. He said his wife liked tea. What if it were left over from her time? Was it okay to drink old tea? One had to be careful when ingesting something that was being shared with a baby.

26

"Is this Red Tea, Charlie?" I took another bite of the ginger biscuit because it helped to dispel the strange taste.

"No, why? Do you only like Red Tea?" Charlie frowned in apology and started to rise from his chair.

I put out a hand to encourage him to sit back down. "No, no. I like all sorts of teas."

Charlie settled back in his chair and pulled a rueful face. "I got a box of mixed teas from my neighbor for Christmas. To be honest, I threw a couple of them out already. I'm not sure which one this is, but I guess I should have checked and asked you first."

Feeling better knowing the tea wasn't old, I waved away his concern. "No, it's fine. I was just trying to place the flavor."

Charlie nodded in understanding. "It does taste a bit weird, doesn't it?" He chuckled at the situation. "I thought it was just me."

We laughed together and when he took a sip, as if to say he would drink it anyway, I did the same. He nodded with approval and tapped the plate of biscuits with a finger. "These help."

Once again, we shared a laugh and finished off our tea. I was feeling so much better about things, despite that earlier plea for help. In fact, I was feeling almost giddy. I might have pondered that a bit more, but I was suddenly dealing with a bout of nausea.

"Another contraction?" Charlie leaned forward in concern.

"No, no. Just a wave of nausea. It happens from time to time. That and the Braxton Hicks."

"What's that?"

Laughing at the confusion on his face, I explained to him about the "practice labor pains" and though he smiled, he didn't seem convinced. Instead, he seemed … calculating? That made me cringe a little because it sounded rather sinister. He was probably just trying to work it out in his mind if he should take me to the hospital. But there was going to be no need for that. I was going to leave right now.

"Thank you for the tea, Charlie, and also for the biscuits, but I think I better get back to my car." I went to push myself up from my seat but was having trouble coordinating the maneuver, and Charlie quickly rose to assist me. His movements, I noticed, were not quite as slow and hindered as they seemed earlier.

"Are you sure that's a good idea? I don't think you are in any condition to be gallivanting through the woods."

Maybe I rose too quickly and that would explain the sudden rush of wooziness that went to my head. Though I didn't want to admit it, I was thinking he was right. "Wow, I'm not feeling all that well, Charlie." I slumped against him, noting that his strength seemed far surer than when we'd helped each other into the house.

"I think you should lay down."

No, I didn't like that idea at all, though it sounded heavenly. "No..."

"Look, I will go over to the house and get your car, bring it back here, and if you are feeling better, then you can be on your way. But you are in no condition to be walking through the woods or driving a car right now."

"I could go with you in your truck..."

"You think you are in any condition to do that right now?"

His tone was gentle and reasonable, and as much as I didn't like it, I did need to lie down. "Okay, but I feel bad making you walk over there to get my car. Maybe if I just lay on your couch for a few minutes, I'll feel better."

28

Since he had placed his arm around my shoulders and was urging me to go with him, I grabbed my purse and held it clutched in my hand, the desire to keep it close making me tuck it under my arm.

"No, I think you need to lie in a bed. It will be far more comfortable."

The whole time he talked, he led me through the living room (darn it, I forgot to look at those pictures again!) and then up the carpeted stairs. It was no easy task. The more I walked, the woozier I became. It made no sense, but I felt I could just go to sleep right there on the spot. I wasn't even sure I was going to make it to the bedroom he was obviously leading me to.

At the top of the stairs, he paused to let me catch my breath. "You doing okay, my dear?"

My dear? Even in my woozy state I didn't like him using endearments on me.

"Yes, just very tired."

"You'll be okay. You just need to rest."

He sounded awfully certain of that, like he understood exactly what was going on. That foreboding from earlier was now full-fledged alarm. Something wasn't right here.

Charlie passed the first two doors, one on the right and left, and opened the second one on the right, which would put it above the dining area of the kitchen if I wasn't mistaken. Although it didn't look like it had been in use for a long while, the room obviously belonged to a girl at one time.

He led me to a queen-size bed with a white, ornate headboard and matching footboard, covered with a quilted coverlet adorned with small embroidered pink roses. "Okay then, there you go. Your nice, comfy bed."

Why did he word it like that … *your* nice comfy bed? It wasn't *my* bed.

Charlie helped me lay down then removed my shoes, which I would have protested against him doing if I had the energy to so, but I didn't. When he reached for my purse, I held it firmly in my grip, dredging the strength up from somewhere. "No, I want to keep this with me."

Charlie frowned. "I will just put it with your coat…"

"No, I want to keep it with me."

"What's in there that's so important? You have a cell phone in there? Do you want to call someone?"

Why did I sense that he was fishing for information? "No, my cell phone is on the seat in my car. If you could just bring it to me when you come back, I'd appreciate it." I was going to have to call Kade and have him come fetch me. Better yet, I'd call Robin. She was only minutes away and he was over forty minutes from Charlie's house.

Charlie nodded that he'd do that, his sudden alertness relaxing. Was he glad that I didn't have my cell phone on me? Why should that matter to him?

Our eyes met, and though I felt too woozy to say much more, he must have seen my apprehension for his expression gentled. He pulled a pink throw blanket from the bottom of the bed and tucked it around me. "There you go, sweet girl, just relax now."

Sweet girl? What was with the endearments all of a sudden? Though they were spoken with gentleness, something was strange about the tone. I wanted to think about it some more, but my thoughts were scattered, and I was so darn tired.

Charlie leaned down and kissed my forehead. "Get some rest, my sweet girl. You've nothing to worry about. I will make sure of it."

30

Oh dear, that just sounded far more worrisome than he probably intended. But he was coming across as a bit possessive, and I didn't like that at all.

Charlie left the room and a distinctive clicking noise followed, sounding suspiciously like he'd just locked the door. Surely not! If only I wasn't so tired, I'd get up to investigate.

It didn't seem natural, this sudden tiredness. I thought about the tea and became suspicious as I remembered the odd taste. But he drank it too. Then I remembered something that made me force my heavy eyelids open. The room was blurry. Something was definitely not right here.

Though it was hard to concentrate, I thought about our trek across the kitchen when Charlie was helping me towards the stairs, and I'd glanced over toward the stove, which was a matching model to the refrigerator. A tea box was right there next to it. *Red Tea.* Hadn't he said it was some sort of strange tea his neighbor had given to him? I knew the taste of Red Tea and the flavor I'd tasted had nothing to do with it.

Think, Tess, think. I was looking around while he prepared our tea, and he'd asked me how I liked it. But hadn't I seen him put something in my cup before I mentioned the sugar? Why did I just now remember that? I knew better than to not zero in on stuff like that. But he was distracting me, and his house was distracting me.

Another contraction started but I was too tired, and strangely relaxed, to concern myself over it. I wanted to look at my watch, but I just couldn't gather up enough energy to lift my arm. Besides, I don't think I could have read my watch anyway because my vision was so blurry.

There was only one conclusion to make here. Charlie had drugged me. But why? *Why?*

Sleep clawed at me, pulling me under, but I fought to maintain consciousness, refusing to give in. Then I heard *her* again.

Please help me! Please!

She was here in this house and she wasn't a ghost. At least, I felt pretty sure she wasn't a ghost. If only my mind wasn't so muddled. It actually surprised me I could still hear her cries for help considering the condition I was in.

"I'm so sorry," I mentally replied. *"But I think I'm now in the same mess you are in."*

How could I have allowed this to happen? I was very likely in the initial stages of labor, and I was very likely under the influence of some drug, which I prayed most fervently wouldn't harm my daughter, and I was very, very likely under the complete mercy of Charlie—if that was even his name.

Kade was going to be very upset with me, and I wouldn't blame him one bit. I was upset with myself.

Oh, Tess, what mess are you in now? It was my last clear thought before succumbing to the drug I was certain Charlie had given me.

Chapter 4

"Tess, wake up."

It wasn't a loud voice, more like an echo in my head, but it was effective enough to get my attention, and I opened my eyes. The room was so dark I couldn't see anything beyond the bed, yet I could clearly see the pink throw blanket, my hands resting on my chest, and even the white footboard.

"You have much to do."

I looked around for the source of the voice, but I knew there was no one in the room with me. Whoever was communicating with me was doing it in my mind. Since their voice was distinctly different from my own internal voice, I knew it wasn't me talking to myself. So, who was it?

"It doesn't matter who I am. What you do from this point on matters."

True enough, and though I would have liked to know who was talking to me, I let it go and tried to sit up. Only my body was very lethargic, my muscles weak, and I reluctantly relaxed against the mattress. "What's happened?"

"The effects will wear off soon enough."

"Was I drugged?" But the voice didn't need to answer that. I already knew. Whatever Charlie gave me, my biggest concern was that it would bring harm to my baby.

"She is fine."

That was reassuring, even coming from a disembodied voice in my head. "How much time do I have?" Even as I spoke, I felt another contraction coming on and looked at my watch. Was that real time? If I recalled correctly, over an hour had passed since I last looked at it.

"As much as you need."

"That isn't a satisfactory answer. I can't control when my daughter will enter this world. As for spending more time here in Charlie's house, I've had my fill of it."

"Obviously you haven't, or you wouldn't be here."

That made me huff out a frustrated sigh. "I do not want to give birth to my daughter in this house, not without my husband, and not with just Charlie to assist. In fact, if it came to that, I'd rather be alone."

"You don't always get what you want."

Wasn't that the sad truth.

"You get what you expect, or what you have agreed to prior to birth."

"Yeah, well, if I agreed to this before my birth, I've changed my mind and no longer want any part of it."

Gentle laughter floated through my mind. *"Then change it."*

"How? I'm no Genie." Even as I said the words, I was disappointed with myself for saying them. Maybe it was the drug Charlie gave me. It was messing with my emotions and making me dismiss all that I'd come to learn over the past few years.

"You are a worried mother-to-be. It's understandable that you are feeling powerless and fearful. But don't hang onto those feelings or things will get much more disagreeable."

I understood the warning. Our prevalent emotions attracted more of the same, which is why negative thinking often brought on more problems,

34

making us think the world is working against us. But geez, I had a right to be upset about all this. I was about to have a baby, possibly while being held captive, and no one knew where I was. It would be a distressing situation for anyone.

"Everything happens for a reason, as you well know, and the trick to dealing with the challenges that confront you is to understand why they're happening. Once you have acquired that understanding, the issue becomes resolved."

Well then, I hoped I would figure this out soon, because I wanted to go home, and I wanted to go as soon as possible. "Why is everything so dark around me?"

"That which you cannot see it yet to be determined. There are no absolutes. Your destiny has infinite possibilities. Your choices determine what you do and do not see, what you do and do not experience, and what you will or will not learn."

"Why darkness?" It was, perhaps, a useless question, a waste of time to even ask, but I really was curious about the fact that a black nothingness, which apparently represented infinite possibilities, surrounded me.

"Light reveals answers and represents the end journey. The lack of light is the beginning of a journey, for all is unknown until revealed, until your choices are made."

Impatience was diminishing my interest in continuing this conversation. As the voice said when I first woke up, I had much to do, and I needed to get on with it. My life had become a mess in just a few short hours. A mess resulting from bad decisions. "Just so long as we, my daughter and I, make it out of this situation unscathed, that's all that matters to me right now."

"That cannot be 'all that matters' or your lesson will continue."

"Can't you at least give me a hint as to what lesson I'm supposed to be learning?"

"No."

Well, that was a short answer. "Is Sheila here?"

"Always."

She was being awfully quiet.

"Do you need her to speak to you?"

"No." Ha! There was my short answer. But then I sighed in apology. "I'm sorry, I am just really worried."

"And what is 'worry'?"

"Fear of the unknown."

"Just 'fear' will do. There are lots of unknowns that do not cause fear."

True enough. I gave it some consideration then came up with what I thought was a better answer. "Worry is the expectation of an unwanted outcome."

"That's a better explanation, though it encompasses so much more."

Was I talking to an angel? It was definitely a voice of reason, but from where? Obviously, the spirit realm, and honestly, it truly didn't matter. Then again, it was a human trait to want to put names to things.

"It's time to wake up."

What? I thought I was awake, though the blackness surrounding me should have told me that I wasn't fully aware of the physical world.

"Hello, my sweet girl, can you open your eyes now?"

That was Charlie. My eyes flew open as my heart began pounding, the noise loud in my ears. I pressed my hands to my chest and did my best to regain some inner calm. Seeing that Charlie was carefully watching me, I figured it best to act as if I was nothing more than a guest in his home. I'd play along with him, hopefully relax his vigil, and then work out an escape. The fact I was even using the word 'escape' in my plans was very alarming, but despite my rising fear, I somehow managed to give Charlie a small smile. "Sorry I got so tired on you, but I feel much better now. Did you get my car?"

He smiled in return, though his was more pronounced, and he leaned in to slide his arm behind my back. "Here, let me help you sit up. I made you something to eat."

Right, as if I'd ingest anything else this man wanted to give me. "Oh, that's so sweet of you, but I'm really not hungry right now."

A contraction began and I didn't want him to know about it. I didn't want him to know anything more about me. Like, nothing at all. Not even the fact that I could possibly be in labor. So, I used the excuse of getting more comfortably settled while he tucked pillows behind me, to glance at my watch. It was 30 minutes from the time I'd had the previous one while talking to "the voice" (for lack of a better label) and yet, that couldn't possibly be right. I mean, I was still talking to the voice when Charlie interrupted us, so thirty minutes couldn't have possibly passed. Then again, while in a vision, time didn't mean anything.

"There you are, my dear. Are you comfortable?"

Oh, the concern he exhibited. It seemed genuine, from the gentle tone of his voice to the kind expression on his face. But he was holding me here against my will. Or was he?

"I really need to be going, Charlie." Once again, I made to get up and Charlie placed a firm hand on my shoulder.

"No, you need to be resting. I am not letting you out of here when you are obviously not well."

Obviously not well? Right. He knew darn well there was nothing wrong with me. Perhaps he meant that I couldn't leave while I was still under the effects of the drug he gave me. As to that ... why? I had a very strong, unsettling suspicion that he wasn't going to let me go at all, and it made no sense. I showed up at his house unexpectedly. We'd never met despite living so close to each other, so I couldn't possibly mean anything to him. What reason could he have to keep me here?

And then I thought about *her*. Maybe she was the reason he was keeping me here. "Charlie, do you live alone?"

Since he was busy organizing my tray, which contained a glass of milk, a slice of toast, a bowl of diced fruit and what looked like a blueberry muffin, he took his time answering me, though I could tell by his stiffening posture that he didn't like the question.

"I mean, you told me your wife died, and I am so sorry about that, but did you not have children?"

Charlie straightened the tray on the stand beside my bed, then stood back, his pale brown eyes narrowing just enough to leave me feeling uneasy. "Come now, my dear. Surely you know the answer to that, hmmm?"

What on earth was he talking about? Did he know I was a medium? Did he suspect that I knew about the girl?

A strange light entered Charlie's gaze as it traveled over my face, his expression becoming increasingly tender as the seconds ticked by. "You've come back to me, Lindsay." He lifted a hand when I was about to correct him and wagged a finger. "Now don't go denying it. You've let your hair grow out and you've lightened it quite a bit, but I would know you anywhere. Did you think I wouldn't recognize you?"

38

My heart pounded as I fought against my rising fear. *"Keep a clear head, Tess. Reason through this with calm and care.* "Charlie, I am not trying to trick you about anything. My name is Tess…"

"Enough." His barked command made me wince and Charlie visibly fought to regain his composure. "You've always given me a tough time, and you twist everything I say." Frustration battled with bewilderment. "I don't deserve this, Lindsay." He scrubbed his hands over his face and ran them up through his gray hair. "You were gone so long, and I've been worried sick."

As I didn't want to upset him further by seeking information, I figured the best thing I could do right now was keep him talking. "How long has it been?" Did my pregnancy mean nothing? He wasn't surprised by it, nor did he express any curiosity about my condition. I mean, what was Lindsay's story? If only I could learn more about Charlie's situation, I might figure a way out of this mess.

Giving a nod toward my belly, Charlie reached over and gave it a gentle pat, withdrawing quickly when he saw me frown. "You'd just found out about your pregnancy, remember? Since it is obvious you are about to have it at any time, that makes it about what … seven months?" Charlie looked away and scanned the room, then he walked over to the rocking chair near the window and pulled it close to the bed. Once he settled in it, he rocked quietly back and forth, back and forth, and stared at me with expectation in his gaze, as if waiting for me to say more.

"That's about right then," I said, hoping my playing along would keep him calm and talkative. "I … I've had some memory relapses. Could you tell me about our last meeting?" It was, perhaps, a bad idea to play along with his delusion, because it would only solidify his belief that I was his daughter. At least, that is who I was assuming Lindsay was, but denying it only agitated him, and I needed to get as much information as I could and then use it somehow to get out of here.

"I came to Boston to see you. Remember? I came as soon as I could." He leaned forward, his voice rising defensively, as if he were expecting an argument and wanted to press home his side of the story. "You didn't come right out and say it, but I knew you wanted me to come, and I did. I came right away."

I gave him an encouraging smile. "That's right. You did what any concerned … father would do." When he didn't correct me, I knew I had it right. Lindsay was his daughter. Despite his claim to the contrary, my gut was telling me she hadn't wanted him anywhere near her.

"He's been here twice, Lindsay." Charlie pushed himself up from the chair and started pacing. "I thought for sure he was the one who took you and yet here you are." He swung around and threw his hands up in the air, his eyes fired with emotion. "You told me you were going to pick up something for us to eat and be right back. Then he shows up wanting to know where you were, and I told him." Charlie rushed to my bed and grasped one of my hands, which I tried to resist, but his grip tightened. "You don't know the guilt I've been feeling for telling him that. I mean, he left so quickly, and I knew he was going after you. I knew, honey, I knew he was coming for you. But I didn't think he'd take you away." A smile wreathed his anguished face. "And after all this time … here you are." His smile morphed into a frown, deepening the lines in his forehead. "Did you get away from him? You must have, because he's been here fishing for information. He knew you'd come home to me."

I could only guess that this man he was talking about was the father of Lindsay's baby. Since she was obviously still missing, it worried me that Lindsay might no longer be alive. Perhaps it was her from whom I'd

40

received the plea for help. Murdered victims … if that's what she was … often wanted their bodies found so their families could have some closure. Charlie was obviously suffering greatly over her loss, to the point that he was losing his grip on reality, convincing himself that a complete stranger was his daughter. In that, I could feel sympathy, but he was holding me here against my will and that dulled some of my empathy for what he was going through. "Why did you suspect him?"

Charlie sank onto the chair, though he continued to hold my hand, his grip gentle. I didn't like him touching me, but I allowed it. Besides, it would probably agitate him if I drew away.

"He was never good for you, Lindsay. I told you right from the beginning that I didn't like him, but you are always out to prove me wrong." He gave me a reproachful look. "You must know that anything I do is always in your best interest."

Even keeping people captive? Did he really think that wouldn't upset his daughter? "Yes, I know." Oh, how it galled me to agree with him.

"I knew he wasn't treating you right." His expression hardened, his mouth firming before he spoke. "Your black eye was proof enough." As if he expected me to argue that point, he gave me a look that was quite clear … he would brook no argument about it. "I knew you were lying when you said it was an accident and that he didn't mean to hit you." His hand tightened on mine. "I knew something was wrong when you came to see me after I had that stroke. And I knew you rushed back to him because you were afraid staying any longer would make him mad." His eyes darkened with sympathy and his voice softened. "I wanted to help you, Lindsay, but I couldn't right then. That's why I came as soon as I was released from the hospital." He glanced away, the look in his eyes telling me his mind was fully engaged with memories. "When you told me you were pregnant, you tried so hard to pretend you were happy about it, and you worked too hard trying to convince me that he was happy too. But I knew, Lindsay. Men like that … they don't take things they can't control very well."

He leaned forward, reaching his free hand toward my hair and it was all I could do not to flinch away. But he was gentle as he brushed some of my hair back from my face, tucking it behind my ear. "Where did he take you? How did you escape him? He's been here twice in the past few weeks. He says he's looking for … someone else, but now I know … he was really looking for you!"

Who was the 'someone else' he was looking for? The shiftiness of Charlie's eyes told me that could be relevant information.

Charlie squeezed my hand, which prompted me to try and withdraw it, but when his eyes narrowed in warning, I stopped resisting. "He must have known you would come back to me." He sniffled and stared at me with glistening eyes, his emotions real, even if they were displaced. "So, tell me—did you escape from him?"

How was I to answer that question? I had no idea what Lindsay's current situation was, and I certainly didn't want to implicate someone for a crime I wasn't sure he'd committed. But I had to say something, and whatever it was, it needed to keep Charlie appeased enough that he wouldn't become agitated and do something rash. As if holding me here against my will wasn't rash enough. Who knew what else he was capable of? "I really don't want to discuss it."

Charlie's mouth firmed with disapproval. "Don't tell me you are still trying to protect that man, Lindsay."

"I'm not…"

"Tell me then, why is he coming around here all of a sudden, pretending to be looking for someone else?"

42

"Who is he saying he is looking for?"

Charlie's mouth firmed and he looked away. "It doesn't matter, because now I know that it's you he wants."

It most certainly did matter. Probably more than I was thinking it mattered. But now I was left to wonder ... was this man Charlie was talking about someone I, too, needed to be concerned about? "Is he causing you trouble?"

Charlie returned his gaze back to me, his brown eyes burning with the intensity of his emotions. "What do you think?"

I gave a shrug and shook my head in a manner that implied I didn't know what to think. "He is probably just looking for answers." That, at least, had to be the truth of it.

Charlie nodded in agreement, his expression grim, his brown eyes hardening. "He wants to know where you are and he knows, Lindsay, that if given the opportunity, it is here you would come." He leaned over and patted my arm with affection. "The police tried to convince me that you left of your own free will, but I didn't believe it."

Well, that was some interesting information. Perhaps Lindsay was still alive after all. Right now, however, her whereabouts were not my concern. "So ... what is your plan? You don't intend to keep me here in this bedroom forever, do you?" I was almost afraid to hear his answer, but I needed to know what was going on in his mind.

"Oh no, no!" His eyes widened in surprise that I would even ask such a question. "Of course, I wouldn't do anything like that to you." And then he drew in a breath, and the way he looked at me, I knew, as he did, that I wasn't going to like what he was going to say next. "But until I can deal with him and make sure he cannot harm you again, you need to stay here."

I wasn't sure what Charlie meant by "until I can deal with him," but I didn't like the sound of it. "No, that won't work. I need to get to the hospital, Char …" Oh God, what do I call him? I couldn't bring myself to call him dad or pop or anything of that nature, but as his daughter, calling him by his name might jar his mind or anger him, making him do something harmful.

He was quick to utter reassurances, patting my shoulder as he did so. "Don't you worry none, my dear. You will be fine. Women used to have their babies in their homes all the time."

Now that was alarming. Was he intending for me to deliver my daughter here? "Something could go wrong. I need to be with professionals. Promise you'll call for help if it should come to that." If he wasn't going to let me out of here and Kade didn't find me in time, then perhaps I could rely on emergency services to lend assistance. If it came to that, though I prayed fervently that it wouldn't.

"I can't risk it, my dear. He might find out. But don't worry, nothing will go wrong. Between us we will figure it all out." He released my hand and stood, nodding towards the tray. "You really need to be sure and eat."

"How do I know you didn't drug it." I was feeling a little bitter and that slipped out before I could stop myself from saying it. The moment the words were out of my mouth, I looked up at him with what I hoped was a contrite expression. "I'm sorry … that was … it was wrong of me to say."

Charlie drew in breath then let it out in a long sigh, his eyes softening in apology. "You've a right to be upset, but I had to drug you. I didn't want you to fight against what I knew had to be done. That could have put you and your baby at risk, the upset and all that." He tapped the tray with a finger. "I promise you there is nothing in any of it. I will taste it first if you prefer, just to show you that you've nothing to worry about."

44

I wanted to say yes, to have him eat every last bite of it, but I forced myself to smile. "No, that's fine. But whatever you gave me earlier, I hope it didn't harm the baby. I won't tolerate you doing anything to hurt her." On that I was firm, and I didn't care if it angered him or not.

"No, no. It won't hurt her, or you, and I won't use it again."

But his eyes shifted away, and I knew he was lying. The threat was clear. If I did anything that alarmed him, he would do whatever was necessary to keep me under control. There might not be anything in the food on that tray, but it didn't mean future offerings would be that way. I looked at it and wondered what I should do.

Charlie pushed the tray a little closer to the bed. "It's all good. There's no reason to be drugging you, right? You know it is safest to be here with me. Don't you?" His eyes were practically begging me to agree with him. "I love you, Lindsay. You are my only child, my only living relative, and I am looking forward to being a grandfather."

I closed my eyes so he wouldn't see how horrified I was feeling. How angry I was for being in this situation. How could I have walked blindly into this mess? "So where do you think he is now?"

Charlie frowned. "Who? You mean Dean?"

Dean. So that was his name. "Yes, Dean."

Charlie's mouth tightened into a thin line. "He'll be back. He said if he didn't find…" He shook his head. "Don't you worry none, I'll take care of him."

Now why didn't he finish that sentence? "He said if he didn't find me, he was coming back?"

Charlie's gaze fell on my handbag lying next to me on the bed. "He's looking for trouble is what he's looking for, and I don't want you to worry about it. I will deal with him. You just focus on you and the baby."

He moved around the bed and reached for my handbag, but I snatched it away, removing it from his reach. "What are you doing?"

"I just want to put it somewhere safe with the rest of your things."

What about my car? Did he go and get it or was it right where I left it? I hoped it was still parked at the Wheeler house, that would tell anyone searching for me that I was still in the area. Kade would leave no stone unturned, he'd eventually come talk to Charlie. Though, come to think of it, that might be a matter of concern. If Kade came looking, I had no idea what Charlie was capable of, but I didn't doubt he'd stop at nothing to eliminate anything or anyone he perceived as a threat. His convoluted ideas about me (as his daughter) needing protection were in the realm of near insanity. "Did you bring my car here?"

"Don't you worry, I will be very careful in ensuring Dean doesn't find you." Charlie patted my shoulder then grabbed my purse while I was distracted. Backing from my reach, he rummaged through it, ignoring my repeated requests to return it to me.

Charlie pulled out my digital notepad. "What's this?"

"It's just an electronic notebook. It isn't connected to any cell towers so I can't use it to contact anyone if that's what you are worried about. I use it to write notes without the distraction of the internet or social media."

Charlie shoved it back into my purse. "I will keep all your things safe for you." A sly look entered his eyes, and I knew that whatever caused it pleased him but probably would not please me. "If they find your cellphone, though, they will be wicked confused."

"What do you mean?" Oh God, what did he do to it?

"I 'spect you told other people you were going to that house, though why you felt you needed that cockamamie story I can't imagine." His expression turned thoughtful. "You always did love that place, didn't you?" He shook his head, clearly not understanding his daughter's apparent fascination with the property next door. "So anyway, I dropped your cellphone in the bushes by the front steps. Took me a while to figure out how to shut the dang thing off. I know all about them using cell phones to find people." Charlie grinned and actually looked like he expected me to praise him for his actions.

What I wanted to do was bonk him on the head and knock some sense into him. "But why would you do that?"

"They'll think you left the house so fast you dropped your cellphone." He chuckled over the images that seemed to be running through his mind, then snapped his fingers as another idea came to him. "Or maybe they will think you struggled with someone … like Dean … and dropped it when he grabbed you." He seemed to revel in that idea for a moment, then his expression became somber. "Not that it will matter. They don't look for people the way they should."

"What about my car?"

"I took care of it. I told you, Lindsey, not to worry about it."

"But how did you take care of it?" I rather liked my car, I hoped he didn't do any damage to it.

"I took it someplace they won't even think to look." He chuckled again and gave me a beaming smile. "It's all fine, Lindsay. I'm watching over you now."

I turned my head away and squeezed my eyes closed in disappointment. Darn it. How was Kade ever to find me? Despair was a self-defeating emotion, and I had to force it away with focused determination. Charlie would not win with this … this … horrible plan of his.

Once I felt in control of my emotions, I turned back to Charlie and smiled in entreaty. "Just let me have my notepad. If I am to be tra … if I'm to stay here in this room for however long I must, I will need something to do, and I like to write. Please just let me have that." Though I'd wanted to say 'trapped', I didn't figure Charlie would appreciate me using it.

He looked indecisive but at least he hadn't said no. Yet.

"Please." I forced myself to meet his eyes and he smiled.

"Okay." He pulled it out of the bag. "But I need you to turn it on and show me that it has no capability of connecting to a cell tower. I don't have that internet stuff. Don't know anything about it."

I turned it on and showed it to him. "It's just something to write on. See? I use this stylus pen. It's basically an electronic notebook and nothing more."

Charlie nodded, satisfied, and handed it over to me. "Fine. You go ahead and write poems or whatnot. I can bring you up some magazines if you like. You always liked to read *Birds and Blooms*. Remember those? They kept coming even after you left, and I stacked them in the closet."

"Sure. That would be nice." Another strong contraction seized my attention, and I turned my head hoping he wouldn't catch the wince I couldn't suppress. Breathing through the pain was difficult without giving anything away.

"You okay?" Charlie pressed a comforting hand to my shoulder. "Can I get you anything?"

Yes, a ride out of here. My cell phone. My freedom. "No, I just need to rest some more."

"Okay. I'll leave you alone for a bit. I need to see about dinner. Do you still like pasta?"

48

"I really can't eat anything, Ch… um, the idea of it makes my stomach churn." How to stop myself from calling him Charlie? It was hard to address him without using his name, and I was not going to call him anything else.

"You probably shouldn't be filling your tummy up with food if you are about to give birth. I remember your mother got pretty sick just before you were born." He gave a fond chuckle. "She had a hankering for a boiled dinner and made herself a big plate. Later that night she went into labor with you, and it all came back up."

Our conversation sounded so normal, yet it was so messed up. How did Charlie get to this delusional point in his life?

"I'll come check on you in an hour or so. Okay?" He leaned down and pressed a kiss to my forehead. "I do love you, my sweet, sweet girl."

Tears filled my eyes, and I squeezed my eyelids closed. It was just so sad. For him, for me, for my baby. And Kade, oh my gosh but he had to be frantic by now. How long had it been since I last messaged him?

Once Charlie left the room and locked the door, taking no pains to hide the fact he was doing so, I looked at my watch and did some calculations. It was over three hours since I last messaged Kade, having told him I'd made it safely to the house. That was the last contact I made with him. He would know I would not spend more than half an hour there, at the most, so he had to know by now that something was wrong. Since he was about 45 minutes away, he probably first called Daniel or maybe Robin, since she was closer, and asked them to come check on me. They'd drive to the house and my car would not be there. Would they just leave? Would they look for signs of my being there? Would they find my cell phone?

My hands tightened into fists as frustration grew to such a point that I didn't know what to do about it. Darn it all anyway. How did I get myself into this situation? I knew better. I had all sorts of warning signs, and I ignored them all. Stupid. Stupid. Stupid. How many times have I told people not to ignore their gut instincts, or any strong feelings they may get about something they were doing, or were about to do? And what do I do? The very thing I tell others not to do!

Please, someone help me! Please.

It was *her* again. Could it be Lindsay? I wasn't so sure after hearing Charlie say the police believed she might have disappeared of her own volition. Even so, that didn't mean something didn't happen to her. I closed my eyes and took a few deep, calming breaths. Since I had nothing else to do, perhaps I could connect with her, and then, well, I'd go from there if we made contact. *Hello? Can you hear me?*

I did not sense her in the room, nor did I get any sort of feeling that I was dealing with a ghost. Her energy was so strong it felt … alive.

After a good deal of time had passed without any further messages, I thought about what Charlie had told me. He wasn't telling me everything, and it was the things he was leaving out that I needed to know.

Another thing to consider when it came to the state of Charlie's mind was the fact he'd suffered a stroke. It could have affected his memory in such a way that he was easily confused. That and the fact that he wanted his daughter so badly, he didn't see me when he opened his front door, he saw her. That certainly explained the joy I'd seen in his eyes.

Dean coming around must have made him desperate and suspicious. As to that, why was he coming here? Charlie said he had come on the pretext of looking for someone else. Who? Did it matter? I felt that it did. Even more worrisome was the fact Charlie believed Dean was involved with Lindsay's disappearance. If that were true, he could make this whole mess even worse if he came back, which Charlie seemed so sure he would do.

Try as I might, I just couldn't get a strong feel for the situation, my emotions were too overwrought with what was happening to look at it with a clear mind. Given Charlie's mental state, I wasn't totally convinced he had nothing to do with his daughter's disappearance. Guilt can do terrible things to the mind, to one's sanity.

She was crying. I couldn't hear her clearly in my head and felt it in my soul that she was afraid and feeling hopeless. Who was she and where was she? If only I hadn't run off looking for her without my phone or telling anyone!

I wanted to give in to the tears stinging my eyes. I wanted to scream out my frustration. I wanted to react to the panic fluttering through my chest, churning my belly and making me feel like I wanted to throw up. Somehow, I managed to hold it down—with the help of some deep breathing, and eventually the feeling passed.

She was still crying. I couldn't make sense of the fact that I was unable to make a connection with her. It was surprising, honestly, because her pleas for help and my answering the call should have opened the lines of communication between us. But it didn't.

Much as I wanted to help her, I needed to help myself. Right after I made it through this next contraction. Thirty minutes again.

I was in labor.

I let that sink in, feeling anticipation, excitement and absolute dread. I was trapped in a room in a strange house with a delusional old man who thought I was his missing daughter. The man who may have had something to do with her disappearance was making a nuisance of himself and could show up again at any time. That could spell trouble for me if, that is, he was indeed the bad guy that Charlie thought he was. How was I to know what he'd do if he came back and discovered me here. He could either help me get out of this mess or he could make matters worse, especially with Charlie determined to keep me safe. Top all that off with the fact that absolutely no one knew my location, and it all put me in a fine pickle.

The familiar adage "everything happens for a reason" (which 'the voice' had reminded me of earlier) did nothing to calm my fear and rising panic—neither of which would do me a bit of good. I could not let fear take hold for it derailed my faith, and giving in to panic was worse, for it would lead me down a darker path. Besides, my logical self argued, fear is the loss of faith, and I knew better than to believe I would never get out of here, or that any serious harm would befall me and my daughter. This was a temporary setback, that's all. One way or another I'd get out of it. I just needed to do it soon … before my daughter decided to enter the melee. Therein was the trigger for those debilitating emotions. I did not want to have her here in this awful place, under these stressful conditions, and without my husband, her father, present.

If this was a test of faith then I needed to believe I was going to get out of it, and right now I just didn't feel that way. Ughhhh! Why didn't I feel that way?

I looked at my watch. Almost three and a half hours since I last texted Kade. By now he had to be in a complete state of panic, yet handling things with calm, sharp focus. No doubt he had everyone we knew looking for me. And with that being the case … why hadn't they come here yet? Charlie's house was the closest one to the Wheeler property. Surely, they would at least check to see if he'd seen anything.

It was just short of a half hour later that my door swung open, and Charlie came in with a cup in his hand. "I brought you some tea. It's safe, I will even pour some in this glass I brought (he held up a small glass) and drink it with you if you like. But you really need to stay hydrated." He handed me the cup and though I took it, I did not want to drink it. I did not trust him. His offer to share it with me could be a ploy.

Charlie must have read my thoughts, my expression probably giving them away, for he sighed and considered me for a moment. Then his eyes drifted over to my digital notepad on the bed beside me. "Tell you what, you drink that, and I will let you keep your writing thingy there. Refuse to drink it and I take it with me."

"Why?" This bargaining thing only made me more suspicious.

"Because I do not want you getting dehydrated. You know as well as I do that it could cause some serious problems, and quite frankly, Lindsay, we can't afford for you to have any serious problems." His expression gentled, though the look in his eyes told me he was not going to accept any arguments from me. "You have your baby to consider. My grandchild."

I had to grit my teeth not to say anything to that. I didn't like him laying claim to my daughter, delusional or not.

When I did not react right away, Charlie reached over and snatched up my notepad. "Okay then." He started for the door while speaking over his shoulder. "When you drink that tea, I will give it back to you."

"No, don't go. I'll drink it." He was right about me needing to stay hydrated, and considering he already had me under his control, there was no reason for him to drug me. So, I downed the tea and raised the empty cup towards him. "Done. Now give it back to me." I had some writing to do. If anything were to happen to me, I had some things to say. Things I wanted passed on to my daughter if I wasn't here to do so myself. It was a morbid thought, sounding rather defeatist, but I just wanted to be prepared, even for the worst, though I would, of course, hope for the best.

Charlie smiled, pleased with my cooperation, and took the empty cup from my hands. "Now there's a good girl." He handed me the notepad. "What are you writing?"

"I'm working on a story for a book I hope to publish someday, and if I have to lie here in this bed, I might as well do something useful." It was true what I told him. I was working on a book, but that wasn't what I wanted it for today.

Charlie set the cup on the dresser by the door and came back to sit in the rocking chair. "What sort of book? I didn't know you liked to write. Your mother liked to write. She wrote some beautiful poems. Do you remember?"

"Do you still have them?" I was very curious to know what sort of poetry his wife had written. Would it give me any clues concerning Charlie and Lindsay? Something that might help me through this?

"She wrote poems about lots of things. She wrote several during her cancer treatments, before she got too sick to write anymore." Tears glistened in Charlie's brown eyes. He blinked them away, though his Adam's apple was bobbing in his throat, revealing the effort it took to contain his emotions. "I miss her so much."

Of course I was sympathetic. I hated him locking me in this room, holding me here against his will, but he wasn't a monster. He was a confused, delusional, sad old man.

"I could read to you," Charlie said, clearing his throat and regaining control of himself. "You used to like that."

The last thing I wanted was to spend more time with him. I had things to write, and I couldn't do that if he was in here talking. "I'm actually a bit tired." That much was true, I was feeling a very strong wave of sleepiness. It was incredible that I could just lay here and take a nap when I was in this awful situation, but as the seconds ticked by, I was having a tough time keeping my eyes open. And then the realization hit. He drugged me again! With droopy lids, I managed to turn my head and look at him. "Not again, Charlie."

He smiled in apology. "It's just a sleeping pill, Lindsay. It's nothing harmful. You need to rest. I don't want you in here getting all worked up."

As he was talking, I thought I heard a car and then knew that was exactly what I was hearing when Charlie got up and looked out the window.

He stood in a tense pose for a few seconds then relaxed and turned to wink at me. "Our groceries are here." He walked to the door. "Isn't it great when you can just order groceries over the phone and have them delivered? Who would have thought that would ever happen." He looked back at me as he was pulling the door closed. "Go to sleep." But suddenly the door opened again, widening enough for him to make eye contact with me, his voice not so gentle this time. "You might as well give in to the pill because I warn you, if you think to make that delivery person aware of your presence, I will have to take stronger measures to control you." He noted my alarm and his voice gentled. "Just until you see that what I am doing is best for you." He pulled the door closed and locked it.

I closed my eyes, though tears squeezed through anyway. I wanted to be defiant, but I was pretty sure I wouldn't make it safely to the window, and I couldn't risk hurting my baby. I also did not want to provoke Charlie's wrath.

The lethargy claiming my consciousness was too much to overcome. As I drifted into sleep, I heard banging on the front door and the thought passed through my mind that Kade was here. Just wishful thinking I was sure, and though I wanted to rally and stay awake, I couldn't fight the effects of the sleeping pill. I just had to trust the universe to keep us safe while I slept.

Chapter 5

When I fought my way into wakefulness, the room was awash in the gray shades of late afternoon. On a day like today, when the sky was heavy with cloud cover, the winter light was cold and depressing, especially when locked in a room filled with the harsh reality of someone's delusional machinations. Shaking off the melancholy such thoughts encouraged, I wondered how much time had passed and looked at my watch. Another couple of hours lost.

Worried these sleeping pills Charlie was slipping me might cause harm to my baby, I put my hand over my belly and said a quick prayer, then followed it with a protective spell. She moved beneath my hand, as if to let me know she was okay, and immediately a contraction followed. The pain in my back was really becoming an issue, and I sucked in a sharp breath in response. If it was this bad in the early stages of labor, what was it going to be like when things really got going? At least my water hadn't broken and for that I was grateful. Surely it meant I had a little more time to figure a way out of this … this horror novel I'd landed in. I mean, what was happening seemed more like a book plot or suspenseful movie than real life. Maybe I was having a long, never-ending dream. I pinched myself and nothing happened other than having to wince over the pain. Geez, did I have to do that so hard?

Okay then, if this really was happening, then I needed to keep positive. No matter how dire this situation was, or might get, I had to believe that someone would eventually rescue me. Either that or I would rescue myself. In the meantime, I needed my daughter to wait just a little longer before joining us in this crazy, beautiful world.

Not sure when Charlie would put in another appearance, I switched on the lamp next to my bed and reached for my digital pad, but before I could decide what to do with it, I felt *her* again. No message came through, but I could sense that she was in distress. Even stranger, she felt very close.

Good Lord, was Charlie holding someone else captive besides me? The idea of it terrified me. If that was the case, then Charlie's rational mind was far more gone than I thought.

Where are you? If only I could get her to engage with me, but all I got was silence.

After waiting for several long minutes, the time stretching to the point that I couldn't focus any longer, I turned my mind to other things that were equally pressing. Like writing a letter to my daughter, an idea that had been percolating for a while, even before this situation with Charlie.

Feeling a little guilty for not trying harder to connect with the sender of those messages, I switched on my digital pad, but before I could write so much as a single word, I remembered that I'd had a strong impression that Kade was here earlier. The idea of it was thrilling, though the feeling was a fleeting one. If he had come looking, Charlie must have done an excellent job convincing him that I wasn't here. Otherwise, I'd be with him right now.

How was this all going to end? The uncertainty of it had me getting to work on that letter … just in case. There were things I needed to ensure our daughter knew, and if something happened and I wasn't here to teach her those things, then I'd leave her a letter explaining all I'd come to understand about the spirit world, for I felt quite strongly that she was going to be gifted. How could she not when the "SPORCE" (using that word made me smile) was bound to be strong within her.

And now I couldn't help but indulge in the memories of how the SPORCE acronym had entered my vocabulary. Kade and I were enjoying our honeymoon on Prince Edward Island when we met a very special woman named Seleneh. She told us that the spiritual forces (aka "SPORCE") were accessible to all who learned to utilize its power. She thought her acronym was funny, and laughed even as she'd explained it, and here I was months later smiling at the memory. Until a contraction reminded me that time was short.

So, I wrote, pouring everything I felt would be useful to my daughter on my handy little pad. I wrote through two contractions, still coming every 30 minutes, and I wrote even when my hand began to cramp, and my stomach growled. And then, finally, I just couldn't write anymore.

It was with reluctance that I set my digital pad aside and looked at the tray Charlie brought earlier. Like it or not, I needed to put something in my stomach because I was beginning to feel nauseous. I drank the milk first, thinking it must be alright, or he'd have forced me to drink that instead of the tea. It was lukewarm but tasted fine. Then I ate the fruit and finally the muffin. Was it a good idea? Perhaps not but being fortified with food did make me feel better, stronger, and more capable of handling things.

I was about to pick up my pad and write some more, when Charlie entered the room. He looked tired, and a little stressed.

"Hello, my dear. Did you have a nice nap?"

"I really need you to stop drugging me. It can't be good for the baby." Though I did suspect it was slowing down my labor, which I didn't mind. Even so, I wanted no more of it.

"I'm sorry, Lindsay. But I didn't want you to leave me like before..." He stopped abruptly and frowned, then turned away to pull the curtains closed.

"Like before?" Of course, I was not going to let that slip go.

Charlie turned back to me, his smile not as kind, his eyes a tiny bit harder. "You left me to go to Boston, though I begged you to stay, and what did that get you? It brought Dean into your life and look what happened with that." He came to sit in the rocking chair, dropping into it with a heavy sigh. He looked incredibly tired. "I was right there, Lindsay. I went to Boston for you. You could have come home with me. I would have kept you safe."

"How? By keeping me captive like you are doing now?" I had to concentrate hard on not letting my voice show the bitterness and distaste his actions made me feel.

Charlie's expression hardened. "Maybe, I don't know. You always were a stubborn child. But I love you, Lindsay, and I promised your mother I would keep you safe."

As I looked at Charlie, his eyes bright with delusional madness, made all the brighter with his misguided passion to protect his daughter, I could easily believe that she might have run from him that day he visited her in Boston.

Charlie reached over and gave my arm a squeeze, like he wished he could infuse some sense into me. "Why are you looking at me like that?"

"Like what?"

"Like you think I've done something terrible." His face scrunched into a wounded mien. "We used to be so close back when your mother was alive. I don't know how we've fallen so far apart."

Everyone had a story, a reason for being the way they were, and I needed to be more cognizant of that. It was our journey through life that helped shape us into the person we are, influencing our thoughts, actions and beliefs. "I think we just want different things. That's all." Seeing him nod in aggrievement, I softened my voice in an attempt to appeal to the love he swore he felt for his daughter. "Do you intend to keep me locked up in this room forever?"

Charlie chuckled, as if finding the question ridiculous. "Obviously not, Lindsay."

"Then let me out." I challenged him with my eyes, and we stared at each other for a long, uncomfortable moment.

"When you settle down and accept that this is where you need to be, especially now, then I'll consider it." He pushed himself up from his chair. "Right now, I need to see about dinner." He started walking towards the door then stopped to look at me. "You still having contractions?"

I didn't want to share anything to do with my pregnancy with him, but since he wouldn't leave without an answer, and I didn't want to be in his company any longer, I gave a brief nod. "Now and then, but that's been going on for weeks."

Charlie nodded, satisfied with my answer. "Well, that's good then. Maybe we won't be having a baby tonight."

We? I gritted my teeth. Oh, how I hated this whole thing.

Once he left, again locking the door behind him, I laid my head back against the pillow and conducted some breathing exercises to calm my mind and emotions. Resenting this situation would only keep it going, for the things we give energy and focus to, will only persist. If I wanted things to improve, I needed to let go of that negativity. I didn't have to like the situation, but I didn't need to be hating on it either. Besides, all that did was increase my stress, and the more stressed I became, the less clear my mind was for problem-solving. I wasn't going to come up with a way out of here if my mind was clouded by worry and stress and angry thoughts.

Once I felt calmer, I looked at my digital notepad and picked it up. My letter was coming along nicely, bringing up memories that were good for me to remember, especially now, for it was going to help me as much as it would help my daughter someday.

I wrote for about a half hour, having only one contraction in that time, and then I set it aside when my fingers began to cramp.

After staring off into space, wondering what I should do, I finally came to the decision that I was not going to spend all my time in this bed. I was not an invalid, and I wouldn't act like one. So, I pushed the pretty pink throw blanket aside and swung my feet to the floor. My shoes were gone. Of course, Charlie had taken them. He might be suffering some serious delusions, but that didn't stop him from thinking smart. At least, not in regard to the ways of keeping me here.

I walked over to the window and looked out, wishing I would see signs of people looking for me. There were none, but I knew people were looking. They just didn't know where to look and they had no reason to believe I was here.

What I did see was that the sun had gone down, and evening was setting in. The days were still short for this time of year and the people that were out looking would be returning home for the night. Except Kade. He would still be looking. My poor, dear love. He must be out of his mind with worry right now.

Had he come here earlier? It would make sense if he had. Charlie's house was the closest to my last known location. I wondered how that meeting went and had to smile at the images playing through my mind. No doubt Kade's emotions were running high, which could make him very intimidating to those who didn't know him well. But Charlie was a sly one, a good actor. He fooled me and he had to have fooled Kade as well, otherwise, he'd have found me by now. Even so, despite Charlie's wiliness, Kade's gut instincts must have confused him. I didn't doubt that he'd sensed my presence, but it followed no logic to suspect that I was being held captive here. And so, he left.

Poor Kade. I focused on sending him some calming energy, wrapping him in spiritual love. He needed to know I was okay. We would find our way back to each other eventually, but for now I couldn't bear the thought of him torturing himself, fearing something had happened to me or our baby.

Speaking of our baby, we really needed to settle on a name. It had to hold the vibrational energy of something positive and spiritually meaningful, a name that would do well for her as she traversed through the challenges and lessons that life had in store for her. Whatever she decided to do with her life, we wanted her to have all the spiritual reinforcement we could give her to succeed. No doubt we would decide by the time she was born, and I could only pray that Kade would be with me when that happened.

That last thought triggered a rise in determination, to the point that I felt bolder, stronger and capable of whatever was necessary to get back to Kade and out of Charlie's clutches. I would not allow some strange man, whose mental faculties were mired in delusion, to control this entire situation.

And so, with that, I turned to look at the locked door and sent out a silent plea to the spirit world. Surely someone 'over there' would come to my aid, though it wouldn't be Sheila. My spirit guide could not interfere in such a way, for her 'job' was to give guiding counsel, the type that makes me think 'outside the box' and on a deeper level. As she often explained, and as I'd learned the hard way, this life was ours to live via the decisions we make, the thoughts we cultivate, the beliefs we accept. And they, our spirit guides, could only work within the confines of those parameters. Otherwise, we'd reject outright any suggestion that might counter those decisions, thoughts and beliefs. What spirit guides could do was help calm us and put us in a better frame of mind to think through our situation. Sometimes that was enough. Other times, it wasn't. But that wasn't their fault.

Sheila was with me. I felt her presence and that gave me peace of mind. It was enough for now. It was to the others in spirit – those souls who still sought to interact with us – that I sent out my plea. Just as the girl, whoever she was, sent out silent pleas for help – one I'd surely answer if I could only figure out how – I, too, sent out a silent plea for assistance.

Please, if anyone is here, please unluck my door.

The spirit world was a place where mysteries, magic and untold wonders resided. I had either learned or figured out some of it, and there were other things I was still discovering, but one thing I did know for sure—those who dwelled there could manipulate matter in our world. Such manipulations were the stuff of ghost stories, poltergeist activity and supernatural magic. I was seeking something simple, a little thing for a crafty spirit. Surely, I could encourage one of them to do me this one small favor.

64

I felt her presence almost immediately, her emotions so strong they bombarded mine, putting me on edge, and I took a step back, feeling wary yet hopeful. She was quite distressed and somehow tied to Charlie. His wife perhaps? My wariness made her withdraw and I rushed to the door and put my hands upon it.

Let me out. I won't hurt him.

She hovered close but her presence was weakening, and I worried that this was my only chance at getting the assistance I was seeking. In hopes of encouraging her help, I opened myself to her spirit energy. It would help her discern that I was no danger to Charlie, whom I believed was her chief concern. No indeed, I would do nothing to harm him. It wasn't in me to go on a violent defensive. But that didn't mean I would not defend myself if it should come to that. As long as he did not seek to physically harm me, he had nothing to be concerned about. Yes, I wanted out of this awful situation, but I had no shoes, no coat, no car, no phone and I was very close to giving birth to my baby. It was freezing outside and very dark and we were miles from the closest known home with people in it. I would do nothing to put myself in even more jeopardy.

Please unlock the door.

She could do it if she wanted to help me. But she wasn't here for me. She was here for Charlie. I felt quite certain that it was his wife. A mental image began to form in my mind's eye, becoming clearer as I continued to focus on her.

She had short, chestnut brown hair, very thin and fine, but it framed her head in a neat but carefree style. She wore earrings, their shape in a specific design, and with a bit more concentration I could see that they were dolphins. On her left hand she wore an engagement ring inset with a teardrop diamond and her wedding band was in a braided design. Both bands and her earrings were made of yellow gold. Why those particular details were being shown to me, I didn't know, but I committed them to memory.

Her eyes were blue, bright and gentle and filled with love. She was short in stature, perhaps around five feet, and her shoulders were very thin, boney. The loose blue sweater she wore did nothing to hide her thin structure. As her image became clearer, I could almost physically see her. She stretched an arm toward me, and I heard a soft clicking noise, which broke my concentration, and she disappeared from my mental vision.

With my heart pounding in anticipation, I wrapped my hand around the doorknob, knowing it would turn freely, and took a moment to calm myself. Charlie wasn't going to like it, and I needed a good explanation. One he'd not question. The last thing I wanted him to know was that I was a medium. He wasn't ready for that, and he wouldn't accept it. As far as he was concerned, I was Lindsay, and unless I learned otherwise, she did not practice this ability.

Once I felt calm enough to deal with the next few minutes, I opened the door and stepped out into the hallway. Though I wanted to see what was behind the other doors, I didn't want Charlie to hear me walking around. I couldn't risk it and earn his ire and distrust. What I needed to earn was the freedom to move about and discover what I could to get myself out of here.

Very carefully, holding strong to the banister along the right-side wall, I made my way down the carpeted stairs. I could hear Charlie moving about in the kitchen and when I got to the floor, I stopped to again calm my pounding heart. The importance of gaining a bit of freedom had me on edge.

I can do this. He will not lock me back up in that room.

66

With that mantra echoing in my head, I took a deep breath, let it out slowly and stepped into his view, walking slowly and calmly towards him.

Charlie looked up and froze.

While maintaining eye contact, I continued to make my way across the room, stopping just short of the kitchen island that separated us. He'd just drained water from a steaming pot and was in the process of setting it on the counter. "Hi."

"How did you get out?" Charlie frowned, his displeasure with this unexpected development quite evident. "Did you damage my door?"

"No, I got up to stretch my legs and I decided to try the door, and it just opened." I gave him my most innocent smile, at least, that's what I hoped it looked like. "I thought maybe you'd decided not to lock me in anymore."

"But I did lock it, Lindsay."

I shrugged that it was as much a mystery to me as it was to him. "I thought so too, and yet, I figured maybe I was wrong, and so I went to the door and turned the knob, and it opened." I spread my fingers in supplication. "I guess it didn't latch. I don't know. But, please, let me stay down here with you." I gestured with my hands to indicate my state of dress. "I am in no condition to go traipsing outside in the cold, dark night. Besides, where would I go?"

Charlie's eyes darted about the kitchen, and I knew exactly what was going through his head. He was thinking about all the things that could cause him harm if I was to get hold of them.

"Surely you know I won't do anything to hurt you. Besides, you could easily overpower me." If he believed I was his daughter, then he had to believe I cared enough about him not to do him harm, regardless of his actions and what he was doing to me. "Trust is a two-way street you know.

You want me to trust you, then you need to trust me too." Drawing in a breath and hoping I sounded convincing, I looked straight at him. "If you want me here, so be it, but I cannot stay upstairs locked in that room."

We stared at each other, unblinking, for a long tense moment and then Charlie gave a stiff nod. "Fine. I'll trust you until I can't."

And what would he do if he decided he could no longer trust me? Unease shivered along my spine, and I shut down the thoughts such a question evoked. Best not to know. Besides, I'd do nothing to bring about his wrath. All that would do was make things worse, and I was in enough of a pickle already. For whatever reason, the universe put me in this situation, and the quickest way out of it was not to propagate more conflict. No, what I needed to do was figure out what lesson was to be learned from all this. That was the best way to resolve the issue and get on with my life.

But I needed to do it before our daughter was born.

So, stop worrying about all the things that could happen, Tess, and do something that moves you in the direction of freedom. You can do this! That bolstered my resolve. Sometimes giving myself a pep talk was the best motivator.

"I'll be a good girl." I gestured towards the bathroom and began moving in its direction. "I really need to take care of some business, if it's okay." My bladder was screaming for relief, and I wasn't even sure I was going to make it, but I did, thank goodness, or that would have caused some embarrassment.

When I came out of the bathroom, Charlie was getting plates out of the cupboard. "Hey, why don't you let me set the table."

Charlie thought about it for a few seconds then gestured for me to have at it. "Sure. You do that and we'll talk over dinner."

68

Yes, we would. I had a lot to learn about Charlie and Lindsay and maybe even Dean. And I had precious little time to do it.

Another contraction was coming on, and it was very hard to get through it without giving it away. The last thing I wanted was for Charlie to know the contractions were continuing. Though he indicated he was excited about the pending birth of his "granddaughter", I just didn't know him well enough to trust those paternal feelings.

After all, Lindsay was still missing and possibly no longer alive. Though Charlie contended that Dean had something to do with it, I wasn't so sure. Obviously, he and Lindsay had relationship issues, otherwise, he wouldn't be thinking there was a need to hold her here against her will. And there was that girl to consider too. What did she have to do with any of this? I had a lot to figure out, the task looming impossibly large before me, but I would resolve it. One way or another. I had to.

Chapter 6

With Charlie busy getting the food ready, I fetched the silverware, remembering which drawer they were in from when he made our tea earlier. Good thing I watched him get those spoons out! If only I'd continued to watch him, I might have seen him slip in that drug he'd given me.

We worked in silence though I would not say it was a companionable one. Whatever thoughts were running through Charlie's head, they couldn't be all that pleasant. He looked far too serious, and every now and then, the frown lines deepened on his forehead.

As for me, I was trying to think of the questions I wanted to ask while simultaneously concealing my back pain. My instinct was to soothe it with a hand rub, but I didn't want him to think it was related to my labor, which I felt pretty certain was the case.

Charlie had made penne pasta with a ratatouille sauce and toasted garlic bread. Though it smelled quite delicious, I had to take care not to eat too much. The last thing my body needed right now was the added task of digesting food. My friend Mary told me I would later regret it when in the active stage of delivery. Even Charlie had said as much.

"Okay then. I hope you are hungry."

Charlie's voice startled me, and I looked up from where I'd seated myself, nodding to confirm I was hungry, even though it was going to be a chore to eat so much as a bite. Seeing he was about to load up my plate, I placed a hand on his arm to draw his attention. "Just a little for me. I don't have as much room in there as I used to have." I made a rueful face and indicated my belly, which was protruding so much I had to keep the chair slightly away from the table.

Charlie smiled in understanding. "Yes, of course."

He could be so nice and yet he kept me here against my will. And he'd issued a veiled threat that things would get worse if I didn't behave myself.

Once our plates were prepared, Charlie bowed his head. "I'll say grace."

Grace? That was rich coming from him. But I bowed my head.

"Thank you, God, for this food and for bringing Lindsay back to me. I ask that you keep her safe and … and anyone else needing protection. I offer myself as a protector. Amen."

Anyone else needing protection? Now what did he mean by that? Did he have anyone in mind? My heart was pounding again, a telling response to something my psyche knew but my conscious mind did not. This was exactly why I needed to ask the right questions.

We ate in silence, the time stretching past a couple of minutes, which made me anxious. Charlie was shoveling his meal down with ravenous enthusiasm, his only concern being the food before him—not the conversation we had yet to start. I needed to get things going, or he would be done eating, and my opportunity to talk over dinner, when he'd be more distracted, would be lost.

"So, when was Dean here last?"

72

Charlie paused mid-motion, a loaded spoon suspended before his lips, and looked over at me, his face firming with distaste. "A few days ago." He frowned in thought, ate what was on his spoon and followed it with a sip of milk. "Three days ago."

"And before that?"

Charlie shrugged that it didn't matter. Not to him. "I don't know, a couple weeks or so."

"What does he want? What does he say when he comes? When do you think he might come back?"

Charlie set his spoon down, propped his elbows on the table and steepled his hands together. "Well now, that's a lot of questions."

"I am trying to figure out what he's up to. Aren't you curious too? I mean, you think he's a threat to me so shouldn't we be concerned about why he's coming here?"

"Yes, I suppose." He lifted his spoon in one hand and a piece of his garlic bread in the other, then used his spoon to scoop some sauce onto the bread before stuffing it in his mouth. "The first time he came, he said he was just wondering how I was doing and wanted to come in and visit for a bit, but I wouldn't let him in the door. He didn't like that and asked me why I wouldn't let him come in."

When he didn't elaborate any further, I had to stop myself from rolling my eyes and hoped he couldn't hear the impatience in my voice. "What did you tell him?"

"I told him we had nothing more to say to each other, what with you being gone." Charlie shifted in his seat, looking a tad uneasy. "He knows that I've never liked him. He never liked me either."

"Never? You two never liked each other?"

"You know the answer to that, Lindsay. I am never going to like a man who doesn't treat you right, and he didn't like me calling him out on it. As much as you tried to hide it, the abuse he was inflicting on you was obvious." He reached over and patted my hand. "I knew it was because of him that you told me not to come visit." He gave my hand a squeeze. "I think you knew, too, that I wouldn't stay away."

"On the day I disappeared, what did you think happened?"

Charlie's expression showed the heartache he'd gone through, had dealt with, for however long his daughter's been missing. "What do you think I thought, Lindsay? Dean showed up and discovered you weren't there, demands to know where you'd gone to then storms out. Obviously, he went after you and then you never came back." His eyes flared with indignation. "He tried to blame me for you not returning."

"For some reason, my mind is foggy about everything that happened that day." I wasn't sure what else to say, but I hoped that was enough to keep him talking.

"I shouldn't have let you leave like that, especially not after telling me about the baby. Oh, how you tried to convince me that you and Dean were happy about it, but I knew better." His eyes closed briefly, and he rubbed his mouth, the memories of that day still hard on him. "I felt wicked bad that our last words were not good ones."

"I'm sorry." This time it was me squeezing his hand, which rested beside mine, though his fingers were fidgety, a sure sign of his anxiety.

Charlie looked at me with bewilderment. "I don't understand why you didn't just pack up and come home with me. I told you that I would keep you safe."

74

Oh, how I needed to navigate through this conversation the right way. "Don't you think Dean would have stopped me from leaving, especially with me pregnant with his child?"

Charlie scrubbed his hands across his face, our conversation frustrating him for some reason. "Where did he take you, Lindsay?" He looked at me with genuine curiosity. "There's no sense in denying his involvement. I'm not the only one who knew he'd taken you."

Who was he talking about? And what was I to tell him? I sat there, my brain scrambling for a reply, and then an idea dropped into my head, and I went with it. "I did go with him initially, though I didn't want to. I really didn't, but you were pressuring me to come home, and I wasn't ready." I paused to see how he took that, and since he didn't react with indignation, I knew I was right about his role that day. Now to go with the other part of the story. "But eventually I knew that I couldn't stay with him either."

Charlie leaned forward, his expression easy to read. This was exactly what he expected me to say. "So, you did escape from him. It must have happened before his first visit here. It's why he came … he was looking for you, despite what he was telling me." His eyes narrowed with curiosity. "So where have you been?"

What was Dean telling him? "I do have other friends, you know."

Charlie scowled. "Other friends? What kind of friend helps you hide from your own father, who is worried that you might be dead?" Suddenly agitated, he pushed his chair back and stood up. "I prayed for you to be alive, and I have been a wreck wondering about it." He grabbed our plates, not taking much notice that I'd barely touched my food, and headed towards the sink. "You could have called me or something."

"I'm sorry. I was afraid."

That made him go still, and then he turned to look at me. "Of who?"

I let my gaze drop to the table, as if I was ashamed, but it was more because I didn't want him to see that I wasn't being truthful with him.

When he spoke again, his voice was hoarse. "Of me?"

I looked back up at him and did my best to convey an earnest expression. "No! Of Dean." But was Lindsay afraid of her father too? It was hard trying to pretend to be someone I wasn't and who knew things I didn't. "I'm here now, aren't I?" But was it a good idea to let this illusion of his continue? Then again if I were to deny it, his reaction could be volatile, especially after entertaining it this long. I just couldn't risk him losing his temper with me. Best to pretend to be his cooperative daughter until I found a way to make it safely back to Kade. Or him to me.

"Don't worry about the dishes," I urged gently. "Come sit with me some more so we can talk this out. I need to know what our plan is." I had to make this about "us" and what "we" would do, otherwise, I would be at Charlie's complete mercy and that I did not want.

Charlie put our plates next to the sink and returned to his chair. "The second time he came he was really mad."

"About what?"

Charlie's gaze shifted away. He was hiding something, and he wasn't going to share it. Not yet. When he looked at me again, it was to convey the seriousness of his next statement. "He means to do harm. You may have managed to escape him, Lindsay, but I am stuck here. He knows where I am and at some point, he'll be back."

That sounded so ominous and rightly so. Dread washed through me, and another contraction came on, this one hitting quickly and hard. I gave a little gasp and looked away. It was hard to control my breath and impossible to hide my discomfort.

76

"You having another contraction?" Charlie covered my hand that was gripping the edge of the table, and though I didn't want him touching me, I let him think he was giving me the comfort he was intending to administer.

With my other hand rubbing my hardening abdomen, my skin feeling as though it were being stretched nearly beyond its limits, I breathed through the pain and squeezed my eyes closed, wanting to hold back the tears blurring my vision. Not only did I not want to cry in front of Charlie, but I was supposed to be stronger than this. Darn it all anyway. I did not want to go through this without Kade!

"I wish there was something I could do for you, Lindsay, but I promise you won't remember the pain when you are holding your baby in your arms."

As annoyed and frustrated with him as I was, his words were just what I needed to hear. He was right, this discomfort was temporary and was leading to something wonderful. I would deal with it and carry on. So, I continued to focus on my breathing exercise while Charlie rubbed my hand, and once the pain receded, I opened my eyes and saw that his face was wreathed with worry. "I get these all the time."

"So, you aren't in labor?"

"I don't think so." But I definitely was. *Please, dear God, let it be a very long labor!*

"You want to go back upstairs and lie down?"

Though I'd been happy to escape that room, the suggestion did sound tempting. But not yet. "No, maybe in a little bit." I gently extricated myself from his grasp. "So, what are we going to do?"

There, it was said. I needed to know Charlie's plan. What did he intend to do with me?

"We need to keep you hidden. Just until I can figure out what to do about Dean. We can't risk him finding you."

"But seriously, what can you possibly do about him? We can go to the police..."

"No." Charlie stood abruptly and grabbed the pasta dish. "They are useless. I told them I suspected Dean had something to do with you not coming home, and after listening to his lies they decided he was not involved."

How was I to get Charlie to let me go? If I could just have some time to think. The urge to pee suddenly diverted my attention, and then it hit me that it was as good an excuse as any for a reprieve from this conversation. I stood and started across the kitchen. "I need to use the bathroom."

Charlie took the dish he was holding to the counter, and just before I closed the bathroom door, I could see he was thinking deeply about something. For some reason, that made me shudder.

I closed the door and enjoyed the relief of being out of his sight. And though it didn't take long to do my business, I continued to sit a little longer to think things through. I needed to come up with something that might convince him to let me go, but it couldn't anger him in the process. And then an idea came to me, and I flushed the toilet, washed my hands, drew in a fortifying breath and exited my sanctuary.

Charlie was nowhere in sight.

Wondering where he'd gone off to, I made my way back to the table and sat down. A few seconds later, I heard him approaching and turned to see him coming through a door in the pantry. Now what was he doing in there and where did that door lead?

Charlie saw me at the table and smiled, like it pleased to see me waiting for him. "Everything okay, Lindsay?"

"Yes, thank you."

He rejoined me at the table, and we sat in silence for an uncomfortable minute.

Since his mood seemed calmer, I figured it best to take advantage of it, keeping my voice gentle as I spoke. "You know, at some point someone is eventually going to come looking for me." His eyes narrowed on me as I spoke, and though I was starting to get a bad feeling, I persisted. "I told you, I do have other friends, and they are going to start wondering where I am…"

"Yes, yes, I know all about it." His calm mood over, Charlie stood and began pacing between the kitchen and the dining table, his hands running up through his thinning gray hair, his pale brown eyes flashing with emotion.

I don't know what I said to get him so riled up, or what was running through that confused brain of his, but I had a strong feeling it wasn't going to bode well for me. "What do you mean that you know all about it?"

"They were already here."

My heart was pounding so hard I wondered if even Charlie could hear it. "Who was here?" But I knew. Kade.

"When I told you it was someone delivering groceries, it wasn't. But I needed you to give in to the effects of the sleeping pill." Charlie's lips pursed in consideration, his eyes regarding me with calculation. Whatever he was cooking up in his delusional mind, it wasn't going to be anything I liked. "It was Janice, and I have to say, Lindsay, that I am very disappointed that she knew your whereabouts and said nothing to me. Why you two felt you needed to use that convoluted story of checking her grandparents' place in order for you to come here to see me, I don't know."

I started to speak but was glad when a sharp wave of his hand cut me off. Just as well, I wasn't sure what I was going to say anyway. It was a human trait to speak before we think and though that was fine sometimes, it wasn't at others. Like now.

"She wasn't alone. A man was with her. I can't remember his name, but he said he was married to some girl named Tess." Charlie's eyes narrowed on me. "That's the name you first used when you tried to make me think you were someone else. Have you been pretending to be someone named Tess, Lindsay? Is that how you've been hiding from Dean? And I don't mind telling you, if you've hooked up with that man, then I am very disappointed with you. How could you go from one disagreeable man to another?"

A lump was in my throat, making it hard for me to speak. I had to look away and blink a couple times to clear the tears away. *Stay calm, Tess.* "What did they say?"

"Janice said that Tess (he gave me a pointed look) was supposed to look at her grandparents' house and help her decide about selling it, or some such nonsense, and that she … you … hadn't been heard from since." He stared at me, and I stared back not knowing what to say. "At first, I didn't put it together that the girl they were talking about might be you." His eyes narrowed on me. "It's how you've managed to stay in hiding from him, isn't it? You took on someone else's identity." Before I could formulate an answer, he rushed on, getting more agitated as he spoke. "Janice is in on it, too, of course, but I don't think that man has any idea who you really are." Muscles in Charlie's cheek twitched with tension. "Was she the friend you ran to? And why would you convince that man, who told me you were his wife, by the way, that you are someone named Tess?" Realization dawned, his mind coming up with his own

80

answers. "You've convinced him to help you hide from Dean, haven't you?"

Charlie slapped his hand on the table in front of me, making me jump and place my arms protectively about my stomach. His anger was building momentum, and I needed to diffuse the situation. Since he'd already decided on the story, it was best not to refute it. What I needed to do was smooth things over and calm his riled emotions. "I haven't been staying with her. I've been mostly on my own, but then I met Kade, and he's been so kind…"

"Kind?" Charlie gave a short bark of laughter. "I think you may have gone from one bad egg to another, Lindsay! He sounded difficult, angry and suspicious." Charlie sat down in his chair, his posture stiff with tension. "He doesn't know your real name, does he?" He didn't wait for me to give him an answer. "He definitely has no idea that I am your father."

"No, he doesn't know." I couldn't let Charlie's impression of Kade go without correction. "If he sounded disagreeable it's because he's worried about me. He loves me."

"Ha!" Charlie let out a bark of laughter. "If he loves you so much, then why is he letting you go running around the countryside by yourself, especially when you are about to have a baby?" He shook his head with disparagement. "How is it that he's become involved with a woman who is pregnant with another man's baby?" When I started to speak, he sliced his hand through the air, effectively cutting me off. "It doesn't matter. Obviously, you've been lying to him." Again, I tried to speak, and he waved me into silence. "What I don't understand is why you thought you needed to use the excuse of going to the Wheeler house." And then he snapped his fingers as he came up with his own answer. "That cockamamie story was for his benefit, wasn't it? Since he doesn't know I'm your father, you and Janice cooked up a stupid story about looking at her house so you could come here without his knowing the real reason."

I figured the best reaction was none, so I sat quietly and let him rage on.

"He acted quite concerned, so I can see why you fell for him, and Janice played her part well, pretending that you were someone named Tess." He shook his head with disgust. "And honestly, Lindsay, did you and Janice really think I wouldn't recognize you? Did you really think changing your hair color was going to fool me?"

If Charlie was being rational, he'd realize how crazy his thoughts were about this whole thing. But he wasn't rational, and he wasn't using any logic in this at all. How to argue against lunacy? "What did you tell them?" If he really believed that Janice and I were pulling the wool over Kade's eyes, then how did he handle the confrontation?

"I told them I hadn't seen you, that I thought I saw you walking up around the woods, but when I went out to see, I no longer saw anyone." Charlie's mouth twisted into a smirk. "I thought that was a nice touch by suggesting that I had seen you. And, of course, my taking your car away has really thrown them off."

"Is it on the property somewhere?" It was possible, due to the proximity of Charlie's place to the Wheeler house, that the police might search the entire area. If they found my car close by, then Charlie's game would soon be over for surely, they would come here demanding a closer look.

"I took it a few miles away, to a place down the road, somewhere no one ever goes in the winter."

My heart sank. Why did he feel it necessary to do that? And how did he get back to the house?

82

Charlie scratched the back of his head and looked away. He was scheming again, and that made me very nervous. Not that there was anything about this situation that didn't make me nervous.

"That man didn't seem to believe me and that has me wicked worried." Charlie turned back to me and gave me a long considering stare. "He could come back at any time. Dean too." Heaving a resigned sigh, Charlie stood and began pacing again. "I can't risk him showing up with you walking around down here. I wouldn't be able to hide you fast enough, and anyways, I think you'd want him to find you, wouldn't you?"

"No, Charlie, I'll do whatever you tell me to do."

He came around behind my chair and placed his hands on my shoulders. "Don't call me Charlie. Since when have you stopped calling me dad?" His grip tightened. "Up you get." Giving me no choice, he helped me up from my seat.

"Are you going to lock me in the bedroom again?" My spirits fell at the idea of it.

"No, I think that isn't going to work either."

"A different room then?" I felt desperation racing through me. He wasn't leading me toward the stairs.

"I've somewhere safer in mind. Don't you worry none, it will all be fine." We stopped in front of the door he'd come through when he rejoined me in the kitchen earlier, which I could see now was located in what seemed to be his pantry and laundry room combined. "You'll be safer here and I'll feel better about that."

Charlie opened the door, revealing a steep staircase leading down into darkness.

"You are going to put me in the cellar?" Shocked that he'd come up with something like this, I couldn't control the rush of fear that charged through me. What sort of conditions was he putting me in? Expecting the worst, considering Charlie's state of mind, I went right into the throes of a hard contraction. It was so bad I had to bend over, unable to stifle my groans as the pain increased.

"Don't get yourself all worked up. You'll be comfortable. I promise." Charlie waited until the contraction was over before pulling me along with him, and since I didn't want to go tumbling down the stairs, I went without a fight, though my sense of security was fast dwindling. How was I ever going to be found if Charlie was going to hide me in his basement? Unless the police came up with something to make them suspect him, there would be no reason for them to believe that Charlie was holding me captive. And thus, no reason to search his home.

After going down the first step, Charlie reached over and snapped on a light, for which I was grateful. The fear of falling while heavy with a baby terrified me. We went slowly, Charlie being remarkably patient and helpful. I loathed his touch but had to accept it.

At the bottom of the stairs, Charlie turned on another light, revealing a finished, tidy basement, a fact that eased my fears just a bit. The tiled floor was swept clean, the walls were finished with sheetrock and painted white. A drop ceiling hid the heating ducts and house wiring. We crossed over to what looked like a large, old cabinet.

Charlie opened the doors and there was nothing inside, not even shelves. "Do you remember what is here, Lindsay?"

I shook my head, unable to speak past the lump forming in my throat. Fear, grief, panic. They were all clambering through me. All the negative emotions that I knew better than to give into, especially as they did no good and resolved nothing. If anything, those emotions made matters worse.

84

"You know me, Lindsay, always prepared for anything. You never know when you need a place to hide things." He shook his head at the irony of his words. "Of course, I'd never thought it would be you or …" He shook his head, cutting himself short. "Life is funny sometimes."

There was nothing funny about this situation. Not a darn thing.

Charlie reached inside and ran his hand along the left edge of the cabinet's back wall, stopping when his fingers found a recessed pocket. He gripped it and slid the entire back panel to the right, revealing the cellar wall behind it. I noticed a keypad mounted in the top left corner of the wall and a funny feeling fluttered in my solar plexus.

Charlie grinned. "The back panel slides right into the wall between the sheetrock and the cinder blocks. So even if it's left open, no one would notice it from outside the cabinet. Clever, isn't it? I came up with that all on my own." He punched in the code on the keypad, not bothering to hide it from me, for which I was grateful as it might come in handy later, then he pushed against the wall, and it opened inward, revealing a room that was lit by a bulb hanging from the ceiling.

It wasn't a very big room, and it was completely empty. It terrified me to think he was going to hide me in there with nothing to even sit on! If it weren't for my pregnancy, and the fact I was in labor, I would have tried to overcome him, but I was in no condition to do anything but be compliant.

With his hand on my back, he urged me to step forward. "There's nothing to trip you up. Just move ahead enough to let me in too."

As soon as I stepped into the room, I noticed a door on each side of the entrance, and that gave me hope that I was going to be hidden in a furnished room of some sort.

Charlie reached for a shelf above the coatrack next to the entrance, and lifted the top, revealing a hidden compartment. From there he retrieved a key and used it to unlock the door on our right. "I've been working on this a long time, Lindsay. I think you are going to be surprised." He pulled the door open and reached in to turn on the light, revealing a sizable, furnished room.

It contained a full bed, for which I was grateful, a nightstand with an oil lamp, and a bookcase full of books and magazines. A small dresser was placed right beside the door, and a rocking chair was next to the bed. Tucked in the corner to the left of the door was a tiny kitchenette, containing a refrigerator bigger than what was typical in dorm rooms, but smaller than what one would see in a kitchen, a small two-burner gas stove and a sink. Several cupboards were built around them and it seemed he'd stocked it with the usual kitchen paraphernalia.

Seeing all that scared the heck out of me. Just how long did he intend to keep me down here? I looked at Charlie, my eyes pleading with him to have mercy. "I can't stay down here. I cannot."

"It won't be for long, Lindsay. Just until I can figure out what to do about Dean. We'll figure out what to do about that other fella afterwards."

That made my blood run cold, a cliché I now fully understood. "What do you mean that we will figure out what to do about Kade? He is no threat. I promise you."

"I know you believe that…"

"No. I know that. I know it. He … he's as protective of me as you are." Oh, how it galled me to make any sort of comparison between Charlie and Kade.

"Okay, okay. We'll address that later. Right now, we need to worry about Dean." He shook a warning finger at me. "He is a threat and make no mistake about it. You know as well as I do, Lindsay, that he is not a good man."

86

So, what did Charlie intend to do? Was he thinking of eliminating Dean somehow? Regardless of what the man had done, I did not want Charlie to go down that road. Somehow, I needed to convince him to let the authorities handle it. Aside from holding me against my will, Charlie hadn't done anything so grievous that he'd be locked up for the remainder of his days. At least, I hoped this was the worst of his sins. The fact he wasn't in his right mind meant the law would likely be forgiving. But if he did anything to Dean, Charlie's days of freedom would be over. Unless, that is, he got away with it. And if that happened, then my freedom wouldn't happen any time soon, for I feared he didn't intend to ever let me go. Oh, I knew I wouldn't be here forever, but it was possible I might be here when my daughter made her entrance into the world. That worried me more than anything.

A lump grew in my throat, making it hard to breathe. It was all I could do not to give in to the tears of despair building momentum within me. Blinking rapidly to clear the moisture from my eyes, I glanced around the room, my spirits sinking lower by the second. I was going to go crazy in here. "I'm pregnant and that means I must go to the bathroom a lot. This isn't going to work."

Charlie grinned. "That isn't going to be a problem either." He opened a door that I had assumed was a closet and inside was a long narrow bathroom. Charlie turned on the light and let me peek inside. "Not bad work for an old guy, huh?"

It had a toilet, a vanity sink, and a walk-in shower was located at the far, left side of the room, right across from another door. I pointed at it and looked at Charlie. "What's in there?"

The bathroom showed signs of use. A damp looking towel was hanging from a hook, there was a wet washcloth folded on the sink and there was tissue in the wastebasket. I looked at those clues along with Charlie, who had yet to say anything.

With lips compressed, Charlie motioned for me to step back into the bedroom. "I guess we need to have another talk."

I thought I heard something as he ushered me out and closed the door, but Charlie was urging me over to the bed, so I let it go for now. Whatever this talk was about, I had a strong suspicion it had something to do with the girl sending me those messages. My psychic senses were going crazy, making my heart pound, my breath come quick, and bringing on another contraction. I dropped onto the bed and rubbed my tightening belly in a soothing caress.

Charlie waited, saying nothing, until I let out a releasing breath and looked over at him, indicating I was ready to hear whatever he wanted to say.

He nodded in approval and offered me an encouraging smile. "You are handling that so well. I am very proud of you."

I wasn't a violent person and rarely lost my temper, but I wanted to snarl at him and let him have it. How dare he sit there and smile at me like nothing was wrong with this entire situation, like we had no issues between us, like he was doing everything he could to help me through my labor. But, of course, I couldn't say anything to upset him because he was holding me against my will, and, for now anyway, he was calling all the shots. So, I squeezed my hands into fists and fought hard to maintain control of my emotions. "What more do we need to talk about?"

The smile vanished from Charlie's face, and he actually looked uneasy, like he was worried about my reaction to whatever he was about to say. "Well, Dean showing up wasn't entirely a surprise."

"No?"

Now, finally, he was going to tell me about her. And I also knew, with unshakable certainty, that this is why I was here.

Charlie sat and rubbed his mouth a few times, looking undecided, even reluctant, but then he shook his head as if a decision was finally being made. "She didn't want me to tell you, but I feel you should know." Another long pause as he considered his next words. "A couple of months ago a girl showed up. She had some of your things in her car." He waved a hand to stop my attempt to ask a question, then held up a finger in a silent request to give him a minute to speak. "I'm not sure why, but, like I said, she asked me not to tell you she was here, but she's your friend and I should think that you would like to have a friend here with you." He shrugged in confusion, clearly not understanding her request and seemed conflicted about not honoring it. "Maybe it's because she has been trying to convince me that Dean did something bad to you, and with you being here, obviously quite fine ... well, that's made her wrong on those assumptions, hasn't it?"

My heart continued to pound with excitement, making it hard to breathe and triggering another contraction, though it wasn't as strong as the others.

Charlie waited until my contraction was over before continuing. "She knew Dean was responsible for your disappearance, just as I did. She said she got ... feelings, vibes I think she called them, about his involvement, and its why Dean is looking for her. He doesn't want her going to the police with what she knows, but now it doesn't matter anymore because here you are!"

"You said she got vibes about Dean?"

Charlie chuckled. "That's what she said. I don't know what any of that mumbo jumbo stuff is all about, but she said she felt like Dean had done something bad." He let out an unamused laugh. "I have to tell you, she about had me convinced that I might never see you again, so when you showed up this morning, well you just don't know how wicked relieved I was." He leaned forward and patted my leg, his joy over his daughter's believed return evident in his expression. "I couldn't even believe it at first. When I opened the door and saw you, I just couldn't believe my eyes! In fact, it took me a bit of time to recognize you." His face twisted into an expression of apology. "It's why I didn't react right away, you know, when I first saw you."

Was this girl still here of her own volition, as Charlie seemed to be intimating? Then what were those pleas for help all about?

Charlie's thin lips split into a smile, his fondness for the girl evident. "But she did have it right about one thing, didn't she? You said that Dean took you away and that's exactly what she said too." Charlie barked out a short laugh. "Guess her vibes about something bad happening to you were wrong, huh?"

"So where is she?" But I knew.

Ignoring my question, he continued on with his story. "I don't know why she did it, but she told him that she suspected he'd taken you and he got upset with her. Luckily, she already had your things loaded into her car when their argument took place." Charlie gave me a smile, looking happy to impart what he said next. "We put all your stuff in the small bedroom at the top of the stairs."

"So where is she now?" Why wouldn't he just come out and say it?

"She is afraid of Dean." He gave me a significant look, one that said if this girl was afraid of him, then I should be as well. "So, anyways, she's been staying here, and I don't mind telling you, Lindsay, that I've enjoyed her company. You chose well making her your friend." His scowl returned.

90

"After Dean showed up the first time, though, we knew we had to be more careful." His eyes were grave as they met mine. "He came here looking for her, but giving I now know that you got away from him, I think he was looking for you too, though he didn't say so."

"Is she still here?"

Charlie was silent for a long time, and it was very hard not to prompt him along. "She wanted to leave after he showed up the second time and urged me to call the police, but I told her the police would not do anything and to let me handle Dean. But she didn't agree with me. So, I had to do what I had to do."

"Which is what?" But I already knew, and my heart sank for her. How awful that she was in the same pickle as me.

Charlie sighed, like he was tired of keeping the secret any longer. "She's in the room across the hall."

I ran my hands up through my hair and pressed my fingers to my skull. I was filled with so many jumbled emotions. Fear for her, fear for me, fear that we were not going to make it out of this awful mess anytime soon. "What are you thinking? You can't keep us down here forever."

Charlie stood, his body stiff with tension, his hands clenched at his sides. "I am doing what needs to be done to keep you both safe. Her going to the police wasn't going to do anything. Just as they did nothing to protect you, Lindsay."

"What do you mean?"

"I mean that when I told them Dean must have taken you somewhere, they didn't believe me. They did nothing." He went to the door but paused in the open doorway. "He's a sly one, and I must outsmart him. I will keep you and Dawn safe. I promise."

Dawn. Her name was Dawn. "Are we sharing the bathroom?"

Charlie nodded. "Yes, but right now her bathroom door is locked." He frowned as if he wasn't quite sure why then gave the back of his head a scratch, like he was as baffled as I as to how we got to where we were. "I didn't plan any of this, Lindsay. It all just sort of happened, but it will work out fine, and you both will be safe here until it's over."

That didn't sound the least bit comforting. "Until what is over?"

The lines in Charlie's face deepened with his scowl. "Well, Dean of course."

"And just how is Dean going to be 'over'?" I air quoted that last word and he didn't look impressed.

"He'll be back, and I'll be ready for him."

I closed my eyes in despair. I really was caught up in some sort of crazy, terrifying dream. "What will it take for you to let Dawn and me go?" Did he intend to kill Dean? Was that where he was going with all this? How was I supposed to stop it?

"Go?" Charlie bristled. "And where, exactly, do you want to go?"

"Well, I am sure that Dawn has a home. As do I."

"You know as well as I do that Dawn doesn't have a home. And you can't possibly mean to leave me and go live with that unfriendly fellow who came here looking for you, do you?" He looked away, unable to meet my eyes. "I will keep you here until you both understand the situation and stop fighting me about it."

Oh God, he really did mean to keep us captive forever! Because we were never going to agree with any of this. "What are you saying?"

Charlie's gaze returned to mine, his expression softening, his hands circling the air in a calming motion. "Don't get all worked up about it. We'll take things one day at a time. Okay?"

92

At this point, all I wanted was for him to go away. I was overwhelmed with emotion and didn't want to talk to him anymore. Besides, I needed to get to Dawn. Between the two of us, perhaps we'd figure a way out of here. The poor thing. It sounded like she's been down here at least a week. The idea of being here even a few hours was horrifying.

Charlie heaved a frustrated sigh and stepped out into the hallway. "I'm sorry, my dear. I know you don't like this and neither do I. But it will be fine. I'll take care of it." After giving me one last smile, he closed and locked the door.

The moment I no longer heard any noise coming from him, I struggled up from the bed and (thanks to the fact it felt like my baby was a lot lower than she used to be) I waddled my way through the bathroom to the other door. It surprised me that Dawn hadn't yet made any noise. What threats had Charlie made to keep her quiet?

"Dawn? Are you there?" When I didn't get a reply, I jiggled the doorknob, though Charlie had told me it was locked. "Hello?"

It worried me that I was getting no reply, because I could sense her presence, so I spoke a little louder, wondering if maybe Charlie had drugged her. "Dawn? Are you in there?"

Finally, a hesitant reply came back to me. "Yes, I'm here."

Chapter 7

Relieved as I was to hear her voice, the reality of our situation had just become painfully clear, spiking my anxiety. It wasn't just me Charlie was holding captive, and that changed everything, especially knowing he'd been keeping her down here for a while. And now, on top of everything else, I had her to worry about too. "Are you okay?"

"Yes."

Thank God for that. Before we went any further, though, I made sure she knew straight away who I was. "My name is Tess Sinclair."

"I don't understand," she said, sounding confused. "Charlie told me Lindsay was here."

"He thinks I am Lindsay for some reason, and I played along because denying it only agitated him." A sudden sharp contraction forced a gasp, and I braced my hands on the door as the pain intensified.

Dawn's voice rose with concern. "Are you okay?"

It took me a moment to answer, my voice breathless when I finally could speak. "I'm in labor…"

"What do you mean?"

I had to smile at that for it couldn't be anything she would have expected to hear. "I mean I am going to be giving birth soon, and I am praying it doesn't happen here in this house, let alone in this basement."

"This doesn't make any sense," she said, her voice sounding even more confused. "Lindsay had her baby already. Charlie must know that."

What? If that was the case, then Charlie really was lost in delusion. "How long has she been missing?"

"Almost a year."

"Wow." This was incredible. How could Charlie possibly think I was Lindsay? "I don't understand how he could think I am his daughter with me still being pregnant – not if she's been gone that long."

Dawn let out a loud snort. "Charlie's sense of time is warped. His entire brain is fried I think."

"His mental state is definitely in question." I had to let this new information sink in before rousing myself to ask another important question. "Can you tell me about this Dean guy?"

She didn't answer right away, and when she did, she sounded like she was doing so with a great deal of reluctance. "He was Lindsay's boyfriend."

"Yes, I've gathered that much, but do you know him very well?"

"Well enough." Her voice rose defensively. "I mean, after Lindsay disappeared, I got to know him a little better." A short pause and then she muttered her next confession. "He's really handsome."

It made me curious, her saying that. What exactly did his looks have to do with anything? As I didn't know what to say, I just waited, rubbing my aching back as I did so and letting out a small groan. Gosh but it hurt!

Perhaps it was my groan that did it, but suddenly she was talking a little faster. "I actually got a temp job at his workplace, so I kind of worked with him, though I didn't really see him much there. I met Lindsay in a yoga class not long after, and we became really good friends, but..." She let out a long sigh, like she was glad to get this off her chest. "I never told her that I worked with Dean, or that I even knew him."

Aah, so this was why she didn't want Charlie telling Lindsay she was here. She was afraid of her learning that one rather big detail. "I see."

"Charlie doesn't know I worked with Dean either. I'm surprised Dean hasn't told him, though I am sure it will come out if they get a chance to talk for any length of time."

Why did Dawn think it necessary to keep that information from them? What would be the harm in them knowing that?

"After Lindsay disappeared, I started getting … I don't know, a feeling about things. It's hard to explain."

Those 'vibes' Charlie mentioned. She was probably psychically sensitive. "Gut instincts were kicking in," I suggested, hoping she'd open up about her gift.

Though her tone was hesitant, I could tell she was going to open up to me. "I have to tell you, so you'll know, that I am a psychic."

It certainly explained why her message had come through so loud and clear. Her skill at picking up on my replies, however, was not yet developed. I could help her with that.

As I had yet to respond to her confession, she must have taken my silence as disbelief, for she sounded a bit despondent when she spoke again. "Most people don't believe me when I tell them that."

"I can imagine." Though psychic ability was often regarded with skepticism, mediums like me often faced even greater disbelief.

"Dean was worried about it. You know, the fact that I knew things." Frustration and perhaps even exasperation became evident in her tone. "Ugh! I just wish I'd listened to my gut when it warned me to keep my distance, but he was so upset about Lindsay, or so I thought, and I felt bad for him." Her voice lowered with feeling. "Lindsay was always talking to me about their relationship, and at work I'd heard talk that he wasn't happy either, and then when she disappeared, I got a bad feeling."

"I'm sure it was a very hard time for all of you," I said gently, sensing she needed to know that I was on her side.

"I started getting visions of Dean and Lindsay fighting. Then I had a dream that he was driving away with her..." She let out a frustrated sound. "I didn't know what to make of it, you know, all those visions, and like an idiot, I told Dean about them. I should have known better. Everything in me was telling me to stay away from him." It sounded like Dawn struck the door with her fist and I mentally sent her some calming energy. "I should have listened to my feelings."

"Don't beat yourself up over it. I'm here for the same reason … ignoring my gut instinct while at the same time going with it."

A note of teasing sounded in her voice. "Are you a psychic too?"

"I'm a medium, actually, and to some degree, I guess you can say that psychic abilities come along with that."

I heard her gasp in surprise. "No way. A medium? Like, you see dead people?"

"Yes, like that."

"Wow, that's cool." But she sounded wary, and then silence stretched between us. "I don't know how long Charlie is going to leave us alone."

"I don't imagine we'll have a lot of time." But I really needed to know a little more about Dean, especially if he could become a problem for us. "So, after Lindsay disappeared you continued to work with him and talk to him?"

"Yes, and the more time I spent with him the more the … visions … continued. I was really worried about her, and he was pretending to be

98

worried about her, and so we were just keeping tabs on each other more than anything I think."

"So, how did you end up here with Charlie?"

"I told Dean I would help him pack up Lindsay's things and bring them to her father and he agreed to it. The night before I came here to Charlie's, right after getting Lindsay's things in my car, we somehow ended up in an argument. He got a little mean, and I just blurted out about knowing he was responsible for Lindsay's disappearance, and that really set him off."

"And he let you go?"

"Yeah, well, there were people around– he didn't have much of a choice."

Thank God she managed to get away from him. Though coming to Charlie wasn't the right move either.

"When I got here, me and Charlie sort of hit it off. I mean, he was so happy to have a friend of Lindsay's here. He's very lonely."

"But then Dean came, and everything changed."

"Yeah, Charlie just sort of flipped out thinking he needed to protect me. At first, I was okay with it, coming down here to hide the first two times he came, but then Charlie wanted me to stay down here and I didn't like that. I suggested that I go and stay with my mother in Florida and Charlie didn't like that. So, he drugged me and got me down here and I've been here ever since, which is about a week I think."

I felt there was more to the story, but we didn't have time to hash it all out, which was a shame because something was bugging me—a sense that I needed to be probing things more. "Has Charlie shown any signs of not being mentally stable since you've been here?"

"I've realized his sense of time is off and he's a bit weird, but in a quirky kind of way, that's all."

"So, when exactly did you get here?"

"I got here about two months ago. As to why Dean is suddenly looking for me, I have no idea unless it's because he wants an update on my visions." Her voice rose with annoyance. "After Dean's second visit, Charlie smashed my cellphone. He said that it sent out a location signal and that's how Dean knew I was here. I guess that's when I got my first real hint that he's something of a nut case. I mean, who does that? Who smashes someone's cellphone like that?" She made a low growl of aggravation. "But, though I'm not happy about him doing that, I really don't want Dean finding me. As for Charlie, well he is just a mixed-up, crazy old man whose view on reality is becoming somewhat warped."

"So, until a week ago you were staying here willingly?"

"Yup." She uttered a derisive snort. "I felt quite safe until he decided to lock me in down here, but I do understand that he's convinced this is the safest place for me to be. At least until he can figure out what to do about Dean."

I didn't know what to say, I was too discouraged to even speak.

"Just so you know … I don't want any part in what I think Charlie has in mind. To be honest, I really thought I could convince him that we should go to the police."

"Only things have escalated in the wrong direction," I said in understanding.

"Charlie showed me these rooms not long after I got here, and at first, I was quite impressed. I think he had plans to make a basement apartment for Lindsay at one time, but she left him right after she graduated from high school. So instead, he put in that false door, which was pretty clever I

100

thought, and was making plans, I think, to make a safe space for himself for when Armageddon came. Well, either that or the aliens." She laughed at that, and I couldn't help but smile, though it was really all quite sad. "Obviously he's been slowly losing it. I've noticed a decline in his mental state just in the past week, starting with him locking me in down here. And now look, he is holding you captive and calling you Lindsay." The sadness in her voice told me she was grieving the loss of a relationship she had higher expectations for.

After a moment of reflective silence, Dawn began talking again. "I never would have thought he'd lock me in here. Something must have snapped in him after Dean's second visit. That's when he forced his way in the house and searched it." Her next words sounded quite ominous. "He'll be back just as Charlie says, which is why I've pretty much resigned myself to this … this prison. For now."

A chill went through me, and I knew that things were indeed going to get worse. "The last place we should be is locked in an enclosed space!" How were we to defend ourselves? It was a question I quickly berated myself for asking. *Come on, Tess, you most certainly are not helpless in this situation. You do indeed have the means within you to protect yourself.*

"But," Dawn began, pulling my attention back to her. "The good part about this is that Dean shouldn't find us if he does search the house." Her next words made me feel very cold inside. "Then again, no one else is going to find us either."

"We need to convince him to let us go to the police."

"He's not going to agree to it. I mean, he has to know he'll get in trouble for keeping us here against our will."

She had a point, but I had to believe that we'd be rescued. Somehow. We just had to. In the meantime, we needed to stay safe.

"Charlie was a suspect in Lindsay's disappearance for a while too. Did you know that?"

"No."

"Although I felt pretty sure Dean did it, I didn't get a good feeling about coming here. I felt, I don't know, like I shouldn't have come, but I came anyway. Obviously."

I nodded in complete understanding. "Yeah, me too."

We had a moment of mutual commiseration before Dawn continued with her story. "The night I ended up down here, Charlie had me convinced that he was on board with me going to my mom's." There was a slight pause and then she spoke almost under her breath, as if speaking more to herself than to me. "I never thought I'd ever go back there … you know, to my mother's place. It's probably just as well that I ended up down here."

Although I felt there was more to explore with that little confession about not going back to her mother's, we just didn't have time for me to pursue it. Hopefully, we would have an opportunity to address it later after this was all over. For now, I was curious as to how Charlie was managing to keep her here without being overcome by someone so young and spry and smart. "Have you tried to overtake him at all?"

"No, because he always closes the hallway door which automatically locks, and I don't know the combo to the keypad. So, even if I managed to get past him, I wouldn't be able to get out of this area." She heaved an aggrieved sigh. "Besides, I couldn't bring myself to hurt Charlie."

Dread bloomed into near panic, which I fought to suppress, though my thoughts didn't help. But how many times had I heard about people being held captive, sometimes for years, and in places where even close neighbors had no clue? It would be even easier for Charlie because he

102

didn't have any close neighbors. His home was well isolated from curious eyes.

But, I reminded myself, I had Kade, Tara, Anya and Shay, plus an arsenal of spiritual knowledge. One way or another we'd be found, or we'd escape. Since Charlie indicated that Kade hadn't believed him, I didn't figure it would be long. He would come back.

"I have friends who are gifted like you, Dawn. They will find us." We might even get help from the spirit world. After all, someone unlocked my bedroom door earlier, but I decided to keep that information to myself, at least the part about the lock. "I think Charlie's wife is here and she might be able to help us."

Dawn uttered an uneasy laugh. "Now wouldn't that be weird. I mean, who would ever think of getting help from dead people." Her voice rose with defiance. "We need a plan."

"Yes, we do."

"But first, tell me how you came to be here."

"There's a house not far from here, through the woods a ways."

"Yes, yes, I know about that. Charlie said that Lindsay was always over there as a kid. She really liked the people who lived there. I got curious one day and took a walk over … it's really nice. I can see why she liked it so much."

"Well, my friend Janice owns it and plans to sell it. She has someone who is interested in it, but she thinks it might be haunted." I heard Dawn snicker and wondered about it but continued on. "She asked me to check it out. I came to do that, with no intention of leaving my car, but I got your message."

"My message?"

"I heard your plea for help."

"My message?"

"I heard your plea for help."

Dawn's voice rose with contrition. "Oh no! It's my fault you are here?"

"You called for help, and I answered the call, there's no fault involved. It's my choices that put me in this situation. By coming here alone, without a phone, without telling anyone, and coming inside with Charlie when I felt quite strongly that I shouldn't—that's all on me."

"So, when he saw you, he saw Lindsay? He's seriously messed up."

"Yes, he is. He certainly isn't thinking straight, that's for sure." Heaving a sigh, I rubbed my belly in a reassuring gesture to my daughter and to myself. "Like you, he thinks he is keeping me safe from Dean by holding me here."

"Are you really in labor?"

"The initial stages of it. My contractions are thirty minutes apart and have been all day." We lapsed into a short silence, then I spoke with conviction. "I will not deliver my daughter in this house or on this property. We will be rescued, and Charlie will get the help he needs. As for Dean, well he will get whatever the universe feels he deserves."

"What's that mean?"

"It means, if he truly is responsible for Lindsay's disappearance, then the truth of it will come out."

Once again, we lapsed into silence. I hated not being able to see her. I was better at reading people's emotions when I could see them.

"So, no one knows you are here then?" Though a question, I could hear a hopeful note in her tone.

"No, but they knew I was at the house next door."

"What about your car? You must have driven here."

104

"Yes, but Charlie took it somewhere and hid it."

Dawn sighed. "Yeah, he pushed my clunker into a quarry pond."

"That's terrible!"

Dawn actually laughed. "It died just after arriving here, so it didn't really matter."

Now was the time to give her some hope. "I have good friends who are very gifted spiritually. Tara and Anya will find me if Kade, my husband, doesn't beat them to it."

"Who are Tara and Anya?"

I couldn't help but smile because I expected her to be intrigued by what I was about to tell her. "Tara is a witch and part of a coven that's been around this area for over two centuries. Anya is her sixteen-year-old daughter, who is a witch by birthright and under the tutelage of her mother."

Dawn sounded impressed and maybe even a little fearful. "Wow, that's so cool to have real witches as friends."

"Shouldn't your family be looking for you too, Dawn? Did you not tell anyone about any of this?"

Her voice became quite subdued. "I don't have a relationship with my parents. Well, maybe my mom a little bit but I don't have anything to do with my father. They are divorced, thank God, but mom should have left him when we - my brother and I - were little kids. I do have some step siblings because my mom is remarried, but I am not close with any of them either." She tried to sound like it didn't matter to her, but it did. It mattered. "I really don't have any close friends, or anyone really."

How very sad to be so alone in the world. I wished I could open the door and wrap Dawn in a hug. "I'm sorry, but you have a friend in me now, and things are never going to be the same. Life will get better. But first, we need to get ourselves out of this situation."

"So, let's make a plan."

Before I could respond to that, we heard sounds that indicated Charlie was coming and Dawn's voice dropped to an urgent whisper. "Go back to your room so he won't know we've been talking!"

As I turned to waddle back to my room, I heard Charlie open Dawn's door and speak to her.

"We've got company."

Chapter 8

I kept thinking about that, the way Charlie addressed her. *We've got company*. Like they were a team. He didn't stop at my door to say anything to me, and he thought I was his daughter!

And then I spotted my digital notepad at the foot of the bed—Charlie must have tossed it there on his way to Dawn's room. I couldn't believe I'd left the bedroom upstairs without it, especially after fighting so hard to keep it with me. I hadn't even thought about it, which was unlike me. Still, I was grateful for this one small act. It gave me hope that he might have enough clarity left in his mind that, with the right help, he could recover from this breakdown. I prayed with all my heart that Charlie would soon be in the hands of people who could help him—and Dawn and I would be free from this nightmare.

Since I hadn't yet heard Charlie leave Dawn's room, I settled onto the rocking chair and waited. Once he returned upstairs, I would go find out what was going on. Who was the company? Kade? The police? Dean? Hopefully one or both of the first two.

It was only about five minutes or so after sitting down that I heard noises in the hallway, and then there was a knock on my door. It was tentative, light handed, which made me curious because Charlie hadn't knocked any other time. I heard the key turn in the lock and then the door inched open until it was wide enough for me to see my visitor. It was Dawn.

She looked no more than a teenager. Her form-fitting jeans—slit raggedly at the knees—and a loose-fitting black sweater that hung off her shoulder, revealing a black lacy tank top beneath, showed off a slender, curvy body. She was perhaps five feet tall and very pretty. Her short, dark hair, cut in a pixie style, emphasized her large blue eyes, made all the more dramatic with black mascara and eyeliner. She stared at me curiously, her gaze sweeping over me as thoroughly as I was going over her.

"You don't look like Lindsay at all." She sauntered into the room with far more confidence than she felt for her smile was tentative, as if wondering about her welcome.

I pushed myself up from the chair and held out my hand, beckoning her to come closer. She did so quickly, her small, slender hand—so cool to the touch—clasping mine briefly before she perched on the edge of my bed.

"How old are you?" I couldn't believe Charlie could be putting someone so young through this nightmare.

"Almost twenty-two."

Older than I thought but still, she shouldn't be in a situation like this. Then again, neither should I! "Charlie let you out?"

"He was in such a hurry, he forgot to lock the door, and I know where he keeps the key to your room." Her pouty mouth widened into a grin. "I figured I might as well take advantage of it." The smile didn't last as she uttered her next words. "Dean is here."

Darn. The one guest I was hoping it would not be. "What do you think is going to happen?"

108

Dawn shrugged a bony shoulder, her sweater (which I now could see was cashmere) doing nothing to hide how thin she was. Even so, she was curvy in all the right places. I could imagine how much attention she must attract, for there was something so impishly appealing about her. "I told Charlie not to argue with him and to let Dean search the house again if he wanted. I mean, he isn't going to find us and that's what Charlie is worried about."

I had no idea how much time we had before Charlie returned to us, or what would happen between him and Dean, but I felt we needed to make the best use of the little time we had. "I need to do a quick protective spell for us and send some positive energy to Charlie and Dean."

Dawn's eyes widened in fascination. "A protective spell? Are you a witch, too, like your friends?"

"No, though they are teaching me stuff."

Dawn's fascination faded to a wary expression. "What kind of stuff?"

"Protection spells for one." I gave her a wink, hoping to ease whatever concerns were running through her mind. "It's simply a matter of directing spiritual energy to a specific intent."

"How?"

While moving my hand in a circular motion and using my index finger to direct the ensuing energy, I spoke the incantation of intent, "Safe we'll be, Dawn and me, a protective shield so mote it be." Satisfied with the spell, I looked at Dawn who rose one slender dark brow in skepticism.

"That's it?"

I nodded with confidence. "It doesn't take much, just some focus and a clear intention."

Dawn let out a small noise, its tone apologetic, and I knew her argument was about to commence. "But if you know how to do all this and it works, then why are you here? Shouldn't you have been able to avoid this or get Charlie to let you go?"

"I can do nothing to overcome another's choice, though I can certainly strive to influence it. Our lives are ours to choose, so exerting our will over another is not what we are supposed to be doing here in this world." I lifted a hand to halt whatever she was about to say so I could make one final point. "We are here, Dawn, in this basement, because you and I made a decision to be here."

I could see that she didn't agree with that at all. "Charlie forced us here. We didn't choose to be his prisoners. Yet, here we are."

"Right, Charlie is carrying out his own plan, making his own choices and exerting his will over ours, but to some degree we are allowing it. I mean, I haven't tried to overcome him or even stop him. For the most part, I've been going along with it and will continue to do so until I can see a safe way out."

"But now we are locked in the basement. It doesn't matter if we are going along with him or not." Her eyes dropped to my belly. "And you are about to have a baby. There really isn't a lot you can do."

"I can certainly influence him with light energy and spell work. As for getting into this situation, well, unfortunately, when it came to Charlie, I didn't realize the danger I was in. I did get some signs telling me not to trust him or to even come here, but I ignored them." I didn't want to voice a cliché, but I was going to anyway. "You know the saying that everything happens for a reason, well there's a reason for this—for what is happening to us—and if we can figure out what it is then all will be resolved."

A strong thought passed through my mind that my reason for being here was Dawn. As for her reason, well, I had no clue unless it was about meeting me, which would open her to a whole new world of possibilities.

110

"Do you really believe we can get out of this okay and before you have your baby?"

"I hope so. Unfortunately, I don't have the gift of seeing the future." I looked at her curiously. "Do you?"

Dawn looked away, her posture hinting that my question had unsettled her. "I get feelings about things, but not always, and never for myself." She briefly met my eyes before lowering her gaze to her clasped hands, which were twisting nervously in her lap. "Like you, I didn't feel right about coming here, and yet I also felt that I had to." She looked back up at me, her expression filled with contrition. "I am truly sorry that it was you who heard my plea for help, especially as I didn't expect anyone to hear that—other than God that is." She let out a derisive snort then lowered her eyes, her voice subdued when she spoke again. "I hate that I am the one who attracted you here."

"I answered the call of my own free will. We cannot take responsibility for other people's decisions, Dawn. We are responsible only for the choices we make." And then I figured I better amend that a little, though it didn't pertain to us. "The exceptions to that are children and those who are mentally impaired in some way, since they cannot make rational decisions for themselves, but none of those apply to us."

"Okay, fine, but you cast a spell to ensure that others wouldn't harm us so, isn't that taking their decision away from them?"

"I cast that spell for us. We have every right to decide if we want protection, and we have every right to reject someone else's decisions concerning us."

"So, Dean and Charlie's decisions concerning us don't matter?"

"They matter because it affects us and what we decide to do about it." Was any of this making sense to her? She didn't look convinced. "They only have absolute control over their own lives, not ours."

Dawn gestured with her hands to emphasize our situation. "And yet here we are."

"Because we both made decisions that brought us here," I reminded her.

"So, let's make some new decisions."

Now she was talking the way I wanted her to talk. "We will certainly keep our focus on getting out of here, but now we must work within the parameters that have been set by Charlie, whom we have allowed to call the shots up to this point."

"What does that mean?"

"It means I have no idea what to do at this moment."

"So, what did you mean about sending positive energy to Charlie and Dean? Shouldn't you be casting a spell on them? Something that will make them let us go?"

"As I've already said, I cannot overcome their free will, but I can send positive, loving energy to them, which will encourage better behavior, though they still can reject it if they choose." I meant them no harm, I just wanted our freedom. "Besides, casting spells that seek to override another's will or cause harm to others, will reflect back on the spell caster tenfold." I gave a visible shudder. "We most definitely do not want that kind of energy working against us. We've enough to deal with as it is."

Dawn's expression turned glum. "Yes, we do."

"Have you ever heard the saying that 'as your focus goes so your energy flows'?" Dawn shook her head, indicating she had not heard it. "It is truly a profound saying, and one we should always keep in mind."

112

Dawn's voice dripped with sarcasm. "Charlie's energy is focused on protecting us, and he's doing it without using a rational mind. What does that mean for us?"

"It means we need to stay focused on our own intentions, not his. Charlie's mental decline makes him unpredictable and possibly dangerous, but we have the means to protect ourselves and that gives us an advantage." Seeing Dawn's eyes darken with worry, I was quick to dispel the gloom that descended between us. "My protection spell will help keep us safe."

"Do spells overrule destiny?"

Wow, what a question. When I didn't answer right away, because I was trying to figure out how best to answer it, she went on to explain why she'd asked.

"I mean, if we are supposed to die but we cast a spell for protection, does that change the fact that we were supposed to die? Do we have the right to change destiny?"

"Dawn, we are not going to die. Not anytime soon anyway. I mean, we all die sometime but not from this." And yet I got the worst feeling in the pit of my stomach. It made me very nervous, and a contraction started.

Dawn didn't seem convinced, but she remained quiet while I focused on my contraction, and then continued her silence while I sent loving energy to the two men upstairs. Once done with that, I opened my eyes and looked at her with compassion. "I am so sorry you've been down here so long."

She waved away my apology. "It isn't your fault." She heaved a sigh and slid off the bed. "Charlie will probably be back soon, and I don't want to upset him by having him find me here."

I struggled to stand as well, finding it harder to maneuver my body with a baby preparing for birth. "See if you can convince him to let us be together."

Dawn nodded and accepted my hug, her body stiff, as if unsure about giving in to it, then she wrapped her arms around me and hugged me back.

It was a small victory, but I reveled in it just the same. I wanted her to trust me, and I felt that she was coming around.

When she pulled away, she looked me in the eyes, her expression very serious. "I will do whatever I can to help you get out of here." And then, as we heard the sounds of Charlie's return, she rushed to the door. After giving me a conspiratorial wink, she shut my door and locked it.

Moments later, I heard Charlie enter the outside hallway. He didn't come to my room, however, he went to Dawn's. I was tempted to go into the bathroom and try and listen at the door, but I was worried they'd hear me, especially if I were to have a contraction. Breathing quietly was impossible at this point.

About ten minutes later, someone was at my door. I knew it was Charlie because he didn't bother to knock.

"Hello, Lindsay. How are you doing, my dear?" He came into the room with a glass in one hand and a small bottle of what looked like apple juice in the other. He held them up for me to see. "Your mom craved apple juice when she was pregnant with you, drank it right up until your birth. I thought I'd bring you a glass." He set the glass on the dresser, then twisted open the bottle of apple juice, giving me a "see, it's all good" look when the seal popped. Then he poured some into the glass and handed it to me.

I couldn't help but wonder what he was up to, but I accepted the glass. He raised the bottle as if in salute. "Let's toast to you having a healthy little baby."

114

"Why don't you invite Dawn over and we'll drink it together?"

Charlie looked amused by the suggestion and chuckled. "That's pretty funny because she's the one that suggested I give you something to drink."

"Why?" He had to be lying and that made me suspicious.

"She said it was important that you stay hydrated, and so I thought you might like what your mom liked." He raised the bottle again. "So, let's drink up and have a talk."

"About what?"

"Dawn says I shouldn't keep you down here."

My heart started racing with excitement. Was he going to let us go? Or at least free us from the basement?

"Come on, Lindsay, drink up. I don't think you've had anything since dinner, and you didn't drink much then either." He went over and sat in the rocking chair and finished the bottle of juice.

Since he didn't seem inclined to talk until I drank the juice, I did as he requested and finished it off. I showed him my empty glass before putting it on the dresser and walking to the bed, dropping onto it gratefully. Even standing was becoming a chore.

Charlie smiled approvingly. "There, see that wasn't so bad, was it?"

"Are you going to let me and Dawn go upstairs?" Between the two of us, we should be able to figure out a way to escape him, but could we do it before my daughter was born?

Charlie nodded slowly, like he was considering it. "You don't feel safer down here?" He seemed genuinely puzzled that I was not happy with this arrangement.

"I feel … safe, being here in the house with you. There's no need for us to be locked in down here." A wave of dizziness came over me and I swayed unsteadily.

Charlie was immediately by my side, urging me to lay down. "Why don't you relax while I give it some thought. I'll go talk to Dawn and see what she thinks. Okay?"

I wanted to protest, to tell him I didn't want to lay down, but I couldn't get up the energy to do it. As I relaxed against the mattress, feeling the lethargy overtake me, I knew he'd duped me yet again. "Cha…Charl…why?"

Charlie kissed my forehead. "I'm so sorry, my girl. But you need to sleep for a little bit."

"H…how?"

His expression was apologetic. "The medicine was in your glass already."

I couldn't talk, but I could think, though that was getting difficult, and I was terrified that the drug would interfere with my labor or hurt my baby. Though I tried to fight the effects of whatever he'd given me, all I wanted to do was sleep.

"Don't worry, honey. Your mother had the same thing when she was in labor with you. It was taking so long, and they wanted her to rest … so she'd have the strength later to deliver you. So, you see? This will help you too."

That was all I remembered before I drifted into sleep.

Chapter 9

It was a contraction that woke me up. I wasn't sure how long I'd been out, but I was relieved to know that whatever Charlie had given me hadn't stalled my labor, though I was pretty certain it was slowing things down. I didn't want to have my baby here, but I also didn't want anything to interfere with the process. Aside from that, my biggest fear was that the drugs might harm my daughter in some way.

I looked at my watch to note the time and saw that over an hour had passed since I'd fallen asleep. Worry bloomed, making my heart pound. Why did Charlie feel it necessary to drug me when he had me trapped in a room unable to escape?

I looked toward the bathroom door and forced myself to get up. I needed to go check on Dawn. And I needed to pee.

Once my bladder was emptied, I felt ready to deal with whatever drama was in store for me, and after drawing in a fortifying breath, I tapped on Dawn's door. She didn't respond so I knocked a little louder. "Dawn? Dawn are you in there?"

"Dawn isn't here but I am."

That was a male voice and one I did not recognize, though I knew instantly who it was. "Dean?"

"Well then, so you know my name, what is yours?"

Oh God! What happened to Dawn? My heart thrumming with anxiety, I backed away from the door. "Where did Dawn go?"

"I wish I knew."

"How did you get in there?"

"Charlie drugged me. At least I think that is what must have happened."

This was a very unexpected turn of events. Though worried about Dawn, I was equally concerned about my safety. Dawn didn't trust that man and it made me wary as well.

"So again, who are you and how do you know my name?"

Did Charlie not tell him about me? He had to know that I'd come to this door at some point, so why would he not tell Dean about my presence? And what did he do with Dawn? "Charlie didn't tell you anything about me?"

"Yeah, well, we probably didn't get to it before I passed out." There was a pause and then his voice sounded louder, like he was trying to speak through the gap around the door. "If Dawn was in here then I think she's in trouble."

I didn't just think it, I knew it, and a surge of fear went charging through me. Almost immediately a contraction followed, and that's when I understood what was happening. Highly charged emotions were triggering them, and thus, moving things along, which meant I needed to stay calm. The one thing I did not want to do, no matter what, was accelerate my labor.

My ensuing silence, thanks to the need to breathe quietly through the contraction, must have concerned him because his raised voice sounded anxious. "Hey, are you still there?"

It wasn't easy to speak, but I forced out a reply. "Yes."

His tone softened. "You aren't here by choice, are you?"

Ha! Dawn and I just had this discussion about choices. "No. I am pretty much in the same situation as you are."

He heaved a loud, rumbling sigh, which was followed by a short silence. His mind, no doubt, was trying to make sense of things. "Since he is also holding you here against your will, like me, I would say we are all in trouble."

"That pretty much sums it up." At least he understood the direness of the situation we were in.

The doorknob jiggled and I stepped back, worried he'd open it. But it remained solidly closed between us. There was a thump against the door, and I was pretty sure that he'd just hit it lightly with his fisted hand. More silence followed and then he finally spoke. "Can you please tell me what is going on?"

If only I knew! "I don't know."

A short pause and then it sounded like he had slumped against the door. "Can you at least tell me who you are?"

The question brought me back to my initial shock of learning that Dean had taken Dawn's place. If Charlie thought I was Lindsay, then why did he put Dean in such close proximity to me, especially considering he believed Dean was a threat? And what did he do with Dawn? "My name is Tess Sinclair, but Charlie thinks … he thinks I am Lindsay."

"What? I can tell you aren't Lindsay by your voice. I know Charlie is somewhat crazy, but I didn't think he was crazy enough to believe that someone else is his daughter."

He sounded confused, somewhat dumbfounded, but not angry. He certainly didn't sound like someone out to cause harm to anyone.

"Do you look like her?"

Now it seemed he was trying to rationalize why Charlie thought I was Lindsay. "I wouldn't know. I've never seen her."

"There's pictures of her on the walls, you didn't notice?" He sounded skeptical and suspicious.

I wanted to laugh at the irony of it ... him being suspicious of me. "I was a little preoccupied at the time."

"So, how did you come to be locked in a room in Charlie's house? At least ... we are in his house, aren't we?"

"In his basement. I came here because ..." What to say? I was extremely reluctant to tell him about my ability, especially after the way Dawn said he acted when he found out about hers. "I was looking at the house next door to see about buying it, and I figured it wouldn't hurt to check out the closest neighbor. Only the moment Charlie saw me, he thought I was Lindsay, though I didn't know that until after he got me in the house."

"So how did you end up here in the basement?"

"Like you, he drugged me."

"And Dawn was in here?"

"Yes."

"Damn it. He's a slick dog."

There was a thump on the door, and I figured that Dean had just slapped his palm against it. The action frightened me, and I turned to go back to my room. Hopefully my door would lock from my side.

"I shouldn't have given Charlie all that information. Damn it. I had no idea he was losing his fricken mind."

That stopped me in my tracks, something telling me to turn around and listen to what Dean had to say. Not only that, but I needed to ask the right questions, which was another important thing I needed to add in that letter to my daughter … the importance of asking the right questions!

"What did you tell Charlie?"

"I told him that Dawn is a fricken lunatic, and he better be careful, or she'd wreck his life like she's trying to wreck mine."

He was probably talking about Dawn's visions, the fact she could uncover his involvement with Lindsay's disappearance. Of course, he would make her out to be the bad one. That's how people like him operated. And yet, even as those thoughts passed through my mind, I felt wrong for thinking them. I was making a judgement based only on hearsay, and I knew better. Though my empathy was all for Dawn, it was possible her impressions about Dean were wrong.

"Listen, can you tell me the layout of our situation? How many rooms are down here? What is your room like? Is it the same as mine?"

Considering all that Dawn had shared, I didn't trust him, but I would give him a chance. Besides, he didn't have any reason to turn against me. Given that, did I really have anything to be worried about?

"Are you still there?" Another pause and then he groaned. "Did Dawn tell you all the bullshit she's spouting off about me kidnapping Lindsay?" His voice softened to a plea. "I swear to you that I did not kidnap her, and I certainly didn't hurt her. I loved her. Yes, we were having issues, but I was hoping we'd figure it out, especially since she was carrying my baby "

It wasn't unexpected that he would deny it, so it would be folly to not question his truthfulness, and yet he might be my only ticket out of this basement. "We didn't really get a chance to talk much. We only managed one short conversation before Charlie came down and I went back to my room."

"You went back to your room? So, you aren't locked in there?"

"Yes, I am. This is the bathroom, which is between our rooms. There's a hallway outside our bedroom doors, and the door to get out of this area of the basement is at one end of it."

"Look, we need to combine forces before Charlie returns. Step away from the door or go back to your room if you've not a lot of space. I am going to try to break through this door."

My heart was pounding hard, concern for my safety overshadowing everything else. If he managed to break through the door, how could I know for sure that he wouldn't hurt me? Surely, he wouldn't for there was no reason for him to do so. But the uncertainty of it was making me feel sick. Oh why, oh why, did Charlie put me, whom he believed to be his daughter, in this precarious situation?

When I didn't reply, he spoke again, his voice gentler though firm, his next words telling me he was getting tired of defending himself. "Look, I don't know what Charlie has told you, or Dawn, but I promise that you don't have anything to worry about where I am concerned. I am not the kind of man they are making me out to be."

All criminals said that when trying to lie their way out of their sins. Surely, I should know better than to accept his word as truth. Then again, what reason could there be for him to lie? It was times like these when I wondered what was the good in being intuitive if I couldn't figure out whether someone was a threat to me or not?

Let him in.

Wow, that came quick, especially considering I hadn't had much help from the spirit realm since my arrival here at Charlie's house. It did make me feel better, though, and I sent out a silent, heartfelt thanks. Now to placate, Dean. If we were going to team up, then it was best that I ease his concerns as to what I knew about him. "Charlie hasn't said anything but

122

speculation. Considering his mental state, I don't hold much weight to anything he says. As for Dawn, well I already told you we only talked briefly. We barely got through our introductions and Charlie showed up." The less he knew about what I knew, the better.

"Can you safely stay out of the way while I try to break this door in?"

"Yes." I moved into the open doorway to my room, positioning myself so that I could see Dean's progress, or lack thereof, and hear Charlie return.

Dean slammed against the door several times, muttering an oomph with each impact, but the door didn't give. I glanced around my room to see if there was something that might be helpful and called out to Dean. "Do you have a chair in your room? Maybe that will help. I mean, you could use it to ram the door."

"I think it will make too much noise and alert Charlie." A short pause and then, sounding winded, he spoke again. "I am trying to force it open from the wrong side. The door opens in my direction and the frame is solid. It's not going to splinter."

"So now what?"

"Damn it." His frustration clear, Dean kicked at the door, at least that's what it sounded like. "I just don't know."

Okay, time to try something else. "Give me a minute, Dean. I've got an idea." I pressed my palms against the door, closed my eyes and visualized it opening. Maybe because my emotions were running high, it worked faster than usual—within seconds, but I felt the door respond almost immediately, and I knew it had worked. I should've done this upstairs. Asking spirits for help was unreliable; trusting myself and what I knew was possible was the better choice. "Dean, give the door a hard yank. I think it'll open this time."

I stepped away, moving toward the door to my room and prayed he would be true to his word and work with me. Just in case, though, I reinforced that dome of protection I had put in place earlier then sent protective energy to Dawn as well. I was very worried about her. Why would Charlie take her away and where did he take her?

The doorknob rattled as Dean grasped hold of it. "Okay, I'm going to give it a hard yank. Wish me luck."

Two seconds later the door swung open, which obviously caught Dean off guard, for he let out an expletive as he lost his grip. The door slammed into the wall and nearly bounced closed, but Dean never appeared, nor did I hear him hit the floor. Wondering what had happened, I rushed over and found him sprawled across the bed.

Giving his head a shake, his expression incredulous, Dean twisted about and pushed himself upright. "Wow, I should have tried that sooner." Once he was on his feet, he gave me a rueful smile and gestured towards the door. "Guess I don't know my own strength."

He was a handsome man, just as Dawn had said, and tall, about Kade's height, at just over six feet. He had a lean fit body that suggested a very active lifestyle. And though I probably shouldn't notice such things, he filled out his jeans quite nicely. His checkered flannel shirt, though loose fitting, did nothing to hide his muscular build. He exuded quiet sex appeal, which was made all the more charming because he seemed unaware of it, and I appreciated how his arms hung relaxed at his sides, his stance unthreatening, as if to show me he meant no harm.

My eyes traveled back to his face, which was framed by chestnut brown hair that was styled to suit his chiseled features and square jawline. He was probably close to thirty, the maturity about him suggesting it more than anything, for he had a boyish look to him that made him even more

124

appealing. I took all that in at a glance, but it was his chocolate brown eyes, hooded with thick lashes, that caught and held my attention.

His regard was openly curious as his gaze moved over my face, and I knew he was looking for similarities between me and Lindsay, wondering, no doubt, why Charlie mistook me for his daughter. Then his gaze dropped down to my belly and his eyes widened, his thick dark brows rising in shock. "Jesus, you are pregnant?"

I wrapped my arms protectively about myself. "How astute of you."

He lifted his hands, palms outward and fingers spread in apology. "Sorry, it's just … what the hell is Charlie thinking taking a pregnant woman hostage?"

"Hostage?"

"Prisoner then." He ran his hand through his thick wavy hair. "I have no clue what that crazy old man is up to." He dropped his hand back to his side and gave a nod towards my belly. "When are you due?"

"Soon. Anytime actually."

"I hope the stress of this situation doesn't put you in labor. I know nothing about delivering babies, and I would think Charlie is the last man you'd want doing the honors. Not that he'd know any more than me."

I didn't want anyone to deliver my baby except a doctor, or Kade if it came down to it. Or Mary. She'd know what to do, and it would be rather nice having her do the honors. If I managed to get out of here, it was probably going to come to that, for I felt quite certain that my daughter's birth would be happening before the day was over. The ache in my back was telling me time was running out. I gestured towards the chair. "Do you mind if I sit down?"

"No, no of course not." Dean went to fetch the chair and brought it to me. "I'd offer you a drink, but I'm not set up for entertaining anyone." He gave me a lopsided smile, and I got a sense that his attempt to be funny was meant to put me at ease, which it did.

"What do you think Charlie is doing with Dawn?" We needed to get down to the business of figuring out a plan, and we needed to do it before Charlie returned.

Dean lowered his tall frame onto the edge of the bed, his hands lightly clasped between his knees. "I've no idea." He gave a nod, indicating the room at large, which looked like a bedroom and sitting room combined. "I wouldn't have believed he would do something like this – drug people and lock them in his basement, which seems to be set up for a long-term stay! But I'm glad to know that Dawn is okay."

Was he?

He must have seen the question in my eyes for he let out a sigh. "I don't know what she's told you about me, but there's always two sides to a story."

Yes, there was, and I knew better than to dismiss one side out of hand. He had a right to have his say. Sometimes people just perceive things in a way that was unintended. Maybe that was the case with Dawn, and Charlie, and even Lindsay, if what Charlie and Dawn said about her feelings towards Dean were true. Maybe they all had it wrong about Dean being the bad guy. The odds, though, were stacked against him.

"I met Dawn in a bar."

A bar? She didn't say anything about meeting him in a bar.

"I work for a security surveillance company and a bunch of us decided to stop in after work for a drink. Dawn was there." He looked at me with a sheepish expression on his face, clearly not proud of his part in the story. "She's very pretty and I admit, though I was with Lindsay, I was flattered by her interest."

One of them was lying about where they met. I suspected it was Dean, but I gave him a small, encouraging smile anyway. Time was ticking and I was having another contraction. Twenty-five minutes. My labor was progressing.

"I knew she was more interested than I had a right to let her be, so after she waited for me outside the men's room and wrapped herself around me for a kiss, I had to call it quits and tell her about Lindsay." He glanced away, lost in thought. Thinking. "The following week, she showed up at the office where I work."

Ah, so that part did match her story. If the other part was also true, why did Dawn leave that out?

"She said it was a coincidence, but I don't know if I believe that. She's a very persistent girl. A go-getter if ever there was one." He let out a sigh and ran his hand up through his hair. "I don't know what was happening with Lindsay and me, but she was suddenly suspicious of everything I did." He looked at me, holding eye contact, and continued. "I did not start an affair with Dawn. Other than that night at the bar, I behaved appropriately around her. I did nothing to encourage her interest." Another long pause followed, one which I was hard pressed not to interrupt, but I really wished he would talk a little faster. Time was ticking away.

"When Lindsay told me she was pregnant, I thought it might help us regain the closeness we had, but she just became more distant. We were arguing all the time. She didn't trust me at all, and I was constantly defending myself and resenting her for having to do that. Besides, I was feeling guilty about Dawn, though all we'd done was kiss, which she'd instigated - not that it matters. I mean, I shouldn't have let it happen." He let out a disgusted sigh. "It was enough of a betrayal that it weighed on my mind, and I think Lindsay picked up on that, which only made things worse. I will admit that if it weren't for her pregnancy, we probably would have split up. I mean, we just weren't working anymore, but after learning about the baby, I wanted to be there for her through the whole thing." He gave me an earnest glance then dropped his gaze to his hands, which were fisting and unfisting with agitation. "I wanted to be in the baby's life and support Lindsay through her pregnancy."

His tone was sincere. I felt like he was being honest with me, and he didn't strike me as someone who would bump off his girlfriend, but I told myself to just keep listening.

"Lindsay's dad has never liked me, but I don't think he would like anyone that kept his daughter from moving home with him. Not that Lindsay would have done that, even if we had split up, and even if she'd not disappeared that day. She said he was too suffocating, too controlling, and yet loving enough to make her feel bad about not going along with everything he said."

That was Charlie. Lindsay's description of him fit perfectly. He was so sweet and caring that it made me feel bad that I wasn't more appreciative of his concern. But he wasn't rational about how he went about protecting his daughter. Or Dawn for that matter.

"Dawn stopped working at our office shortly after Lindsay disappeared, but she stayed in touch with me. I shouldn't have encouraged her texts, but she seemed so concerned and was so supportive and I needed that. I mean I was a wreck, so any kind words and a sympathetic ear was appreciated." He pushed himself up from the bed and went to the door, giving it a hard yank, as if hoping it would work as well as it had on the bathroom door. It didn't so much as creak. He turned around and leaned against it, tucking his fingers in the front pockets of his jeans.

128

"A couple of days before Lindsay disappeared, we were supposed to go to a dinner party. When I got to our apartment there was a car illegally parked in my spot." He glanced at me briefly, letting me know that this was important. "Another car was pulling away a short distance up from it, near an alley, which comes into play later, so I waited and pulled into that spot and went to get Lindsay. When we came out, there were three older teens hanging around in the alley near my car. They asked for money, and I told them to take a hike. They didn't take too kindly to that suggestion and became aggressive. One of them began antagonizing me while another one seemed to be blocking Lindsay, keeping her from backing away. The punk aggravating me came in for an attack and I made a swing for him, but he ducked at the last second and one of the other kids pushed Lindsay in the way. Though I tried to stop the swing, I ended up hitting her. The moment that happened they took off."

He ran both hands across his hair, revealing his anxiety over the incident. "I felt so bad about hitting her. She knew it was an accident and didn't blame me at all, but I felt bad anyway. We didn't go to dinner. We went back to the apartment and ordered out." He closed his eyes and laid his head back against the door. "It was probably our best night together in ages, and I was so hopeful that things were going to change."

He didn't say anything for so long that I felt it necessary to prompt him along. "That was two days before she disappeared?"

"Yes. I had to work a late shift the next night and Lindsay was in bed when I got home, and she was still sleeping when I went to work the next morning. Since I didn't want to disturb her, I slept on the couch, but I did go in and kiss her on the cheek before heading to work. The bruise on her face was pretty nasty by then and it made me feel like crap. It didn't matter that it was an accident. I did that to her, and it tore me up."

He pushed away from the door and paced in the small space available, though he did avoid moving around me, which I thought was considerate of him. "Anyway, it was the last time I saw her. When I got a message from Lindsay asking me to meet her at the apartment, I was feeling hopeful, thinking she was coming around and we were going to work things out. But when I got to our place, only Charlie was there."

As Lindsay had a bruise on her face, I'm sure Charlie was not pleasant with Dean when he arrived. The look on Dean's face told me as much.

"He was being an overprotective, unreasonable ass. Lindsay told me he was a very sweet, overprotective father, but I didn't see anything sweet about Charlie. I saw his so-called overprotectiveness as being overbearing and controlling. And if he was 'sweet' he sure never showed any signs of that when I was around." Dean dropped back down on the edge of the bed. "Naturally he thought I put that bruise on Lindsay's face on purpose."

Another long pause told me he was thinking back on that day, letting it all run through his mind. No doubt telling himself all the mistakes he made and what he should have done to change it. We do that to ourselves, especially when a tragedy happens. We think of all the ways we could have stopped it, or changed it, or avoided it altogether.

"I couldn't stay there with him. He told me Lindsay was headed to the food stand by the park entrance. It was a couple blocks away, so I figured I'd walk there and meet her. Only I never encountered her on the walk over, and when I got to the food stand, she wasn't there either." He scrubbed a hand over his face. "Charlie thinks I had something to do with it. He said I rushed out of the apartment to get Lindsay and that I must have taken her away somewhere."

"So, what does Dawn have to do with anything? I mean, you came here looking for her, right?"

130

"Dawn was probably the only person, outside of work and aside from family, that didn't think I was guilty of any wrongdoing. At least not at first. She was supportive and kind and didn't make any inappropriate advances, not since that night we first met. I probably shouldn't have, but as time went on, after Lindsay disappeared, I saw her from time to time. She was a great sounding board for all the thoughts running through my mind—what I should've done, what I shouldn't have done, going over every detail I could remember before Lindsay vanished, searching for any clue of what might have happened to her." He shook his head as if still trying to understand it. "Dawn even went through Lindsay's stuff, packing up anything worth keeping and offering to take it to Charlie's. She said she'd always wanted to visit Maine." He closed his eyes briefly and heaved a sigh. "I should have known where her mind was heading ... about me—us—but I was too blind to see the signs."

With a frustrated groan, he stood and commenced pacing. "I swear to you that I never made any moves on Dawn. I gave no suggestions or hints or anything that I was interested in her. But a couple months ago, she started coming on to me like she thought we'd have a relationship."

Okay, their stories were no longer matching at all.

Again, he ran his hands across his hair, an obvious gesture of agitation. "How was I supposed to think about moving on with anyone when my pregnant girlfriend was missing, possibly out there..." he swung his arms wide. "What if she's being held captive like us?"

As I did not know what to say to that, I just gave him a sympathetic smile, hoping it would be enough to keep him talking, though the more we talked, the less time we had to find a way out of here.

"She said stuff here and there that suggested she knew things she shouldn't know, and word got around at work that she was psychic." His mouth twisted, telling me what he thought of that. It wasn't much. "I don't know how she knew the things she knew, but she was getting her information from somewhere. I admit it made me uncomfortable, but when Lindsay disappeared, I figured what the heck maybe she did have a special gift, and if so, maybe she could help find Lindsay. I was desperate for any information that might lead me to her." His eyes searched mine, the raw honesty in his gaze hard to deny.

Despite my reservations, my resolve softened, and I gave him an encouraging nod. I did understand his willingness to use any avenue to find his girlfriend, but was he being completely honest with me? I felt that he was, but it conflicted with what Dawn had told me and therein was my problem.

"Dawn started sharing her 'visions' (his voice dripped with sarcasm) with me concerning Lindsay, but they never led to anything." He heaved a sigh that I understood very well. The weight of Lindsay's disappearance had become a burden he was finding increasingly difficult to bear. "So anyway, the last night I saw Dawn was when she came to my apartment to pack Lindsay's stuff into her car. Afterwards, we were sharing a pizza and she … well, she let me know that she was interested."

As his mind had gone off to thinking again and I was breathing through another contraction, twenty minutes from the last one, I didn't have time to be patient. "And?"

"I told her that I wasn't interested in her that way." He looked completely baffled that he'd even had to have that conversation with her. "She got pretty mad and stormed off." He heaved another sigh and scrubbed a hand over his face. "Anyway, the next day she called to tell me she had another vision. Only this one was of me and Lindsay fighting and she saw me in a car with her." He gave me a meaningful glance. "All a load of crap."

"So, you don't believe she's psychic?"

"I don't know what to believe, but what I can tell you is she was suggesting that I was responsible for Lindsay's disappearance." Dean frowned. "If she thought I could do something like that, then she doesn't think much of me, does she?" He looked at me askance. "Would you be interested in a guy like that?" He waved his hand telling me it wasn't necessary to answer.

Since he looked pretty put out by the implication of Dawn's visions, it left me wondering what to believe. Their stories didn't match, but it could be he was leaving out details she hadn't and was giving details she didn't. Although Dawn had said Dean was attractive, that didn't mean she was hoping for a relationship with him, but he was saying otherwise.

"Dawn said she was going to tell Charlie, and I tried to talk some reason into her, but she hung up on me. I didn't hear from her again though I sent several text messages and tried calling her." A frown marred his forehead and if I didn't know better, I would think he was worried, though not for himself. "I knew she came here and since it was going on nearly two months of silence, I figured I better come check on her. But Charlie said she wasn't here, and he seemed more certain than ever that I was responsible for Lindsay's disappearance." Dean looked at me, his brown eyes dark with emotion and burning with an indignant light. "I had nothing to do with it. I've been trying to find her since she disappeared. Christ, she was having my baby!"

"Why did you think that Dawn was still here?"

"She told me she wasn't close to her family. Her father had been very inappropriate with her, if you know what I mean, so she wouldn't go to him, and she didn't like her mother's new husband. In fact, she was convinced that he hated her as well. I just suspected that she and Charlie were a perfect fit for each other. She needed a dad, and he needed a daughter."

"So, you came back a second time?"

"Yes. I had a feeling she was still here, and I was very worried about her. I just needed to know she was okay."

"Dawn said you forced your way in."

His expression was indignant as he shook his head, denying the claim. "I did not force my way in, but I was persistent, and Charlie gave in, letting me search the house." He gestured to the room around us. "I didn't find any of this."

"The door to get into this part of the basement is hidden behind an old cabinet."

"Aah." I could see that he remembered the cabinet and shook his head in reluctant admiration. "Clever."

"So, why did you come back today after having searched the house on your previous visit and not finding her?"

"I came to beg Charlie to tell me where she'd gone so I could check on her." He gave a derisive snicker. "The sly dog invited me in, making me think he was going to cooperate." His expression was sincere as his eyes met mine, his attitude telling me he had nothing to hide. "I feel responsible for her, and don't ask me why, I just do. After losing Lindsay, I didn't want another girl I knew going missing." He paused for just a moment, as if he wasn't sure how I'd take what he had to say next. "I also needed to be sure that he hadn't done anything to her."

I remembered Dawn telling me that Charlie was on the suspect list with the police, though he obviously was cleared, just like Dean. It was

134

ironic that each man suspected the other. Yet, I didn't believe either of them was responsible for Lindsay's disappearance, despite Charlie's actions and Dawn's beliefs about Dean. "Charlie was so concerned about Dawn after your second visit, thinking you were out to harm her, that he locked her in down here."

Dean's mouth tightened with derision, his opinion concerning Charlie's beliefs about him unmistakable. He ran his hands over his hair again. "I don't know what I did to earn his hate, but that old man cannot stand me."

As I listened to him recount his story, especially where Dawn was concerned, he appeared sincere, and I found myself instinctively believing his account – or, at the very least, his perception of it. Although his interactions with Dawn were not how she expressed them, it didn't necessarily mean that either of them was lying. It could be that they were misinterpreting each other's responses. One thing I was beginning to believe, though, especially after meeting him, is that Dean was not responsible for Lindsay vanishing on that fateful day. "Why did you come back today?" I meant why this, of all days, but he took it wrong.

"I told you, I figured Charlie knew where Dawn had gone, and well..." He looked a little sheepish. "To be honest, I just had the biggest urge to get my ass over here and demand the truth, and I came before I talked myself out of it. Dawn's been missing for nearly two months, and he was the last one to see her, despite his denials that he hasn't. I figured he knew exactly where she was."

"Did he invite you to have tea, or coffee with him?"

Dean nodded, his disbelief about it evident. "Yeah, a beer actually. I should have known he had something up his sleeve. Not that I ever thought he'd be capable of something like this."

"You obviously trusted him enough to drink his peace offering."

"I should have questioned it when he served it to me in a glass."

That made me chuckle. "Did you wonder at the brand when you tasted it?"

"I thought maybe it was cheap beer." A grin tugged at Dean's mouth for a fleeting moment, but the seriousness of our situation didn't allow it to linger. "I figured I better tell him about my interactions with Dawn, minus the nightclub part. Since I knew she'd been here, I figured she'd probably told him stuff – lies – and I wanted to give him my side of it."

He must have told Charlie stuff that Dawn hadn't told him, like the fact she'd worked with him. Had that angered him? Is that why she was now gone from her room? "How did he take it … the stuff you were telling him?"

"He didn't look like he believed me but was attentive and accommodating." Dean gave a derisive snort, casting his gaze around the room with disgust. "Now I can see it's because he was planning this." His eyes met mine, and I could see the worry going on behind that gaze. "What do you think he is planning to do with us? He can't keep us down here for long. The man is 72 years old, how long can he keep this up?"

It was a good question and a very worrisome one. "What do you think he's done with Dawn?"

"I don't know, but I wish to hell I hadn't told him everything I told him."

Yeah, me too. I was very concerned about the state of Charlie's mind and what was going on in it.

"He was very intrigued about Dawn's visions," Dean said. "I could see this … I don't know how to describe it … an almost calculating look in his eyes while I was telling him about it."

"Dean, we need to get out of here and find her."

He heard the urgency in my voice, saw it in my demeaner, and nodded with infused purpose. "Right." He shot off the bed and looked around. "But how?" Then he looked up, as did I.

Charlie used sheetrock for the ceiling but that didn't deter Dean. He jumped up on the bed and gave it a series of knocks. After a few moments, he nodded with satisfaction, fisted his hand and gave several swift upward punches, his fist going right through the sheetrock, though it took several more punches to make a decent-sized hole. He then grabbed the broken edges and yanked hard, pulling large chunks of it down onto the bed. After working at it a bit more, he had a hole big enough to crawl through and grabbed hold of the cross beams. With determination hardening his features, he hoisted himself up far enough to look inside, his arm muscles corded tight and his back rippling from the effort. Thank God he was physically fit and tall, or he wouldn't have been able to do that. "I think I can make it over to the other side."

He lowered his feet onto the bed then looked down at me, nodding at my chair. "I hate to make you get up, but I'm going to need that."

Waving off his concern, I stood and pushed the chair towards the bed. "Please take it but do be careful."

Dean set the chair on the bed and carefully stood upon it.

Worried it would topple over and send him flying onto the floor, I put out a steadying hand, though I don't know how effective I was for my strength was nothing to brag about.

Dean glanced down at me with concern. "If the chair starts to topple over, let it go and move out of the way, don't try to stop it. I don't want you to get hurt."

His consideration made me feel better about putting my trust in him. Would he really care about me if he was such a cad?

Dean hoisted himself up until just his legs were left dangling. "It's going to take some careful maneuvering, but I think I can make it."

I gave him all the details he needed to get back into this area from the basement and told him, yet again, to be careful.

"Okay then, off I go. Wish me luck." His legs disappeared and I heard him grunting his way towards the outer room.

It worried me that Charlie would come back while Dean was crawling through the ceiling, but there was nothing to be done about it.

Since I wanted Dean to find me in the same room he left me, I ran to retrieve my digital pad, making it back in time to deal with another contraction, a hard one. It nearly took my breath away, and I had to grab the edge of the desk for support, leaning over it and stifling the moan I wanted to make. Gosh, but it hurt. Under normal circumstances it would be a pain I'd welcome, knowing it meant my daughter would soon be joining us in the world, but right now it frightened me. This was the worst time to deliver a baby.

"Oh, please my sweet little one, be patient just a little longer. Let me get back to your daddy before you join us in this crazy world." I gently rubbed my rock-hard belly and heaved a big sigh when the contraction finally subsided.

Sounds coming from the hallway alerted me that someone was coming, and I prayed it was Dean. Then he opened the door.

"Let's get out of here."

Chapter 10

With Dean leading the way, we headed towards the stairs while listening intently for any signs of movement from the rooms above us.

"I did a quick check to see if there was another way out of here," Dean said. "But there isn't. At least, not that I could find. If there's another hidden door somewhere, I didn't see it."

"Well, if it's hidden, I wouldn't think so." It probably wasn't the right time to tease him, but it helped ease some of the tension flowing between us. Our current predicament was far from favorable, and neither of us knew what to expect next. On the heels of that thought was the realization that someone was nearby.

With my heart in my throat, I looked toward the stairs, expecting to see Charlie, but it was the woman that I suspected was his wife. She stood at the top of the stairs, her hand urging us forward, indicating we should hurry.

"I think we are good for the moment, Dean, so go on up."

Dean didn't even question me about it, he just nodded and rushed up the stairs, stopping at the door to listen. When satisfied it was safe to proceed, he quietly turned the knob and pushed the door open. After peeking into the room beyond, he gestured for me to wait where I was, which was about halfway up the stairs, and stepped out of sight. Seconds later his arm appeared from behind the door, motioning for me to join him.

I did so as quickly as I could, considering my condition, and by the time I was at the top of the stairs I was out of breath and dealing with a contraction.

Dean poked his head around the door to check on me, saw what was happening, and waited patiently for the contraction to end. His expression was sympathetic though he was concerned about the time it was taking, his worried gaze shifting between me and the kitchen. But to give him credit, he didn't utter one complaint or express his impatience in any way.

As soon as the pain began to recede, I nodded that I was okay to continue, and he put out a hand to help me up the last step into the pantry, ensuring I was okay before letting me go. The gesture was a thoughtful one and it just wasn't in keeping with everything that Dawn had told me.

"Let me walk ahead and keep watch for Charlie." He met my gaze to see if I would argue his direction, but I gestured for him to have at it. I was more than happy to hang back and let him clear the way.

As Dean stalked through the kitchen, I shut the cellar door then fetched the key and locked it, putting the key in the detergent cup holder that was on a shelf above the washing machine. The likelihood of Charlie looking there would have to follow an intense search first. If he thought of forcing us back into the cellar, it wasn't going to be as easy a task as he might think. I was not going down there ever again.

Satisfied that I'd done what I could to prevent a return to the basement, I turned to watch Dean as he moved through the house. He crept about with the stealth of a cat burglar. At least that's what he put me in mind of as he went from the kitchen to the living room and beyond.

The house was enveloped in silence, except for the rhythmic ticking of the wall clock in the living room, echoing the passage of time and reminding me of how little we had before my daughter's pending birth. Through the windows, darkness stretched endlessly, creating an abyss of nothingness. The scene reminded me of my dream, and I glanced at my watch. I couldn't help but wonder about Kade and what he might be doing. He wouldn't be sitting idly at home waiting for news. No, he'd be out searching for me, his determination unwavering, relentless, and, knowing him, bordering on desperate. Where, though, was he looking? What place would he be scouring for clues to my whereabouts?

Dean reappeared and stopped to peer out the window, taking precautions to stay out of sight. "I don't see Charlie's truck. Or mine for that matter. He must have taken Dawn somewhere."

But where? And why? A sense of unease settled in my stomach, and it made me anxious, which was an annoyance I couldn't afford right now. Clear thinking and composure were vital tools to getting through this. I needed to stay focused on getting out of here, finding Dawn and giving birth to my baby, though I only wanted that last part to happen after reuniting with Kade.

But first things first and that meant securing our safety. "Dean, we need to do a few things before we get out of here … in case Charlie comes back before we make our escape."

Dean nodded and rejoined me in the kitchen.

I pulled open the drawers closest to me and collected every knife I could find, placing them in the wash basin and gesturing for Dean to get to it. "We need to hide anything he can use as a weapon against us."

It didn't take long to go through all the drawers and cupboards. Once we identified everything that we deemed hazardous to our safety, Dean stashed them into the dishpan and hid them in the dryer. "He might find them eventually, but hopefully we won't be here long enough for him to think of looking there."

I went to the cupboard where Charlie had fetched the tea supplies and found his stash of bottles and baggies, all filled with questionable substances. Seeing them made me sick with worry. He had to have obtained them from a nefarious supplier, and I could only pray they weren't contaminated with anything that would cause lasting damage to our bodies, or to my baby.

Taking care to scoop up Charlie's ill-gained goods without dropping any of it, I contemplated washing them down the sink then figured I better not. Once rescued, it would be useful to have them analyzed to find out what Charlie had given us. So, I placed them in the dryer as well. With any luck, the police would get them before Charlie did, which was a more likelihood if the cobwebs and dust covering the dryer were anything to go by.

Dean reached around me and pulled out a big butcher knife. His expression was apologetic when he turned to look at me. "I am hoping we don't need this, but we need something to keep him away from us, you know, if he comes back before we can get out of here."

He was right, of course, but it made me nervous. He had a weapon. I did not. Well, that wasn't entirely right either. I had my ability, and I had knowledge of how to do things that should keep me safe. Besides, I didn't feel like Dean was someone I needed to worry about. He just didn't give off that sort of vibe. As for him taking Lindsay, I was not convinced of it despite Dawn's convictions on the matter.

When we were nearly to the front door, Dean glanced back at me. "Should I check upstairs? I only secured this floor."

142

"I think you should. We need to make sure Dawn isn't drugged somewhere up there."

Dean nodded, his expression grim. "Right. I'll go look. You keep a lookout for Charlie."

I waved him on, though I hated to be alone, and stood watch for any oncoming headlights. The blackness beyond the window stayed that way until Dean returned minutes later.

"There's no one up there."

"We need our shoes and jackets." I looked in the closet in the mud room area, but our things were not in there.

Dean raced back up the stairs, speaking to me over his shoulder as he did so. "I think I saw them in his closet. I wasn't really paying attention, I was looking for Dawn, but I'm pretty sure I saw stuff that didn't look like it would belong to Charlie." He came back down a few minutes later wearing a jacket and heavy boots. In his hands he held my things, even my purse.

Dean helped me with my coat then bent down next to me and picked up one of my boots. "Use me for balance and I'll help you with these."

After slipping my digital pad in the deep pocket of my coat, I placed a hand on his shoulder and let him slip on my boots, which he then tied securely. It was weird having a man besides Kade help me dress, but I was grateful for his assistance.

In no time at all we were stepping out of the house. But where in the heck were we going to go?

Chapter 11

We stood on the porch, considering our options, and Dean ran a hand across his hair. "I wonder what the hell he did with my truck. I couldn't find my cell phone either, and Charlie's house phone has been disconnected." He gave a nod towards my purse. "I don't suppose you have a cell phone in there."

"No. Charlie threw it out at the other house."

"What other house?"

I pointed towards the woods on our left. "Through there is a house a friend of mine is getting ready to sell. I stopped there to look at it but got drawn to Charlie's house, and I left my phone in the car. When Charlie moved my car, he said he threw my cell phone near the outside steps."

"Why would he do that?"

"I guess he thought it would make the people looking for me think I had left in haste. I'm not really sure why that would matter, but it did to Charlie."

"Then let's go there." He put an arm around me, and after storing the knife in his jacket, he offered his other arm for additional support. "Let me help you."

Grateful for his assistance, I put my arm around his waist and clung to his other arm as we made our way across the driveway and the short distance to the tree line. It worried me that Charlie would come back before we made it to the trees, but those worries never materialized. And that's when I berated myself for even worrying about it. How much time was spent worrying about stuff that never materialized?

"I think we are supposed to get some freezing rain, it certainly has that feel about it," Dean said. "I hope we get rescued soon. I know you are about ready to pop, aren't you?"

"Yes, and all this physical activity is just encouraging things along. But we've no choice." Even as I spoke, I felt a contraction coming on and let out a low, despairing groan. I just didn't want to deal with this right now.

"It's okay. Just do what you need to do." Dean stopped walking and waited for the contraction to end, his hands rubbing my arms in support. He even breathed with me, the thoughtfulness of him doing that making me grateful, for it helped me to stay focused.

When the pain receded, I nodded that we should continue. "Where do you think Charlie took Dawn?" I hoped it wasn't to dump her body somewhere. Good Lord, why would I think such a thing! They'd spent a couple of months together and had forged a friendship of sorts. He wanted to protect her after all.

"I don't know, but Dawn is a crafty girl, so who knows what ..."

"Shhh!" I tightened my hand on Dean's arm and drew us to a halt. "That's Charlie's truck at Janice's house!" There was another vehicle in the yard too, but it was behind Charlie's truck, and it was too dark for me to see what it was. Not mine. Dean's maybe?

We both crouched low behind some densely growing pine trees and searched for signs of movement. Though we didn't see or hear anything,

146

Charlie was there somewhere, and I wasn't moving from this hiding spot until I knew where.

It seemed like forever - though it was probably no more than five minutes - that we waited for signs of Charlie, and in that time, Dean tried twice to persuade me to let him go investigate the situation. Though I managed to hold him back, he was running out of patience.

"You need to let me …" but he stopped abruptly and pulled me deeper behind the trees. Seeing my questioning look, he put a finger to his lips.

Charlie had appeared from behind the house and was running to his truck. He was in a very great hurry, his movements jerky and his anxiety so high it hit me like an emotional tidal wave. Something happened to frighten him and that frightened me.

Once Charlie was in the truck and started the engine, I voiced my concern to Dean. "Do you think he brought Dawn over here and did something to her?"

"Where else would she be? Once thing's for certain … she's not with him now, unless she's tied up in the back of his truck."

I hadn't considered that and pressed a hand to my stomach as nausea overcame me. It was too much to deal with, especially while in the throes of labor.

"There's another car in the driveway."

"I see that."

"It's not Dawn's – she has a small car and it's not mine, I have a truck."

"It's not mine either. Charlie said he took mine somewhere and left it."

As soon as Charlie's truck was out of sight, Dean and I left our hiding spot and headed for the other vehicle.

While still helping me along, Dean spoke quickly. "He's going to get to the house and discover that we've escaped. We need to get the hell out of here."

Yes, we did! And maybe that other car meant someone else was here who could help us. Maybe it's why Charlie was in such a rush to leave. Then we got close enough to see the other car more clearly, and fear charged through me, stopping me in my tracks and freezing every muscle. No! Please, God, no! As I stood there, contemplating the worst and clinging to Dean, it felt like all the blood in my body was draining down to my feet, making me feel faint.

Dean's arms tightened and kept me from sinking to the ground. "What's wrong?"

"That's my husband's SUV."

"Let's see if the keys are in it. We'll drive to the police station..."

"No, there's no time. Charlie might have done something to Kade!" Regaining my strength and pulling away from Dean's grasp, I headed for the back of the house. That's where Charlie came from, and it's where I was going.

"Tess, Charlie is going to come barreling after us the moment he discovers we are missing. He's going to come here first, it's the most logical place for him to come looking. We need to escape. What good are we going to be for your husband if Charlie comes back?"

"He'll have to find us first. We have the advantage at the moment in that he doesn't know where we are. He'll check his house to be sure we aren't hiding there somewhere and then he'll probably check the garage. It buys us a little bit of time."

"Okay, but we must hurry. First though, let's get the keys out of your husband's car. In case Charlie comes back and thinks to do it himself."

He took my arm in an offer of support, but I pulled away and gestured towards Kade's SUV. "You go ahead and check for the keys. I am going to look for Kade."

"I don't know if it's a good idea to separate..."

"As you said, we don't have much time, and I can't waste another second here when Kade might need my help."

Dean nodded and rushed off. "Okay, I'll join you in a few seconds."

There was a large barn behind the house, and since Charlie had come from that location, I was hoping, praying that Kade was there. Otherwise, he could be anywhere, and the area was too vast to search in the dark. Not to mention how little time we had to do it. I was in no doubt that Kade had returned to look again because he'd sensed my presence. It wouldn't matter to him if the area was thoroughly searched by the police. As for why Charlie, and maybe Dawn too, had come here, I didn't know, but I sensed in my very soul that something was seriously wrong.

I didn't get far before a contraction began and it was going to be a rough one. I braced my hands on the side of the house and started my breathing exercises, annoyed and excited at the same time. As much as I was looking forward to holding my daughter in my arms, I didn't want to have her here!

Dean rejoined me before my contraction was over. He placed a hand on my back and knelt to look at me since I was bent forward, facing the ground, the position seeming to help with the pain. "You okay?"

"No, I am not okay," I snapped between breaths. "I am in labor, and I think my husband is in trouble." I sucked in another breath and let it out on a groan. When I could speak again, I continued my tirade. "And a fricken lunatic could be bearing down on us at any moment." Could things get any worse? I looked up at the night sky. *Don't answer that!*

Undaunted by my tirade, Dean's voice was calm but urgent. "When you are able, we need to get out of sight in case Charlie comes back. There were no keys in the SUV by the way."

I was not surprised about the keys and could have saved Dean from the bother of looking, though he would have looked anyway, which is why I said nothing. "I figured he'd keep them on him."

When the contraction finally ended, we rounded the corner of the house and headed for the huge old barn. Though it was only about a hundred yards away, it looked too far for me to reach in my condition. But Kade was probably in there, and since he hadn't made an appearance, he was likely in trouble, and nothing was going to stop me from getting to him, not even hard labor. Even so, we weren't even halfway there before I had to stop and deal with another contraction. It was all the damned walking. It was speeding things up!

Dean maintained a firm hold onto me and murmured compliments on how well I was handling things, which annoyed me to the point of gritting my teeth, and yet I didn't want him to stop. His voice was soothing, and it gave me something to focus on. When I felt ready to walk again and indicated we should continue, he peered at me with concern.

"Do you think you can make it? I mean, it seems like your labor pains are coming a lot faster."

"It's going to trigger more contractions but what choice do we have?" It bothered me that I was getting annoyed about my labor. This was an event we'd been looking forward to since the moment I found out I was pregnant, and thanks to Charlie I was not able to enjoy any of it.

Dean knelt low and placed a hand behind my legs. "Put your arms around my neck."

150

"No! I weigh a ton." It horrified me that Dean was thinking he could carry me to the barn.

"I lift weights more than what you weigh, trust me." He scooped me up, forcing me to put my arms around his neck, then rushed across the grass towards a gravel path leading to the barn. Once on the path, and after ensuring it wasn't slippery, he made his way quickly to the barn, though he was getting winded by the time we made it to the barn doors, which were partially open.

If Kade, and perhaps even Dawn, were inside, their unnerving silence could only mean one thing–they were in grave trouble. Feeling sick to my very soul, I pressed my face into Dean's shoulder and squeezed my eyes shut. I couldn't give in to the tears surging for release because despair would follow and that wasn't going to help anyone, least of all myself. But oh, how I wanted to open the floodgates.

"Ssh now, it's going to be fine," Dean assured me. He sat me down very carefully and waited until I was steady on my feet before letting me go. "You okay?"

I couldn't speak past the lump in my throat, so I gave him a nod and turned to look into the yawning darkness beyond the barn doors. Kade was in there, I just knew he was.

Dean put a hand on my arm, prepared to assist me, but suddenly his head snapped up and he turned to listen. "I think I hear a car coming."

That got me moving, and I squeezed through the barn doors, but it was pitch black inside, making it impossible to see anything, and I drew to a disparaging halt. "Kade? Kade are you in here?"

Dean gave my arm a quick squeeze and let me go. "I'm going to try and get into the house and attract Charlie's attention if that's him coming. I should be able to keep him away from here long enough for you to find your husband. If he's even in here."

"Dean, no." I didn't think it was a good idea for us to split up, especially if Charlie was coming back.

"I'm stronger than that old geezer and he won't get me by surprise this time. I should be able to overtake him. Be careful walking around in here." He grabbed my hand and pressed a small flashlight into it. "I always keep a pen light in my coat." After giving my hand a quick, reassuring squeeze, Dean took off running for the house. As for how he planned to get into it, I didn't know, but that was his problem. I needed to find my husband.

Chapter 12

Dean's little flashlight didn't offer much in the way of light, but it was better than nothing, and it shouldn't be noticeable enough to draw Charlie's attention. I didn't even question whether it was him returning, I only hoped Dean could handle him okay and prayed neither of them got hurt.

"Kade, are you in here?" I shined the small beam into the dark space around me, my heart sinking at how large an area there was to cover. If he was unconscious somewhere, it was going to take forever to find him, and I didn't have but minutes at best.

Broken hay bales were scattered everywhere and to the left of me, taking up a good portion of space, was an old tractor. The barn's height indicated an upper section, but I didn't figure I'd need to worry about it. Charlie was of an age when getting up there would be too difficult and dangerous, especially given the dilapidated condition of the structure. Janice concentrated her renovation efforts on the house, leaving the barn for its new owners to deal with. Besides, if Kade had gone up there to get away from Charlie, he would have answered my calls by now.

"Kade, where are you?" The approaching car still sounded a ways off, and I figured Charlie was driving slowly so he could scan the woods for Dean and me. Good, it gave me a little more time. "Kade! Kade, can you hear me?" But only the hollow echo of the wind coursing through the rafters followed my calls.

What if Charlie had drugged him (though I couldn't figure how he would have gotten Kade to take anything from him), and if he had managed it, why? What was Charlie's end game? And where was Dawn? Perhaps I should call out to her as well. "Dawn? Dawn, it's me Tess."

I went further into the barn, wondering where to look and feeling overwhelmed by the sheer size of the barn, when I sensed someone coming up behind me. I swung around and a shape loomed before me, coming closer, and though a scream became lodged in my throat, it soon dissipated with relief. "Dawn!"

Blood was trickling down the side of her face, which was a concern, but not enough to raise my alarm, and though she stood in a relaxed stance, her voice was bordering on frantic. "There's not a lot of time, Tess. Charlie is really losing it."

"What has happened?" I went to hug her, but she rushed past me and stopped just a few feet away, pointing to the floor. "He's down there."

I aimed my flashlight at the area she was indicating and saw an iron ring lying in a recessed circle. A closer look showed me that a square access panel was cut into the floor. My heart thudded with alarm. Kade was down there? But how? Why? And how did Dawn come to know this?

As I could not grasp the ring from a standing position, I struggled to kneel before it, the task was no easy accomplishment for someone in my condition, and once I had managed it, I looked at Dawn with desperation. "Can you give me a hand?"

But she remained where she was, her hands clenching and unclenching, her expression remorseful.

154

Though I wished I had time to talk to her about whatever she was feeling, I didn't have a moment to spare. Charlie would be here at any moment and Kade was my first priority. "Dawn, please!"

But she continued to stand there looking tragic.

I lifted the metal ring and gave it a hard tug, but the panel was much heavier than expected. I looked at Dawn, about to plea once more for her help, when she suddenly turned about and hurried towards the barn door. "Where are you going?"

"Dean is in danger. Charlie has a gun."

A gun! Oh God, this was getting worse. "Dawn, stay here with me. Dean can handle himself."

"Take care of your baby and your husband."

I wanted to argue with her, stop her from going toward more danger, but if Kade was beneath this floor somewhere, I needed to concentrate on helping him. "I wish you'd stay."

"You saved me, Tess. And now I need to help save you."

I returned my attention to the heavy ring in my hand and gave it another hard tug. The panel lifted about an inch, but the effort triggered a contraction, and I had to let the ring go to deal with it. Tears spilled from my eyes as I breathed through the pain and worried about Kade.

With the contraction intensifying, I dropped my hands to the floor, finding this position slightly more helpful. It was unbelievable how tight my belly could become, and I focused on my breath for it did help deal with the pain. Even so, it still hurt a lot. Our daughter was on her way. More tears flooded my eyes, and I couldn't stop them from trickling down my face. I didn't want to have her here in this cold, dark barn.

The pain finally receded, and I returned to my task, lifting the panel enough to get my hand under it, which gave me more leverage in lifting it high enough that I was able to prop it on my knees and rest.

Down below I heard sounds of movement. "Who's there?"

Kade. Tears of relief spilled from my eyes and emotion clogged my throat, making it impossible to answer him.

"Hello?"

Though I wanted to succumb to sobs of despair, relief, worry and joy, I sniffled them away and finally managed to speak. "It's me."

"Tess! Oh my, God, Tess! Are you okay, honey?"

Since he was not making his way up to me, I could only ascertain that he was restrained in some way. "I'm okay but it might take me a minute to get this thing open enough for you to get out of there."

Closing my eyes, I focused on raising my strength via help from spirit, envisioning the panel lifting without effort. And in the silence of the moment, I heard Charlie's truck getting louder. That sent a surge of power charging through me, and I lifted the panel enough to reposition my grip and get my weight behind it. Seconds later I was able to shove it backwards onto the floor.

A gaping dark hole yawned before me and I grabbed my little flashlight, which I'd set aside while grappling with the panel, and saw there were no stairs nor was there a ladder. "Kade?" My little flashlight didn't reach the bottom, but I could see movement.

"Thank God you are okay, Tess! I've been out of my mind with worry."

"I know, I'm so sorry…"

"You've nothing to be sorry about. All that matters is that you are okay."

"Well, we have a few other things that matter too, but for the moment I am just going to enjoy the fact that we are together again."

"I think I've got either a broken ankle or a very sprained one."

That wasn't good news, but it wasn't the worst either. In any case, it was going to present a huge problem. "How long have you been down there?"

"I can't say for sure how long it's been. Someone pushed me and the old man I was with just left me here. I may have lost consciousness because I don't remember how the panel became closed."

"I need to figure out how to get you out of there." What was I going to do? More tears blurred my vision, and I brushed them away with annoyance. If only my emotions weren't so easily riled. I didn't have time to indulge in useless tears.

"You'll probably need to call for help."

Before I could tell him that I didn't have a phone, nor did we have time for help to arrive even if we did have a phone, I heard Charlie's truck get loud enough to indicate that our time had run out. "Charlie is back, Kade. Dean and Dawn are trying to keep him away, but we need to hurry."

"Don't let him see you, Tess. I mean it. He obviously can't be trusted. As for those other people you mentioned, I don't know who they are, but I hope they are on our side."

"They are. Do you know how far down you are?"

"Not sure ... maybe eight feet."

Oh dear! That was an awfully long way down. "I'll see if I can find a ladder." But where to look? "Hold on."

It was a chore to get back on my feet and as I struggled to do so, I heard the slam of a truck door. I glanced out the barn door, taking care to stay out of sight, and saw nothing, no flashlight bobbing this way, no signs of movement anywhere. Hopefully Dean would be successful in keeping Charlie away from the barn, though for how long he might manage that, it was impossible to say.

With a sense of urgency, and borderline panic, I began my search for a ladder, figuring if there was one it might be propped against a wall or lying next to it. So, I concentrated on my search around the inside perimeter. But the going was slow because I was worried about tripping over something. The last thing I needed to do was fall.

Feeling discouraged, I looked about with a heavy heart. The barn was so big, it would take ages to look with only this pen light and we didn't have that kind of time.

Suddenly Dawn came rushing towards me, motioning for me to follow her. "Dean needs help."

"I can't leave Kade and what can I do anyway?" The last thing I wanted to do was run towards someone who had become completely unhinged.

While motioning for me to follow her, Dawn turned to her right and disappeared into the shadows.

I hurried after her and prayed she knew where to find a ladder.

When I got close enough to see her again, she pointed at the floor next to the wall and I shined my flashlight in that direction. A ladder was laying atop the strewn hay. "Oh, thank you Dawn!"

How she knew that was there, I couldn't imagine and though I was getting a weird feeling, a sense that I needed to be careful, I rushed to the ladder. "Can you help me with this?"

"I must check on Dean."

I turned to argue with her, but she was already gone.

158

Dragging the ladder across the floor was a struggle (and I had to deal with yet another contraction, which was about ten minutes from the last one). All the physical exertion was accelerating things, but it couldn't be helped. So, I focused on the task at hand and pushed aside my fears, which would do nothing but cripple my efforts, and I wasn't going to let anything distract me.

Finally, I got the ladder to where Kade waited. "I have a ladder. I will try to lower it slowly, but I probably won't be able to stop it from falling."

"Ok, Sweetness, I'm ready for it."

I positioned the bottom end over the opening then moved to the top end and lifted it high enough to sink the other end into the opening. As heavy as it was, I couldn't maintain control of it once a good portion of the ladder was in the hole, and it began to slide from my grip. In a panic, I called out to Kade, in as loud a voice as I dared. "It's going to fall…"

But suddenly I didn't feel it pulling from my grip anymore and I knew that Kade had hold of it.

"I've got it, Sweetness. Let it go and let me handle it from here."

While Kade made his way up the ladder, grunting with the effort it was costing him and making me worry about the condition of his foot, I went to stand watch near the barn door. It was impossible to see anything, it was so dark, and it was beginning to sleet, the ice-cold rain making me shiver. Fear charged through my veins. I couldn't have my baby in these freezing conditions.

"How are you doing, Kade?" He hadn't yet appeared above the floor and that made me worried.

"I'm almost there, just catching my breath."

Wishing I could be more helpful, I did the only thing I could do and that was keep watch for trouble. Seconds later, a popping noise made me jump in abject fear. Was that a gun going off?

I didn't hear anything more or see any movement up at the house, but knowing Dawn and Dean were joining forces to thwart Charlie made me hopeful they were successful. That gun shot was worrisome though. That and the fact that neither Dawn nor Dean were coming to join us.

When Kade's head appeared, I rushed to his side, love and heartfelt relief washing through me at the sight of him. Though we weren't out of the woods yet, I felt more confident that we'd get there, especially now that we were back together.

Once he made it up high enough to grasp the floor and hoist himself upon it, I sank to my knees, using his shoulders for support, and wrapped my arms around him. How wonderful it was to be back in the safety of his embrace.

After enjoying a brief reunion, Kade pulled away and looked me over. "Are you okay?"

"Yes, but I am in labor."

"My God, Tess, what is going on? Where have you been?"

"It's a complicated story, but we need to stand up and get out of here." It was a struggle for both of us, with his injured foot and another hard contraction complicating things, but we finally managed it, and once upright I leaned on him heavily as my contraction intensified.

Between breaths, I tried to speak. "How's your back? Your legs…"

"I'm okay. It's you I'm worried about. Are you sure the contractions are the real thing?" He held me close, his hands rubbing my back, my shoulders, while pressing kisses to my temple and whispering his love and encouragement.

160

When it was finally over, I fell against him with relief. "It's the real thing. They are about ten minutes apart, though activity brings them on even quicker."

Panic made his voice hoarse. "My God, Tess, are we going to make it out of here in time?"

"I sure hope so." With his arm around my waist, we made it to the barn door, taking care to remain out of sight, and stopped to assess our situation.

As Kade peered into the darkness, taking note of the worsening weather, his body tensed with worry. "I don't know what to do at this point. I don't quite understand the situation." His arm tightened around me in both a protective and reassuring gesture. "Give me a rundown on what's been happening."

"Charlie's been holding me and another girl captive. Her name is Dawn. But then Dean showed up and he became a captive too. Charlie took Dawn away, which is when he showed up here, and in his absence, Dean managed to free us. Now Dawn is trying to help Dean subdue Charlie, but Charlie has a gun, and I think I heard it go off."

"Good God, Tess!"

"I know, right?" As dire as our situation was, I was so happy to be with Kade that I wasn't as terrified, though I needed to get into a better situation for the birth of our daughter. With my head resting against his shoulder and my eyes keeping watch of the house, I had to ask how it was he came to be here. "Why are you here alone? In fact, why are you even here at all?"

"I knew you were here somewhere, though the police are concentrating on the graveyard where your car was found."

"Charlie took it to the graveyard? The one by Silver Lake?"

"Yes. But when I went over there, I just didn't feel your presence and I told them as much but, well, they don't operate on people's feelings. Besides, they'd done an extensive search of this area earlier—them and all our friends—and they were quite certain you were not here."

"I was at Charlie's."

Kade's arm tensed, his hand tightening on my waist. "I knew it. I sensed you were there, but it didn't make any sense." His mouth firmed with annoyance at himself for not giving his gut feelings the merit they deserved. "Why was he keeping you there?"

"He thinks I am Lindsay, his daughter who disappeared a year ago. I'm worried that something's happened to her though."

"So how did you end up over there?" This time, I detected a note of censure in his tone.

"He was holding Dawn captive in his basement, and I tuned in to her call for help." I twisted slightly in his arms to look up at him. "I'm so sorry that I went over there without calling you first…"

"We'll hash it all out later. So, there are two people in that house needing our help?"

"Yes, Dean, who was Lindsay's boyfriend, and Dawn." Another contraction came on, quicker than the others, giving me little warning, and I let out a gasp, unable to hide the pain it was causing me.

His voice sounding strained, Kade gently rubbed my back. "It's not been ten minutes since your last one."

"I've been in labor all day. It's just in the past hour that it's really started progressing." Now, with him here at my side, I wanted to give in to the tears of despair. There was so much that needed to be done. I didn't have time to deliver a baby.

162

With Kade talking me through the pain and rubbing at that spot in my back, which intensified with each passing second of the contraction, I got through it well enough, though it wasn't over by any means. It was only going to get worse.

It was impossible not to cry, for I was feeling incredibly emotional, and I pressed my head to his chest, letting his jacket soak up the tears. "What are we going to do?"

Before he could answer, we heard a car start up then go spinning out of the yard. Someone had just escaped. As I couldn't believe that Dawn or Dean would leave us here, I guessed that it was Charlie, which made me worry over the condition of the other two.

Then I heard Dawn calling us. "It's okay. Charlie is gone. Dean needs you."

I started to exit the barn, but Kade refused to budge, which made me look up at him. "We need to get up there before Charlie decides to come back."

"Maybe I should go check it out first."

"No, it's fine and you are not leaving me here by myself. I am not letting you out of my sight again."

"Hurry, Tess!" Dawn's voice was frantic and that put me in motion.

This time Kade didn't hold me back, but we had to help each other, which was an interesting fete considering our condition. We were both winded, and quite soaked, by the time we made it to the back porch, where I had to stop and breathe through yet another contraction.

Once again, Kade rubbed my back and murmured encouragement, sounding calm and collected though I suspected he was a wreck inside.

Even as I dealt with the pain, I was checking out the situation and saw that one of two doors was standing wide open. Dawn must have done that so we'd know where to enter the house.

Once my contraction was over, I gave Kade's arm a grateful squeeze then made my way up the steps, stopping near the open doorway to call for the others and wait for Kade to catch up. "Dean? Dawn?"

Silence.

Once Kade made it to the top of the stairs, I walked through the door.

The moment I did so, I knew exactly why Janice was worried about the house.

It most definitely was haunted.

Chapter 13

"Now who is it we are looking for again?"

"What?" I was so focused on trying to get a read on the otherworldly inhabitants, it took me a second to get my mind back to what we needed to stay focused on. "Dean and Dawn."

Thanks to the beam from my little flashlight, I could see we had entered a spacious kitchen. Janice's generous remodeling was evident in the sprawling, two-tiered island, its polished granite surface gleaming even under the poor lighting from my flashlight. Stainless steel appliances shimmered in sleek contrast to the white cabinets that framed the room, and my mouth dropped open in awe. I loved my kitchen, but this was a chef's dream.

Beyond a widely arched doorway to our right was the dining room, where a long, elegant dining table matched the heavy, high-backed chairs that flanked it. A sturdy matching buffet stretched along the opposite wall, its surface set with tiered candles on a mirrored tray adorned with dried flowers.

"Do you think it's safe to turn on a light?" Kade felt around the wall near the door and located a couple switches.

"Yes. Charlie's gone and he's the only threat." As for the entity, lights wouldn't bother it in the least.

Kade flipped the switch, and a recessed light above the sink, set in the same polished granite as the island, cast a warm glow over much of the kitchen.

Directly ahead and expanding to the left of the island was a spacious living room. A grand stone fireplace took center stage on the left-side wall and a large ornate domed light fixture hugged the ceiling.

After a quick glance into the dining room and seeing no one, Kade returned to my side. "We need to find them …"

"I can't, Kade. Walking is encouraging my labor, and the contractions are too close." I reached for him and wrapped an arm around his waist. "I need to sit down." Another contraction was already underway, and it was shaping up to be as strong as the last one.

Kade assessed our surroundings and gently steered me towards the living room, which was not furnished. "That bay window inset on the wall facing the front porch has a wide sill. You can sit there."

I managed only a few steps before the contraction grew too intense to continue walking. Holding firm to his supportive arms, I bent forward to alleviate some of the agony. As with the others, it began as an intense ache in the small of my back, then quickly expanded to engulf my entire midsection, each passing second increasing the tightness of my skin until my abdomen was rock hard and incredibly painful. Difficult though it was to speak, I forced the words through gritted teeth. "I feel like a vice is tightening around me and my muscles are going rigid to resist it."

"We need to get out of here. Thank God Charlie didn't get my car keys from me."

With the pain receding, I motioned for us to continue to the window and sat down with a sigh of relief. "What about your cell phone?"

166

"Charlie has it." He snorted in disgust, which I knew was aimed at himself. "I have a flashlight ... or had one, but it broke when I was shoved into that blasted hole. Charlie asked if he could use the flashlight on my phone and I stupidly handed it to him instead of giving him my flashlight."

"Wait, you were shoved? And you were cooperating with Charlie?"

"He showed up while I was looking around in the house. I heard a vehicle approaching, so I went out on the porch to see who it was. Charlie got out of his truck and asked me what I was up to, and I told him. That's when he offered to show me a couple of secret places in the house where we, of course, didn't find you. Then he told me he knew of another place where you might be. That's when he led me to the barn. He showed me that blasted room under the floor and though I didn't see you and you didn't answer me, Charlie said there was another room down there, which there is, but it's not that big. In fact, it's smaller than the one in our basement."

"And you believed I might be down there?" That really surprised me but then he was desperate, and he would leave no stone unturned, or rather I should say he'd leave no secret room unchecked.

"We have looked everywhere, Sweetness, and it's here, well this area anyway, that I felt your presence. I felt it even more when Charlie showed up."

"Because he's been with me all day."

"I had to at least make sure."

"So, when you were looking down into the room, Charlie pushed you into it?"

Kade shook his head, and though the kitchen light didn't extend as well into the living room, I could see how baffled he was by his expression and by the sound of his voice. "No, he was across from me, and I was shoved from behind."

That was a very worrisome detail, but we didn't have time to chat about it. We needed to find Dawn and Dean and get out of here. I didn't know how much time we had before our daughter arrived, but it wasn't much.

"Go find the others. We need to hurry, Kade."

"It's not going to be easy for me either, Sweetness." He indicated his foot, which he was keeping his weight off of by holding onto the window frame next to me.

I glanced around for something he could use for support but saw nothing suitable. The house was nearly empty, and then I looked up. "Kade, take that curtain rod down and use it to help with support."

"You are so smart, my love." Kade reached up and popped the heavy curtain rod from its bracket and tested its sturdiness. "This will do. Are you going to be okay for a few minutes?"

"Yes, but hurry!"

A noise on the second floor caught our attention and Kade hobbled from sight. He'd no sooner gone out of my view, and Dawn came towards me walking slowly, as if uncertain of my reception. I glanced past her and guessed she must have been hiding somewhere behind one of the doors in the kitchen.

"Dawn! Why didn't you come out earlier?"

She looked so sad that I wanted to give her a hug, but I didn't dare stand up. It could trigger yet another contraction and I needed to stay as calm as possible until we got out of here.

"I have to tell you something, Tess, and I am ashamed to admit it."

"Can it wait until we get out of here? Kade is looking for Dean. Do you know if he is okay? Did Charlie shoot him?" The sounds coming from the second floor suggested that he was not incapacitated because it wasn't just Kade causing that amount of noise.

"He'll be okay," Dawn said, drawing nearer.

Her eyes were shadowed with a mix of sadness and regret, her gaze holding mine so intensely that I extended a hand in a gesture of encouragement, urging her to come join me. "Come sit with me."

"Dean is innocent, Tess. He did not take Lindsay or hurt her in any way."

I figured as much, he'd been so helpful and considerate from the moment we met each other. "I know."

Dawn's lips curved into a slight smile. "Yes, I'm sure you do."

Kade interrupted our discussion when he called down to me from the stairs. "I found Dean. He's been shot, but he's going to be okay. It's going to take us a few minutes to get down there. Are you okay?"

"I'm fine." The energy exerted to answer him was enough to trigger another contraction. I braced one hand on the edge of the windowsill and the other on my belly as I prepared for it.

"I ran away from home when I was fourteen," Dawn said, her voice tinged with the emotional pain her confession elicited. "I didn't have any money and so I had to use what I had to make some." She gave me a significant look and I knew what she meant. Her only asset was her body.

Though I was breathing through the contraction and not doing it as quietly as I wished, I did my best to convey my understanding and sympathy. "I'm so sorry, Dawn, that you had to go through that."

Dawn waved away my empathy. "I did things to live, Tess. Things that I am not proud of." She looked away and paused, and I had the impression she was choosing her words carefully. "One day I met a woman who claimed she was psychic. People willingly gave money to her, just for saying stuff that anyone could say. I mean, she never gave out any extraordinary information. It was all hogwash, but she made enough to live on. So, I figured I'd give it a try. It was better than what I was doing." She shifted her stance, looking uncomfortable. It pained her to come clean with me and yet she was doing it. For that I was proud of her. "I started following people, learning a little about them, then approaching them and acting like I knew things. People are so easily impressed that they really do just hand over their cash."

"So, you aren't really a psychic?"

"No. But I wished that I was." She gave me a wistful smile. "So anyway, it was a better way to earn money than the other way, so I got better at it. I mean, you can pretty much just read people and know what they want to hear. Then I saw Dean in that bar and I just …" Dawn paused, struggling for the words to express what she wanted to say. "I developed a major crush. He was so nice, and kind, and I tried really hard to attract his attention." She gave a sharp little laugh. "I scared him off when I cornered him outside the bathroom and pretty much plastered myself to his body. He kissed me back but only for a few seconds. In all honesty, I think he was just trying to let me down kindly."

Relief filled me at this revelation. I'd come to like Dean, and I wanted him to be the man I thought he was.

"Although he claimed to love Lindsay, I didn't want to give up. He'd told me where he worked, and I managed to get a temporary job there." She let out another sharp laugh. "Dean wasn't thrilled when I showed up at his workplace, but I behaved myself and just tried to be a friend, you know?"

170

"Were you hoping he'd leave Lindsay for you?"

"Yes. And to ensure that happened, I made friends with Lindsay too." She paused to see how I reacted to her confession, and I kept my expression carefully schooled, revealing nothing of my disapproving thoughts, and she was encouraged to continue. "I used a different name when I was with Lindsay and I wore one of my blond wigs, one that I used to wear when I was doing other stuff."

She looked so contrite and ashamed that I again patted the space beside me, inviting her to come sit. "Please come join me."

"No, I need to get this out." She pressed on before I could object. "I did the same thing with Lindsay that I'd done with other people, following her around, gathering information then bumping into her and posing as a psychic, feeding her what she wanted to hear. I was able to say quite a bit. After all, I was working with Dean, and he spoke about her often, so I knew lots of things she didn't think I should know." She looked past me, to the shadowy, wet world beyond the window. "I started planting doubts in her mind about Dean, making her think he was having an affair, and she fell for it. I knew from rumors going around at work that Dean and Lindsay were fighting a lot, and it was easy enough to see that neither of them was happy."

"Dawn…"

"No, please let me finish. As you said, we don't have much time."

"But we'll have plenty later…"

"No, we won't." She held up a hand to halt my next question and rushed on. "When Dean told us at the office that she was pregnant, I was scared that I'd lose him forever. Not that I ever had him, but he did like me, so I clung to that, thinking I could make him love me if I could just split them up. But the pregnancy made it so much harder."

An awful feeling began to rise in my gut about what she was going to say next, and the anxiety of it triggered yet another contraction.

Dawn continued speaking, seemingly oblivious to my plight. "I came up with the idea of scaring her back here to Maine. You know, to be with her dad. Dean said Charlie was always begging her to come home. So, I made a deal with some guys to help me with a plan."

"Which was what?" It was very hard to keep my voice neutral, especially when dealing with a hard contraction.

"I knew they were going to a company dinner one night, so I fixed it that Dean would have to park his car near an alley instead of his designated parking spot. Then I had a few guys wait for them there. I told them to instigate a fight with Dean and to make sure Lindsay got in the way." When she saw me narrow my eyes with disapproval, she dropped her gaze to the floor. "I told them not to hurt her…"

"But you instructed them to have Dean hurt her?" It was disappointing to hear this and I wasn't sure what I wanted to do about it.

"Yes, I told them to do that, but I didn't intend for her to be seriously injured."

"Oh, Dawn…"

She held up her index finger, silently conveying her wish that I allow her to continue uninterrupted. "I know. I'm not proud of myself."

Our eyes met and I could almost read her thoughts, our connection was that strong. She was genuinely contrite over her past behavior. I hoped she could read my thoughts as well, telling her that it was going to be okay. She wasn't alone anymore. She had a friend in me. Besides, she wasn't the same person she was then. Her confession and how she felt about it told me as much. This whole situation with Charlie, and our meeting, had changed her. "Dawn, please come with us when we leave here."

172

She squeezed her eyes shut and was silent for a few seconds, as if gathering inner courage, and when she opened her eyes, I saw her resolve to continue with her confession. But I also saw secrets. "That incident didn't scare her away. I met up with her the following day and she told me about what happened. She said she and Dean had a really nice evening afterwards." Dawn rolled her eyes in remembered exasperation. "Obviously that is not the result I was hoping for. So, when she went off to use the bathroom and left her cell phone on the table, I made a call to her dad, hanging up when he answered. Lindsay told me he was crazy paranoid, and so I figured he'd get worried, wondering why she hung up on him, which he did. He must have called her like five times after that. She ignored them all."

"But Lindsay would see that a call was made to her dad on her phone."

"Yes, but she thought she must have dialed him by accident." Dawn laughed though there was no amusement in the sound. "People are funny. They try to logically explain everything away, even if they don't believe it."

She reflected on that before continuing. "The next day, Lindsay told me her father was coming to visit, and she was worried about him and Dean getting together. She knew Charlie was going to make a big deal about her black eye, and he wouldn't believe it was an accident. Since I was hoping Charlie would come and convince her to go home with him, I told her I was getting a psychic message about Dean being in Providence, Rhode Island, so it would be fine for Charlie to come. She corrected me, said that he was going to a conference there but not until the next week, which she was right, but I convinced her Dean was lying to her about the dates."

"But why?"

"So, she would let her dad come and to instill distrust about anything Dean said to her." She peeked at me through her lashes and looked away, unable to meet my disappointed stare. "With her thinking Dean was going to be hours away at a conference, she let her father come."

"She never questioned any of your so-called messages?" It was people like Dawn that gave people like me a bad name, and I was doing my best not to resent her for it. She was just a kid when she went out into the big, bad world on her own, and she'd adapted to it by coming up with a scam that helped her make a living. I didn't agree with it, but I understood.

"No, by this time she was so convinced I was the most gifted psychic she ever knew—not that she knew any others, mind you—that she believed everything I told her."

"But why, Dawn? Why lie about that?" I wanted so very badly for this not to go where I was worried it was going. Lindsay vanished the same day her father showed up, and I hoped with all my heart that Dawn didn't have something to do with that.

"I just told you, I wanted her to think it was fine for her dad to visit, and it worked out really well. He came and Dean showed up, thanks to me leaving a message at his office. I pretended to be Lindsay and said I wanted him to come to the apartment for lunch."

"Dawn, do you know what happened to Lindsay?"

She started to speak but the men had made it to the bottom of the stairs, and we could hear them making their way to the living room. Dawn glanced towards the sound and backed away.

I motioned for her to stay where she was, though I knew she was probably nervous about facing Dean, and didn't hold much hope that she wouldn't bolt.

174

When the men came into view, I looked at them in alarm. Dean's face was covered in blood and his forehead was wrapped in what looked like a torn-up t-shirt. Dean's left arm was not in the sleeve of his jacket because he was using it as a sling Kade must have fashioned for him. Being in the Marines, he learned all sorts of things, especially when it came to administering first aid, which he'd learned while 'out in the field' as he called it. Kade was leaning on Dean's other arm, using him for support instead of the curtain rod, though I think they were both actually supporting each other.

"Dean, what happened?"

"I didn't know Charlie had a gun when I jumped him. We struggled over it, and it went off. I fell when the bullet hit me and banged my head on the windowsill, and it knocked me out cold."

"He must have thought he shot you in the head." Now that he was close enough, I could see his heavy dark jacket was also soaked in blood but that would have been impossible to see in the dark.

"We need to get out of here," Kade said. "Dean told Charlie that you were hiding in the garage back at his place. He might come back when he figures out you aren't there."

I turned to look at Dawn, intending to urge her to come with us, but she was gone. Given everything she'd just told me, she probably wouldn't come anyway, not until she was ready to face the consequences of her actions. I wished we'd had just a minute more of time, though, for I believe she was about to tell me what happened to Lindsay.

"I didn't see Dawn anywhere," Kade said.

"No, she won't be coming with us."

"She's here in the house though, isn't she?" Kade asked, and I nodded that she was.

"Dawn is here?" Dean looked from Kade to me. "You saw her?"

"Yes, but she doesn't want to see you right now, Dean." Or any of us, really, and that made me sad, but there wasn't anything I could do about it right now. I had a baby on the way! "We need to get to the hospital." I struggled to stand but had to wait for another contraction to be over before we could head out of the house.

As we made our way to Kade's car, an ordeal for all three of us, considering the state we were in, I prayed we'd get to it before Charlie returned. I was nearly out of time and couldn't afford any extra to deal with him. As it was, I knew we weren't going to make it to the hospital.

After helping me into his SUV and ensuring Dean was settled in the back seat, Kade managed to get in behind the wheel without too much difficulty.

There was still no sign of Charlie, thank God, and Kade took a moment to catch his breath before starting the vehicle. We all let out a collective sigh of relief when the engine started right up.

"Guess this horror show is over," Dean said, giving a small chuckle.

"Not yet," Kade muttered. "We still need to make it past Charlie's place." His exit from the driveway was similar to Charlie's, and it was another huge relief when we passed the entrance to his driveway and did not see his truck barreling towards us.

Now was the time to voice a new concern. "We aren't going to make it the hospital, Kade." Another contraction rendered me unable to say more, for all I could manage at this point was panting and groaning.

Kade stepped on the gas. "We'll go to Tara's."

It was a great idea, and I nodded my approval. She'd know what to do for all of us.

Ten minutes and two contractions later, we pulled into Tara's driveway.

As if expecting us, she came running out, an umbrella in hand, and spoke to Kade the moment he opened his door. "Kade, where have you been?" And then, at the same moment he answered her, she glanced past him and saw me.

"Saving my wife. Or rather, she was saving me. And she's about to have our baby!"

Chapter 14

Tara came running around to my side of the vehicle and opened my door. "Tess, oh Tess, I am so glad you are found, and you are safe!" She wrapped her free arm around me and pressed a kiss onto my cheek. "I did a protection spell right after Kade called and said you were missing."

"Thank you, I appreciate that." With Tara's help, I slid from the vehicle, an awkward maneuver with the baby's impending arrival making everything more difficult.

Dean climbed out from the back seat, catching Tara off guard, and when she saw his head wrapped in the remnants of Kade's t-shirt (thank goodness he was one of those guys that still wore t-shirts under his clothes) and all the blood on his face, her eyes widened in shock. "Hello there, and who are you?"

"Tara, this is Dean, he helped me escape and he's been shot in the shoulder. The injury to his head happened when he fell. Dean, this is my very dear friend Tara."

Nodding to him in acknowledgment, Tara shook her head in confusion and looked to me for answers. "Shot? Escape what?" Then she saw Kade limping his way around the SUV, using the vehicle for support. "What's happened to you, Kade?"

"Not sure, either a bad sprain or it's broke." He slid his arm across my shoulders. "We need to get her out of this freezing rain."

"How close are you?" Tara asked, slipping her free arm around my waist.

"My contractions are about two minutes apart." As she was exclaiming over that, I heard the slushy patter of approaching footsteps and looked to see Daniel and Mary hurrying toward us, their expressions morphing from elation to concern.

Tara gestured for them to step up the pace with an urgent toss of her head. "Tess is about to deliver a baby." She then started barking orders and everyone scrambled to comply. "Kade, let me help Tess into the house. Daniel, assist Kade, his foot is either sprained or broken. Mary, you help Tess's new friend Dean, he's been shot in the shoulder."

"What happened to your head?" she asked, going straight to him.

"Hit it on the windowsill when I fell." He waved off her concern as she sought to look him over, her medical training kicking in. "It's not that bad."

"You lost a lot of blood and could pass out on us," Kade said.

"What is going on out here?" Robin came out onto the porch and peered at us through the rain, then when she realized who she was looking at, she came running. "I go in the kitchen to fix some tea and come back to find the answer to all our prayers! Thank God!" Then her eyes landed on Dean. "Good Lord, what's happened and who are you?"

"His name is Dean and he's been shot," Kade told her. "The injury on his head happened when he fell."

"Shot? Oh my God!" Robin splayed a hand across her chest in shock. "I'm so sorry!" She saw that Mary was taking charge of him and nodded in reassurance. "You are lucky to have Mary here, she'll know what to do."

Before Dean could respond to that, she was looking at me, her elation returning. "I am so glad to see you!" Then she noticed the way I was leaning on Tara and her face became wreathed with concern. "Are you in labor?"

Seeing my astonishment over the presence of so many friends, Tara offered an explanation. "We've been together all day trying to find you." She shot Kade a little glare. "Mr. Man there said he'd follow us here from the cemetery where they found your car, but he never showed up. So, we've been sitting here wondering and worrying where he went off to and fretting over the fact that he wasn't answering his phone."

"I felt I needed to go back to the Wheeler house," Kade said, his tone unapologetic. "And as you can see, I was definitely needed there."

"Sounds like you should have called us, bub." Daniel nodded at Kade's foot and Dean's shoulder. "Who had the gun?"

"We'll tell you all the story when we get Tess settled in the house," Kade said. "If we keep yammering, she's bound to deliver out here in the driveway."

Right on cue, another contraction started, and Tara let me cling to her while she motioned for Robin to come around to my other side for additional support. Although Kade wanted to stay with me, I waved him on. "Go, I'm going to need you all settled when I get inside."

I felt blessed to have so many of my close friends with me, especially now, when I was about to bring our daughter into the world. I'd been so afraid she'd be born at Charlie's place, and I should have known that it would work out. We still had to deal with Charlie and find Dawn, but those things could wait just a bit longer. We had other very important things to do.

When I was finally able to walk again, Tara and Robin helped me into the house and immediately started disrobing me of my sodden clothes. As I was almost too numb to move, my teeth chattering uncontrollably, I was glad for their assistance.

Kade was perched on the edge of a bench that was located just beyond the entryway. He'd already removed his jacket and was now dealing with the discomfort of having Daniel remove his boot from his injured foot. His jeans were soaked, and I worried about him having to stay in them for an extended period. Few things were as miserable as being clad in cold wet clothes.

Our eyes met and locked in a moment of mutual support, and a sense of calm settled over me. It was going to be okay. We were safe and right where we needed to be. And as our friends continued to assist us, we exchanged smiles, our eyes conveying a wordless message of profound gratitude for each and every one of them.

A door slammed, and then Anya came bouncing down an open set of stairs. The headphones she was wearing must have made her oblivious to our arrival because when her gaze lifted to take in the room, she faltered into a stunned pause. Her eyes, as beautiful and expressive as her mother's, widened in much the same way that Tara's had earlier. She yanked the headphones off and darted her eyes across each of us, settling her gaze on me, her wide mouth curving into an excited smile. "Tess, I am so glad you are found!" Then she noticed that something wasn't quite right with what was going on. "What's happening?"

"She's about to have her baby," Tara told her. "Fetch that waterproof pad from the linen closet." She looked at me and shrugged in apology. "I am excited for you to have your baby, and I am honored to be helping you, but I need to protect the furniture. I'm rather fond of my couch."

Suddenly I realized just what was going to happen and what it all entailed, and heat flooded my face.

Tara understood right away. "No worries, Tess, we'll protect your modesty." She gave me a wink then turned to address Mary, who was asking Dean a bunch of questions and helping him get his sodden jacket off. "Mary, take Dean to the guest bathroom. I've a nice first aid kit in there. You'll find it under the sink." She took in Dean's pale face and glanced at Mary. "You can handle it okay?"

Mary nodded and gave Dean's good shoulder a gentle, reassuring pat. "I'm a trained Army medic, did it for twenty years and saw much worse than you over in Afghanistan. I'll take care of you until we can get you to the hospital."

With a visible sense of relief, Dean gave her a grateful smile. "I'd appreciate that, thank you."

"Once you've taken care of him, Mary, go to my room and find a dry shirt, yours is soaked, then come join us," Tara instructed. "We'll get Tess comfortable and then we are going to take advantage of your expertise." She then looked over at Kade. "I've a pair of sweats that should fit you. You need to get out of those wet jeans. Daniel, follow Mary to the guest bedroom." She glanced over at Anya. "Take them there after you get me that pad. Your uncle left some clothes here from his last visit, I think they'll fit Kade. You'll find them in the dresser." She waved them on. "Get going, we don't have much time."

Tara's efficiency at taking charge was comforting, not just for me but everyone involved, and everyone scattered to do as she instructed. My fears at delivering my baby calmed down to nothing. Tara was a great organizer and knowledgeable about many things, and Mary was a highly trained medic. Though delivering in a hospital was the safest option, it wasn't one open to me and this was the next best thing, better actually because I could have all my friends with me to share in the experience.

And so, while Tara prepared the chaise lounge section of her sofa, Robin led me into the bathroom and Anya brought me one of her mother's lightweight robes. She and Robin assisted me with removing the rest of my clothing then helped me into the robe, though we had to stop a couple times while I dealt with a contraction.

When I returned to the living room, it was to see that Kade was wearing a pair of dark blue sweatpants and a gray t-shirt. He was settled next to the chaise lounge and lit up when he saw me heading his way.

"I looked at his foot," Tara said. "I'm pretty sure it's just a bad sprain."

She helped me settle on the chaise lounge while Robin wrapped a bandage around Kade's foot and ankle to keep it more stable.

"Shouldn't we call the police?" Anya asked.

"Not yet," Tara said. "They'll swarm this place, and I will not have them all in here while Tess is giving birth."

"But they are still looking for Tess," Anya pointed out.

"Actually, they aren't," Kade assured her. "They suspended the search until tomorrow morning. When I left the cemetery to join you guys here, I felt a strong urge to go back to the Wheeler place, and though I intended to come by here first, I just found myself driving straight there."

Mary came running back into the room. "It's a clean shot, the bullet passed right through. Luckily it didn't damage anything crucial. Daniel is bandaging him up. He's got a bad cut on his head too, but I put a couple butterfly stitches on it. He will need to see a doctor, but he's going to be fine."

184

She saw that I was in nothing but a robe and propped on the chaise lounge with Kade sitting next to me and nodded in approval. "Right then, I guess we are ready!" When Daniel came back into the room with Dean close behind him, she motioned with her hand that he head for the door. "Daniel, we need you to run over to Tess's place and get her suitcase, the one she has packed for the hospital. It's got stuff for the baby in it."

"Where will I find the suitcase?" He was already at the door, pausing just long enough for my answer.

"In the hallway next to the front door. And can you let Alex out too before coming back here?"

Kade tossed him his keys, since he had parked behind Daniel's car. "Thanks, Bud."

Dean, who looked much better now that he was cleaned up and properly bandaged, stood awkwardly, looking uncertain as to what he should do, and Robin motioned for him to take a seat in Tara's reading nook. He would be able to see some of what was going on but situated behind me so I didn't need to worry about my modesty, which Tara and Mary assured me I wouldn't worry about anyway when the time came.

Tara placed a soft fluffy blanket on the large hassock next to where I was located. "We'll put her there to get her all situated after you've had some bonding time." She asked Mary to sterilize the scissors in the first aid kit and then asked me if I had one of those little suction tubes for the baby's nose in my suitcase.

"Yes, I have everything in it that I thought we might need." Tara told me that the hospitals provided everything, but one could never know when a baby might arrive, so she suggested that I have everything I might need for a car birth. She must have had a gut feeling that something like this would happen.

"Anya, put some towels in the dryer," Tara instructed. "We want them nice and warm for when the baby arrives."

Minutes later, my contractions were coming one after another and when I complained about feeling pressure, Mary knelt before me, waiting until a particularly hard and long contraction was over before giving my knees a gentle pat. "I am going to have a look, Tess, and see where you are at."

I barely had time to part my legs and let her have a look when another contraction followed, this one accompanied by a very strong urge to push. "I have to push!" It felt like I had no control over my body as it did what it needed to do to help our daughter enter the world.

"She's crowning, Tess!" Mary's excitement was contagious as everyone cheered, expressing their awe over this amazing moment.

"Kade, help her sit up a little more so she can put more power behind her pushes," Tara instructed and then she lifted one of my legs and slipped an arm under my knee, telling Robin to grab the other. "We'll just help her keep these out of the way while her baby makes her way out to us."

"Dig your heals into the couch, Tess," Mary instructed. "Do whatever you need to do for leverage, and when you feel the urge to push again, draw in a breath, hold it and push as hard as you can, letting your breath out slowly and quietly."

"I'd be screaming about now," Anya said, her voice hushed in awe over what she was witnessing.

"Screaming lessens the energy needed for pushing," Tara told her.

"My water hasn't even broken yet." I couldn't believe I was about to give birth without that having taken place. I'd heard so many stories of women's water breaking in the most embarrassing of places and I'd been a little concerned about where I'd be when it happened to me. Apparently, I

186

had nothing to worry about, which was why worrying was a useless waste of time, the things we spend hours worrying over often never come to pass.

"Perhaps she'll be born en caul," Tara said softly.

"What's that?" Kade asked.

"She might still be encased in her amniotic sac," Tara explained.

Kade leaned down until his mouth was near my ear. "I am so incredibly proud of you. I love you."

I pressed my head against him, and he kissed my temple. "I love you, too, Kade, so very, very much." Tears filled my eyes though I didn't know why. As they spilled down my cheeks, I let out a little embarrassed laugh. "I don't know why I'm crying."

"Happy tears," Robin said and gave a little sniffle of her own.

I looked around to see that they all, including Kade, had tears in their eyes. But it had been an emotional day and now we were having the most amazing moment.

And then I had to push again.

"She's coming, Tess!" Mary said. "Draw in a breath and bear down!"

"Anya, note the time when she's all the way out," Tara instructed quickly.

"Oh my, God, Tess, I see her!" While keeping his arm firmly around me and providing his much-needed support, Kade's focus was all on our daughter, and I wanted to see too.

I leaned as far forward as I could, which wasn't far, but my belly made it impossible to see anything. She might be on her way out, but my belly was still pretty big, as if she were still stuffed in there. The pain was intense, almost unbearable, but pushing against it did offer some small relief.

"What is on her?" Anya asked, leaning close to see.

"She's en caul," Tara breathed.

"I've never seen such a thing," Mary said.

The door opened and Daniel came rushing in. "I have the suit … oh my God!" He hastily shut the door, dropped my suitcase at his feet and came further into the room, the fascination on his face matching that of everyone else.

"One more push, Tess," Mary said. "Her head is out but we need to get her shoulders out too, then the rest will follow."

With Kade and everyone else offering encouragement, I drew in another breath, held it, and bore down. And our daughter slid right out, her birth giving instant relief. Just like that, the pain was gone.

"Wow, I've never seen anything so amazing in my life," Mary said.

"Anya, did you note the time?" Tara asked, glancing at the clock.

"Yes. 9:13," she said.

Kade helped me sit up higher while Tara and Robin lowered my legs so I could see.

Mary held our daughter in her hands, and she was completely encased in her amniotic sac, her tiny body folded up, her feet tucked under her chin, one hand flattened against a cheek and the other resting on her head which appeared to be covered in hair. Her tiny little face was pressed against the sac, which was stretched around her like a clear balloon.

I was in awe and completely, totally, madly in love with her.

Chapter 15

We all wanted to touch her, and did so with gentle fingers, all while marveling over the miracle of her, the wonderment and magic of this special kind of birth. It was like she had yet to be born. Her eyes were closed, and she seemed to be asleep.

Dean had come close enough to see over the back of the couch and Kade motioned for him to go ahead and lean over and touch her, which he did with reverence, the look on his face completely mesmerized. "This is the most amazing think I have ever seen in my life."

"Anya, bring me a warm towel," Mary said. "Daniel, bring me that suitcase." As soon as he handed it to her, she fished out a baby blanket, a beanie hat and the little suction tube for her nose.

When Anya returned, Mary spread the warm towels next to me and gently placed our precious baby upon it.

"Anya, note the time the sac is punctured," Tara said, her focus completely absorbed on my daughter.

Mary carefully punctured the amniotic sac, and the water instantly drained away, soaking into the towels. Like a flower unfolding, our little girl spread her arms and legs and lifted her chin, her eyes opening in wonder. We all welcomed her to our world, expressing our love for her, and she looked around her as if she was as fascinated as we were.

Mary gently unwound the umbilical cord, which was wrapped around her body, and once it was completely free, she held out a pair of scissors and offered them to Kade. "You want to cut the umbilical cord?"

He accepted the scissors then leaned down and tenderly pressed a kiss to our daughter's forehead. His lips lingered as he murmured softly against her skin then he cut the cord.

Mary promptly clamped it with a clip she'd sterilized earlier then cleared fluid from our baby's nose and ensured her airway was clear.

Our precious little one voiced her protest with her first cries, and I thought it was the most exquisite sound I'd ever heard.

Kade and I locked eyes, our love for each other and our little girl so powerful it fused us together, an unbreakable bond that went beyond words. "What did you say to her?" I had to know, just watching him interact with her that way had touched me deeply.

"I told her that she could always rely on us, as she had relied on that cord, and that we would give her all the tools necessary to live a safe and happy life."

Tears blurred my vision as emotion surged within me, welling up from my very soul, and I blinked several times to clear them away. I had to be one of the luckiest women in the world. "I love you both so much."

"I know. I feel the same."

We shared a lingering kiss, then Mary interrupted the moment as she laid my daughter on my chest. "It's time for you three to bond."

My sweet baby tilted her head up to look at me, and I knew, when my eyes met hers, that she could see me. I felt as if I'd known her my whole life, in this one and in others. We were soul mates, she and I, traveling through many lives together.

190

She seemed curious about everything, her round little eyes open wide, her elfin chin quivering, her bow mouth parting and closing as if she couldn't quite express how she felt about what was occurring. She was absolutely perfect.

Kade was touching her all over, running gentle fingers along her back, her arms, her legs and her head, which was covered in dark, downy soft hair. She grasped his finger when he got to her tiny hands.

"She's already got a grip on my heart, Tess. She's the most perfect thing I have ever seen." He bent to kiss her brow, and she tried to lift her head to look at him. Whoever said babies couldn't see clearly couldn't possibly know what they were talking about, because she seemed very aware and alert and very cognizant of what she was seeing.

"I love you so much, sweetheart." Kade's arm slid down behind me and hugged me to him. He kissed the top of my head, then slid his lips to my ear so he could whisper his love some more.

I pressed my head to him, enjoying the feeling of him beside me as our daughter squirmed about on my chest. I was so worried about this moment not being like this and I shouldn't have doubted it. I should have known that I would never manifest anything but this for such an important moment in our lives. "I love you, Kade. Thank you so much for this precious little girl."

"What are you going to name her?" Anya asked, her voice hushed with reverence for what she'd witnessed.

Kade and I looked at each other and in unison we announced her name. "Autumn Belle."

We'd talked about it several times, and we talked about other names we liked, but we knew when we saw her that the right name would come to us, and it did.

"That's beautiful," Tara said. With a finger, she gently caressed Autumn's downy hair. "Autumn represents change, for energy is ever changing. The Autumn month is a time when the world explodes in splendor, spreading joy and wonder to all who view it. Autumn represents a time for harvesting all that we've nourished through the spring and summer, and it's a time of glory before the rest and introspection of winter. It's a wonderful name for her."

"We need to finish a few things," Mary said. "And then we need to call the police and Tess's doctor."

An hour later, Tara's house was swarming with the police and two paramedic units, one of which tended to Kade and Dean, while the other checked on me and Autumn, who had nursed earlier and was now sleeping in my arms.

Though I hated the intrusion on this special time, we needed to address the ugly side of reality.

Chapter 16

It was chaotic with the paramedics doing their thing while we were talking to the police, but we wanted to give our statements while our memory was fresh and before we all went to the hospital.

Despite everything that had taken place, I worried about what was going to happen to Charlie. He was an old man with serious mental health issues. In the end, he didn't seriously hurt anyone, though the potential to do so was there. And though he didn't intentionally shoot Dean, he had left him after doing so. He'd done the same with Kade, leaving him without bothering to see if he was okay.

"So, Charlie took you down to the barn to show you a room below the floor and someone pushed you into it?" The police officer taking our statements seemed skeptical as he gave Kade a long look, like he was waiting for more. "If he didn't push you, then who did?"

"Well, that's a good question, Officer ..." Kade looked at his nametag. "Milton, and I have no idea as to its answer. Charlie was across from me, and whoever pushed me did it from behind."

"Do you know if Charlie was aware that someone was behind you and if he saw that person push you?"

"I have no idea if Charlie saw it happen or not."

It worried me that a malevolent spirit might be involved, but it didn't make sense. I felt nothing like that in the barn, no sense of anything evil or dangerous. But I did feel something…

"You are certain he isn't the one to push you?" Officer Milton pressed.

"He was looking down into the room, using my cellphone as a flashlight, and it happened so fast, I don't think he was aware of anyone coming up behind me. He never gave off a reaction like he heard anyone as far as I can remember." After taking a few seconds more to think about it, Kade nodded, doubling down on his conviction that Charlie was not responsible for his fall.

"What did he do with your cellphone?" Milton asked.

"I don't know what he did with it, but then again we haven't really looked for it."

"So, he still might have it on him then." Milton made a note of it. "What's your cell phone number? We might be able to locate him through that."

Kade handed him a business card from his wallet. "All my information is on there."

"Thank you." He secured it to his clipboard. "So, did you see him replace the cover back over the opening?"

"No. I didn't see him do that. I heard him say something when I fell, maybe expressing concern, I don't know, but he sounded alarmed."

"Do you think he was under duress?" Another officer, whose nametag said Dutton, was also taking notes.

"It's certainly possible," Kade answered. "As to who put the lid back over the opening, I can't say. It's certainly possible that whoever pushed me might have done it after chasing Charlie off. I just don't know."

194

"Charlie was in an awful hurry when he left, like he was scared of something," Dean said. "He tore out of there like the hounds of hell were on his heels."

"But then he came back and shot you," Officer Milton said.

"Well, he came back with a gun, but I don't know if it was to shoot me. I mean, he couldn't really know for sure where Tess and I were. As for shooting me, the gun went off when I jumped him, and I do believe it was an accident."

"The fact he came back with a gun shows possible intent to shoot someone," Officer Milton persisted. "Why come back with a gun otherwise?"

"It's something you'll need to ask him," Dean said. "He might have come back to help Kade and had the gun to protect himself. But again, I don't know. I didn't confront him or have a chance to talk to him. I just didn't want him to go down to the barn where Tess was looking for her husband. My job was to keep him distracted until I could overtake him." He indicated his bandaged arm. "Obviously that plan didn't go all that well." Looking a little sheepish that he couldn't subdue a 72-year-old man, Dean shifted on his feet and shrugged. "I didn't want to hurt him. He is Lindsay's father, and she loved him. So, I was trying to be careful, and as I just said, I don't think he intended for the gun to go off."

"When he realized he shot you, what did he do?" Milton asked.

"I don't know. I hit my head on the windowsill when I went down, and I think it knocked me out."

"Dean was still on the floor when I got to him," Kade said. "He was bleeding from the bump on his head and Charlie might have thought he'd shot him in the head. There in the dark, he probably didn't even notice the blood on his dark jacket."

"So, he left someone for dead," Dutton said.

"We still don't know who pushed, Kade," I pointed out. "It's possible that person appeared and scared him off." I couldn't place blame on someone without knowing all the facts, and though it looked bad for Charlie, I just couldn't believe that he'd leave someone like that, even if he thought he was dead, without having a good reason, like the fact he was scared himself.

"But he drugged you, and Dean and this other girl Dawn, and was keeping you all prisoners in his home," Officer Dutton said. "Obviously he isn't a good guy."

"He's mentally ill," I felt compelled to point out. "He thought I was his daughter, and he thought Dawn was in danger..."

"Why?" Officer Milton asked, interrupting me.

I was reluctant to answer him and sent an apologetic look to Dean. I shouldn't have said anything about Charlie thinking Dawn was in danger. But, at this point, not saying anything would probably make it worse. "Well, he thought Dean had something to do with Lindsay's disappearance."

Both officers looked at Dean, but it was Dutton who asked the question. "Were you involved with that?"

"No, of course not," Dean said, looking frustrated that he was again defending himself over this issue. "I was cleared by the police in Boston, you can call and ask them about it if you want."

"So why do you think Charlie locked you in that room?" Dutton asked.

"I'm not sure. I went to his place to talk to him about Dawn..."

Officer Milton cut him off. "What about her?"

196

"I was trying to discover where she was so I could confirm if she was okay." He ran a hand through his hair showing his anxiety over the whole thing.

"So you thought she might be in danger?" Milton asked.

"No, I didn't think that. We parted with a misunderstanding, and I was concerned about her."

"What kind of misunderstanding," Milton persisted.

"If you must know, she was hoping to have a relationship with me, and I turned her down."

"Why did you go to Charlie's house looking for her?"

"I went there because that's where she was headed when she left my apartment. She was bringing Lindsay's things to him. But aside from that, I wasn't sure what she had told Charlie, and I came to talk to him."

"What do you mean?" Dutton asked him.

Dean bristled defensively. "I mean that she was saying stuff that wasn't true. And she knew things that she shouldn't know…"

"She was spying on you," I told him.

Dean cast me a confused look. "What?"

"She told me that she watched you, followed you around, and listened to stuff you talked about at work. That's how she knew things about you. That and she also had made friends with Lindsay."

"She what? She told you that?" Dean shook his head, not understanding. "But she never said anything about knowing Lindsay personally, and Lindsay wouldn't have kept that from me, she just wouldn't."

"She used a different name with Lindsay."

"What name?"

"She didn't tell me. She just said that she was hoping to break you two up because she thought you were meant to be together. She was just pretending to be a psychic."

"She was pretending? Then she really didn't have a special gift." His tone matched his expression, and both said he knew as much. "Did she make him think she was a psychic and fill him with a load of crap?"

Remembering Charlie's dismissal of that 'mumbo jumbo stuff,' I felt pretty sure that if she had mentioned it to him, his reaction would have silenced her in that regard. "If she did, I can say with confidence that Charlie wouldn't have been impressed."

"Well, even if she didn't tell him, I did," Dean said. "I told him a lot about her so-called psychic claims. I told him she was accusing me of kidnapping Lindsay and hurting her, using her 'visions' (he sarcastically air quoted that) as proof that I was involved."

For some reason, Dean looked uneasy about the fact he'd shared that information with Charlie, and it made me curious. "Why does it concern you that you told him that?"

"Because that might be why Charlie took Dawn away. He said Dawn knew, just like he did, that Lindsay was fine, and he also felt certain that it was me who took her. Of course, I now realize that he believed Lindsay was okay because he thought you were Lindsay." Concern was etched in the deep frown lines that appeared on his forehead. "Did she tell Charlie she thought Lindsay was dead or did she just tell him she thought I was involved with her disappearance?"

"I know she thought you were involved with her disappearance, but I also think she was worried that something bad might have happened to her." At least, that's what I remember her saying, though I wasn't totally sure it mattered. Or did it? Maybe Charlie wanted to gloat about how

198

wrong her mumbo jumbo stuff was, or maybe he wanted to ask her what to do about Dean now that they knew (to his mind anyway) that Dean hadn't killed her. Who could know what was going on in that mixed-up mind of his.

"I just remember him being really upset while I was talking, and then the effects of the drug he gave me kicked in and my mind became really muddled."

"When he came back down in the basement, probably after drugging you, Dean, he went straight to Dawn's room." What if she had tried to tell him that I wasn't Lindsay? It might have triggered him to do something crazy. But I still didn't know why they went to the Wheeler place or how they got separated. It made me really worried about Dawn's safety, especially considering that wound she had on her head. She never explained how it got there. And now she was hiding again. What if Charlie found her first?

Officer Dutton got a phone call and excused himself while he took it, and Officer Milton went with him, leaving the rest of us to talk among ourselves.

"Do you think Dawn is in danger from Charlie?" Mary asked.

"She didn't appear to be afraid of him," I said, thinking back to when we talked in the house before the men interrupted us. "She was too busy wanting to come clean with me, though I don't know why she was bothering."

"She connected with you down in that room," Tara said. "She wanted her secrets out because she didn't want there to be any between the two of you."

"But why did she run away? She knew I was on her side and that I hoped she'd stay here with us." It didn't make sense to me that Dawn had run, which she must have done because no one had seen her.

"I know you said she was in the house at one point and that she came down to tell you I'd been shot, but I never saw her," Dean said.

"She probably didn't want to face you, Dean." But why did she go to the Wheeler house with Charlie in the first place? She must have done, though when he'd left, he was alone. I voiced as much to the others.

Tara was the first to give her thoughts on it. "Maybe she didn't go there with him. That might be why Charlie showed up there, he could have been looking for Dawn and found Kade instead."

I nodded that it was possible. "I'd told her that Charlie had thrown my cell phone in the bushes next to the front stairs. Maybe she was hoping to find it to call for help." It would explain why Dawn never returned to the basement and why me and Dean were left detained. Unable to rescue us, she ran for help and Charlie took off after her.

"If that's the case, then she was hiding there when I arrived," Kade said. "Don't you think she would have come to me for help?"

I nodded in disagreement. "She could have gotten there after you arrived but didn't have time to find you before Charlie showed up, or she arrived after Charlie did. He drove over in the truck, and if she wasn't with him, then she would have had to run through the woods to get there."

"Okay," Kade said, his voice patient but wanting me to hear him out. "Let's say that was the scenario. She must have been aware that we had gone down to the barn because she was the one who showed you where I was. So why didn't she help me after Charlie took off?"

"Tess and Dean showed up as soon as Charlie left, so maybe she didn't have time to rescue you," Daniel said. He'd been quiet up to this point but was listening and processing and thinking. Everyone was, which was good because they saw things from a perspective that were not influenced by high emotions and stress, like those of us who were directly involved.

"I think that's likely what happened, Daniel." I couldn't explain it, but I felt very strongly about defending her. "We don't know where she was when Charlie took off, and Dean and I came out of hiding as soon as he sped away. If she saw me with Dean, it probably prompted her to stay in hiding."

"This, of course, is assuming that she didn't arrive with Charlie," Tara reminded us.

"I met Charlie almost as soon as he pulled into the driveway," Kade said. "I was in the house looking around when I heard him coming and went to see who it was. I didn't see anyone with him."

"Then she must have gotten there on foot, which means she probably had escaped from Charlie." It was the only plausible explanation I could come up with, though there was a niggling sense that we weren't completely right about our assumptions.

Kade spread his hands. "It seems rather suspicious that she knew where I was."

"That's a good point," Dean said. "How did she know where you were?" His distrust of Dawn was quite evident, but then it would be, they did not have a good history.

"I'm still trying to puzzle that out," I admitted. "I mean, she did have an injury, there was blood on her face, so something must have prevented her from helping Kade before we got there." Maybe whoever pushed Kade had done something to her as well. But then … who pushed Kade and who hurt Dawn?

"Okay, if we go with that, it still doesn't explain why she didn't come with us," Kade said.

"I don't think she was ready to face Dean. She was very ashamed of what she'd done to him and Lindsay." If only I could find her and talk to her. There were so many questions to ask and, more importantly, I wanted to help her.

The officers came back into the room, and we all looked at them expectantly, knowing that they were likely to have news.

"They couldn't find Charlie or Dawn," Officer Dutton told us. "They searched both properties."

"Did you look in the rooms in the basement?" Charlie not being found didn't surprise me, but I was hoping that Dawn would have revealed herself when the police showed up.

"Yes, they were empty," Officer Milton said. "They even went down into the rooms under the barn floor that Mr. Sinclair fell into. There's no sign of either of them."

"Was Charlie's truck gone?" Kade asked.

"There were no vehicles at his house when they got there," Milton said.

"What about my truck?" Dean asked. "Have you found that?".

"No, we've not found any vehicles," Dutton told him.

"Are you going to continue to look for Charlie and Dawn?" I couldn't imagine they would not, but I wanted the reassurance of his word.

"We will continue looking for Charles Templeson. As for Dawn Conway, we are still working to determine if she is a person of interest," Milton said.

Templeson and Conway. So those were their surnames. Charlie's last name held the word 'Temple' in it, which was a sacred space, and 'son' traditionally indicated descent—marking someone as the son of the original namesake. I was curious as to how his family came to identify with that surname. As for Dawn's surname, it contained the words 'con' and 'way' and both fit her well. She made her way in life doing cons. "We need to know that Dawn is okay." I looked at the two officers to ascertain if they even cared. "Charlie might be looking for her too."

"We are actively looking for him, Mrs. Sinclair," Dutton assured me. "If we find him, we'll question him about Dawn. If she's found, we'll let you know." Dutton closed his clipboard and made it evident that they were wrapping things up.

"Did they find Tess's cell phone?" Kade asked.

"Or mine?" Dean added.

Milton shook his head. "No, we have not found any cell phones." Seeing I was about to speak, he rushed on. "We looked around the steps of the Wheelers' house, Mrs. Sinclair, but did not find it."

"I'll need your phone numbers," Officer Dutton told us. "We'll put a trace on all your phones."

After the police officers left, the medics began readying us for transport to the hospital, but I was reluctant to ride in an ambulance with my baby and Tara offered to take us.

The medics weren't too happy about that plan and tried to talk us out of it. "But what about the baby?" One of the medics asked. "Do you have a car seat for her?"

"Yes, Daniel thought to grab it when he went to our house earlier to get my suitcase." They still didn't look convinced. "I'm fine. She's fine. There's no reason for us to take up space in your ambulance."

Kade and Dean, however, went with the paramedics. I think Kade agreed to do so for Dean's sake, not wanting him to go alone or feel isolated from our little group. We were all in this together, and I think Dean was grateful for all the support.

After the men left with the ambulance and the police soon after, the remaining paramedics, who insisted they follow us to the hospital, ensured that Autumn and I were settled safely in the back seat of Tara's car.

Mary insisted she ride with us—with Daniel following in their car—and soon we were on our way to the hospital. During the journey there, our discussion revolved around the day's unfolding events. And then Tara posed a question that cast a somber mood over our little group.

"Do you think it's safe for you while Charlie and Dawn are still at large?"

For a space of time, the question hung in the air, making us uncomfortable with the thoughts it evoked. And though it was a valid concern, I felt compelled to cast my new friend in a more favorable light. "I certainly don't think Dawn poses any threat. If it wasn't for her, I wouldn't have found Kade, nor would I have been able to get him out of that room below the barn floor. And she did seek to help Dean as well."

"But Charlie is a problem," Mary affirmed. "He has a gun, remember, and has already used it on Dean."

"That was an accident, but yes, he does warrant some caution on our part." Worrisome though it was, I couldn't let it control my life. I'd done enough worrying for one night and most of those concerns did not materialize. Thank God.

Tara briefly met my eyes in the rearview mirror. "Charlie thinks you are Lindsay, not Tess Sinclair. He won't know where to find you."

"But he knows that everyone was looking for a woman named Tess Sinclair, and decided it was my ... aka Lindsay's ... alias." Leaning my head against the headrest, I shut my eyes, wanting nothing more than to give in to my weariness. I was exhausted, sore and emotionally overwhelmed. But Tara was right. It probably wasn't safe for me until Charlie was found and it was something we needed to think about.

"You can stay with me," Tara said.

Mary twisted in her seat to look back at me. "Or me and Daniel."

I appreciated their offers, but it was something I needed to discuss with Kade. "We'll talk to Kade and see what he wants to do." I tried to stifle the yawn that followed that statement but then more followed. I was so tired I thought I could sleep for a week!

"Just relax and take a nap if you'd like, Tess. It's been a very long, tiring day," Tara said. "Enjoy the peace and quiet while you still can."

Nodding my thanks, I made myself more comfortable and tried to do as she suggested, but my mind was too busy to let me sleep. Images of Dawn, the blood on her face, the sadness in her eyes, haunted my thoughts, and I sent out a silent message to her. *"Come to me, Dawn. Let me help you."*

When we were able to do so, Kade and I would look for her. As for Charlie, well, we'd stay vigilant and hope the police found him soon. Until they had him in their custody, this wasn't over by a long shot, and I prayed fervently that whatever happened, Autumn remained safe. She was our top priority now.

Chapter 17

It was closing in three weeks since Autumn's birth and I was finally starting to venture from the safety of our home. Kade put up security cameras around our property and so far, the only thing that triggered them were animals. There was no word on Charlie or Dawn. It wasn't surprising that she hadn't surfaced—she had street smarts. But Charlie was an older man who'd spent most of his life in the same house, so how was he managing to stay under the radar? Where were they? Were they together?

Tara employed several location spells, and though they didn't pinpoint a precise spot, they consistently pointed to the Bucksport area. It was worrisome where Charlie was concerned because the possibility of him discovering my whereabouts remained a looming threat, making it a risk for me to even venture out on my own. Because of that, I didn't dare bring Autumn with me unless Kade was also present, and even then, we proceeded with the utmost caution. Going anywhere on my own was a hard-won concession when it came to Kade. He was very protective and rightly so, but I couldn't live in fear indefinitely. Much as I loved him, I sometimes needed my own space and time.

As for Dawn, I said a daily prayer that she would find her way back to me, and when I allowed myself to think about that time in Charlie's basement, I wished I'd made it clearer to her that she'd always have a place with us here in Bucksport. We—Kade, my friends and I—would gladly take her into our fold.

Although Dawn's behavior with Dean and Lindsay did concern me ... the stalking, pretending to be psychic and trying to split them up ... I had to take what I knew of her into consideration. She was young and alone, and such conditions would make anyone do things they wouldn't normally do, especially if they didn't have a supportive network of family and friends. I realized I was excusing her behavior, and though I understood why she'd acted as she did, I also knew it didn't make it okay. Still, I liked her and truly believed she was a good person at heart.

Charlie turning on her, locking her in that room, and whatever followed that caused her injury were sure to leave her mind and emotions in turmoil, making her both vulnerable and afraid. If only she'd trust us— we could help her work through it all. I just needed her to call me.

The police were still on the lookout for Charlie and his truck, neither of which had been seen. Dean's truck was discovered on an old woods' road not far from Charlie's house. His cell phone and ours were still missing. We ended up discontinuing service to them and acquired new numbers.

As for Dean, he stayed in touch, especially via video calls, because he loved seeing Autumn. He was committed to our budding friendship, and doubly so because our precious daughter held a special place in his heart. His being there to witness her birth, something he never got to do with his own child, was an experience he swore he'd never forget.

Through extensive discussions and careful analysis of everything we knew, the scope of Dawn's subterfuge concerning Dean and Lindsay came into sharper focus. The fact she knew both, without their being aware of it, gave her a considerable advantage, especially in maintaining her façade as a psychic. They had no reason to doubt her, and she exploited that, by using their trust in her, to break them up, and it was deeply unsettling. If not for Lindsay vanishing on that fateful day, her scheme might have succeeded. Given the fact her relentless efforts to dismantle their relationship were on the brink of accomplishment, we couldn't find any logic in her being involved in Lindsay's disappearance. What motive would such an act serve, and what outcome could she possibly anticipate, especially when it wasn't necessary? Lindsay's disappearance did nothing but throw a wrench into Dawn's carefully laid plans, for Dean's focus became fixed on finding his pregnant girlfriend, leaving nothing for Dawn to gain.

As for Lindsay, I was conflicted. Logic told me she was likely inhabiting the spirit world, and yet a niggling doubt persisted that it was possible she'd made herself invisible, blending into obscurity until she no longer willed it. I prayed it was the latter. Tara said my emotions were too involved to sense her spiritually, and that was why I couldn't say for sure if she was dead or alive. Perhaps that was indeed the case, for I'd certainly been guilty of it before. Three years ago, when I lost Mike and Tootsie, the tragic blow had completely derailed my spiritual connection. Although I thought I was overcoming that issue, it seemed that wasn't the case, and I hoped most fervently that I could someday master this particular problem.

In the meantime, we were constantly brainstorming the possibilities. If Lindsay was still alive, then where was she? Was it really that easy to hide in this world? Apparently so, considering how long it's been since Charlie was last seen. And, of course, there was no trace of Dawn either.

As for the Wheeler house, it went under contract about a week after everything went down. Janice informed the buyer, whom she still hadn't met, that it was part of an active investigation, as well as admitting her concerns about it being haunted, and it made no difference, they still wanted the property. And so, following the advice of her realtor, who was also a close friend, Janice agreed to sell it.

It didn't seem to matter that it might be necessary for people to enter the premises if the investigation required it, the buyer agreed to the terms, and the closing date was set to happen in just over a week. A quick sale if ever there was one, but then it was a cash buy. As they did not intend to move in until the weather was better, they granted us free access to the house and grounds, even allowing Janice to keep a key until they took physical possession of the property.

It was such an odd thing, their willingness to allow strangers free range of their property, that we discussed it whenever we all got together. Why was this mysterious buyer so generous and understanding? If only more people were like that, the world would be a better place.

On this glorious day, still cold but sunny, it felt good to be out of the house. I needed to do some much-needed grocery shopping and though Kade offered to come along, I felt it best for him to stay at the house with Autumn. I needed to be out on my own again, to feel like life was getting back to normal, and besides, I wanted some time to myself.

When I reached the main road at the end of our long driveway, I paused there to look in the direction of the cemetery where Charlie had taken my car. What if he'd taken it there because he had an affinity for the place? If so, then it might be possible to connect with Charlie's energy and get a clue to his whereabouts. The idea swirled around in my head but before I could decide what to do, my cell phone rang.

It was Janice, and with a pounding heart, hoping she'd heard something new, I put my car in park and answered it. "Hello, Janice."

"Hi, Tess. Is this an okay time to talk?"

Since there was no urgency in her tone, and knowing how much she liked to talk, I wasn't sure how I wanted to answer that—though I felt bad for hesitating. Whatever she had to say, no matter how long it took her to say it, was bound to be important, or she wouldn't have called. "Yes of course. I am headed out to do some grocery shopping but haven't yet turned onto the main road. What's up?"

"I've been doing some digging and talking to people who knew Charlie, you know, to try and figure out where he might be hiding. Well, I found out that someone in the assisted living facility here in Bucksport knew him quite well, or she used to anyway, and I finally got a chance to talk to her today. She's been ill, the poor thing, and they've been restricting visitors. So anyways, she's doing better now, thank goodness, and she agreed to see me. Turns out I kind of knew her! She knew Charlie's wife Andrea too, which was helpful."

Andrea. It was the first time I'd heard her name.

"Esther, that's the woman I met with, used to live in that first house you pass going to my grandparents' house. I don't think anyone is living there now. But anyways, that's how I kind of knew her. I used to see her from time to time while waiting for my bus or getting off it in the afternoon. She befriended Andrea after she and Charlie got married, and Esther said Andrea thought of her like a second mother. I guess Andrea's mother died when she was young, just like she died when Lindsay was young. So tragic, don't you think?" She didn't wait for me to answer. "So anyways, she said that Charlie was 38 when he married Andrea, who was 22 at the time, so he was considerably older, which I knew, of course, but never paid much mind to." She stopped to ponder something, speaking mostly to herself. "I wonder how they met?" Another moment of silence, then she continued. "So anyways, she was 33 when she died, and Lindsay was 11. I didn't move in with my grandparents until I was 16 so I never got to meet Andrea, and I met Charlie only a couple times when he came over to fetch Lindsay. He wasn't a very sociable man, keeping mostly to himself." She paused long enough to draw in a breath. "Lindsay came over all the time to hang out with me, though she was several years younger, and after I started dating my husband, I never saw much of her during her last couple years of high school. So anyways, Esther said Andrea's death really affected Charlie, as it would anyone, obviously, but he took it especially hard. Esther said he just wasn't right after that. I asked her to explain, and she said it was like he didn't know what to do with himself after she died. According to Esther, Charlie doted on his wife, letting her run the show, if you know what I mean."

She paused again, but this time it was to give that last revelation a quick moment of appreciation. "I thought it was sweet, you know? He never argued with her, never complained, just did whatever she wanted him to do. You don't find men like that anymore." She let out an aggrieved sigh, which then became an exclamation of disgust. "Hard to believe he became the man he is now. How awful that people can spiral into madness like that. I mean, who would have ever guessed that he'd turn out like he has."

"We can't rightfully pass judgement on someone when we have not walked in their shoes and experienced what they experienced," I gently reminded her, and thus, reminded myself. "We don't know all that's happened to make Charlie the way he is, plus, it's a mental illness he is suffering from."

Janice was immediately contrite. "Oh my, yes, you're absolutely right." She paused again, probably to gather her thoughts, but was soon forging on. "So anyways, Esther tried to stay close to them, mostly because she felt so sorry for Lindsay, but Charlie's strange personality change disturbed her. Losing his wife made him afraid of losing Lindsay, too, and Esther said he just smothered that poor girl, to the point that she left home the day after she graduated from high school. She took off with a friend who had family in Boston, and she stayed with them until she was able to get a place of her own. That's how she ended up there. So anyways, Charlie became even more unhinged—Esther's words not mine—after Lindsay left, acting strange and talking like he wasn't aware of time in relation to things that had happened in his life. She didn't think it was dementia or Alzheimer's though. Esther said he became so emotionally unstable that it frightened her, and she stopped visiting him completely. In fact, she hadn't seen him since shortly after Lindsay moved away. She feels bad about it because I guess she promised Andrea she'd keep an eye on him for her, and she feels guilty that she hasn't kept her promise."

As if realizing she was rambling, something Janice was known for, much to my amusement, she made a dismissive noise and continued. "So anyways, when I told her about what he did to you and Dawn and Dean, she wasn't surprised at all."

I found this all interesting but was wondering about the point of it, and hoped she'd get to it soon.

"So anyways, why I called is that someone in Andrea's family owned a house in Orland, on the river, and it passed on to Andrea when they died, which was many years ago, of course, way before Andrea died. She and Charlie used to go there for little getaways, though they didn't go far, did they?" Janice laughed. "I mean, the Orland town line is just a few miles from their house, and they only had to travel about twenty minutes to get there."

"Do you think that's where Charlie might be hiding out?" But why hadn't the police checked that out already?

"Well, it could be, don't you think? The house actually belongs to Lindsay, but with her missing, it's just sitting there not really belonging to anyone. Well, other than Charlie, I suppose, what with him being next of kin."

"I wonder why the police haven't checked that out?"

"I'm not sure they know about it. I mean, the house belongs to Lindsay, not him."

"Do you have an address for this house?" I pulled my digital notepad out of my purse and waited to write it down.

"You aren't thinking about going there, are you? Let the police go…"

"Not yet on the police. We need to give it a quick check first. Covertly, of course."

"But why? He has a gun, and he's already used it once!"

"It accidentally went off when he and Dean struggled," I corrected, pointing that out as much for her benefit as mine. "But I'd be very careful. I'm not thinking to confront him, just maybe check things out."

What I really wanted to know was if Dawn was with him. If she was, the police might scare her off and I'd never find her. Going over there probably wasn't the smartest idea, but I didn't really believe Charlie was seriously dangerous. Unstable, yes. Delusional, yes. But dangerous to the point of murder, no. Given he was hiding, though, it was hard to say what was going on in his mind. He needed help and I prayed he'd get it. But until then, Dawn was my priority. "Can you give me the address?"

"Okay, but if you go over there, please take Kade with you."

After jotting down the address, I thanked her for the information and promised I'd let her know if anything came of it. Then, as soon as I disconnected from the call, I sat for a moment and contemplated my next move. Out of curiosity, I punched the address into my navigational app and knew exactly where it was. I thought about it a little more then came to a quick decision and pulled onto the road. But I didn't turn towards town, I turned in the direction of Orland.

No matter how much I pleaded or reasoned with him, Kade would absolutely refuse to let me go anywhere near Charlie, even with him in tow, and though I knew I shouldn't be doing this without talking to him first, I couldn't risk him keeping me from checking it out. He just didn't understand how I could dismiss Charlie's actions as something he'd done out of love and desperation, and I didn't know how to make him see beyond the fact that Charlie had held me captive.

The difference now was that I was going into this knowing far more than I knew the last time I went near Charlie. Besides, I had no intention of going to the house or even setting foot on the property. What I would do, though, was call Robin so at least someone knew what I was up to. She wouldn't like it, but I knew I could trust her not to tell Kade.

As expected, she didn't like the plan.

"If anything happens to you again, Kade will never forgive me," Robin said. "And I will never forgive myself."

"Nothing is going to happen because I know more now than I did when I went to Charlie's house that day. Besides, I am not going to go to the house, I'm just going to check things out from a distance."

"Not that I don't trust you or anything, but you did promise Kade you wouldn't go off on your own that day and yet you ended up in Charlie's house."

I couldn't blame her for bringing that up, but it wasn't a true statement, not exactly. "I did not promise him I wouldn't go wandering off. I promised him I wouldn't enter the Wheeler house, and I didn't."

"Come on, Tess, you are nitpicking the word choices. You know very well that he wouldn't have wanted you going off to the neighbor's house either."

Trying not to be frustrated, especially as I was getting close to the Orland River and the turn I needed to make, I hoped my next promise would appease her. "I will not step foot on the property, and I will stay well hidden from view. I promise." Since she had gone silent, which meant she was close to accepting my plan, I offered some more reassurance. "Trust me, I no more want to get into another situation like before than you want me to. When I went to the Wheeler place that day, I had no idea about what was going on next door. I walked into that totally blind. I am not walking into anything blind this time. I know what Charlie is capable of and I have no intention of seeing him or talking to him or getting anywhere near him. I promise you."

More silence and then she sighed in resignation. "Okay, but you better promise me that even if you see Dawn, you won't talk to her until the police have dealt with Charlie."

That was going to be a hard promise to keep. The moment I saw her, if I saw her, I'd want to talk to her, but Robin had a good point, Charlie needed to be taken care of first. "If she's alone and nowhere near Charlie, I will probably try to talk to her, I won't lie about that. But if there's any chance that Charlie is nearby and could possibly see us, then I will not approach her." It was the best I could do in the way of promises on the matter.

216

"You'll do what you feel you must, regardless of what you promise…"

"No, that's not true. I don't break promises, which is why I am explaining exactly what I will do."

"I didn't mean that I didn't trust your word, Tess. I just know that sometimes situations warrant the changing of promises."

"I will not put myself in danger again. Not knowingly anyway. But, just to help you feel better about it—when I get there, I'll let you know exactly where I am, and then I want you to wait a half hour and call the police, give them the address and tell them that Charlie might be there. That should give me enough time to case out the situation and see if Dawn is with him."

She liked that idea. "Okay, Tess. A half hour and then I'm calling the police."

"Please don't tell them that you think I'll be over there though." It would probably be best if I was gone by the time the police arrived, though I would tell Kade what I'd done.

"I will give you a call before calling them. If you don't answer the phone, though, I'm calling them asap."

"Okay. That works."

Five minutes later, I came to the road where Lindsay's camp was located. It was unpaved, with trees on one side and the river running parallel on the other. Janice said I'd come to it about a hundred yards in.

Now that I knew where the road was located, I turned around and went back a short distance to where I saw what looked like an old woods' road. I pulled into it and found a small clearing where I could park my car and have it hidden from the main road.

This is where I had to be stealthy and careful. If Charlie was nearby, I didn't want him to see me. My advantage was that I knew where he might be, and he had no clue as to my whereabouts.

Staying within the cover of the trees, I followed along the main road until I was across from the dirt road leading to Lindsay's camp.

After ensuring the coast was clear, I ran across the road and entered the trees on the other side, making my way through the thick growing pines and shrubs until the house I sought came into view. Feeling well concealed, I knelt low and waited it out. Hopefully one or the other, preferably Dawn, would put in an appearance.

From where I stood the camp looked empty and Charlie's truck was nowhere in sight. The surrounding yard was being overtaken by spindly alder trees, a growing cluster of raspberries, several wild rose bushes and a huge patch of rhubarb. The house itself sat far closer to the river than was legal these days. It wasn't very big, maybe 900 square feet at most, and rectangular in shape. The roof was sagging, its shingles covered in moss, but the chimney, which was positioned at one end of the camp, looked solid. Chipped green paint covered the clapboard siding, which was severely weatherworn and in need of replacing. Time and neglect had taken its toll on what was probably a cozy little getaway at one time.

Although the camp looked unoccupied, I knew it wasn't and that made me take stock of my hiding place. The pine trees around me, and the tall dead cattail reeds rising from the ditch along the road in front of me, made me feel confident that I was hidden from any eyes that might be looking in this direction, though there were no windows on this side of the camp. If Charlie was in there, there was no way he would be able to see me from inside, even if I was standing out in full view.

Despite my confidence that I was well hidden, a sense of unease crept over me, giving me the jitters and making me glance around. I saw nothing to account for it and yet the fine hairs on the nape of my neck bristled with tension.

Then a noise to my left made me turn my head and I saw a skunk skulking along the edge of the road and heading in my direction! It also revealed the one angle from which I could be seen. The little fella spotted me and went still. I was so worried about being seen from the house that I didn't consider my vulnerability if someone were to approach from my right or left.

Not sure what the skunk's next move would be and not wanting to take any chances that he'd get any closer, I moved deeper into the brush and out of his view. He sniffed the air then turned around and headed back down the road, and that is when I saw that someone was approaching.

It was none other than Charlie.

Thank God for that skunk! If it weren't for him, Charlie would have easily seen me. Not only that, but thanks to the skunk going back in his direction, Charlie was now scurrying towards the camp, taking a path that took him further away from my location. As soon as he went around to the other side of the house and out of my sight, I let out a quick breath and gave thanks, yet again, for the skunk's timely arrival.

Knowing that spirit must have orchestrated that to help me out, I expressed my gratitude then wondered what I should do. Obviously, I wasn't going to confront him, and besides, Robin would be calling the police in about … I glanced at my watch … ten minutes. I couldn't be here when they got here. As it was, when I told Kade what I'd done, I was going to have to deal with his disappointment, and I hated upsetting him. Not that he didn't have good reason to be upset because he did.

"Tess, you shouldn't be here."

I about had a heart attack right there on the spot and swung around the second I heard her voice. "Dawn!"

"What if I'd been Charlie?" She gave me a disapproving frown. "He's not in a good place right now."

"I came to see if you were here."

Dawn's dark blue eyes looked tragic, and I wondered what Charlie had been saying to her. Somehow, I needed to get her to trust me. "Why are you with him?"

"We are the same, he and I."

"What do you mean by that?"

She looked away and while she was thinking about how to reply to me, I noticed she was wearing the same clothes she was in the last time I saw her, though they didn't look dirty, which meant she had access to laundry facilities. It did worry me, though, that the black leather jacket she was wearing wasn't enough to keep her warm in this frigid weather.

"Please come back with me." But I had a very strong sense that she was not going to do that.

Her eyes met mine and after a few short seconds, her mouth twisted into a faint, sad smile. "I can't." She looked over towards the camp. "What will happen to him?"

"When the police come?" When she nodded, I gave a small shrug. "I don't know. His crime isn't too horrific. I mean, he held us captive, but he didn't really hurt us, though giving us drugs without our knowledge isn't a good thing either."

"He shot Dean."

"But Dean has already given his statement that it was an accident."

"But Charlie left him there to die."

220

"He wouldn't have died…"

Dawn let out a frustrated noise, her patience with our discussion wearing thin. "Charlie thought he was dead already."

"Please come back with me." I watched the play of emotions cross her expressive face and wondered what more I could say to convince her. She wanted to, I could tell. "Dawn, you aren't in any trouble…"

"I'm the one who pushed your husband." She said it in a rush, her mouth quivering, her eyes bright with unshed tears. "I thought I was protecting him, getting him out of Charlie's clutches. I was going to come back and get you and Dean out of the house and tell you where to find him, but then suddenly you were there."

I wasn't happy with her confession, but I was determined not to show it. "Well, I can understand you were under duress, and you did what you felt was right at the time…"

Dawn's expression darkened with anger. "Don't make excuses for me!"

Worried that we were getting too loud, which could attract Charlie's attention, I lowered my voice and hoped that this time I would say the right things. "I'm not making excuses. In the heat of a moment, especially when we think we are in danger, we make hasty unthought-out decisions, and you did what you felt you needed to do. He got a bad sprain, that's all. He isn't mad at you. I promise."

She looked at me for a long moment, as if she couldn't figure something out, and I was about to ask her what was bothering her when my phone began vibrating in my pocket. Robin.

"I have to answer this." Dawn nodded and took a couple steps back. Without taking my eyes off her, I answered my phone. "Hello?"

"Tess, thank God you are okay. Are you over there?"

"Yes, I am in the woods across the street from Lindsay's camp." After giving Dawn a reassuring wink, I looked over at the house, worried that all this talking would carry over to Charlie. "He's here, Robin."

"Oh my God, he's with you?"

"No, no, he's in the house."

"Are you sure? If he's in the house, how do you know?"

"He was walking outside, and a skunk came along and scared him back around to the side of the camp that faces the river. He must have gone inside because he hasn't reappeared."

Wanting to let Dawn know that I would not mention her, I glanced in her direction, and she was gone. Darn it! I wanted to go rushing through the woods after her, she couldn't be too far, but I couldn't risk moving from my hiding spot.

"I'm going to call the police and let them know Charlie is there," Robin said.

"Yes, do that, but give me about five minutes to get out of here and back to my car."

"Yes, go back to your car and go home."

"What do you think they will do with him?" Despite everything, I was worried about Charlie's fate.

Robin made a small sound that told me she didn't really care what they did to him. "Put him in the looney bin I suppose."

"Robin, I wish you wouldn't call it that. He has mental health issues. He isn't loony, he's sick."

She gave a little chuckle. "I knew you were going to protest that the moment I said it. But okay, I think they will send him to someplace where they can determine his mental state."

222

While keeping her on the phone, I cautiously retreated, my eyes in constant scanning mode as I headed for the road. Though I was hoping to see Dawn, it was a futile wish. Despite our ordeal together, she didn't trust me. "I'm almost back on the main road. My car is close by. You can call the police now."

"It's fine, I'll wait until you are actually in your car."

I stepped out of the trees, while still looking for signs of Dawn behind me, and when I turned back to the road, I came to an abrupt, alarmed halt.

Charlie stood at the beginning of the dirt road, looking about as surprised as me and perhaps even a bit ... relieved?

My eyes went straight to his hands. No gun. I could outrun him, but I hoped it wouldn't come to that. Staying poised for action, I spoke in a low controlled tone, alerting Robin to the fact that something was happening. "Rob, call them now. Charlie is here."

He made no move toward me. In fact, he seemed more interested in what I would do, which was to take a couple steps back. As he didn't seem to care, I took a couple more.

Charlie spread his hands as if to tell me he meant no harm, even so I was ready to make a sprint for it if I had to.

"Oh my God, Tess. Stay on the phone, I'm going to call them from my house phone right now." Robin's voice sounded loud in my ears, startling me. I forgot for a few seconds that she was still on the phone, or that I was even holding it to my ear.

Everything else in my world had gone totally quiet. Even the trees were hushed.

"It was only a matter of time before you showed up here," Charlie said, his tone conversational. "I'm a little surprised it took you so long though."

Was Dawn still nearby? Would she help me if it came to that? Surely, she had to know that we were now facing each other.

Then a concerning thought sent a shiver of panic racing through me, making my blood drain from my face. Had she been acting as a decoy in order to allow Charlie time to get past me and out here onto the road? She had to have seen him for she was facing that direction while talking to me. And now that I was thinking about it, it did seem weird that Dawn just happened to be walking in the woods while Charlie was walking on the road. Maybe they'd been waiting, expecting that I'd show up, as Charlie just intimated.

"I'm not going to chase you, Lindsay. You've made it quite clear that you don't want to be with me." Charlie dropped his arms to his side, looking dejected and forlorn. "I was only trying to protect you. It was never my intention to hurt you or anyone."

"Then why are you hiding here?"

"I killed Dean." His eyes shimmered with tears, and he looked away, sniffing and swiping at his eyes with the sleeve of his checkered jacket. "It was an accident."

"He's not dead. You hit him in the shoulder."

Charlie swung his head back around to look at me. "But … I saw blood on his face. I … I thought I hit him in the head."

"He hit his head on the windowsill when he fell."

Charlie squeezed his eyes shut in relief, then reopened them to lock onto mine, his expression marked with worry. "What about Dawn?"

"What about her?"

"Are you going to look for her too?"

"Maybe." Dawn was fully capable of taking care of herself, but I was not giving up on the hope that she would come to me one day.

Charlie frowned and looked down to the ground. "The poor thing. All she's ever wanted was for someone to love her."

She wanted Dean to love her, though I believed she'd moved past that obsession. Granted, she hadn't done a good thing by stalking him and Lindsay and doing her best to break them up, but she was genuinely contrite for having done that. People learned from their mistakes, and I believed Dawn had definitely learned a lesson in all this.

As I was not sure how long it would take for the police to arrive and I didn't want Charlie going anywhere, I kept him engaged in idle conversation, about the weather, the rising cost of food, the crazy gadgets we'd all come to rely on, anything to fill in the time. I tried a couple times to get information out of him concerning Dawn, but he clammed right up, and I let it go.

Finally, in the distance we heard sirens, and they were getting louder by the second. Charlie turned his head towards the sound then looked at me. "I'm done running. I'm done hiding. Besides, she won't leave me alone until I do the right thing."

I figured he was talking about Dawn and nodded that he was probably right. Maybe she'd been staying with him in the hopes of getting him to turn himself in. He needed professional help.

Two police cars came into view, slowing down when they saw us. Behind them were other vehicles. One of them was Kade's car. My heart sank a bit when I saw it. He was going to be pissed, and I couldn't blame him one bit.

Charlie turned to them and raised his hands. "Time to face the music I guess."

As Kade rushed to my side and pulled me close in a hug, I accepted his loving embrace with a fervent prayer that this whole thing was truly over. I wanted to focus on him and our daughter and enjoy being a family. And I wanted to do it without so much drama hanging over our heads.

Chapter 18

It was three days before I was given approval to see Charlie. He was being held in a mental health facility in Bangor and they had to determine if he was safe to see visitors, especially me, before allowing it. He still thought I was Lindsay, and his case workers were hoping that I could help him see me as me and not as his daughter.

I was more than happy to help, but I also wanted to talk to him about Dawn. Since Charlie's capture, I'd dreamed about her every night, and in each dream, she seemed to need help. I knew my concern for her could be influencing those dreams, but what if she truly needed me?

Kade came with me, but I told him I needed to speak to Charlie alone. He didn't know Kade, and I was worried he wouldn't talk freely if he was in the room with us. Despite his protectiveness, he reluctantly agreed, though he made it clear he was allowing it only because someone would be stationed nearby and prepared to intervene if necessary. With further assurance of a live camera feed, which he would be watching from a room across the hall, he didn't argue against my wishes. Besides, Charlie's medical team believed he wouldn't pose any problems.

And so it was that I found myself moments away from facing my captor once again. I stared at the door, knowing he was waiting on the other side, and strove for inner calm, though my heart was pounding hard, its racket loud in my ears.

Okay, Tess, you can do this. Just breeze on in there and treat this like a normal meeting, one in which you will do your best to conduct in a civil manner. He has information you need, and you cannot mess this up. Dawn's life may depend on it.

My pep talk over, I grasped the doorknob, turned it with confidence and entered the room.

Seated at a table and facing the door, Charlie was attired in a set of green scrubs. His hair was neatly trimmed, his face cleanly shaven, and a welcoming smile was plastered on his mouth. The sight he presented looked like that of a kind and innocent grandfather. If not for the trials I had endured by his actions, it would be difficult to imagine him capable of holding people captive in his home.

"Lindsay! I have been waiting for you to come see me."

I settled in the chair opposite him and extended my hands, which Charlie accepted without hesitation, gently wrapping his fingers around mine.

The police officer stationed behind Charlie was instantly on guard, his posture tense as he took a step forward. When it became apparent that Charlie posed no threat, he relaxed his stance and stepped back.

"Charlie, I need you to really look at me and listen to what I am going to say." It was hard holding his hands like we were friends, but it helped me make a better connection with him.

Charlie's pale brown eyes widened at my use of his name, but he nodded that he'd listen.

"I am not Lindsay."

"Sure ..."

228

"No, Charlie, I am not. My name is Tess Sinclair. I moved to Bucksport a couple of years ago, about a year before your daughter disappeared."

Charlie's wrinkled face, which looked more aged than when I first met him, turned into a mien of confusion. "I don't understand…"

"You miss her very much, Charlie, I understand that. You want Lindsay back so badly that you somehow saw her instead of me when I showed up at your house."

"But … but you didn't deny it. Why didn't you correct me?"

"I was scared, Charlie. I didn't know who you were or what you were capable of. I was in labor and not in a position to run away."

Charlie shook his head in disbelief, not yet ready to accept what I was telling him. He did, however, stare at me, his eyes scrutinizing my face, and I watched as dawning realization began to unfold in his expression. Finally, he was beginning to see the truth.

After what felt like the longest minute of my life, he pulled his hands from mine and dropped his head into them, his gnarled fingers grasping at his short, thinning gray hair. "No, no. My poor Lindsay."

"Charlie, we want to help you. Please look at me."

He let his hands drop to the table and looked up. The smiling, kind old man of moments ago looked haggard and defeated. "So where is my Lindsay?"

"I don't know, Charlie, but we are going to try to find her."

"How are you going to find her when no one else has?"

"I have special gifts that might help, and I have friends with special gifts. Sometimes it takes a different approach to what's been tried." I felt strongly that Dawn was somehow connected to Lindsay's disappearance, but how and in what way, I didn't know … yet. My dreams suggested that

I look into it, and I intended to do just that. "Charlie, I need you to tell me what happened with Dawn when you swapped her out with Dean. Do you remember that day?"

He gave me an annoyed glance before looking off into his memories. "It wasn't that long ago, of course I remember."

"So, what happened?" I was hoping to get some clue as to why Dawn was still on the run. If I could understand why she was still running, I might be able to figure out a way to help her stop.

"Dean told me that she was accusing him of killing you ... I mean Lindsay. He said she was using her special powers. I guess she thinks she's some sort of a magician or something."

"He told you she claimed to be a psychic." I had to really focus on not showing my amusement. A psychic and a magician were two completely different kinds of people.

"Yeah, one of those people. He said she was threatening to tell people that he killed you ... I mean Lindsay ... and Dean swore he didn't hurt her or take her. And I didn't believe it, that she was saying those things. Besides, I had you ... I mean, I thought I had Lindsay down in my basement."

"So, Dawn didn't tell you she was a psychic?"

Charlie shook his head, adamant that she had not. "No. She told me she had feelings about things. Vibes I think she said. But she didn't say she had special powers." He looked away and scowled, and I had to explore the reason for the scowl.

"What are you thinking about?"

"Dean said Dawn worked with him, but she never told me that."

"Did that make you angry with her?"

230

He shifted in his seat, looking uncomfortable. "I wanted to ask her about it, but I wasn't mad."

"Can you tell me a little more about the day Lindsay disappeared?"

Charlie took some time to think, casting his mind into the past. "After she left to get us some lunch, Dean showed up and we had words." Charlie gave me a look and I knew he meant they had had an argument, a bad one. "When he left, he said he was going to go get Lindsay and we were going to settle all the misunderstandings. But he says he never saw her and figured he missed her and decided to just go back to work. But I don't know..." Charlie shook his head. "Why didn't he come back to the apartment to see if Lindsay made it okay? And he gave her that black eye..."

"Did he explain how that happened?"

"Yeah, yeah, he said there was a fight with some kids, and they pushed her when he swung a punch at them. Lindsay said that, too, but I knew it was just a story they came up with to cover for his abuse."

"If he was abusing her, Charlie, there would have been more than one incident of it. People like that don't just have one incident of physical abuse, they have many, especially after they've been together awhile and can no longer hold off on giving in to their abusive behavior. Had she ever said anything about Dean hurting her before?"

"No, but then she didn't tell me much of anything."

"Did you know that Dawn wanted a relationship with Dean and so she wanted Lindsay and him to break up?" I was uncomfortable telling him that, for it felt like I was betraying Dawn's trust, but then again, something like that didn't deserve to fall under the guise of a secret. Besides, I was trying to make an important point. "If she believed he was the kind of man who might hurt her, do you really think Dawn would have wanted him for a boyfriend?" I didn't want to paint a bad picture of Dawn, but he needed to know the actual relationship dynamics going on between the three of them.

"I didn't know that and I'm not sure I believe it. Dawn told me she and Lindsay were friends. She said she was trying to convince Lindsay to leave Dean because of his abuse, but Lindsay was afraid of him … afraid to leave him."

"I'm not sure why she told you that, Charlie, about Dean being abusive, because it isn't true, and I honestly don't believe Lindsay was afraid of him. Dawn told me that she liked Dean and felt they should be together, and she befriended Lindsay in order to find a way to break them up." I could tell by his expression that Charlie wasn't buying anything I was saying. Whatever Dawn told him, she'd done a convincing job of it. I couldn't really blame him for being skeptical of anything I said. Why would he believe me over her? They had developed a rapport, and he didn't know me at all.

"Dean told me that too … about Dawn being interested in him." Charlie scowled for he clearly didn't believe it. "He told me that when he turned her down, she started accusing him of killing Lindsay." He looked at me with the saddest set of eyes. "Do you think Lindsay's dead?"

"I don't know what to think, Charlie. No one wants to believe that of someone who is missing. We always hang on to hope until we know for certain." The chances of her still being alive were slim, but slim was better than a zero chance and it was enough to cling to.

"After talking to Dean, I needed to talk to Dawn, let her know what he was saying about her and figure out what to do. So, I put something in his drink and when he passed out, I went down and got Dawn."

"You 'got' her?"

"Well, I went in to talk to her and she told me that I should give you something to help you sleep while she and I took care of Dean." He gave a smile, as if impressed with her suggestion. "She gave me the apple juice because I remembered your…Lindsay's mother liking apple juice when she was pregnant. So anyways, after you fell asleep, we went upstairs. The drug didn't knock Dean out completely, but it made him groggy enough that he didn't give us any trouble when we helped him downstairs and put him in Dawn's room." His expression became defensive, as if expecting an argument from me. "We only put him there so we could figure things out. Dawn didn't need to be in there anymore anyway. I mean, not with us knowing where Dean was and having him under our control."

"So, Dawn helped you take him downstairs?" That bit of information bothered me. "And you decided not to hold her captive but felt I should remain so?"

Charlie frowned with confusion. "Captive? I wasn't holding either of you captive. I mean, I was keeping you there for your own good, until we knew you were safe, but you weren't my captive, Lin... er, um Tess. I kept your door locked more to keep him out than to keep you in."

"Dawn said you had her locked down there for almost a week."

Charlie shook his head. "I think you misunderstood her. She stayed down there, because we never knew when Dean would show up."

Charlie's warped sense of reality was skewering what had actually gone on. To his mind, he wasn't keeping her there against her will, he was just keeping her out of Dean's reach. Me too. It's what made it so hard to be angry with him, or to seek legal justice. He needed psychiatric help, not a jail cell.

"That night you all got away … you misunderstood what I was trying to do, which was protect you. Dawn too, but she knew that and was okay with it until … well obviously, you convinced her that I wasn't to be trusted."

So, something did happen between them. "Tell me what happened that night."

"I was on my way down to give you your tablet thing you left in the bedroom upstairs, when I saw Dean's car on the camera feed. So I ran down to let you guys know, but you were in the bathroom. I put your tablet on the bed then went to tell Dawn that we had company." His eyes begged me to understand. "I knew he'd be back and that is exactly what happened."

"But we were in a locked, secret area of the basement, why lock our doors?"

"You weren't being very cooperative, Lin … Tess, and I couldn't risk you going out and banging on the door and alerting Dean as to where you were!" He shook his head as if he couldn't understand why I didn't understand. "It's the only reason I locked your door."

"But you locked the door when I was upstairs in the bedroom—when Dean was nowhere near us."

"Because I thought you might try to run out into the night and the freezing cold in your condition. I told you, I didn't want you to get hurt, and I wanted you and the baby to be safe."

I felt a strong urge to recall the discussion I had with Dawn, about what she'd said concerning her confinement in the basement, but now wasn't the time to do it. I was only given a short amount of time to talk with Charlie and I needed to use every second of it wisely. "Why didn't you let me out when you put Dean in that room? I mean, didn't you think that you were possibly putting me in danger by keeping me down there with him?"

"No, the bathroom door was locked so he couldn't get to you. We felt you were safe until we got things worked out."

"What things?"

"What to do with Dean of course." He scrubbed a hand about his head, his frustration with our conversation agitating him. "Dawn wanted to call the police, but since you didn't want my protection, I was worried that you would leave me again." He gave me a pointed look, his disappointment with me evident. "I just got you back, Lin... I mean, I thought I'd just got Lindsay back, and I didn't want to lose her again." He looked away, scowling. "Anyway, I wasn't sure what you'd do."

"So, what did you think you might have to do, Charlie?" Could he ever be made to see how many wrong decisions he had made and how illogical it was to do the things he'd done?

"I didn't know what to do," he said, looking at me with exasperation. "I told you. We were trying to figure it out."

"Okay, let's move on. Why did you go to the Wheeler house?" Somewhere along the line, he and Dawn parted ways, at least they did that night, and maybe if I knew why, I would understand Dawn's determination to remain in hiding.

"Well first we took Dean's truck out onto an old wood's road."

"Why?"

"Because we were thinking about saying that Dean had sneaked over to my place in order to do me harm. Since he couldn't do that in his truck, he parked it in the woods nearby and walked over." He heaved a sigh. "We were still working out the details."

"So, after taking his truck elsewhere, you then headed to the Wheeler farm?"

"Yes, to get your cell phone. Dawn said it was stupid of me to put it there in the first place. She was quite upset about it. She said it would encourage people to continue looking around there for you."

Telling him that must have been a ploy on her part, so he'd agree to get the phone, which she could then use. I was still confused as to why they felt it necessary to do what they did to Kade. "Did you guys really think it was necessary to push Kade down into that room under the barn floor?" I was still upset they'd done that to him. He could have gotten seriously hurt.

"When we got there, his car was in the driveway and Dawn said it must be that man that was looking for you earlier." He shifted in his seat, looking uncomfortable. "I wanted to leave straight away, but she said whoever owned that SUV had to know we were there because he would have heard my truck. So, then I told her that I'd have to get rid of him somehow." Charlie looked at me, lifting his hands to show he meant no malice in that statement. "I think Dawn took it wrong. She said that I was right, and that he might be a problem because he was determined to find you. She said we needed to come up with a plan to detain him until we could work out what we were going to do with Dean." He paused at this point, and I think it was to gauge my reaction as to what he'd said so far.

I was careful to keep my expression neutral. "Okay, so then what happened?"

"We came up with the plan about pushing him into that room under the barn floor. Since no one knew about her, Dawn said he wouldn't be on the lookout for her. So, she told me to get him down there and she'd take care of it." He gave me a pointed look. "Now, I did warn her it was a wicked steep fall, and she said she'd throw some hay down to cushion his landing." Charlie gave a nod, as if what he'd just told me was proof

236

enough that they meant no harm to Kade. "She jumped out of the truck, and I drove on up to the house and he came out to greet me. Just as we suspected, he told me he was still looking for you. So, I mentioned I knew about a couple secret rooms in the house, and he asked me if I'd show them to him, which is what I wanted to do in order to give Dawn time to set things up down at the barn." He gave me a meaningful look, telling me he meant what he was about to say. "We never meant for him to get hurt. We just needed to buy some time."

His story matched Kade's so I knew he was telling me the truth.

As for the secret rooms in the house and under the barn floor, Tara told me they were used to hide things that were considered nefarious by those who were completely clueless about esoteric and mystical knowledge.

"We were never going to do anything to your young man," Charlie said, bringing my attention back to our discussion.

But what if things hadn't gone according to plan? We'd never know because with Kade being Kade, he'd insisted on inspecting every secret room, and thus had unwittingly played right into their hands. At least I now knew why they'd done it, though I wasn't okay with it by any means. Now to find out what had happened to Dawn that night. "When Dean and I saw you running to your truck, Charlie, Dawn was not with you."

This is where a strange expression came across his face. He went instantly pale and looked down at his hands, wringing them together in an indication of nervous energy. "We got into an argument on the way back to the truck. Dawn told me that we needed to let you go and call the police and turn Dean in for killing Lindsay. I told her that you ... well I mean, that Lindsay wasn't dead because you were at the house."

He paused at this point, and I knew he was remembering that night, going over the mental visions in his head. Judging by his expression, he seemed unsure how to go on and that made me curious. What was causing his confusion?

"That's when she told me that you weren't Lindsay." His mouth quivered, revealing his nervousness. "Of course I didn't believe her, and she got upset with me." He scrubbed his hands over his head, his agitation increasing. "She said she was going to call the police and tell them about Dean and about you." He went silent, and I knew he was still trying to figure it all out. "She pulled your cellphone out of her pocket…" He stopped abruptly and stared off into space.

"Charlie?"

His gaze returned to me, looking confused. "Yes?"

"She pulled the cellphone out of her pocket and then what?"

"I … I tried to get it away from her and we ended up fighting over it. When she hit me in the face, I pushed her away and realized that maybe we needed to part ways." I could see the fear he'd felt stamped there in his expression as he remembered that night. "She was getting violent, and it was scaring me."

She was scaring him? The irony was not lost on me. "So, what happened after that? Did she run?"

He looked away again and was silent for a long time.

"Charlie?"

He stirred, looking at me then looking away. "No, she – she started to run off I think, but tripped on something and fell on the ground. She got really silent and stared at me, her eyes really big, and I knew something was wrong, but I didn't know what."

Now my heart was racing. "What was wrong?"

238

"I'm not sure. She just stared at me, not moving, not saying anything."

"Did she hit her head on a rock when she fell?" That would explain the blood I saw trickling down the side of her face.

"I don't know, I just don't know. But I didn't push her that hard, honest I didn't." Charlie's eyes watered with unshed tears. "I knelt down to help her, and she suddenly started moving, rolling over onto her knees crawling away from me."

"So, then you left her?" He didn't answer me, and I had to prompt him. "Charlie, did you just leave her?"

"I followed her, because I wanted to help her, and she got to her feet and kept going, but she was walking funny, and I was worried about her. Then she fell again and didn't move." He swiped at the tears shimmering in his eyes. "I thought she was dead. So, yes, I left her. What else could I do?" He looked away, staring off into space and into memories that still disturbed him. "I felt bad about it. I really did. But I had you to think about, Lin ... umm ..." He brushed at the tears trickling down his hollowed cheeks. "Everything was getting out of control."

I handed him a napkin from the tissue box on the table and after he'd wiped his eyes and blew his nose, I reached over and patted his arm. "I know you meant well, Charlie, but then you came back with a gun."

Charlie pressed his thin lips together and nodded, then turned his head back to look at me, a strange look in his eyes. "When I got to the house and found the cellar door was locked, I knew you had escaped, and I looked everywhere for you. When I didn't find you in the house, I opened the door to go check the garage and spotted Dawn on the outside edge of the trees." His expression matched the shock in his voice. It must have really messed with his mind, seeing her like that when he'd thought he'd killed her.

"So, then what happened?"

"I ran down the porch steps, for I was going to go talk to her, but when I looked back up, she was gone."

She'd probably ducked back into the woods to hide from him, and I didn't blame her, I would have done the same. Since she showed up back at Charlie's, she must have run through the trees as soon as he'd taken off, which would explain why she hadn't gone to help Kade. She was probably worried about me and had come to help.

"I yelled to her, hoping she could hear me, and told her that you and Dean got away, then went back into the house to get my gun. I didn't feel safe with Dean on the loose and I didn't know if he would hurt you or not. I know you probably won't believe it, but I was going to ask you what I should do. You know, about that man, your um husband, and about Dean." He wiped at his tears and rubbed a hand across his head. "I figured the only place you could go was to the Wheeler house. I mean, you were pregnant, and it was freezing cold and dark. Where else would you go?" His eyes were bright with annoyance and admiration. "It was pretty smart of him to go up through the ceiling. I didn't think about his height or how strong he was."

"Were you going to shoot him?"

"No! I don't know what I would have done. I think I might have had him go down that hole with the other man and taken you away to safety. I don't know. I didn't have a plan. All I could think about was saving you." He drew in a steadying breath and let it out in a rush, shaking his head at the memories playing through his mind. "I checked the garage first, just in case, then got in my truck and headed back to the Wheeler place, though I drove slow and looked for you in the woods."

Since he had gone quiet again, I gave his hand a squeeze. "Charlie?"

He blinked, pulling from the thoughts consuming his attention and continued with his story. "I looked for you all along the way, because I was very worried about you. I even thought I saw you once or twice. It was so dark, and it was raining. So hard to see." Charlie shook his head, remembering his frustration. "When I got to the Wheeler house, I caught a glimpse of Dean running into it, and I went after him. I heard him running up the stairs and I had my gun ready, in case I needed to defend myself, but he jumped me so fast that I didn't have time to warn him, and the gun went off and, well, you know what I thought … I thought I'd killed him too."

Couldn't this man, regardless of his mental health, not see that what he had done that night was wrong on so many levels? He hadn't made a single good decision.

"All I wanted was for you, I mean Lindsay, to be safe." Charlie's voice dropped, becoming very somber. "When I left Dean and made it back to the house. I wasn't sure what to do. I was still trying to make up my mind when I looked out the window and saw Dawn standing in the driveway." His face went pale as he remembered that moment. "I thought she was coming to hurt me, you know, for hurting her, or maybe for hurting Dean, I don't know. I yelled out to her, telling her I was sorry I'd hurt her. But she just kept standing there. I figured it would be a matter of time before the police came, so I packed what I thought I'd need, figuring I would go to your … I mean, Lindsay's camp she inherited from her mother and wait there for you, I mean Lindsay, to come find me."

"What about Dawn?"

"She was nowhere in sight when I went back out to the truck. I figured she'd run off back to the Wheeler place, and I was really okay with that. I mean, I was worried about you. And believe it or not, I was really glad that Dawn was still alive."

Well, at least I now knew why Dawn hadn't helped Kade right after Charlie went tearing off back to his place. But how did she end up with him at Lindsay's camp? "So, when did Dawn meet up with you again?"

"What do you mean?"

"How did she end up at camp with you?"

"Well, she wasn't exactly with me."

"She wasn't?"

"No. We'd talked a few times about other places she might have to go, to hide from Dean, and I told her about Lindsay's camp. She was all excited about it, and I showed her on her map thing on her phone where it was located. We wanted to have a plan B and that was it, going there." Charlie paused to take a breath. "She obviously figured out that's where I had gone and she ... she came there looking for me."

"So, when you left your place, you never intended to come back to the Wheeler place at all, did you?" We'd been in such a panic worrying about that and once again, as was usually the case, all that worry for nothing.

"I couldn't go back there. I'd caused too much trouble." He paused for a moment and then he looked at me with sincerity. "I wasn't far from Pine Wood Lane when I looked in my rearview mirror and saw that man's SUV go tearing out onto the road. I knew you'd all made it out okay." Taking note of my questioning look, he further explained. "That's the name of the road my house and the Wheeler house is on." He gave me a fleeting smile. "I knew that you'd found each other and that did make me feel better, Li ... Tess, knowing you were okay."

"Why didn't you just call the police and tell them what happened?"

"I wanted to talk to you first. I knew you'd eventually come, but then ..." He shifted uncomfortably in his seat. "Well, Dawn showed up, showing herself every now and then, taunting me."

242

"What do you mean?"

"She didn't come talk to me, but she made sure I saw her."

"If she wasn't staying with you, then where do you think she was staying?"

"I'd told her about another place a bit further down the road that belongs to an old friend of mine. They never go there anymore, too old to bother, and we discussed hiding my truck in their garage, which is where it still is, by the way, unless Dawn took it. She must have been staying there. I don't really know. I never dared to go find out."

That made me excited for it would be my next stop after leaving Charlie. "We'll go check and see," I told him.

"You don't know how glad I was when I saw you coming out of the woods."

I remembered the look of relief on his face, and it actually made me feel better. Charlie knew by that point that he needed to turn himself in, though that didn't explain why I'd found him standing there at the end of the camp road. "Where were you going? I saw you go around to the back side of the camp, but I didn't see you reappear. I thought you went inside."

"No, I just sat on the doorstep wondering what to do. Then I thought I heard a noise and when I peeked around the house, I saw Dawn standing in the woods and she pointed like she was coming for me, so I took off for the main road and that's when we met up."

What was I supposed to make of this? Dawn hadn't run off with Charlie after all, but instead had kept her eye on him, probably waiting for me to show up and take care of it. "Do you think Dawn might still be hiding at your friend's camp?" I could only pray that she was.

"I don't really know for sure. As I said, I didn't dare go find out."

"Do you have any idea why Dawn is continuing to hide?"

Charlie shook his head, looking more confused than me about it. "I don't. She didn't do anything wrong."

But she felt like she had. She hated what she'd done to Dean and Lindsay, contriving to break them up and then placing blame on Dean for Lindsay's disappearance, and she hated what she'd done to Kade, pushing him down that hole, but did she really think those things justified her being in solitude–alone in the world with no one to turn to?

The guard stepped forward, gaining my attention, and when I looked at him, he pointed to the clock on the wall. "Time is up."

Charlie and I stood and faced each other. He looked incredibly sad, and my heart couldn't take it. "We'll do what we can to find Lindsay, Charlie. And I hope we can find Dawn as well."

"If you find Lindsay alive, will you tell her how much I love her?"

I nodded that I would.

"And if you find Dawn, tell her that I'm sorry."

The guard touched Charlie's arm. "Let's go."

I waved to him and remained in place until they'd gone out the door and I was alone. That's when I turned to his wife who'd been standing near him the whole time. "We will take care of him. You can move on and stop worrying about him."

She nodded her understanding then lifted her face up to a shining light, which flared through the room then was gone, taking her with it. The fact that Lindsay hadn't appeared to me yet did make me feel hopeful that she was still alive somewhere. Now to find her. And Dawn too.

244

Chapter 19

Kade and I talked about my conversation with Charlie and headed straight to the property where he thought she might be hiding. It was also possible that she might even be using Lindsay's camp now that Charlie was no longer there. It worried me that she was out in the world, homeless and feeling like she had no one she could trust. I felt I'd failed her somehow in not showing her she had a friend in me.

When I told Charlie that we would try to find his daughter, I meant it. Given Dawn's interactions with Lindsay, I couldn't help but wonder if she knew more about her disappearance than she was letting on. We did not, in any way, believe Dean was involved. He wanted her found as bad as Charlie did. But was she hiding or was she residing in spirit?

Despite placing my focus on Lindsay and using all my skills to try and find her, the only thing I got were dreams of Dawn. Disturbing dreams of her needing my help. So here we were, on a mission to find her.

The property Charlie told me about was easy enough to locate. It wasn't far from Lindsay's camp, and it was on the opposite side of the road. Charlie's truck was indeed in the garage and Kade called the police to let them know about it. The house was locked up tight and there were no signs of anyone having been there in a long, long while.

So, we turned around and went back to Lindsay's property.

The door to the camp house was locked but it looked like it would be easy enough for anyone to force open. We would not be doing that. Breaking and entering were not on our agenda for the day. Instead, we looked in the windows, seeing one large open room, though there were a couple doors, which were closed. A wood stove occupied the hearth in front of the fireplace, a stack of wood nearby. A tiny kitchen took up one corner of the room and a lumpy old couch, placed in the center of the room and facing the wood stove, contained a pillow and blankets. There were food items—bread, boxes of crackers, canned goods and other products— on the table and counters in the kitchen, and the garbage can next to the propane stove was overflowing, but I felt pretty certain that Dawn was not staying there. The mess inside was from Charlie.

Kade scanned the area. "I doubt she's hiding anywhere around here." The only other building was an old outhouse, which was slowly crumbling into complete ruin. In a few years' time it would be compost for the surrounding foliage, which was overtaking it in a rather charming way. Kade made a nod towards it. "I highly doubt she's in there."

I was about to suggest that we go check Charlie's place, which we had yet to do, when a peculiar sensation washed over me. Goosebumps peppered my skin and the fine hair on the back of my neck prickled. I rubbed my hand across my nape to dispel the eerie feeling and scanned the area, moving closer to Kade so I could speak to him in a whisper. "I think she's watching us right now."

Kade immediately went on alert, his body tensing, his eyes narrowing as he covertly surveyed our surroundings. "Can you get a lock on her location?"

I did a slow turn, taking care to act as if I were doing nothing more than a casual scan, and when I was facing the woods where she'd startled me that day, little alarms went off in my head. "She's in the woods across the road, almost right across from the house." The same spot where she'd found me hiding, waiting for a glimpse of either her or Charlie.

"Let's walk to the car, make her think we are leaving." Kade placed an arm across my shoulders, and we walked towards my car, speaking loud enough for her to hear us.

"I guess there's nothing more to see here, Tess. We should get back to the house."

"You're right. Maybe we can go to Charlie's later and make sure everything is okay with the property. No one's been there since he went in the hospital." If Dawn were to continue to elude us, I wanted her to know that Charlie's house was empty if she needed a place to stay, and I wanted her to know that he was no longer a threat. It seemed a better option than for her to be staying on someone else's property, where she ran the risk of being charged for trespassing. At least she'd been a guest at Charlie's house, so if she was to be found there, it wasn't technically trespassing. Was it? In any case, I wanted her to know that I would be going there at some point to check on it. If she changed her mind about avoiding me, she'd know where to go that we might eventually hook up again. She'd definitely be more comfortable there. At least she would have electricity, heat and running water.

When we got to my car, we positioned ourselves by the passenger door and took a final glance around, but we saw no sign of anyone attempting to conceal themselves.

Drawing close to Kade, I wrapped my arms around his neck, as if wanting nothing more than a hug. Titling my head up to him, I playfully nibbled on his ear and spoke softly into it. "You see that cluster of pines across from us? I think she's there."

"Not yet."

The voice caught me off guard, making me spring back from Kade. The sound was loud enough that I thought whoever said it was standing right behind us, but of course no one was there.

"What's wrong?" Kade's arms tightened protectively around me.

"I just got a message."

"What was it?"

"She said, 'not yet' and I'm pretty sure that means she doesn't want us to chase after Dawn."

"She? Do you know who it was?"

I shook my head, and with a finger to my lips, conveyed the need for Kade to remain quiet. Stepping away from him, I positioned myself beyond the influence of his aura, mindful that his energy might interfere with my spiritual connection. As our auras were our individual energy fields, being within the personal boundary of his aura could hinder my efforts to establish a connection with my spiritual messenger. *"Who are you?"*

"One must learn to ask the right questions."

That was Sheila and given she was now talking to me, I figured it meant whoever had delivered the first message was no longer with me. *"Have I not been asking the right questions?"*

One did not ignore the profound advice given by their spirit guide and since she was being specific, I knew that at some point I'd come up short in the questioning department.

"Have you?"

She was really good at that, answering a question with a question. Perhaps I needed to learn how to question HER better!

"When answers given do not give you satisfaction, your questions are the reason."

"Well, Sheila, the problem is that sometimes those who are providing the answers are not willing to divulge the information being sought. What then? We can ask all the right questions, but if they refuse to answer, or seek to mislead, what then? Sometimes people don't want to answer questions and sometimes they lie."

"When one is truly seeking an answer, becoming persistent and asking the right questions will eventually reveal the truth -- in one way or another."

"Thank you. I shall give this further thought. But right now, I need to get back to our daughter." The need to feed Autumn was becoming almost painful, and it would not wait for anything—not questions, nor chasing elusive girls into the woods.

"We need to get home, Kade. It's time to feed Autumn."

"What about Dawn?"

"Now isn't the time." He didn't question my answer, and it was one of the things about our relationship that I loved—how we readily accepted things like this. Even on those rare occasions when I went rogue, like going to Charlie's house without telling him first, or going to Lindsay's rundown camp and again not telling him first, he understood. When spirit calls, I answer it, even if it means breaking the protocols of our relationship. We respected each other, but we also understood that we had the right to make decisions that didn't always include the other. That didn't, of course, excuse those occasions from disappointment or annoyance. In both of my recent rogue occasions I had put myself in danger and that was never going to be okay with him. And it shouldn't. But such things would never get in the way of our love for each other.

So, after giving the woods one last scan and seeing no sign of Dawn, though I knew she was there, we got in the car and pulled out of the driveway. I thought I glimpsed her through a break in the pines and sent her a silent plea to go to Charlie's. We needed to talk and work things out between us.

"Did you see her?" Kade glanced at me briefly, his eyes searching, then returned his attention to the road.

"Yes, I think so."

"So why didn't you at least try to talk to her? Maybe she would have come out with a little encouragement."

"Because a voice told me the time wasn't right and we both know that spirit, unlike many of the people in this world, does not lead us astray."

"So, what's the plan? You told Charlie we would try to find Lindsay. How do you propose we go about doing that? I mean, the police have used all their resources available to them and they haven't found her."

"They didn't have us and our friends."

"Does that mean you are forming a plan?"

"You know, Kade, I think it's time you did another painting." I turned my head to smile at him and reached over to stroke his lean cheek. He was such a handsome man, and I fell more in love every time I looked at him. He appealed to me on so many levels, it was one of many reasons why our relationship was so solid and ever deepening.

"Okay, I'll get on it. Anything in particular you want me to paint?"

"How about the Wheeler house? It would be a pretty painting. The house has an interesting architectural style and with the barn in the background, the fields beyond that and the trees edging the property, it would be a lovely picture." And who knows what other interesting things

250

Kade would reveal in the creation of it. His gifts in that direction were quite remarkable.

"I agree. We can gift it to Janice afterwards."

"What a lovely idea!"

With our plan in place, we finalized the details on the rest of the drive home, then turned our full attention to Autumn, after first seeing off Anya, our enthusiastic babysitter. Feeding my daughter was a moment I cherished each and every time. This fleeting closeness wouldn't last forever, and I intended to savor every second.

When she'd had her fill, we spent some precious, quality time with her and when Dennis meandered in, he sat on the back of the couch and watched us with curious intensity. He no doubt found it interesting that we were as fascinated with her as he was. For an often-aloof cat, his devotion to Autumn was surprising. From the day we brought her home, he kept her in his sight and even approached her every now and then to check her over. Sometimes he even lay next to her.

Alex, too, had become immediately bonded to her. Dogs, I knew, were known to be protective of their family, especially the children, but Alex took things to an amazing level. Wherever she was, there he was too. He even sat watching her during feeding time, looking like a proud little protector. I swear if he could talk, he'd be saying, "There now, what a good girl you are to eat so well. You are amazing. Simply amazing. No one eats as well as you. No, they don't." Such thoughts made me chuckle, for it amused me to put words in Alex's mouth. He may be a dog, but he seemed more in tuned with his human family than we were. He was going to be a devoted companion to her as she grew up, competing with Dennis, no doubt, for her attention.

It was a wonderful time for all of us and when Autumn's eyes began to droop and she started sucking on her dainty little fist, we knew it was time to lay her down for a nap.

Robin's arrival was perfect timing. She was an eager babysitter, often competing with Anya for the job, and someday, when she had a child of her own, she was going to be an amazing mother. Right now, she was an amazing aunt to our daughter.

We hated to leave our precious little girl, even when she was sleeping, but we had things to do, and we couldn't do them with her in tow. One, it was still quite cold in Maine. The March weather was showing signs of thaw, but we still were not there yet, and two, we just didn't know what to expect and it was no place for a baby to be. Besides, I needed to give the next couple of hours my full attention and if Autumn were with us, that would never happen.

So Kade and I loaded up his art supplies and we headed to the Wheeler house.

Even before we got there, before turning onto Pine Wood Lane, I felt the familiar shiver of spiritual unrest. One way or another, we were going to make some sort of contact today.

Chapter 20

It was midafternoon and the sun was high in the sky, its warmth chasing off some of the cold, making it bearable to be outside. The absence of wind was an added bonus. With only a few precious daylight hours remaining, we wasted no time in preparing for our tasks, determined not to squander a single moment.

Kade positioned his easel at the onset of the driveway, choosing an angle that afforded a view of both the house and the barn, as well as a sweeping stretch of the field beyond. He planned to do a quick pencil sketch first, which is how he started most of his paintings. Sometimes unintended things showed up at that stage, before he even got to the paints. We were hoping it would happen this time too.

Later, when we were back at home, he would use photos he took with his phone, which he then sent to his tablet, to do the paint work, coming back at the end of the project to compare his painting to the actual subject and make whatever changes needed to be made at that point. Photographs were nice to have, especially when a good photographer knew how to take them, but paintings added extra touches that were far more personal and harder to add, even with the help of a photoshop application. The additions Kade made were spiritually inspired and offered clues to something we needed to know.

As we set up his things and I mentally prepared myself to try and contact whatever entity lurked here, we both felt a stirring of excitement in the spiritual realm. The very air almost crackled with paranormal activity. It was more prominent than any other time I'd been here, and I wondered what was stirring things to such a tizzy. No wonder the construction crew got spooked. It was an eerie feeling, enough so that even I felt a little on edge.

"I'm going to go out back and see if anyone comes to me." I gave Kade a kiss, which he accepted absently, and it made me chuckle, finding it amusing how completely focused he was on his task. I admired that about him, how absorbed he became when in the creative zone.

We'd put our protective necklaces on before leaving the house, and I gave his a gentle tug, reminding him of its presence. "We are safe. No matter what." I felt it prudent to remind him of that because he was a very protective man, going a little above and beyond in his drive to keep me safe.

We purchased the necklaces at Robin's metaphysical shop. It was the first time we'd met her and now we were such good friends I couldn't imagine her not being part of our lives. She'd wanted to come here with us but was also happy to have Autumn to herself. Besides, she was hoping that when Todd got back from his paranormal investigations in Rhode Island, he would be willing to investigate the Wheeler House, with her help of course. Given our purpose for coming today, she was worried I would cleanse it of ghosts before they had a chance to talk to them. I wasn't here to cleanse the house or perform any sort of exorcism. I was here to connect with the spirit entity I felt the night Dean and I fled Charlie's house and came here.

There was one thing I wished I'd cleared up before coming here though. Ever since learning that Janice's grandfather wished for the house to be burned down after he died, I'd been wondering what drove him to feel that way. The house needed updating, but other than that it was in solid shape, the foundation perfectly fine. So why would he request such a thing? It couldn't be spirit activity that had bothered him, Janice said she was not aware of the house ever being haunted.

But it was now. Or at least, *something* was going on with its auric energy. Sometimes it wasn't a haunting but a response to the energy flux of those connected to the property.

Since I knew that Janice's grandmother used to be part of Tara's coven, staying active until her later years, I figured that had to have a hand in her grandfather's feelings. He hadn't, after all, been on board with her being a witch. But, as his Alzheimer's progressed, he shouldn't have even remembered any of that. Besides, Janice's grandmother stopped practicing the craft even before he got sick. And then, in the end, her mind, too, had become fogged by the dementia which plagued her.

I was rather surprised to learn of a witch getting that kind of mental impairment, though I guess it was rather naive of me to even think that way. My reasoning, though, came from the assumption that their esoteric knowledge would give them the means to acquire immunity for such conditions. And then I remembered a conversation that Tara and I had engaged in, when she explained that the paths we follow in life are hardly ever logical, even to the spiritually enlightened.

For whatever reason, Janice's grandmother went down a path that eventually led to dementia, though it's difficult to comprehend why someone would choose such a pre-birth destination. Then again, some people made choices that were far more perplexing, and sometimes even horrific. Understanding the decisions we made before entering the physical world was a mystery I hoped to decipher someday. But it was more likely that full comprehension and insight would only be gained during my post-life review. Once we cross back into spirit, we have all the time we need to reflect on the 'whys' of our life choices and experiences.

One thing I had come to understand was that we could alter our pre-birth choices—if, that is, we learned the lessons those experiences were meant to teach us. The catch was mastering these lessons before the predetermined events unfolded. If a purpose was woven into all this…and I believed there was…I wished I could figure it out before being led through further trials.

Sheila told me I needed to learn the art of asking the right questions. Given she only gave advice when it was pertinent to the immediate complexities of my life, it wasn't something to ignore or set aside for future reference. Because of that, I couldn't stop thinking about it. I had a strong feeling I hadn't asked Charlie the right questions when we were together at his house, and maybe I didn't ask the right ones when I spoke to him at the hospital either. Honestly, I wouldn't be surprised to learn that I'd failed on asking the right questions with Dawn as well. And now, because of that, I found myself here at the Wheeler house, seeking to communicate with a mystery spirit and putting myself into a situation that could become very unpleasant.

At least I had Kade here with me this time, and together, we can handle just about anything.

The reminder about Janice's grandmother being an active member of Tara's Coven, back when Tara herself was just a small child, made me think that perhaps I needed to give Tara a call and ask her a few "right" questions.

She answered on the first ring, as if she'd been waiting for my call, which, knowing her, she probably was. "Hello, Tess. Thanks and praise for this glorious day and all the blessings held within it!"

"Thanks and praise indeed! Can you guess where I am?"

"You are at the Wheeler House. I felt a shift in the energy field there, though it hasn't been right in quite a while."

It was stuff like that which interested me, and I was glad that I'd called her. Tara's property, which was considerably larger than I'd originally thought, bordered not only my property but also the Wheeler's. Given that Tara had grown up in Bucksport, born and raised right there on her family homestead, she probably knew far more about this place and the families who'd lived here than I realized. Why she hadn't volunteered information, especially after learning what happened to us at this very house, was rather a surprise. She was usually very generous about sharing her knowledge with me.

But first, asking for clarification on what she'd just said had to be one of those right questions to ask. "What do you mean by that … about the energy not being right here in quite a while?"

"Do you feel something there? Something that makes you uncomfortable?"

"Yes."

"So, that's what I mean."

"When did you notice a shift in the energy here?"

Tara was silent for a few seconds, and I knew she was calculating the timeline. "Well, it went a bit awry when Janice's grandmother married Harry, her grandfather. As you well know, he was never on board with her being part of a coven." She gave a sigh, signaling her confusion and exasperation over his objections. "But it's gotten even worse over the past year, and especially so in the past couple months, since Janice started preparing the property for the market actually."

Tara was not happy about Janice selling the property. She was worried about who would buy it and what they'd do with the place. As far as Tara was concerned, a good portion of Bucksport was sacred land, a sentiment rooted in the region's history, reaching back to a time predating the arrival of the first European settlers who, fueled by a misguided sense of entitlement, claimed the land from the indigenous people residing here. Some of these indigenous roots were mixed in Tara's own ancestry, leading her to feel an affinity for the area. She considered herself a guardian of sacred land, and so was very protective of it. Given the chance, she would amass as much acreage as possible, if, that is, she had the financial means to do it. Which she didn't. So instead, she did what she could to protect what she could.

"Do you think Janice selling the property is the biggest reason for the recent change in its energy field? Or do you think Janice's grandfather might be responsible for the change? She seems to think he may be haunting the place."

"Well, aside from Maureen, Janice's grandmother, returning to spirit, I do think Janice's plans to sell it are what's causing the most angst. The land has been in her family for a long time, at least three or four generations, so it's a big deal that it will soon change hands."

She paused at this point, and I figured it was to mourn what she felt was an appalling decision, her silence steeped with disappointment on the matter. "When Janice hired people to do the renovations, the energy shifted even more."

She paused to take a breath and then waited, I think, to see if I had anything I wanted to say, which I did not. "The energies of the land

258

interact with the energies of the people on it, and so who knows, maybe some of the construction crew brought energy that didn't mix well with the property." Tara sighed in a manner that suggested her frustration was more with herself than anything else, then her next words confirmed it. "I wish I knew, and I probably could figure it out if I'd give it some time, but I've been busy with other matters. Besides, I have no control over what happens with that place, and I can't spend time worrying about things I cannot control."

"That is so true, Tara! As for this place and what is going on here, Janice said she was not aware of it ever being haunted."

Tara laughed, the sound light and amusing, making me smile. "Yes, well, as you know, spirits are everywhere, so I guess we could say that there is no place free of spirit activity. But no, I don't believe there are any active ghosts on the property, at least none that are sticking around for any length of time."

"Did you know that Janice's grandfather wanted the place burned down after their death?"

Tara made a little growl of disapproval. "Yes, Janice told me. As I said, Harry was never on board with Maureen being part of a coven, and he hated living on the property. He loved Maureen, though, and she loved him." Another pause as we pondered a relationship that, by all accounts, shouldn't have survived. "Somehow, they made it work, though they never saw eye to eye on spiritual issues. When Harry married Maureen, her parents were still alive, so they rented a house in Orland. He worked in a boat yard, and he loved it. But when Maureen's father died, she wanted to move in with her mother, you know, to take care of her, keep her company and help run their farm. He didn't want to, but they did it, and then when Maureen's mother died, the property went to her. He, of course, wanted to sell the place and buy another home elsewhere, but she wouldn't hear of it." Tara paused again and I wondered what she was thinking about, but her silence didn't last long. "Although Maureen was an active part of my Coven, her participation was minimal because of Harry. He believed what she was doing was evil, and he thought she was polluting the land with evil energy." Tara let out an irritated noise. "People like him irk me to no end."

"It's very sad he felt that way." I was so blessed to have a husband whose spiritual beliefs were in alignment with my own.

"It was very sad indeed. Their son, Janice's father, wanted nothing to do with his mother's activities or the farm, having adopted his father's sentiment, unfortunately. He worked at the paper mill here in Bucksport and they bought a house in Searsport. They pretty much kept Janice away from her grandparents until they died in a car accident her first year of high school. Her mother's parents lived in North Dakota and Janice didn't want to move there, so she went to live with Maureen and Harry. As you know, she came to love them very much."

"I'm surprised Janice never sought to learn more about her grandmother's involvement with your coven."

"Yes, well, her father put the fear of all things paranormal in her, though it never stopped her from being curious. She's a Doughty after all."

"A Doughty?"

"Maureen's maiden name."

"Well, she certainly seems to enjoy the seances that Barb holds at her place."

"Yes, she does. She's warming up to it and besides, she has never rejected all of it ... I mean, she is very interested in herbs and rocks and crystals and how all things hold energy. She just has a healthy respect for ghosts and doesn't want to be involved with them, other than going to seances where people she trusts are in control, of course." We both chuckled over that.

"Very soon this place won't belong to her anymore."

Tara's tone became quite somber. "I know. I'm very eager to learn more about who is buying it."

"I told Janice that I did detect a spirit entity here and she informed the buyer, but he doesn't seem to care."

"Is that why you are there now?"

"Yes, that and I am hoping Dawn might come around."

Aware that we'd spent enough time talking, I needed to wrap it up and get to work. "I called because I was wondering about that comment Janice made about her grandfather wanting the house burned down and you answered that. I thought it might have some bearing on the entity, but now I understand his feelings on the matter, I don't think it has anything to do with whatever is lurking here."

"No, I don't think so either," Tara agreed, her tone firm on the matter, then she let out a regretful sigh. "It's too bad Harry never took the time to learn about and understand Maureen's beliefs and spiritual standing. It does sadden me that he thought of us, the Coven members and everything we do, as evil."

"That is evil at work, Tara, turning people against the spiritual aspects of our lives and closing their minds to natural truths. But we must remember we are all here to travel different paths, to experience different things, believe different things, and, because of them, be stuck within the confines of those experiences and beliefs."

"Until we—hopefully—learn to break free of those constraints," Tara said.

"Yes!" This was one of the things I loved about her, how she constantly reminded me that things were not written in stone, and we actually had more control over our lives than we realized.

"Thank God we are not like that, Tess." The warmth in Tara's voice transmitted through the airwaves, cloaking me in loving energy. "We are so very blessed to be here, in this physical life of ours, with a more accepting, open attitude toward our spiritual natures."

"I love talking to you as always, Tara, but we don't have much daylight left and it cools off considerably when the sun goes down. Thank you for all that information."

"Call me when you get home, so I know you are home safe and sound, and let me know what happened. If you need help with anything, I am not even ten minutes away."

"I will, thank you, Tara. Blessed be to you."

"Blessed be to you as well, Tess."

I'd no sooner put my cell phone in my pocket and Kade was calling for me to come join him.

I took off immediately, wondering what was going on now.

Chapter 21

I met up with Kade at the back corner of the house. "What's up?"

"I think you should take a look at what I've drawn."

Entwining his hand with mine, we headed around to the front of the house and since he appeared relaxed, his stride unhurried, the tension flowing through me dissipated into curiosity. It wasn't anything bad, whatever it was.

"Who were you talking to on the phone?"

"Tara. I called to ask her a few questions about the Wheelers." I gave a nod toward his canvas as soon as it came into view. "Something came through already?"

"You could say that."

Kade stopped just short of the easel and released my hand. "Go have a look."

With my heart pounding in anticipation, knowing that whatever he'd drawn it was going to be relevant, I circled around the easel and caught my breath. As always, I was amazed by his talent and the spiritual gift that came along with it.

The drawing wasn't of the house at all. Well, there was an outline of it in the background, the focus more on the barn than the house, but the main body of the picture was that of a girl. She appeared to be in her later twenties, with long hair, an inch or two longer than mine, which was several inches past my shoulders, and it was very straight. Given the lighter strokes and the way in which he drew it, I had the impression hers was quite a bit lighter than my dark blond. Her eyes, fringed with long thick lashes, were narrowed slightly, as if wishing to convey something, her gaze seeming to spear right into my soul, making me stare back with a silent question … *What do you want from me?*

Her mouth was tilted ever so slightly in a smile, like she wanted to give it more than that but couldn't get there. A smile that said she'd been through stuff, and hard though it was, she was ok. Slender cheeks, a defined chin, and a head tilt just enough to give some of her profile. It was an overall flattering portrait.

I looked over at Kade. "Who is it?" The first name that came to mind was Lindsay, but I knew very well that my hopes of finding her were likely influencing such a guess.

Kade came around to study the drawing for a few seconds then shrugged. "I don't know, but I saw her clear as day, like she was standing right there in front of me, blocking most of my view, though I felt it important to do a rough sketch of what I did see beyond her."

When I looked back at the canvas, I was startled to see that the angle of her head had changed, giving me almost a full profile of her left side. Even as I reacted to it with an indrawn breath, I studied the changes intently. She was looking toward the direction of the barn, and I could see a small dark freckle on her jaw, about an inch over from the corner of her mouth.

"What's wrong?" Kade asked, his voice hushed. He knew me so well. "What are you focusing on?"

264

Taking care not to look up at the actual view, I took note of everything in her direct line of sight. It would've been helpful to compare the views and note the differences, but I didn't want to lose the vision. Instead, I committed each pencil stroke to memory

The outline of the barn was clear enough, then there was the field beyond, which used to be a cow pasture. Tufted clumps were scattered here and there, the grass tall in some areas and flattened in others. Bordering the field was a line of trees. I felt–knew—there was something important for me to see, but nothing jumped out at me. I couldn't see anything unusual or out of place or prominent.

"Tess?"

Kade's prompting for me to answer his question had me glance at him briefly, but it was enough to change what I saw when I returned my gaze to the picture. It was back to the way it looked when I first saw it, though it seemed her smile had faded some, and there was sadness in her eyes that I hadn't noticed earlier.

"It changed for me a bit."

"What do you mean?"

"When I first looked at it, she appeared as you have drawn her. Then, when I looked away and back again, the angle of her head was different. She was turned slightly away, gazing in the direction of the barn." I thought about it for a moment, because it didn't sound quite right as I said it, and then shook my head, retracting that last part. "Actually, she was looking somewhere beyond it." Knowing this new insight came from the spiritual connection I'd made with the girl in Kade's drawing, I quickly scanned the area in question, hoping to pinpoint what she may have been looking at, or trying to tell me.

The field, though trampled by the winter's snowfall, which had mostly melted—apart from a few lingering patches, was wildly overgrown, having seen no mower in years. Clumps of tall, dead grass formed mounds here and there, with scattered tufts dotting the frigid landscape. From what I could tell, there was no significant difference between my vision and Kade's drawing. But there was something out there the girl wanted us to find. I felt certain of it.

"Let's take a quick walk." I captured Kade's hand as we set off towards the field, staying to the left of the barn, and I couldn't help but savor the reassurance of his grip. With Kade by my side, I would always feel protected and safe, though my spirit guide inspired similar feelings, but in a different way.

When we reached the side of the barn, we stopped to look over the field, our eyes scanning for any sort of anomaly. Whatever made her look this way, it had to be something significant. But nothing jumped out at me. So, I looked towards the trees. Was it there she'd been looking? Was Dawn in there somewhere watching us? I didn't get a sense of being watched, but I did sense a presence, though I couldn't get a lock on her location.

Suddenly the sound of a deafening crash, like that of a big tree falling, broke the silence, startling Kade and I and sending us on a run back to the house.

Although we were expecting to find some extensive damage, we could find nothing that explained the noise. The only thing out of place was a pile of boards next to the house, but there was no way they could have made that horrific noise. Besides, I was pretty sure those were there on the ground when we arrived.

Kade went over to examine them. "They put new siding on the whole house. These must be what remained when they were done."

266

We knelt to examine the boards, and I noticed one had several nails sticking out of it. As the end was badly cracked, it was likely the reason it had been pulled off the house and replaced. Since it wasn't safe to have those nails sticking up like that, I wrapped my fingers around it, intending to turn the nails towards the ground, when a sudden sharp piercing pain went through the back of my head. I saw a flash of blinding light and then total darkness.

Stunned, I couldn't move and though I was aware that Kade was speaking, I couldn't understand him or even speak. Then suddenly I was floating upwards, above the boards, above Kade's head, moving higher and faster, until I wasn't going up but forward, rushing through a tunnel of swirling, sparkling light. Good God, was I dead? Panic surged through me. *No! Please no, I'm not ready.*

"Tess, for the love of God, will you please answer me?"

Kade! It was such a relief to not only hear him talk but to understand him, though I couldn't pinpoint his location. *Keep talking, my Love! I will find you. I will, I will.*

"Tess, open your eyes and look at me."

I opened my eyes and saw that Kade's face was inches from mine, his grip on my shoulders firm but not painful. We were both kneeling on the frozen ground, but we were no longer near the house or the pile of boards we'd been examining.

Realizing how rigid I was, I forced myself to relax, and Kade's grip loosened, the relief on his face almost comical, making me smile in reassurance. "I'm okay now, I think."

"Thank God." He pulled me into his arms, holding me close for several seconds. Even through our jackets I could feel the pounding of his heart. After a few moments, he released me and rose to a stand, pulling me up with him. "You scared me for a minute there."

"What happened?"

"I don't really know. You went stiff as a board." He grinned at his silly pun, which was an attempt to lighten the intense mood we were in, and I grinned in return, nudging my shoulder against his and enjoying the closeness we shared, especially during times like these. "So anyway, your mouth was opening and closing, much like a fish does when it's out of the water." His beautiful blue eyes dancing with continued humor, he gestured with his hand to indicate the distance we were from the house. "Before I could determine if you were having a vision or not, you were suddenly standing—and I mean, you were kneeling one second and on your feet the next." He snapped his fingers. "It happened that fast and it was so fluid, like something had lifted you up." He shook his head, indicating he was still wondering over it. "You sort of stood there for a couple seconds and then you were rushing across this field. I couldn't keep up with you and I was terrified I was going to lose you, so I, well…"

His hesitation made me look at him curiously. "What?"

"You were getting so far ahead of me that I yelled our code word, and you stopped instantly and slumped to the ground. The moment I touched you, you went rigid, and I knew you couldn't see or hear me."

I withdrew my hand from his, to gain the freedom to turn about, and sought to determine where my vision had wanted to take me. I wasn't upset with Kade for using the code word even though I didn't reach my destination. We decided a while back, before Autumn was born, that there might be times when it became pertinent for a vision to end. Kade was worried that jarring me from it, by yelling at me or grabbing at me, would be harmful in some way. So, after talking to Sheila, and per her suggestion, we decided to use a code word, one that would bring me back to full consciousness. When Kade expressed concern that I might not appreciate his interference, I promised him I would never question his use of it. He needed to know, and trust, that there would be no repercussions from me, no matter how disappointed I might be to not see things through to the end. Our safety came first, though I did hope that Sheila, as my trusty spirit guide, would prevent any harm from befalling me, especially while ensconced in a vision.

"Do you have any idea where you were headed?" Hands on hips, his stance relaxed, his eyes narrowed against the glare of the sun, he surveyed the area, and I was struck by the handsome sight he posed, taking a few seconds to admire the view.

Then our eyes met and one of his brows shot up in question. "What?"

Smiling, because he made me so happy, I shook my head in answer to his question. "I have no recall of where I was headed. And you look very handsome by the way."

Kade laughed. "I sometimes don't understand your thought processes."

Laughing with him, I reached over to give his arm a loving caress. "I love you."

"I love you too." We shared a moment and then he got back to the business at hand. "Do you think you were headed to Charlie's?"

That made me take note again of where we were standing, which was about halfway to the woods from the barn. The direction I was headed towards would eventually take me to Charlie's property. Was it possible I was headed there, and if so, why? Is that where we would find Dawn?

"What do you think is over there?" Kade pointed to an area just ahead and slightly to the left of where we were standing. The grass there stood tall and dense, unlike the area around it, which was trampled nearly flat. And now that we were focused on it, I could just make out pieces of wood peeking through the grass. Knowing it merited a closer look, we went to check it out, and the closer we got, the more my heart pounded. Whatever we were about to see, it was spiking my adrenalin, making me anticipate an important discovery.

Though the ground was still frozen, and the overgrown grass clumped together, we could see the remnants of an old, long-abandoned well. A few stones remained in place, forming part of the wall around the opening, while decaying pieces of wood lay scattered in such a way that we knew they once bordered the well's rim.

I poked at the rocks with my foot. "Do you think it's been filled in?"

"Not sure. It was probably hand dug and when the invention of well pumps and plumbing came along, they drilled one closer to the house." Kade knelt along the outer edge of one part of the remaining rock wall and brushed some of the dead leaves and grass aside. A round, rusted metal plate, obviously the well cover, became visible but was frozen into the ground. He straightened and rubbed his hands together, blowing into his cupped palms to warm them. "Come the summer, Janice, or whoever owns the property by then, needs to open it and see if it needs to be filled in, otherwise it presents a safety hazard."

"I already made a mental note to mention it to her." Shivers were racing along my spine, my skin prickling with awareness, and I swung about to stare in the direction I'd been heading before Kade pulled me from my trance. "Maybe we should walk over to Charlie's place."

Kade glanced at his watch. "We've got about an hour before the sun is down, so if we're going to do that, we need to get moving." We clasped hands and started out across the field. "Sorry I pulled you from the trance, but I couldn't keep up and I was worried…"

"Don't. You need not apologize."

"So, what did you see? What happened to put you into a trance?"

"I'm not sure. I touched that board that had the nails in it and suddenly I felt a sharp pain in my head and then it was like … I thought I had died." Giving an exaggerated shiver and tightening my hold on Kade's hand, I shook my head to rid it of such thoughts. "It was quite scary. I felt myself floating upwards and then I was zooming forward. That must be when I started across the field."

"You had no idea where you were going?"

"No. I couldn't see anything." But now I was thinking about it, I remember feeling regretful. "I am pretty sure there is something here for us to find."

And then, just as the words left my mouth, I saw it.

Something green was wrapped around a low-lying twig just inside the trees. I walked over and tugged it free, taking care not to snag it, and saw that it was a crocheted scarf.

Kade gestured that he would like to see it and I handed it over to him. He examined it closely then glanced around to see if there was anything else to find. "It's been out here a while. Do you have any ideas as to who it belongs to?"

Although logic was telling me that it was likely Dawn's, I just didn't feel certain enough about it to say. "No, but I think it's an important find." It was frozen stiff and covered in leaves and small twigs, telling me that it had been out here a while. I looked about, getting my bearings and nodded in the direction of Charlie's place. "How far in do you think it is before we get to Charlie's property?"

"Not sure. Didn't you go through the woods to get there? Do you think Dawn is there?"

"I did, but from up by the house. As to whether Dawn is there, I just don't know." I wasn't getting a reading on anything. And yet I felt … something … on the peripheral of my psychic senses. "I feel like I'm missing something."

"Let's get on over to Charlie's place. We are rapidly running out of daylight. In fact, let's go put my stuff away and drive over." He nodded toward the scarf in my hand. "I've a feeling this is what you were meant to find, so there's no point continuing on through the trees."

He was right. Besides, I didn't want to get stuck over there without transportation being nearby. Not that I really expected anything to happen that required a quick escape … but it was better to be prepared. Just in case.

Chapter 22

As we neared the house, I noticed a puzzled expression cross over Kade's face and asked him about it.

"Those boards ... one of them is leaning up against the house."

The board in question was the one with the nails sticking out of it. "You didn't pick it up and put it there?"

"No, I was busy running after you."

When we got to it and looked it over, we saw nothing of note. Although touching it earlier had triggered a vision, it didn't do anything this time. Well, okay, it did send a strange feeling skittering through me, unsettling my senses and making me anxious. The fact it was now leaning up against the house when Kade left it on the ground was another indication that there was something to be gleaned from it.

A tingling sensation on the back of my neck put me on alert and I swung about, scanning the area with my eyes and with my psychic feelers. Had Dawn put that board there? Was she watching us?

Kade dropped the board on the ground, nails down, then stepped on it to drive the nails into the dirt. "At least it can't hurt anyone this way. We need to tell Janice that the contractors need to clean up a few things before the sale goes through."

"She might have to do it herself, the closing date is only a few days away."

"Do you think the buyer is someone who is already familiar with the house? I mean, you said they didn't even request a showing before they offered on it, and they haven't been to see it since their offer was accepted."

I was almost certain of it, my curiosity as piqued as his. Janice, too, was intrigued. The buyer's name didn't ring a bell and since all her correspondence was through his lawyer, she couldn't even ask him any questions. "We'll find out soon enough, I guess."

Once we had all of Kade's art supplies loaded into my car, we headed for Charlie's place, my anxiety increasing the closer we got to it. Returning to a place where something so stressful and unpleasant had occurred was emotionally unsettling. But it all turned out well in the end, so I needed to keep my focus on that.

After Charlie was apprehended, a team was sent to scour his house. They had also collected his drug paraphernalia that we'd hidden in the dryer. Thankfully, he hadn't given me anything harmful, though the drugs were not something one could buy over the counter. In fact, the sleeping pills were his, indicating he was having issues, and since only a few were missing, the ones he'd give me, Dawn and Dean, he hadn't taken very many. Sleep deprivation could become a serious problem over time. It hindered the brain's ability to process information, and as a result, reality can become impaired. It explained some of what happened to Charlie though I think his mental decline began with the death of his wife.

When the house came into view, it appeared cold and dejected in the dimming afternoon light. Not a lot of happiness happened within those walls, and the energy vibrating from it was depressing. I mentally placed a cocoon of protective light around us, ensuring not only our safety, but also keeping that negative energy from infiltrating our aura and affecting our psyche.

Kade parked as close to the front porch as he could get without driving on the walkway leading to the porch steps. I had to shake off the memories bombarding me and concentrate on picking up the presence of others, be they living or dead.

Energy fluttered along my nerve endings, putting me on edge and on alert. Something was here alright, and it wasn't entirely a good thing.

"Are you getting anything?" Kade's voice was hushed as we made our way up to the front door, his eyes scanning the area, his body tensing for action.

It was like we were acting out a scene in a mystery movie, and I wanted to shout, 'Cue the suspenseful music', which made me giggle, and Kade turned his head to look at me, one brow quirked in question.

"I was just thinking that I feel like we are in a suspenseful movie, and this is the part where the music would start building momentum, preparing the audience for something to happen."

Kade started to punch the code in for the lock box but the moment he pressed the first number, the door drifted open. That made us look at each other, our eyes locking in silent communication.

Kade pulled a stun gun from his pocket, something he decided we needed after what happened to us here on this property and over at the Wheeler house. He was licensed to conceal carry a gun but neither of us felt it was necessary, though having some sort of protection couldn't hurt. If I knew how to harness the power within us, elevating it from mere 'belief' to true 'knowing,' we wouldn't need things like that. But unfortunately, I wasn't there yet. I knew we had incredible abilities, of course, but I didn't know how to access them—at least, not all of them. When explaining this to others, I always used the analogy of flying a plane. I know it's possible, and I believe I could do it, but without knowing *how*, I wouldn't be able to fly one.

Kade lowered his head to whisper in my ear. "Let me go first, stay close." He pushed the door open wider, and we peeked into the rooms beyond, taking note of everything within our line of sight. Satisfied the coast was clear, Kade stepped inside and looked to the left where the staircase was located. He held up a finger, signaling for me to stay put, then quietly headed for the area where Charlie kept his jackets and shoes, glancing up the stairwell as he did so.

In the meantime, my eyes scanned the living room and what I could see of the kitchen. The only sounds were the ticking of the clock on the wall across from me and the hum of the refrigerator. The house was clean and tidy, despite being raided by the police.

I was disappointed to see no signs of anyone staying here, though it was an ideal place for Dawn to hide. Charlie didn't get company, and the police were done with the place.

Kade came back to my side. "What's beyond the kitchen?"

"To the left is an open doorway that leads to the laundry room and pantry area, it's also where the cellar door is located. The bathroom is there to the left of the living room."

Kade went to check the bathroom, with me trailing close behind, then went into the kitchen. After a quick glance around, he made his way into the pantry and tried the cellar door, which was locked.

I was about to tell him where the key might be when we heard something fall onto the floor above us. We broke into a run, my heart pounding from the surge of adrenalin, and I knew before we even made it to the top of the stairs that it was someone in spirit that had made the noise.

"You aren't going to need the taser, Kade."

He nodded that he heard me, his arm relaxing to his side, and opened the door to our left. It was a small, sparsely furnished bedroom and contained several bins and boxes, which I guessed were Lindsay's things that Dawn had brought from Boston. After ensuring nothing looked out of place, Kade then opened the door across from it, and to the right of the stairs, discovering a bathroom. Although we could see it held two other doors, Kade didn't bother checking them, instead going to the next door on the same side of the hall as the small bedroom, which was the bedroom where Charlie had first taken me. I didn't' go in, I just couldn't bring myself to enter it, but Kade checked it thoroughly then rejoined me in the hallway.

"I didn't see anything lying on the floor." He gave me a brief hug, then pulled away to look at me. "You okay?"

"I'm fine."

He gave me a kiss on the forehead, then headed for the door across the hall, which turned out to be Charlie's bedroom. Kade went around to open the door on the right side of the king-size bed, and it opened to the main bathroom, solving the mystery of one of the doors we hadn't bothered to check.

I went around to the left side of the bed and lying on the floor next to it was a picture frame facing down. It had to be that which had made the noise.

I picked it up and some of the shattered glass fell onto the floor. After shaking the remaining loose shards into a nearby waste basket, we stared at the photograph. It was that of Charlie, his wife Andrea and a young girl of about ten or so. Lindsay. Mother and daughter were hugging each other while Charlie stood close behind them, a hand on each of their shoulders. They were all smiling into the camera, looking happy and normal. A close-knit family on the verge of having their world torn asunder. It was a happy photo, one that depicted a time in Charlie's life when it was filled with love and laughter. The wood frame was worn on each side of the photograph, and I knew it was from Charlie holding it in his hands, his fingers rubbing the edges as he gazed at the two loves of his life.

Tears blurred my vision, and I blinked them away, wishing with all my heart that things could have turned out different for them. They had no idea, when that picture was taken, that Andrea would be gone within the year, that Lindsay would one day disappear, and that Charlie would lose his mind and end up in a mental health facility.

"It's so sad, isn't it Kade, how badly the fate of their little family turned out."

Seeing someone's past, while knowing their present and where it led them, made one think about how quickly things could change in our lives. Moments of adversity seamlessly transformed into periods of prosperity, which eventually gave way to unforeseen challenges, and so it went, a ceaseless cycle of ups and downs.

"Our lives are based on the decisions we make and the reactions we have to the consequences of those decisions. It didn't have to turn out this way." Kade pressed a long kiss on the top of my head before murmuring against my hair. "We always have choices, Tess, to do things that either make our lives better or worse. If their journey didn't lead towards happiness, then their choices took them down a road they needed to travel, for reasons beyond our comprehension."

He was right and I was glad he knew what to say to bring me out of my melancholy. Whether it was consciously or subconsciously done, the three of them chose the paths they followed, and the consequences of those choices were opportunities for growth. I hoped they learned the lessons they needed to learn so they would not have to go through anything like this ever again. In another life, of course. For Andrea, and possibly Lindsay as well, their choices here were over. As for Charlie, I wasn't sure if his mind was healthy enough to make better choices for himself.

I felt a presence nearby, her energy field vibrating along the edges of mine, and I turned my head to see Charlie's wife Andrea. She stood near the window overlooking the front yard and appeared just like the smiling woman in the photograph, even wearing the same flower-print dress. Her appearance was healthy and happy, the glow around her spirit body bright and warm. Unlike the other times I saw her, the sadness that was so prevalent was gone.

Mentally I greeted her. *"Hello, Andrea."* When she didn't reply, I gestured at the photograph that Kade was now holding. *"Did you knock that onto the floor to get my attention?"*

Andrea looked at the photograph, the brightness around her dimming, and when her eyes met mine again, I saw the regret she was feeling. *"Don't be upset about the choices you made. Our life here is temporary, as you know, and one day we will all understand the whys of the things we experienced."*

She looked a little lost, like she wasn't sure what to do and turned to glance out the window, though I knew she didn't see what was out there for she was seeing into a realm I was not yet privy to. *"Do you have a message for Charlie?"*

Andrea turned back to me, her glance considering, then she touched a hand to her heart.

I understood all too well. It was a common message and a good one. *"I will tell him you love him."*

She fisted her hand and pressed it again to her heart.

Though I understood the gesture, I felt her emotions almost as clearly as I felt my own, and my eyes filled with compassionate tears. *"You've nothing to be sorry for."*

It was hard sometimes, for those in spirit to see the decisions and reactions their loved ones here were making. For them, death was not a regret. It wasn't to be mourned. It wasn't a horrible fate to befall them. They were not in a terrible place or gone forever. Grieving loved ones didn't understand that it wasn't the worst thing that could happen to the one who died ... it was the worst thing to happen to the ones who lived.

What I had come to understand was that when we cross into spirit, we don't miss out on anything because in spirit, we experience everything. The people we loved, the animals we adored, the places and experiences we cherished, all remain a part of our soul forever. Given that, the messages I was most often asked to convey were those of love and encouragement. They wanted loved ones here in the physical world to go on and be happy, because that is exactly what they were doing, and it was all those things that Andrea wanted Charlie to know.

I mentally assured her that I would do my best to explain all of this to Charlie and she smiled, her light brightening to a near blinding brilliance.

And then, because it couldn't hurt to ask, I decided to go for it. *"Can you tell me anything about Lindsay?"*

"It is not for her to say."

Sheila's reply made me feel just a tad bit resentful, though I was quick to squash such feelings. There were rules to follow between the living and the dead and I would never expect them to be broken, especially not for my own convenience. *"Ok, I just don't understand why I can't have some sort of hint, but I'll accept your answer, despite my not understanding it."*

"Some things are meant to be discovered when they are ready for discovery."

"Does that mean that Lindsay is not ready to be found?"

Silence.

I glanced toward the window and saw that Andrea was gone. Would she rest easy now, knowing that Charlie was getting the help he needed and that I would convey her message to him? I hoped so.

"She will always be checking on him. Until he joins her."

"Yes of course, Sheila, I do understand that. I just hope she won't be as concerned for him as she's been. He's been living a very lonely life here."

"Those were choices he made."

"But they weren't the best ones to make. I mean, he wasn't happy."

But I knew, even before she spoke, what she was going to say. Sheila did not like me passing such judgements.

"It's not your call to determine if his choices were good or bad."

"Then what does it matter what I say or do, what anyone says or does, if people are to be left on their own to make the choices they do?" I needed to understand what my role, as a medium, was supposed to be.

"You offer information they can use, or not, to make their choices. Always share your messages, but do not anticipate how those messages are received, processed and acted upon ... or not."

A sudden calamity of noise erupted from downstairs, startling me from my conversation with Sheila and sending both Kade and I running for the door.

Kade motioned for me to stay behind him, which I did, but only by a step or two. I needed to be right at his side if we had to fight off a particularly nasty poltergeist, because only that could make the sort of noises we heard.

It was completely quiet by the time we made it to the bottom of the stairs and as soon as we rounded the corner and could see the kitchen, we stopped to stare in disbelief.

It was in complete shambles and was definitely the work of a spirit. No person could do all of that in the space of the few short seconds it took for us to get down here.

Every drawer and every cupboard door were open. The stuff within them was tossed everywhere. The chairs around the kitchen table had been tossed about and were lying in the oddest places. The table itself was upside down. All the items on the counters were gone, replaced by other objects which had been tossed about, like silverware, spices and the like. This was the work of a very, very upset spirit.

"Do you detect anyone, Tess?"

"No. Whoever did it is no longer here." The entire room was freezing. Such anger, so much fury, had sucked up every bit of warmth and used the energy to do what we now surveyed with dismay. "This is the work of a very unhappy soul."

Although a return to the spirit world was typically a joyful and peaceful experience for most, some people carried their anger with them, leaving them in a state of unrest. It was so ingrained into their soul, their disappointment with the way things went in their life, that they became lost souls, acting out their negativity in ways such as this. These were the souls that became poltergeists, and they became spirits who wreaked havoc upon the living. It was not a common occurrence, but an exception, and if someone's departed loved one fell into this category they would know right away. They were the spirits who needed help from professionals, from people who possessed the knowledge and skills to deal with restless spirits.

"Who do you think did this ... Lindsay?" Kade walked over to where the mess was the worst and gestured at it. "We can't leave the place like this, but it's going to take a long time to clean it up and we really need to get back to Autumn."

"As to who I think did this ... I have no idea. As far as cleaning this up, we'll come back with Tara, Robin, Anya and Mary." They all wanted to check the place out anyway so now they had an excuse to do it. "I'll let Charlie's lawyer know what happened."

Kade turned to look at me, one brow raised in amusement. "And what are you going to tell him, that a ghost got mad and wrecked the kitchen?"

I laughed because I could just imagine the look on the staid lawyer's face when I told him that. "I'm not sure yet, but he does know who I am, so I don't think he would be totally surprised to hear something like that from me."

"Who were you talking to upstairs?"

"Andrea, Charlie's wife. I think she's happy that her husband is in a place that can help him."

"Did she say anything about her daughter?"

I was still bummed about the answer to that question. "No, Sheila said it wasn't her answer to give."

Kade nodded, not surprised to hear that and held out a hand to me. "Are you ready to head home?"

"I think we should check the basement before we go." If Dawn was here, wouldn't that be the place to hide?

Kade gestured toward the locked door. "If she was down there when this door was locked, don't you think she'd be up here asking us to let her out?"

"Maybe." It was a valid point, but I still wanted to be sure.

"Okay then." He picked his way over the mess on the floor, giving me a hand as I followed him, and we found the door to the cellar wide open.

The stairwell was empty and dark. Kade turned on the light then looked at me, his expression clear enough, he would accept no argument to what he was about to say. "I'd like for you to stay here while I check it out. I don't want this door being slammed shut while we are down there." He gave a nod to the mess behind us. "Whatever did that might not take it too well that we are still around."

I didn't like him being down there alone, but I also knew he could handle whatever might happen. If Dawn was down there, she wouldn't hurt him and if the ghost that wrecked Charlie's kitchen didn't want him down there, he could handle things until I could help. "Okay, I'll wait here." I told him how to get into the secret rooms and where the keys were hidden if the doors inside were locked.

Kade gave me a quick kiss then headed down the stairs. I watched him until I could no longer see him then leaned against the door jamb and focused on strengthening the protective energy around him.

Not ten minutes later he was coming back up the stairs. "I can't tell you how it made me feel to see the room he kept you in." He pulled me in

284

for a long embrace, burying his head against my neck and kissing my shoulder. "Thank God Dean got you guys out of there."

"Yes, thank God. I was so scared I was going to have our precious daughter down there, and without you present to see it."

We shared a kiss then Kade withdrew and slid his hand down my arm to entwine our fingers. "Let's go home to that precious daughter of ours. We'll figure out our next step after we've spent some bonding time with her."

It was a great idea. We had a lot to think about. We also needed to gather our friends and see what we could come up with. One way or another, I wanted to help Charlie find his daughter so he could move on with his life, and I hoped to find Dawn so she would know that she was not alone. She had people who would be more than happy to call her a friend.

Chapter 23

I pulled into the driveway at Charlie's house and was instantly disturbed by the fact that there weren't any other cars present. Where was everyone? Did I get the time to meet here wrong? I thought about calling Kade to check on his whereabouts, but caught a glimpse of someone in the living room window and was almost certain it was Dawn. So, she was here!

I jumped out of the car and ran for the house, calling her name and praying she wouldn't hide from me. "Dawn, please wait!"

It was probably stupid to go into the house alone, without my husband or my friends, but this was Dawn, and I wasn't going to lose the opportunity to talk to her.

The moment I stepped into the house, I knew I'd made a mistake. But before I could stop and turn around, the door slammed shut, the sound reverberating with such force that it swelled to a painful intensity. In fact, I was surprised the door's wooden frame hadn't splintered from the force of it.

Charlie stood just inside the living room, dressed in green scrubs and holding a gun, though it wasn't pointed at me, thank God. There was a disturbing smile on his face and a crazed look in his eyes, and yet I didn't feel threatened, though I was very concerned. What was he doing here?

Did he escape the hospital? Panic surged through me, and my brain scrambled with a slew of alarming considerations. There were so many ways this confrontation could end.

Charlie looked at me in surprise, his voice disturbingly pleasant. "Hello, Tess."

Well at least he got my name right. I closed my eyes briefly and fought to remain calm. Now was not the time to become paralyzed with fear or give in to panic. Neither reaction did anyone any good. Had I learned nothing over the past month?

Behind me I heard someone approach, and as badly as I wanted to turn and see who it was, I didn't dare take my eyes off Charlie. It was a very uncomfortable spot to be in, and I mentally placed a protective aura of light around me.

"I knew you'd come back. I'm just surprised you came alone."

Dawn. I wasn't sure if I should be relieved or more frightened. There was something about her voice that didn't sound right.

"Dawn, what is going on? I've been worried about you." I took a couple cautious steps to the side, moving just enough so I could see her and Charlie at the same time. She looked … defeated? Hopeless? What was that look on her face? It held no joy, and her aura, which was visible to me, emanated like a pulsating shadow around her. If I wasn't so stressed about Charlie being here, I would be marveling over it, the fact I could see it so well, and worried about that color, which did concern me. Perhaps Charlie was the problem. He was standing there with a gun, after all, looking pleasantly unhinged. That had to be very disturbing for her. It was for me. "Are you okay, Dawn?"

Charlie laughed. "You think you are friends with her now?" He turned away from us and went into the kitchen. "Would you like some tea?"

288

Tea? What did he think we were going to do, have a tea party and sit like old friends? Speaking of making tea … I looked at the kitchen and was surprised to see it was all back in perfect order, just like it was when Kade and I first arrived here the day before.

"Did you clean up the kitchen, Dawn? Do you know what happened in there?" Had she witnessed the violent spirit activity when it went down? That might explain her current mood, it had to have been terrifying. But when did Charlie get here?

"What about you, my dear?" Charlie asked, looking to his side, the tea kettle in one hand and his gun, pointing at the floor, in the other.

The fact Charlie was obviously speaking to someone else, someone standing next to him, made me concentrate on seeing what he was seeing. And then I saw her, clear as day and looking as solid as the rest of us. Andrea. She looked almost radiant as she smiled at Charlie, responding to his question with an enthusiastic nod.

What was going on here?

"I'm so sorry, Tess." Dawn was suddenly right next to me, taking me by surprise as she cupped my head between her warm hands. Pain pierced into my brain, and I stared into her eyes with confusion. She wasn't holding me in a strong grip, in fact it was rather gentle, but her eyes were begging me to understand. "You need to wake up."

What?

Autumn's cries brought me back to full awareness and I shot up to a sitting position, my eyes sweeping the room as terror shot through me that something was after my daughter. But it was Kade who was seeing to her, and the relief that brought me was so immense my bones turned to jelly, making me flop back against my pillow. He had her on the changing table, cooing softly as he changed her diaper and bending now and then to give her little kisses. He must have heard me sit up for he spoke to me over his shoulder.

"I think she's hungry."

I hated dreams like that, especially when they felt so real. I wanted to discuss it with Kade, try to figure out its message, but Autumn came first.

Holding her to my breast as she nursed did amazing things to my psyche. I felt okay with the world again. I felt hopeful, strong and more determined than ever to put all this business with Charlie and Dawn to rest.

Once she was asleep and snuggled in her bassinet, with Alex laying on watch nearby, we ensured the video monitor was on then went downstairs to make some coffee. It was nearing six in the morning and there was no sense in trying to get back to sleep. I couldn't have anyway, my brain was too busy buzzing over the reasons for that bizarre dream.

I told Kade about it in as much detail as I could remember and he wrote it all down, in case we forgot something later, and then we went over each point that we considered important. Dreams were a way for our soul to communicate with us, especially dreams like that one. They were often more symbolic than straightforward, and though I wished many, many times that they would just get to the point and tell us straight up what their message was, I knew that it was in deciphering these symbols that we gained the most profound insights.

Unfortunately, our thoughts were all over the place when it came to the message behind this dream, and each time we read over Kade's notes, we came up with something else.

At seven, Tara called.

"I had the strangest dream and had to tell you straight away. I know it's early, but you have an infant in the house, so you can't possibly be sleeping."

I knew the moment she mentioned having a dream that it would somehow tie into mine. I put her on the speaker so Kade could listen in. "You are on speaker, Tara. Kade is here with me. What was the dream?"

"I dreamed that I flew to Charlie's house…"

"Flew?"

Tara laughed with delight. "Yes! On a broom no less." She had to indulge in her laughter a bit longer before regaining enough control to continue. "Isn't that just amazing?"

"So, you flew to him in the role of a witch?" That had to be significant.

"I did. If only I could get my broom to cooperate like that!" After chuckling over that a little more, her voice became more serious. "You were there … alone I might add … (she was still upset with me for going to Charlie's house that day), and you were standing outside near the front porch brandishing a wand." More laughter interrupted her ability to talk for a moment, but she recovered quickly and continued. "I think you were casting a spell, I'm not sure, but there were evil spirits flying in circles around you, encompassing the house and … well, I think the whole area, even the Wheeler place was included within their circle."

"Wow, that's pretty epic."

"Isn't it though? When I woke up, I knew I had to tell you right away but it wasn't yet six and so I've been waiting and waiting for seven to arrive."

"We were awake. I'd just come out of my own dream."

"I'm coming over. Do you have the coffee ready?"

"It's all ready. Bring Anya if you can get her up."

Tara's broody teenage daughter was an expert at figuring out dreams and she would love us including her.

"Are you kidding me? She'll be wide awake the moment I tell her that we both had dreams. Yours included Charlie, too, I'm guessing … yes?"

"Yes, and then some."

"She'll come."

Half an hour later, the four of us were sitting around the fireplace in our study—or 'the great room' as I affectionately referred to it—a warm fire crackling, with Dennis in my lap and Alex at Kade's feet. Autumn was asleep in her bassinet, which we'd placed in a dark corner near my desk, away from the wall of windows, which faced the marsh in the backyard.

"So, after you flew to join me at Charlie's, what happened?" I'd been waiting and waiting to hear the rest of her dream, my curiosity only deepening in the half hour it took for them to arrive and get settled.

"I landed right next to you, and then Charlie came running out of the house with his gun, only he didn't point it at us, he was pointing it at the spirits circling us."

"Was there anyone else in the dream?" I was curious if Dawn was part of it.

"I was aware of being watched from within Charlie's house, but I didn't actually see anyone."

"Did he shoot at them?" Kade asked.

"No, I think he realized his bullets were useless, but the gun made him feel safe…." Tara's voice trailed off as she gave it some more thought. Knowing she needed time to ponder it, we remained silent and waited. After a minute or two, she shook her head in confusion. "He never really addressed us, but instead kept his focus on the spirits circling above our heads, like vultures waiting for their prey to die. I think he trusted that we would take care of it."

"That surprises you?" Kade asked.

"Yes, quite frankly. I mean, look at what he did to Tess, holding her there against her will, and Dawn too. But he seemed … I don't know, like he was not surprised by the demons circling his property, and I just can't help but think that is an important detail."

Anya nodded with enthusiastic agreement. "I think Charlie can feel the dark forces that are at work over there. He succumbed to their influence when Dawn showed up and then even more so when Tess arrived." She rose from the hassock next to her mother's chair and began pacing in circles in front of the fireplace. "In mom's dream, he didn't have anything against anyone except the spirits circling his property. It's why he didn't point the gun at Tess in her dream. I think his wife showing up is another sign that he isn't a threat … not to any of us, not anymore. It's why he was doing such a friendly task making tea."

"What about Dawn?" It worried me that Anya was going to say something I wouldn't like, but the question had to be asked.

"She's the dark horse in all this, isn't she?" Tara said, her tone skeptical.

"There's definitely more to her story, but I don't know that I'd call her a dark horse, mom." Anya gave me a sympathetic smile, for she knew I genuinely cared about Dawn, and shot her mother an annoyed glance.

"She's not entirely innocent," Kade said gently, raising a hand in a calming gesture, his eyes telling me to hear him out. "She lied about having psychic abilities, stalked both Dean and Lindsay, and tried to drive them apart."

"Not to mention the fact that she pushed you down into that room under the barn floor, Kade." Tara's mouth firmed with disapproval. "I know you have a soft spot for her, Tess, but she was staying with Charlie on her own free will."

The need to defend her was too strong for me to remain silent. "She pushed Kade to protect him from Charlie, though I agree it was a terrible plan, and I am not happy about her role in it. As for Charlie, she felt accepted by him. He was the father figure she's been wanting and needing in her life. And then he went and betrayed her trust by locking her in the basement."

"Which she basically went along with," Tara said. "At least initially, because she was hiding from Dean, though I don't understand why."

Neither did I, really. According to Dawn, she was over her crush on Dean by the time she landed on Charlie's doorstep, though Dean claimed otherwise. In any case, she needed a place to stay and using Charlie's beliefs concerning Dean earned her an invitation. "I am not excusing her behavior, not by any means, but for her own reasons, she's said and done things to achieve a desired outcome."

"Yes, like claiming to be a psychic," Tara murmured, the disapproval in her expression quite evident.

"She didn't tell him she was a psychic," I reminded her. "She said she got vibes." I was splitting hairs here, but I thought it an important point.

"Right," Tara said, the sarcasm in her tone barely veiled. "Same thing."

I didn't want to be at odds with Tara over this, especially as I understood that her loyalty to Kade and me was influencing her feelings. But what she didn't understand were the circumstances of Dawn's life and what led to her doing the things she'd done and continued to do. "By agreeing with Charlie, it put them on the same side, and she really wanted him to accept her. It also ensured that the two men wouldn't talk, for she didn't want Charlie to discover that she had worked with Dean, because she never told him about that, and she didn't want Dean to learn that she was friends with Lindsay."

Anya gave me a sympathetic smile. "I know you care about her, Tess, and I respect that, but I don't think she and I would be compatible for developing a friendship."

"Okay, okay." Tara waved a hand to get our attention and motioned for Anya to return to her seat. "Please sit, Anya, you make me dizzy watching you." She then turned her gaze onto me, her expression serious but kind, for she, too, did not want us at odds with each other. "We must consider Dawn's role in all this and …" She held up a hand when I started to say something, asking me to hear her out. "And what motivated her actions. In all honesty, I am very curious as to why she is still hiding. What, or whom, is she hiding from?"

"Dawn does factor pretty heavily in this whole thing," Kade agreed, his tone modulated enough to let me know he wasn't making any accusations, just an observation. "I know you took a liking to her, Sweetness, but we need to consider all the angles here."

He was right. I knew he was, but I couldn't stop myself from wanting to defend her. Dawn wasn't under investigation for anything, she was just someone who was part of a terrible situation, one that got out of control, and Lindsay's disappearance complicated the whole issue. "We need to find Lindsay."

"Yes, we do," Tara agreed. "And we can hope that her story here in our world hasn't ended." She looked over at her daughter. "Anya, have you any more insight to share on the dreams Tess and I had last night?" She waved a hand to encourage her daughter to take the floor. "I'm sure something is percolating in that brain of yours."

"I think part of the message in Tess's dream is that she should not be doing anything alone, no matter how safe she thinks the situation is." She tossed me a sidelong glance that spoke volumes and duly chastised, my face heated with chagrin.

"I think that's a great assessment." Kade gave Anya a wink of approval as he patted my leg in a gesture of comfort.

"I think so too," Tara agreed.

I couldn't find any dispute in that assessment, though I felt compelled to mentally defend myself. When I went to Charlie's house that day, I had no reason to believe I'd walk into the situation I did. And the second time, when I went to Lindsay's camp, I had no intention of going anywhere near Charlie—nor did I. Our meeting on the road was a complete shock.

"I don't think Charlie is really a problem either," Anya said. "In Tess's dream he had a gun but was not pointing it at her. And in yours, mom, you saw him with a gun, too, but he was pointing it at the spirits circling his house." She stood again and resumed walking in circles, talking things through. "I think it means that he is as much a victim of things as you were, Tess, and as Dawn was, though I think there's more to her story to consider." She stopped pacing and stood facing me. "You said, Tess, that in your dream she seemed different, and you weren't sure if you should be afraid or not, but Charlie wasn't threatening you at all. He offered you tea and ended up in the kitchen with his wife, whom you believe is a good person. Her appearing next to Charlie was to help you see that you have nothing to fear from him."

"But what about when Dawn grabbed my head? I felt pain even though I don't think she was trying to hurt me." That part of the dream totally confused me.

"She was trying to tell you something," Anya said. "She was trying to convey a message. Did you not get any impressions while she was holding you?"

"The pain in my head was too intense."

"Didn't you say you got a pain in your head at the Wheeler place?" Tara asked, though the question was rhetorical for she was only making a point. "And then you went dashing across the field and found that scarf."

"She expressed regret when you were in the Wheeler house waiting for me to help Dean," Kade reminded me. "Maybe she's trying to tell you that she feels pain for the things she's done..."

"No," Anya interjected. "If she was feeling pain for the things she's done, Tess would have felt it in her heart, not her head."

"In your dream, Tess, Dawn told you she'd been waiting for you," Tara said. "So that makes me wonder if she is, in fact, somewhere on one of those properties waiting for you to come to her." After a slight pause, she shook her head at her own assessment, unconvinced that this was the message. "I just don't know what to make of it. In my dream I knew there was someone in the house, but I didn't know who, though I'm guessing it was Dawn."

"The demons circling the property indicate that bad energy is present there." Anya, who had started pacing again, stopped this time to stand before her mother. "We should do a cleansing spell and try to clear some of it out."

"I agree," Tara said, smiling with approval over her daughter's suggestion. "And we need to find Dawn, and then focus on finding Lindsay."

"I think I should try to contact Lindsay." That announcement was met with silence. Kade's expression told me he thought it was a good idea, but he didn't like it. "If she's in spirit, she'll come to me. She might not tell me where her body is, but she might have a message for Charlie, and maybe Dean as well."

"I think it's a great idea," Tara said, correctly interpreting Kade's expression. "Lindsay isn't the bad person in this. We may not know who it is, but it isn't her. Tess will be okay."

"But I am getting a bad feeling about it," Kade said.

"How did you feel when you were sketching that picture of the girl, whom we are quite sure is Lindsay?" I asked him. "Did you feel like she was someone to be avoided?" Lindsay connected with him while he was drawing her, he surely must have gotten some impressions.

"We aren't positive it was Lindsay," he said.

"Come on, Kade, you know it was her." I stood and went over to the sketch in question, snapped a picture of it with my phone then sent it to Dean, asking if he recognized her.

Dean answered within a minute of my sending it. *Yes! That's Lindsay.*

I messaged him back saying that Kade had drawn the picture while out at the Wheeler farm. Seconds later, Dean called.

"Hi, Dean. I have you on speaker. Kade, Tara and Anya are here with me."

"Hey, everyone, I hope you are all doing well!" And then his voice lowered into a somber tone. "Does this picture mean she's … if Kade drew her then she's an angel now, isn't she?"

I didn't want to put a lid on his hopes of finding Lindsay alive, but I felt it was important to be honest with him. "It's not a certainty, but it's a possibility, Dean. I'm sorry."

298

He was silent for a few seconds, absorbing the news he was expecting anyway, though I knew it didn't lessen his hurt. "Do you have any idea where her body is?"

"Not yet. We were at the Wheeler place when Kade drew that sketch, and we aren't sure why she came through in that location."

"She told me she was over there all the time in her younger years," Dean said. "So, it's not surprising, really. She loved the Wheeler farm."

"What did she love about it?" Kade asked.

"She said she had good feelings while playing over there. She loved the barn. Of course, they had horses back then and she loved horses, so I think they attracted her too."

Now that I had him on the phone and he was able to see Kade's sketch, it was a good time to ask a few more questions. "Are there any special places, besides the barn, that she liked … like a spot in the woods for instance?" Maybe that would explain why we found the scarf in the woods, to lend significance to that area.

"She never mentioned anything like that. Let me enlarge the photo and look." We waited in silence and judging from the time he was taking, he was going over it very thoroughly. "I don't see anything, other than the old well. I see you have that in there."

It was interesting to hear him mention that, and my heartbeat sped up. "What about the well?"

"Charlie was always telling her not to run around in that area in case she fell into it. There's no water in it anymore. Lindsay told me they used it as a hiding spot when they were playing Hide and Seek over there."

Maybe that was the significance of it being added to Kade's drawing. It was yet another place that was connected to her. As for anyone hiding in it, that was quite impossible, it was frozen shut.

"We also found a scarf in the woods," Kade told him.

"You found a scarf?"

There was a strange quality to his voice that I couldn't quite determine. "Yes, a green one."

"Green?" Now his voice was definitely sounding weird.

Kade went to his desk and retrieved the scarf. "Dean, I'm sending a picture of it." His eyes met mine as we waited for Dean's response.

He was silent so long we thought we lost our connection. "Dean? Did you get it? Are you still there?"

"Yeah," Dean said, his voice hoarse with emotion. "That is Lindsay's scarf. Her mother made it for her just before she died. She would never part with it. Never."

Chapter 24

Considering the Wheeler farm's long history of spiritual significance, we decided it was the ideal location to try and contact Lindsay. Its atmospheric energy should be a perfect conduit to someone in the spirit world, especially when that someone was emotionally connected to the property.

Janice asked if she could attend and of course we told her she was welcome. It was her house after all—well, for the time being, and it was very generous of her to let us use it. She was so excited to be included that she called earlier to tell us she'd turned on the new furnace so the house would be warm, and she brought coffee and snacks for us to enjoy when we got there.

Since my arrival in Bucksport almost two years ago, I have discovered amazing connections between the investigations I'd become involved in. Tara, being well-versed in the town's peppered history, was a great source of information, and the more I learned, the more it became clear how intricately woven those connections were. Given the fact that the Wheeler farm and the people who had lived on it were a big part of it all, I felt it important to share what I'd learned with the whole group.

The sense of urgency to resolve things before the property's closing date weighed heavily on my mind. Aside from wanting to learn how

Lindsay's scarf ended up where it did, we wanted to know what fate had befallen her. Thus, the main reason for tonight's gathering. In addition to that, though, we also hoped to learn of Dawn's whereabouts. At least I did. The others, I suspected, didn't have that on their list of priorities. I understood why but I wished they knew Dawn better, for I believed they would be more in her corner if they did.

Another mystery that was of interest to all of us, was learning why the indigenous people of the area had considered this property, along with mine and Tara's, to be sacred ground. If everything unfolded as hoped, we might uncover something about that too.

Aside from Kade and I, our group consisted of Mary, her husband Daniel, Tara, Robin and, of course, Janice. Anya wanted to come but we needed someone to watch Autumn.

After arriving at the house, we helped ourselves to the coffee and snacks Janice had laid out, then gathered in the dining room to talk. Before moving on to our planned activity, I wanted to share what I'd learned about the property and Janice's ancestors. Beyond that, I hoped the conversation might stir interest from the spirit world, drawing in the souls connected to our purpose here—the very ones I wanted to contact.

Once we were settled around the table, I got right to it for we had a lot to accomplish, and no one wanted to be here any longer than necessary. "As most of you all know, we've been uncovering quite a bit of interesting history involving our properties and even some information on a few of our family ancestors." I took a sip of my coffee while considering how I wanted to present all the information without it getting complicated. "Almost all the family connections, which are also tied to our properties, involve Isi Rowan, a woman who lived more than three centuries ago. When I first came to Bucksport, I channeled her story through automatic

302

writing. Her descendants were prominent figures in Bucksport's history, though their stories are not well known. In fact, most of their stories were kept deliberately secret."

"Thanks to Tess's gift, she is bringing their stories to light," Tara interjected, giving me a warm smile.

I motioned for her to go ahead and recount what we knew so far, as she was more familiar with the local history than I was.

Tara was happy to do so because she loved talking about Bucksport's fascinating history. "A large part of the area, especially along the surrounding coastal waters, was once settled by people from the Wabanaki Confederacy. When tracts of land, which included the town of Bucksport, was parceled over to settlers from Massachusetts and New Hampshire, the local indigenous tribes were not happy about losing their free use of the land, which to them was meant for everyone to share."

"So, what's this have to do with my grandparents' property?" Janice asked.

Tara held up a hand for her to be patient. "I'm getting to that." She took a sip of her coffee and finished off a pastry before continuing. "The indigenous people believed certain areas of Bucksport held sacred significance, making them, in their view, ineligible for individual ownership. Of course, this didn't stop settlers from claiming the land, and a few local tribal groups were threatening to retaliate against these encroachments. Sacred ground, they argued, wasn't meant to belong to anyone, least of all to those who had no respect or connection to it."

"Unfortunately, we don't know why they believed the land sacred," I added, and glanced at Tara to see what she might say to that. I felt she knew more than she was letting on, and the way her eyes shifted away told me I was probably right.

Keeping her gaze on Janice, which made me feel she was deliberately avoiding eye contact with me, Tara continued. "To appease the indigenous people that were most upset by the dispute, some of the sacred land—including what is now my property, Tess's property, part of your grandparents' land, Janice, and even a small section of Charlie's—was eventually parceled out to settlers who had married into the tribes."

Janice's eyes widened with surprise. "Are you saying my grandparents' property is sacred?"

Tara nodded sagely. "I am! What is now our properties, eventually became allocated to descendants of Isi Rowan, whose story Tess channeled when she first got here."

Mary indicated she'd like to join the conversation and Tara gestured for her to have at it.

"Unions between indigenous people and incoming settlers were not acceptable by either party. But that didn't stop Ruth, a young woman from one of the families, and Rad Rivers, a respected guide and prominent member of a local tribe, from marrying. To ease some of the growing unrest, town officials approved the request from Ruth's family to allocate a portion of their land—the part considered sacred by the tribes—to the newlyweds."

This is where I jumped back in. "When I learned that Rad River's was Isi's nephew, son to her brother, I couldn't believe it. I mean, I'd first learned of him while investigating the Buck curse. As Tara said, he was one of the first guides the new settlers relied upon. He was respected, admired and well-liked by most everyone." Some of my enthusiasm dimmed when I shared the sad part of his story. "His life was cut short when he was murdered by three men who were passing through the area and not affiliated with the settlement. Later, his grandson, Kitchi would take up the mantle as a respected guide and continue his grandfather's legacy."

Now it was Kade who chimed in. "To maintain trust with the local tribes and to prevent the possibility of retaliation, Rad's murder was kept secret and the three men, unfortunately, managed to evade retribution."

Tara held up a hand to signal that she had something to add. "I know from reliable sources, however, that a private posse later tracked them down and took care of that oversight."

I looked at her in surprise, for she hadn't shared that information with me before, but not wanting to get sidetracked, I let it go. "I just want to touch a little more on Isi's story because her legacy lives on today—through Tara, the Coven, and our properties. Not just Tara's and mine, but also yours, Janice."

The interconnectedness of it all left me in awe. Everything I'd been drawn into—the story I channeled, the people I met, the mysteries I uncovered, and even the land I purchased—was linked in ways that were too significant to be a coincidence. Even those gathered around me realized that. I could see it in their expressions.

"Through writing Isi's story, I discovered she possessed extensive knowledge of plants and their healing properties, and she was well-versed in esoteric wisdom. Her grandmother, whom Isi referred to as a 'Chosen One'—what I believe to be akin to a Shaman or medicine woman—taught her and Rad's father, Isi's brother, everything she knew. This wisdom was passed down through the generations, and I suspect Tara has inherited much of it as well, thanks to the meticulous records kept by the Coven, which was founded by Isi and Rad's ancestors."

Now for the part that I was tickled about. "My property was once inhabited by Rad's family, and people used to go to them for help with ailments and other issues."

"I remember people thinking a witch was involved with your property somehow," Janice said. "We used to refer to the area around your place as Witch Woods."

"That's right, Janice, that is exactly how the woods on my property gained that reputation." While I finished off my donut and coffee, I gestured for Mary to go ahead and share what I could see she was eager to impart.

"Many of my family are Isi's descendants because Clay Rowan, whom Isi married, is in my father's family tree. My maiden name is Rowan."

"That's all so amazing. How exciting to learn all of that!" Janice exclaimed.

Tara's expression became somber. "It's why I have been upset about you selling the property. It's been in your family since the area was first settled." She gave her an understanding smile, one that told Janice she had no ill will towards her. "For the first time in the past three centuries, someone outside the Coven will be in possession of it. But I do understand why you are letting it go, and I am at peace with it."

Janice looked contrite. "I'm sorry, Tara, but I just can't keep it..."

Tara waved away her apology. "I don't blame you, I am just sad. But you've nothing to apologize for."

Janice looked genuinely saddened, though I could see, even before she spoke, that it would not change her decision. "I'm truly impressed by all you've shared with me, I really am. But I feel in my soul that this is the right thing to do." Her face softened with apology. "I'm sorry that I have no interest in my grandmother's Coven activities, though I do find it fascinating. But honestly, it feels like it's all over my head—and far too much responsibility for me to take on."

I thought it unfortunate she felt that way, but she had every right to do what she believed was best for herself, and I respected her for being honest with us.

Tara clapped her hands to dispel the solemn air. "Okay, enough talk. Let's move on to the reason for our gathering."

Chapter 25

While Mary and Janice tidied the dining room and kitchen, Kade, Daniel and I gathered chairs, arranging them in a circle in the living room.

Tara, meanwhile, focused on her own preparations, lighting candles and placing them in strategic spots, then swishing a smoldering bundle of sage and sweetgrass around the room, cleansing it of negative energy. When she was finished with that, she turned to look at us. "If everyone would please sit down, I will protect our circle and then we can begin."

I took a seat, with Kade settling into the chair on my right, then Janice next to him, followed by Mary, Daniel, and Robin. The chair to my left remained empty for Tara, who was walking the outer perimeter of our circle, her supple fingers moving in a melodious dance, like reeds swaying in a gentle wind.

She chanted low, under her breath, her words unintelligible to us, and I knew this was intentional. A witch's words were her own and not always meant to be shared.

As she often told me, casting energy for a specific purpose was deeply personal, and how we chose to do it was up to us. The point wasn't to be focused on reciting something word for word—unless it was a powerful incantation whose strength came from consistent usage—because that shifted the focus to the wording and not on the intention itself. When it came to something like invoking spiritual protection, as Tara was doing, her words alone were all we needed.

Even before Tara had finished, I could feel a soft hum of warm energy vibrating around us. I knew the others felt it, too, for everyone was visibly relaxing, looking comfortable and in a positive state of mind. Even Janice, who I was initially worried about, had become very quiet.

Finally, Tara sat down and nodded for me to begin.

My first order of business was to prepare everyone. "Okay then, Tara has neutralized any lingering negative energy and secured a ring of protection around us, ensuring that malevolent entities stay out." Although everyone understood what Tara had done, I explained it anyways, for voicing it strengthened the intent of her activities. "Now, I want you to imagine that we are sitting within a circle of light, which extends behind us by a couple of feet. Within this light, no negative energy may enter. We are inviting only positive energies to interact with us, and we are seeking to communicate with Lindsay. If, that is, she is residing in spirit. But others who feel they must talk to us are welcome as well." I glanced at each person in turn, even Kade, though I knew he understood this process very well. "Is everyone in agreement with this and okay for us to continue?"

Everyone nodded their assent.

"Okay then. Let's rest our hands on our laps, palms up. This shows an openness for communication and acceptance of loving entities to interact with us, specifically, but not limited to, our loved ones and any spirit who has been active here in this house or in Charlie's. I shall act as the communicator for them, but you may get impressions, thoughts, ideas or pictures in your mind. You may experience smells or physical sensations. Spirit beings communicate with us in many ways and in a manner we can easily accept. Experiencing these things is normal, especially when in a focused group like this, so don't be surprised if someone comes through to you. I ask that if you do get anything, any thoughts or impressions, any mental pictures that suddenly flash through your mind, that you share them with all of us."

Once again everyone nodded their assent.

"Good, I can feel positive vibrations around us and there are many spirits who would love to come through!" This was always the case whenever a circle was opened to spirit communication. Those in the Tri-State were always eager to come through and opportunities like this were rare. It certainly didn't happen often enough. "I think the word is out in the Tri-State and everyone wants to join the party!"

"Tri-State?" Janice ducked her head in apology for speaking. "Sorry, I don't mean to interrupt, I just don't understand what that is. I know you've mentioned it before, Tess, but I've forgotten what it means."

"No apology necessary, Janice. The Tri-State is what you might think of as 'the other side' or the afterlife. I call it that because I believe when we die that we enter a place between life on the physical realm and life in the beyond, which encompasses what many believe to be heaven and hell." I met her eyes and asked her in silence if that answered her question.

Janice nodded that it did and motioned for me to continue, lowering her head and closing her eyes to show her readiness.

"Unfortunately, we cannot speak to them all, for there are many, so I am going to ask Sheila to help determine who may come through." I found this to be necessary over the past few months for the more I did this sort of thing, the more spirits I attracted, their eagerness to come through making it difficult to decide who did and who did not. Sheila offered her assistance in the matter, and I now turned to her during every message circle. She knew whom we needed to speak with the most, whose message was important to hear, and she helped to control the masses. It was rather overwhelming how many Tri-State inhabitants wished to come through.

Aloud I addressed them, as much for the benefit of the others as for the spirits crowding the outer rim of our circle. "To those whom we do not have the time to speak with, we send love and light to you all."

I closed my eyes and focused on Sheila, telling her I was ready for the first spirit to come through.

Most of the entities swirling around us were positive and loving but as always, even negative energy was attracted to situations like this. It was why it was so important to have protections in place and our intent clear and specific. Tara was an expert at knowing exactly what to do. I did not fear something penetrating our circle and bringing with them an unpleasant experience. Everyone here trusted her and that would ensure that fear had no place within our thoughts, which was a good thing because fear weakened the protective shield.

"Now that Tara has done her magic," I paused to cast her a smile and a wink, to which she returned the same, then continued. "Within this circle we are safe."

Speaking the words, saying them aloud, was akin to casting an incantation, for each significant word, beyond the filler that forms a sentence, carries a potent vibrational energy, capable of radiating positive or negative forces. The outcome, of course, depends on the intentions behind them. The adage 'the pen is mightier than the sword' holds a profound truth for words do indeed possess a formidable power. The old saying 'sticks and stones may break my bones, but words will never hurt me' couldn't be further from the truth.

The challenge, and one I often encounter when relaying the messages I receive, was in the interpretation of the words used. The impact of these

312

messages relies heavily on personal context, and it is quite common for certain words to be received in stark contrast to an intended meaning. What one saw as a powerful positive word, another might perceive as a potent negative one. This created the potential for dissent and misunderstanding and often division. It's why spirits frequently communicate via emotional responses and visual prompts, though I found that those, too, could be just as confusing. Their meaning might not be interpreted accurately by the messenger, which was me in this case. It's why I preferred to share what I saw and let people make up their own minds as to what it meant. I did, however, understand feelings quite well, gaining entire concepts through the emotions they conveyed. It was a much more effective method than a string of words that might be taken wrong.

The sudden awareness of a spirit within our midst caught my attention and I opened my eyes. "Someone is here. She wants to speak to you, Janice."

Janice's head shot up, her eyes wide, but she nodded that she was okay with it.

"I think it's your grandmother." I saw her clearly in my mind's eye. "She's about five feet tall and has a stocky build, very robust, having an ample bosom from what I can see, for she's mostly facing you." The forms we had in our earthly existence did not follow us into the spirit world, for "over there" we were light beings and free from the constraints of bodily forms. But, when spirits sought to communicate, they often chose to appear as they had when they were alive, though sometimes they were at a different age than they were when they died. This was especially helpful for purposes of recognition, and it usually encouraged acceptance of their presence.

"That sounds like my grandmother." Janice's expression became worried. "I hope she's not mad at me for selling the property."

"She says the property can take care of itself and you should do whatever you feel is right for you." I looked at Tara. "She says to tell you that you've nothing to worry about as far as the property is concerned."

Tara smiled in gratitude for the message. "That's good to hear. Thank you, Maureen."

Her energy was so warm and caring that it saddened me to think someone like her had suffered the mental degradation of dementia. This was something I was still trying to understand … why people got certain illnesses, especially ones as debilitating to the mental faculties as dementia and Alzheimer's.

"Your grandmother loves you, Janice, and is proud of you for joining us this afternoon." Messages of love are the most important and, in my opinion, the only ones necessary to hear.

"I love you too, Grandma, and I miss you and Grandpa so much." Her eyes tearing up, Janice sniffled, and Tara reached under her chair to retrieve a box of tissues she'd placed there earlier. Janice gratefully pulled a tissue free and wiped her eyes. "I'll never stop missing them."

"They are always with you, Janice." It seemed that was the main reason for Maureen's appearance for once the message was given, she transformed into a bright flare of light, which then condensed into a small orb.

I heard several gasps and then saw what had captured their attention. Maureen's orb was visible to everyone. It zipped around our circle, danced in front of Janice for a few seconds then zoomed out of sight.

"That was amazing!" Janice exclaimed. "I mean, I've seen pictures of orbs but that's the first time I've actually seen one in person, and it was my grandmother! I could see her orb clear as day."

It was a special gift Maureen gave to all of us, letting us see her thusly. "It was amazing indeed, Janice!"

Before I could expound upon it some more, I felt another entity coming through and quickly warned everyone for they were still talking about Maureen's orb appearance. "We've someone else…" He materialized in front of me, and I stood to face him, staring in shock and concern. Why was he coming through? We'd made our peace and shared everything that needed to be said.

Kade grasped my hand, giving it a gentle squeeze, and spoke to me in a low, urgent voice. "Who is it?"

I glanced around, surprised that no one saw him, not even Tara who was getting increasingly comfortable with spirit contact. "Mike is here." It was Mike's passing from a vehicle accident involving a drunk driver that sent me down a dark road just over three years earlier. I'd wanted to talk to him so badly after it first happened, to see him one more time and say all the things I wished we'd had the time to say, but it took two years before that finally happened. Kade had just entered my life and seeing Mike had helped me move on, to accept love into my life again. He wasn't here to confuse my feelings for Kade, that could never happen anyway, but it did seem strange to be standing in front of my first husband while my current one sat nearby.

Mike gave me his lopsided smile, the one that always melted my heart, though this time it just felt familiar and comforting. "Tess, you always want to see the good in everyone, it is one of the things that everyone loves about you, but sometimes it is also one of your biggest obstacles."

"What do you mean?" Was he trying to warn me about something?

"What's he saying?" Tara asked.

I forgot that no one else could see or hear him, which seemed impossible because he was as solid in appearance as the rest of us. "He's telling me that my tendency to see the good in people can sometimes cloud my judgment." I looked at Mike to see if that was what he meant and he smiled again, that beautiful smile I used to love so much. I still did, only it didn't send my heart into a flutter anymore. I smiled back. "You look great, Mike. How's Tootsie doing?"

"She's carefree and happy, content to receive all the attention she gets from every other loving soul she encounters."

Losing my dog had been nearly as painful as losing my husband. I'd loved them both so much and in one fell swoop, in an instant of time … they were gone from me.

"Your daughter is beautiful."

I looked at Kade and gave his hand a tug. He rose to stand beside me, his expression wreathed with curiosity. He wasn't threatened by Mike's appearance, nor should he be. He knew he held my heart and devotion, and he trusted my loyalty to him, but he also knew I would never stop loving Mike. "He's telling us that our daughter is beautiful."

"Well, of course she is." Kade's hand squeezed mine. "But I appreciate him saying so."

"Why are you here, Mike?" He'd shown up on other occasions, when I was most in need, and it did worry me a bit that he was here now, telling me to be careful about expecting everyone to be a good person. Who was he referring to? Lindsay? Dawn? Dean? Charlie? If any one of them was someone to be concerned about, I needed to know.

"As a lawyer, I always had to determine if the people I was defending deserved my defense of them."

Mike was indeed passionate about defending the innocent and exposing the sins of criminals, and given he was reminding me of that, it made me wonder if someone was in a position to conduct criminal behavior against me. Is that what he was here to warn me of?

"You know my goal was always to reveal the bad deeds done by people and end their reign of terror on others," he said, his voice modulated with gentle tones, for he was not here to censure or scare me. "You also need to do the same, but in a different context."

"What is he saying to you, Tess?" Daniel asked.

"He's reminding me how, as a lawyer, he had to determine guilt or innocence when it came to representing someone. His goal was to protect the innocent and expose criminal activity. But sometimes, thanks to the convincing lies criminals make in order to appear innocent, you really don't know for sure if they are innocent or not." I looked at Mike to see if he approved of my explanation and he gave me a smiling nod of approval.

"Why is he giving you that advice, Tess?" Tara asked, sounding worried. "Is there a criminal out there..." She waved her hand about. "That you need to be aware of?"

Mike came closer, until I could feel his vibrational energy trilling over my nerve endings. He was doing it for effect, to make it clear to me that I needed to take heed of his advice. "Trust your gut instincts. Always."

But I knew that and always tried...

"No, you don't." Mike said, reading my thoughts. "Sometimes your mind makes a determination about someone based on your emotional response to them."

"Who are you talking about, Mike?"

"You know I can't tell you that," he said, reproval and regret in his voice. "But I can give you advice, so that is what I am doing. Plus, I wanted to tell you that your daughter is going to do special, amazing things as she matures. Share everything you know with her. You've already started. Don't ever stop."

"What's being said?" Mary asked.

"Mike is telling me that Autumn is going to do amazing things, and he's reminding me to share all my knowledge with her, which I am doing already. I created an email account for her, and I send stuff to it all the time."

"What kind of stuff?" Tara asked, also very interested.

"I've written her a letter for one, but I also send other bits of information I want her to know, or a memory I don't want to forget. I send articles, or whatever it is I feel the need to share with her. I also have a file where I add hard copies of things I don't want to get lost in the ethers of the internet."

"Wow, that's a great idea, Tess," Mary exclaimed, her eyes glowing with excitement over the idea. "I shall do the same for Jewel." Mary's year-old daughter was an unexpected blessing, and I knew they, Jewel and Autumn, would grow to be the best of friends.

"I do something similar by annotating things in my grimoire, which will someday go to Anya," Tara said. "I hope she will continue to add to it and then pass it on to her children." She laughed at that last part, looking a little uncomfortable even saying it. "I am not in a hurry to be a grandmother." She lifted a finger to stop what she figured Robin was about to say. "Yes, of course I want grandchildren someday, but I'm in no hurry for her to give me any. Children consume so much of their parents' lives. Until they leave the nest that is."

"Which some don't do right away," Daniel said, his voice theatrically grim.

We all laughed, but I knew, despite his occasional expression of disgruntlement, that Daniel was in no hurry for his oldest son, who was 19, to fly from the nest.

Mike's energy was beginning to weaken, and I watched as he slowly began to fade from my sight. "You've good friends here, Tess. A good life. I'm happy for you."

"Thank you, Mike. I feel very blessed. Give Tootsie a big hug for me."

He gave me a wink, then he was gone.

"Mike said I was lucky to have all of you in my life." Not his exact words but that's what he meant.

"We are just as lucky in return," Kade said and gave me a kiss. "Is he gone?"

"Yes." We sat back down, and I asked Sheila if Lindsay was available. She was the main target for this session after all.

"She's not here."

"Because...?"

Silence. Ugh. I figured she'd be mum about that. To the others I spoke aloud. "I'm not getting Lindsay."

"Does that mean she is still alive?" Robin asked.

"I don't know. Sheila isn't sharing that information with me."

"How frustrating," Tara mumbled.

I wanted to laugh, for I could totally relate to that, but before I could do so, we heard a loud commotion outside, much like what Kade and I had heard when we were exploring the area near the barn.

We all jumped up at once but stayed within our circle. Then we heard the oddest sound—like a cork popping from a bottle, but much louder, and that sent Kade and Daniel into a run.

My first instinct was to chase after them, but I turned to Tara first. "We need to do a quick protective spell."

Tara nodded and grasped my hands. We did the protective incantation that she'd taught me, with Mary joining in and Robin doing a silent prayer of her own. Then, with a look that we had each other's back, we rushed after the men, telling Janice to stay close as we did so.

It did concern me that we were leaving Tara's protective circle, but we were being led away from it for a reason and could not ignore the call.

As we rushed out into the dimming light of early evening, I wondered what we were heading into, and prayed we were finally going to get some answers concerning Lindsay. After all, the last time we heard that sound, we found Lindsay's scarf.

Chapter 26

Kade and Daniel's mad dash came to an abrupt halt when they rounded the side of the house, nearly causing a collision with us girls, though we managed to skirt around them. I was about to ask what was wrong when I noticed they stood frozen in wonder, their eyes locked on something in the field.

I looked to see what had caught their rapt attention but saw nothing out of the ordinary. "What are you guys looking at?" When they didn't reply right away, I tapped Kade's arm to get his attention. "What are you looking at?"

Kade glanced at me briefly, his expression incredulous. "You don't see it?"

"See what?" Tara asked.

"If I can see it, you girls should definitely be able to see it," Daniel said, his expression as incredulous as Kade's.

Her face etched with exasperation, Tara threw her hands up in the air. "Will you please answer our question and tell us what the heck you are looking at?"

Kade frowned in confusion. "That geyser blowing sky high. You seriously don't see it?"

"Geiser?" What on earth was he talking about? Surely, I misunderstood him. "As in water shooting up into the air?" I looked again but still saw nothing. Why would they be seeing something like that when the rest of us could not?

"Yes, as in water shooting up in the air. Lots of it." Kade pulled his gaze from the field and focused it on us, the vertical frown line between his brows a clear indication of his puzzlement. "You seriously don't see it? I mean, it's spouting like Old Faithful at Yellowstone, coming straight up from that old well we found." He turned back to stare at his vision (for that's all it could be), his awe over the sight making me wish I could see it too. He shook his head in amazement. "So much for thinking it's run dry."

"You see water spouting up from the well?" Tara asked, her skeptical delivery telling them that what they saw could not be real.

It was Daniel who answered, though he didn't bother to look our way. "There is definitely water shooting up into the air, whether you see it or not."

Okay then, it was time to find out what this vision of theirs was all about. So off I went, with the others following in my wake, except for Kade who kept pace beside me.

"Is the water still gushing?" I asked him.

"Yes. I can even feel the spray." He was fascinated by the phenomenon, and I couldn't blame him. It wasn't often that he could see something I could not, other than when he was painting that is.

When we were just a few feet away, Kade wiped his face with both hands, his steps faltering. "The water is pouring all over me and it's cold as hell."

"Yeah, buddy, me too," Daniel said, and ran his hands through his hair as if wringing excess water from it.

"There's no water coming out of the well," I assured them.

Kade continued to swipe at the water he believed was spraying over him. "Yeah? Well, explain to me what I am seeing then, and why I am covered with freezing water."

Daniel had stopped several feet away and was holding an arm up to shield his face from the spray. "This is crazy." He looked at his wife, then the rest of us, incredulous that we could not validate what he was experiencing. "Can't you see that I am soaked?"

"No. You look very dry to me." Mary reached out and touched him. "Yup, dry."

Robin, Tara and I surrounded the well, getting as close to the metal cover as we dared. It looked like it might still be frozen to the ground, but when I leaned down and grasped the edge of it and yanked, it easily lifted from its resting place.

"It stopped!" Both men said in unison.

I turned to see them staring at each other in amazement.

"You don't look wet, Daniel," Kade said.

"Neither do you, Kade," he replied.

"But I feel like I am soaked," Kade told him, holding his arms out and surveying himself in disbelief and confusion. "I mean, I can feel it and see it."

"Me too," Daniel said.

I tightened my grip on the cold, rusted edge of the cover and lifted it high enough to push onto the grass, leaving the well open for our inspection.

It was deeper than I thought it would be, and the dimming daylight made it impossible to see very far into it. A cold shiver and a feeling of dread washed over me, and I stepped away.

"What's wrong?" Tara asked, as she, too, took a step back, gesturing for Robin to do the same.

"I don't know, but I have an awful feeling in the pit of my stomach." I continued to back away until I bumped into Kade, who put his arms around me.

He was shivering so badly I could hear his teeth chattering, and I twisted in his arms to look at him. "You are freezing!"

He gave me a quivering smile, his face scrunching into a grimace. "Y-yes, the w-wet clothes are m-m-making it worse in th-this c-cold weather."

"But your clothes are dry." I couldn't believe he was still under the effects of his illusion.

"I h-hear you, T-t-tess, and I b-believe you, but that d-doesn't change how I f-f-feel or what I s-see."

"This is truly fascinating," Tara said.

"Mary, would you mind going to our truck and getting the flashlight that's sitting in the console between the front seats?" Figuring she was the most agile among us, I gave her the task, which she readily ran off to complete, and then I turned to look at Kade and Daniel with concern. "You guys need to go to the house and get warm."

Kade managed to stutter his protest between violent shivers. "I don't … want … t … to … l-l-leave you … h-here a…a…alone."

"You won't do us any good if you get hypothermia! I am only going to look down in the well, that's all. We'll rejoin you once we've done that … no matter what we see." It was that last part that made his eyes narrow, indecision warring with the cold wracking his body. "Seriously, you need to go warm up."

Kade resisted for only a couple more seconds then nodded. "F-fine, b-b-but Daniel a-and I w-w-will be w-watching you fr-from the w-w-

324

window." Though agreeing to it, he clearly didn't like the plan, but his shivering was increasing. "P-promise me, n-no matter w-what, you w-w-will come r-right back t-t-to the house after you've seen i-if there's a-a-anything d-down there."

"I will do what needs to be done, but I promise to be careful. Besides, I'm not alone and you will be watching us."

Though his shivers were as violent as Kade's, Daniel couldn't ignore his curiosity. "Wh-what d-d-do y-you e-expect t-t-to f-find?"

"I don't know." But I did have a suspicion, one I hoped was wrong.

Though both men were reluctant to leave, they were eager to head back to somewhere warm, their movements stiff with cold, and I prayed they suffered no lasting effects. It really wasn't so surprising they were responding as they were. The mind cannot differentiate between a vision and actual reality, so their bodies were responding to what they believed they saw and felt.

Mary met up with them when coming back from our car and paused to speak to them before running to join us. "Did you see how bad they are shivering?"

"Yes, and I hope they come out of it soon or we are going to have to treat them for hypothermia." Worried as I was about the men, I switched my focus to the immediate task at hand. First, we'd have a look in the well, because I think that was the point of this whole thing … to get us out here to have a look. I also suspected that it was spirit's plan for the men to return to the house, and I didn't like it. Why were we being separated?

"I have a weird feeling," Tara said, speaking low, her focus on the well.

Before I shined the light into it, I reached out to Sheila. *"Are you here?"*

"Always."

"Are we in danger?"

"The only thing you have to fear, Tess, is the fears you create."

"I'm not creating this."

"We won't get into that right now. But you will agree, will you not, that how you respond to it is your creation?"

"What are you waiting for?" Robin asked, peering down into the well and glancing up briefly to question my hesitation.

"I was just having a chat with Sheila." I stepped forward, my heart pounding so hard it was loud in my ears, and I shined my flashlight into the abyss.

And there she was. Dawn.

"Oh my God!" Mary gasped.

She looked like she was sleeping, curled up on mounds of hay that lay beneath her.

Robin grasped my arm in shock and dismay. "Is she dead?"

Tara, though shocked, was the calmest among us. "Do you know who that is, Tess?"

I turned my light off and on, focusing its beam on her face, praying she was just sleeping, or at worst, unconscious. Either way, she looked at peace.

And then her eyes opened. The moment she noticed us, they widened in surprise, and she struggled to sit up. "Oh my gosh! You found me!"

"Are you hurt, Dawn?" I was so relieved to find her alive that I felt weak in the knees and dropped to the cold ground, though I leaned over the edge to keep her in my sights.

326

"I have a headache but other than that, I think I'm okay." She braced her hands on the wall of the well and got to her feet. "Can you get me out of here?"

Standing fully erect, with her hands extended up to me, she was only a few inches out of reach. I looked at Tara and Mary as a plan formed in my head. "Can you each keep hold of a leg while I lean into the well and pull her out?"

They readily agreed as I got down onto my stomach and they positioned themselves in place. "Dawn, I am going to pull you up. Do you think you are okay for me to do that?"

"Yes, I think so."

With Tara and Mary each holding a leg, ensuring I didn't fall into the well, I extended my reach, and we easily locked arms. She was surprisingly warm, her grip firm. How long had she been down there and who put her there?

Luckily Dawn wasn't very heavy, being slight of build, and I easily managed to pull her up. Once we were all back on our feet, I wrapped my arms around her, relieved to see she was okay. "Thank God, we found you."

"What took you so long?" Dawn pulled away and looked at me with accusation in her eyes. "I thought you were a psychic."

"She isn't a psychic, she's a medium," Tara said, her tone as defensive as her posture.

It was quite obvious to me that Tara had taken an instant dislike for Dawn, and that made me sad. She needed a community of support, and I wanted it to be me and my friends.

"I thought you would never come," she said, ignoring Tara and looking only at me.

"How long have you been down there?" I asked her, doing my best to temper my guilt for not sensing her presence sooner, as she obviously had expected.

"Long enough. Even a few minutes is too long."

"Who put you there?" Tara asked her.

Dawn turned her head to give Tara a long, considering look. "Are you the witch she told me about?"

Tara's eyes widened and she looked over at me, clearly not pleased that I'd shared that information with her.

I shrugged in apology. "We were trapped in Charlie's basement, held there against our will, and sharing information seemed the thing to do at the time."

"Who are these people, Tess?" Dawn gestured toward them with an attitude just short of disdain, which had me concerned. Her personality was different than what I encountered in Charlie's basement.

"These are my friends, Dawn." I pointed to each as I gave their name. "That is Tara, Robin and Mary. Janice owns the property."

I could tell by the uncomfortable feel in the air that none of them liked her and I, too, was getting second thoughts about … everything. Mike's words came to mind, his warning that I tended to only see the good in people, my judgement sometimes clouding my emotions, and I glanced at the house, thinking now that I wished the men were still with us, though why I would feel that way I couldn't say. It wasn't like Dawn was going to turn on us and do something the five of us together couldn't handle.

Thinking it might go better if we were somewhere warm, I gestured towards the house. "We should go in the house. It's cold out here and…"

"I am not going in that house ever again!" Dawn said, interrupting me and backing away, as if she expected me to force her.

"It's cold out here and getting colder as the sun sets." We had all run out here without jackets and were beginning to feel the effects of the chill air.

"I'm going back to Charlie's." Dawn turned about and started across the field.

The rest of us exchanged looks, incredulous that she was acting that way, especially after we had just rescued her.

I couldn't just let her go. "Dawn, come back and we will take you over there in the car!"

But she kept going, her steps increasing in speed.

Not wanting to lose her again, I started after her, tossing instructions over my shoulder as I broke into a run. "Go get the men, grab your cars and meet us over at Charlie's!"

Tara's voice rose in alarm. "Tess, don't. Come with us and we'll drive over together and deal with that bratty girl."

I couldn't stop to argue with her for I was determined to keep Dawn in my sight, so I yelled my response hoping Tara heard me. "She might disappear on us again!"

"Just let her go," Robin said, her voice barely carrying to me.

Dawn disappeared into the trees, but I knew where she was going and stopped to deal with my friends' objections, calling to them across the distance. "She's been through a lot. You don't know her like I do." Not that I knew her well, but I knew things about her that they didn't, things that made me want to help her.

I saw a quick discussion ensue between the four of them, then Robin and Janice set off for the house, while Tara and Mary came running towards me.

Satisfied that I wouldn't be alone, I turned and headed after Dawn. I thought I heard Kade calling me, but kept going, knowing the girls would explain.

When I heard Tara and Mary's footsteps growing louder behind me, I spoke to them over my shoulder. "You guys could have driven over there."

"We aren't letting you out of our sight," Tara said, catching my arm and linking hers through it. "I'm sure Kade isn't happy about us running off like this." She glanced back at Mary then slowed our pace, giving her a chance to catch up and flank my other side.

"Janice and Robin are filling the guys in," Mary said, her breath a little harsh from the sudden excursion.

I didn't say it aloud, but I was relieved to have my friends with me. I wasn't afraid of Dawn, but I didn't know what we would encounter once we got to Charlie's, and it was nice to not be alone.

Like the last time.

Chapter 27

When we broke through the trees, Dawn was nowhere in sight, so we stopped to look about, seeing no sign of her. Then I spotted a movement on the front porch and urged my friends in that direction. "She's going in the house."

As we neared the porch, we saw that the front door was wide open and came to a stop at the bottom of the steps. I looked at my two dear, loyal friends and they stared back at me with reserved expressions, waiting for me to give them direction. "The last thing we need to do is rush in on her. Let me try and talk to her first. If you two could just hang back a bit so she doesn't feel like we are ganging up on her, maybe she will be more comfortable."

"I don't know about this girl, Tess," Tara whispered. "I'm getting some bad vibes from her."

Mary nodded. "Me too."

"There is nothing good about this whole business with Charlie, so it isn't so surprising you feel that way…"

"But I don't get bad vibes from you, Tess," Tara cut in, her glance darting at the house to ensure Dawn didn't appear in the doorway.

"I want to help her if I can." I glanced from Tara to Mary, and they reluctantly gave a nod that they would honor my request. Satisfied they had my back, I headed up the steps with them following a few paces behind.

The house was cold and dark, and I worried that Charlie's electricity had been turned off. If the temperature remained below freezing, his water pipes would freeze. Then it hit me that I was worrying over things I couldn't control and shook it off. I had enough to deal with, the fate of Charlie's water pipes being the least of my concern.

It was eerily quiet, which put me on edge, sending shivers of unease skittering along my spine. Dawn was near, I could sense her, and I wasn't leaving until we had a chance to talk. "Dawn?"

The only sounds were those of Tara and Mary entering the house.

"We need to find the light switches," Tara muttered, her hands feeling along the wall. A few seconds later, the living room light came on.

From my vantage point, I could see most of the kitchen and the entire living room, and Dawn was nowhere in sight. The bathroom door was open so I could see she wasn't in there either. Then a sudden thought popped into my head that she'd gone down to the basement, and it made my blood run cold. I didn't want to go down there, and I wouldn't.

"She might have gone upstairs," Mary said, though her tone was doubtful.

Before I could reply that I didn't think so, the front door slammed closed, and the three of us swung around, expecting to see Dawn.

But we saw no one.

Mary tried unsuccessfully to open it. With a groan of frustration, she turned back to us, her face wreathed in worry. "I'm getting a bad feeling..." A gasp of surprise cut off whatever else she was going to say, for the light in the room began to grow dimmer and dimmer, fading fast.

332

I hurried to be near my friends, worried that we would lose each other in the darkness. But I didn't make it.

Plunged into pitch black, with no visible light anywhere, not even from the windows, I stretched my hands out in front of me and waved them through the air. "Tara? Mary?"

Silence.

I should have waited for everyone to get here, especially Kade. But once again, I ignored all the safety rules and cautionary measures one takes in these kinds of situations and came on my own. Well, with the exception of Tara and Mary, though I couldn't take credit for them being here. And now, thanks to their loyalty to me, they could be in peril. Worried as I was, I reminded myself that they could handle whatever we were facing. Mary was close enough to Tara that they should be together, and they would use the knowledge of their craft to ensure their safety.

Concerned as I was for my friends, I felt quite strongly that this was happening for my benefit, to separate me from them. Fine. So be it. Standing erect and drawing strength from the SPORCE (I still loved using Selenah's acronym for Spiritual Force), I mentally placed a protective ring around my auric field and sent out a silent message that I was ready to talk. Who or what was doing this, I didn't know, but I wondered if Dawn was caught up in it too. She wouldn't know how to deal with the dark energy swirling around me.

"It's time, Tess, for you to leave the physical world and join us in the spiritual realm."

The voice sounded friendly, almost loving, but it didn't sit right with me. Such a message was nothing I welcomed hearing. *"I don't think so."*

"You question the plan?"

"What plan?"

A figure was approaching, I felt her disturbance before I saw the swirls of energy cascading around her. As I focused on it, the swirling mist slowly parted, allowing light to filter through, revealing an approaching figure. Though she appeared in silhouette against the ever-increasing light, the closer she came to me, the better I could see her.

My heart skipped a beat then sped up, my initial joy at seeing her turning to concern. Why show herself now? It was Sheila. I'd always imagined how she'd look, and this was the exact image I had of her in my mind. A tiny voice in the back of my head told me not to take everything at face value. Those tiny voices, when lucky enough to notice them, should not be ignored.

"Hello, Tess. I've come to bring you into my world. It's time."

No. I didn't believe that. I wouldn't believe it. I had a daughter who needed me. I had a husband I wanted to grow old with. I had friends I wanted to get to know better. I still had things to do, places to see, stuff to learn. *"I'm not going with you."*

Sheila smiled in response, though I didn't think it reached her beautiful blue eyes. *"Attachment to the physical world is the hardest of things to let go of. I understand. But this is our plan."*

It didn't feel right. I always believed that when the time came for me to transition to spirit, I'd be ready, and I was most definitely not ready. *"Then I am changing the plan. It is my right to do so."*

Sheila's eyes narrowed ever so slightly and that made me wonder if it was really her. She wouldn't get upset over this. She'd accept my decision. *"Who are you?"*

The question made her features harden and I could swear a shadow dropped over her. She came closer, moving in an instant, and suddenly she was inches from me. I instinctively wanted to step back but held my ground. I would not give in to my fear.

She offered me her hand. *"You don't want to change the plan. You'll see when you are in spirit with me that this is best."*

I could sense a distant voice telling me to resist and it was that voice I focused on and listened to. *"No, and I don't believe you are Sheila."*

Our eyes locked, my gaze defiant, and she began to fade before my eyes, the light around her dimming, becoming darker and darker until she blended with the shadows, then getting darker still, until I was once again in complete darkness.

This was when I needed my Spirit Guide. My true Spirit Guide. *"Sheila! Help me out of here."*

"You have only to change your focus, Tess. You allowed this vision to come and now unallow it."

I closed my eyes and imagined myself back in Charlie's house and when I opened my eyes, that's exactly where I was.

Tara and Mary were near the door, arms locked, staring at me with concern. Dawn, however, was nowhere in sight. "What happened?"

"You went into a vision I am guessing," Tara said. "It got seriously dark for a moment, and then that cleared away. But you have just been standing there not responding to us."

"How long was I in the vision?"

"No more than a minute," Mary said and turned to try the door once again. "It isn't locked, but it isn't opening either."

What on earth was that strange vision all about?

Taking note of my confusion, Tara took a step towards me. "What did you see in your vision?"

"Nothing at first, I was in complete darkness, but then a light appeared, and a person came through that I thought was Sheila. I mean, she looked just like I have always pictured her, but it wasn't her."

Intrigued, Mary forgot about the door and gave me her full attention. "What did she want?"

"She wanted me to join her in the spirit world. She said my time here was done."

"A demon," Tara muttered. "It knew how you saw Sheila in your mind and manifested that image to fool you." She grasped Mary's hand and gently tugged her along, crossing the room to stand next to me. "Give me your hand, we need to do another quick spell. We are in their territory here."

"Whose territory?" But I knew enough to understand that Charlie's land was open to anything when it came to the spiritual realm, unlike the Wheeler farm, which was protected thanks to Tara and Janice's grandmother.

Tara's answer to my question confirmed my suspicion. "The Dark Ones. They come after people like you, Tess, because they don't want you here in our world. You hinder the spread of their evil energy."

"Then let's do what needs to be done to stay safe from them," I told her.

We clasped hands and Tara spoke a succinct clear message of intent. "The light of love protects us from the forces of darkness. This we decree, so mote it be."

The room seemed to become a bit brighter, even warmer, and then from the corner of my eye, I sensed a movement and turned toward it.

From Charlie's pantry, Dawn came into view. She stood framed in the doorway, poised for flight, her body tense, her eyes watchful as our gazes connected.

Relief washed through me. Thank God. "Dawn, we only came to talk to you. You've no need to run from us."

"I don't know them, Tess," she said, her voice hesitant, like she wasn't even sure she wanted to talk with me.

Motioning with my hand for Mary and Tara to stay put, I slowly made my way towards my new skittish friend. At least I hoped we'd be friends. "I told you about them, remember? You've nothing to fear from them."

"I've everything to fear, Tess. No one is my friend."

"What are you talking about? I am your friend."

"No, you are not." She took a step towards me. "You let me stay in that well…"

"I didn't know you were there, Dawn!"

"But I heard you!"

"What?" I stared at her blankly, trying to understand. "You heard me when?"

"When you came to the well with Kade. I begged you to help me, but you just left me there. You left me there!" Her voice rose in pitch, finishing with a shout of accusation.

Was she talking about when Kade and I had gone to check it out and found the scarf? "Dawn, I didn't hear you."

"How could you not hear me? How?" Tears rained down Dawn's tortured face. "All my life people have ignored me, dismissed me, lied to me, abandoned me, used me …"

My sympathy for her deepened. "I am not one of those people, Dawn. I promise you…"

"I showed you where your husband was and helped you find a ladder."

"I know and I appreciate that so much." We'd just ignore the fact that he was in that predicament because of her.

"I know Charlie is crazy, but I thought he liked me, and what did he do? He turned on me!" Her agitated voice was nearly too hysterical to understand. "All I wanted to do was help you."

"And you did! I appreciate what you did for me, for us, and now I want to help you." How to get through to her? As for her belief that Charlie turned on her, I could understand why she'd feel that way. When she got hurt and fell, instead of tending to her, ensuring she was okay, he'd taken off and left her for dead.

I moved closer to her, feeling her pain and seeing the dark energy, which was so prevalent in the house, swirling about her, attaching itself to her aura. Naturally it would be attracted to her negative emotions. It's how evil energy worked, it fed off those who were unhappy, discontented and angry. "Come with us, Dawn, and we will help you."

Dawn's head snapped up and then she shook it hard, her jaw firming with her resolve. "No. You come with me. Prove to me that you are my friend."

"Where are you going?" Did she really expect me to leave my family and friends and take off with her?

"Tess, don't." Tara took a step closer to me, though she halted when I gestured for her to stay back. She didn't come any closer, but she continued to protest. "If she doesn't trust us, or you, then going with her is not going to change that."

Dawn rushed forward and flung her arms around me. "I need you to be with me!"

338

Her arms were suffocating in her tight embrace, her body so tense it didn't seem natural. I started to put my arms around her when they were grabbed from behind by Mary and Tara. A tug of war commenced between my friends and Dawn, and I felt helpless between them, unwilling to choose a side.

"Let her go, Dawn," Tara commanded.

"She's my friend. She told me so." While tightening her hold, Dawn put her mouth close to my ear. "Come with me. Please."

I felt torn between them and none of it felt right. Why weren't Tara and Mary more understanding of Dawn's emotional instability and wellbeing? She'd been through so much lately and we'd just pulled her from a well. She needed someone she could trust and believe in. I wanted to be that person.

Then the words Mike told me earlier came back to me. I trusted the good in people too easily. When it came to Tara and Mary, though, I knew them very well and trusted them completely. If they felt compelled to keep me from going with Dawn, then I would not go.

As if aware of that decision, Dawn's arms dropped from around my neck, and she stepped back. Sadness, disappointment and utter sorrow were all there in her expression, in her eyes and in the drooping of her shoulders.

"I'm sorry, Dawn. I can't go with you. But you can come with us."

She shook her head. "No, I can't."

The door burst open, and we all spun around to see Kade and Daniel rushing in, with Robin and Janice close behind them, alarm written all over their faces.

"Tess, for frig sake, you are going to be the death of me!" Kade crossed the room and pulled me into his arms. "You promised you would come back to the house right after looking down that damn well."

"But we couldn't leave Dawn in there!"

He pulled away just far enough to look at me. "Dawn wasn't down there."

"Yes, she was! Didn't Janice and Robin tell you? Didn't you see us pull her out?"

"No, Tess. You did not pull anyone from the well."

"Sure we did..."

"No, Sweetness." Kade shook his head, giving emphasis to his words. "Daniel and I watched you from the house, wondering what you were doing, but when you all finally stood up again, you and Mary and Tara, there was no one with you."

This confused me. "What?" I looked at Robin and Janice. "Didn't you tell them about Dawn?"

Janice and Robin nodded their heads, indicating they had, but then Robin spoke up, speaking softly. "Of course we did, but then Kade told me to look out the window and all I could see was you, Mary and Tara. There was no one else."

"I knew it!" Mary exclaimed. "She wasn't real. I knew something wasn't right."

"Oh, she was real alright," Tara muttered. "She was a spirit."

With my heart sinking at the implication of what they were saying, I turned to where Dawn had been standing, but she was gone. And then I looked at Tara as sorrow washed through me, making me tremble. "She's dead."

Tara nodded, her eyes meeting mine with sympathy.

340

I gently withdrew from Kade's arms and looked over at the window. It was getting dark for the sun had already set. "We need to go back to the well."

"Why?" Kade asked.

"Because I think Dawn is still there."

Chapter 28

As the sun's last rays faded in the horizon and the shades of night rushed to darken the barren, frigid landscape, we drove across the field towards the well, the ground crunching beneath our tires. Kade parked my car so we could use its headlights to see, but we didn't get out right away.

I found myself unable to move as I stared at the well in trepidation. With all my heart, I did not want to see what I expected to find.

Kade reached across the seat and covered my hands with his. "Are you okay?"

"No, Kade, I am not. I don't want to look down that well, and more than anything, I don't want to see what I am fairly certain I will see."

"I'm sorry, Sweetness. You can stay here…"

"No, I have to do it." Drawing in a deep breath and praying for my suspicions to be wrong, I opened the door and stepped out of the car.

Kade came around to join me, a flashlight in his hand, and the others gathered behind us, allowing us to lead the way. A heavy silence hung over our little group, and it was with subdued ceremony that we surrounded the well's opening, our heads bowed in deference to the solemnness of the situation.

As we stood there in the chill night air, its frigid cold seeping into our bones, we looked at each other in mutual support, the beam of Kade's flashlight casting eerie shadows on our faces.

The presence of those around me was comforting, giving me the strength I needed to do what needed to be done, and my gaze dropped to the well's dark opening. The thought passed through my mind that it was a sinister portal to the unknown, and perhaps, in a way, that is exactly what it was.

Kade reached for my hand, entwining our fingers and holding tightly. When I gave him the nod that I was ready, he turned the flashlight's beam down into the well.

At first, we saw nothing but rocks and old, moldy hay. Then, a bit of black hair caught our eye. She was down there. I didn't question that. What I did question was … how? And why? I thought she and Charlie had made a connection. When Dawn said he'd turned on her, I didn't realize she meant this. How could he have done this? He just sat there in front of me and lied to my face, and I had no clue, no inkling, that he wasn't being truthful.

"What should we do?" I stared at that little bit of hair peeking through the hay and sorrow pierced my heart. I didn't know her for long, but it was an intense period of time, the memory of which would stay with me forever.

"We need to call the police and let them handle it," Kade said. "Come on, let's go back to the house where it's warm and wait for them to arrive."

An agonizing hour later, Dawn's body was pulled from the well. Though she still had to undergo identification, I knew it was her. The question haunting us was why? Why would Charlie commit such a heinous act? I know it was presumptuous to think that, but what else could have happened to her? It made me think about all the time I'd spent with him, and the potential danger I had unknowingly faced. And now, given light of all this, I was wondering if he'd shot Dean on purpose too.

Needing answers and still wondering where Lindsay could be, we made arrangements to talk with Charlie the next day. He agreed to talk to me, but no one else.

This time, when I entered the room where he was waiting, his feet and hands were shackled, and I was instructed not to touch him. Not that they needed to tell me that. The very idea of touching someone who had ended Dawn's life made me ill inside. It was bad enough that I'd done so the last time we met.

The large mirror hanging on the wall behind me concealed the presence of Kade, the police and whoever else they felt needed to be there.

I sat across from Charlie and saw panic in his expression and shining through his eyes. "Hello, Charlie."

"I didn't hurt her on purpose." Charlie's eyes watered and he blinked rapidly to clear them.

"Why didn't you say so before?" Didn't he realize that lying during the first round of questioning made it hard to believe anything he said thereafter?

"Because I didn't think anyone would believe me." He grabbed his head with both hands. "Hell, I don't believe it either."

"So, what happened?"

I asked the police not to give me any information. Whatever happened to Dawn, I wanted Charlie to tell me. They could corroborate his story later. Or not, as the case may be.

"After she pushed your young man into the room under the barn floor, she dropped the trap door back down and we headed towards the truck.

Like I told you before, we were making plans on what to do next, because we didn't plan any of that. We didn't. I mean, we didn't know that man was going to be there looking for you when we arrived. But anyways, Dawn said we needed to let the police know where he was. She said that he didn't see her or even know about her, and he would know that I didn't push him because I was standing across from him, so I had nothing to fear and neither did she. She said I could say I ran away because I was scared, because a ghost must have pushed him."

"You were going to call the police and tell them that a ghost pushed Kade, and you left him there because you were scared?" It still angered me that they'd done that.

"Yes, I mean no. I didn't agree to it," Charlie said. "It was Dawn who wanted to do that. She said that you and him believe in ghosts because you talk to them."

"So how did Dawn end up dead in that well?"

"We started arguing about what to do and she told me she was going to call the police. She pulled your cell phone out of her pocket along with Lindsay's scarf. I went crazy inside when I saw that and tried to take it from her. But she backed away. Then she told me she was going to call the police, and I rushed at her, but I didn't care about the phone anymore, I just wanted that scarf. My wife made it for Lindsay shortly before she died."

"Why didn't you mention the scarf before, Charlie?"

"Because I thought you'd think it made me mad enough to hurt her." He shifted in his seat, his hands moving restlessly on the table. "I demanded that she give it to me, but she would not. So, we fought over it…" Charlie's voice gave out and his Adam's apple began bobbing in his throat.

346

I felt no empathy for his emotional anguish, though I didn't want to push him any further either. It was obvious that he felt bad about what happened, but it didn't exonerate him. "So, you killed her?" A wave of nausea rolled through me, this whole conversation a sickening reminder of the ugliness in this world.

"No!" Charlie leaned forward in earnestness. "I swear to you it was an accident."

"So, what happened?"

"She just started saying crazy stuff and attacked me."

"What sort of crazy stuff?"

"She said that I was a stupid old man and a rotten father, and it was my fault Lindsay wouldn't come home. She said that I had to let you go because you weren't Lindsay, and she was going to tell the police about you when they came to let your husband out. She said that you were a witch, and I was in danger from you, and it served me right." Charlie shuddered, his pale brown eyes bright with confusion and sorrow. "I didn't know how to take all that foolishness, but I wanted her to stop hitting me, so I pushed her away."

I thought about that board with the nails in it and how I felt when I touched it. The pain that shot into the back of my head. "Did she fall onto the boards on the ground?"

"Yes. She tripped over something when I pushed her away from me and she fell right on top of them." The horror of that moment was reflected in his eyes. "She just went silent, and she stared at me, saying nothing, her mouth open but nothing coming out." He ran shaky hands through his hair. "I didn't understand what was going on, why she was acting that way, and when I bent down to help her, she rolled away from me and got to her feet. When I tried to get near her, she began running, though she kept stumbling.

I knew she was hurt bad and followed her, begging her to let me help her, but that made her try harder to run from me." He closed his eyes in anguish. "She was making weird noises, and then suddenly she fell, and I heard her hit her head on one of the rocks around that old well. When I got to her, she wasn't moving, and I felt the blood coming out of the back of her head." He stared at me with the horror of that moment shining from his eyes. "I didn't know what to do."

"And so, you tossed her into that well?" Disgust shot through me, and I looked away. What would make him do such a thing?

"I didn't know what else to do! If I left her there in the open, I was worried the police would find her. I figured they might come back to my house, especially as I'd been there on the property with your husband, and they would accuse me of killing her. But I didn't kill her, she fell on those nails and then hit her head on a rock when she fell again. I swear it."

"But, Charlie, you put her in that well and left her, a person who thought you loved her!"

He nodded with complete and utter dejection. "I know and I am torn up about it. I feel wicked bad. I really do, but I didn't know where else to hide her body. I figured she'd be found eventually, but until then, I had time to work things out, you know, about how to convince you to stay with me … you know, when I thought you were Lindsay."

"I'm surprised you left the scarf behind." I mumbled that as I was thinking about everything he said, and Charlie heaved a sigh.

"I sat it on the ground while I pried the lid off the well and I guess the wind blew it away."

"I don't know how you managed to get that lid up. Kade and I couldn't pry it open that day we found it."

348

"We had some rain that night, remember, and it had loosened up enough that I could get it open. Later that night, it must have frozen over." His eyes glistened with tears. "I felt so bad doing that to her. I really did." He stared off into space as he continued. "I covered her with an old bale of hay rotting in the field nearby and a few rocks from around the well." He shook his head in confusion as he glanced back at me. "Later, when I got to the house and spotted her out the window, I couldn't believe it. I mean, how did she get out of the well? I thought she must be really mad at me for throwing all that stuff on her."

"You saw her spirit, Charlie."

He shook his head, not accepting that. "No. I don't see stuff like that. It must have been my imagination."

There was no point in arguing with him. "So, what were you going to do about my husband?" With Dawn out of the picture, I wondered what Charlie's plan was going to be.

"I was going to do what Dawn had initially suggested and tell them that we, you know, your husband and me, were looking around for you and something pushed him into the hole then came after me and I ran away."

The door opened and one of the police officers, the investigator assigned to Dawn's case, motioned for me to join him out in the hallway.

I stood and looked at Charlie's bent head. He'd aged a lot over the past few days, and I did feel sorry for him. But he was a sick man and needed to be put someplace where he could get help and where he wouldn't put others in harm's way.

"Goodbye, Charlie. I hope you get the help you need."

Charlie lifted his head and looked at me, the desperation in his eyes impossible to ignore. "Promise you will still try to find Lindsay."

"I will try." But I wasn't doing it for him. I was doing it for her.

When I joined Kade, a few police officers and a couple of others I was not yet introduced to, they told me that Charlie's confession corroborated their findings. Dawn had punctures in the back of her head and another injury that was consistent with her head hitting a rock when she collapsed. She was dying when she'd run from Charlie, the nail punctures causing grave injury, but the adrenaline pumping through her, coupled with the need to escape him, had given her the strength she needed to run. When she collapsed and hit her head on the rock, it compounded her injury and ended her life instantly.

Her death broke my heart. We never had the chance to help her, and I couldn't shake the feeling that I'd failed her. I knew something wasn't right, was getting all the signs of being with someone in spirit every time she came near me, and I never put it together.

On the ride back to the house, Kade and I discussed everything at length and tried to come up with a plan to find Lindsay. But we didn't know where to look or how to go about looking for her. The one thing I wished I knew was how Dawn came to be in possession of Lindsay's scarf. Charlie and Dean both swore that Lindsay would never have given it to her.

"So, let's ask her," Kade said.

I was looking out the window, watching the passing scenery, wondering about Dawn's role in Lindsay's disappearance, when Kade said that, and I turned to look at him. "Ask who?"

"Dawn. She's been coming to you all along, so let's do it in a controlled situation and maybe she will help us."

I wasn't sure I wanted to do that. She had tried to get me to go into spirit with her, may have even dragged me there if Tara and Mary hadn't grabbed my arms and kept me from embracing her.

"If we do it under controlled circumstances, which you and Tara are very good at doing, then you might get her to come and talk. After all, she was going to help you, Dean and me before her death, it's what she and Charlie were arguing about. If he's to be believed that is."

"I don't know…"

"Tess, it could be that Dawn knows where Lindsey is. I mean, how did she get that scarf?"

An urge to agree blossomed into eager determination. "I think you could be right." Nodding that it was the right thing to do, I picked up my cell phone and created a group message. "I'll get the gang together and we'll figure out a day and time to do it."

Chapter 29

We met at the Wheeler house again, but this time we were not doing a circle. I was hoping instead to go into trance and talk to Dawn myself. Kade and Tara were the only two that would be present. Robin and Mary were at the house with Anya and our daughter, so we could meet up with them later and discuss what happened ... if anything.

I knew, though, as we pulled into the driveway, that she was going to come. I felt her waiting for me and was surprised I didn't see her as we made our way up the steps to the front door, which stood wide open.

As we didn't want to take a chance on her trying to separate us, we held hands as first Kade, then I, then Tara entered the house. It was freezing cold, and I was glad that we decided to bundle up just in case this happened. Janice left the heat on but that wasn't going to make a difference in a house currently occupied with an unhappy spirit.

I knew now that it was Dawn I felt when I entered the Wheeler house on that fateful night. It's why I'd felt uncomfortable every time I interacted with her thereafter. It was why I was uncomfortable now.

We entered the living room where the chairs were left from our last visit and after conducting a short prayer for protection, I sat down and mentally prepared myself for an encounter with Dawn.

Kade and Tara were only to ensure I didn't do anything that might cause me harm. When in the kind of trance I was planning to do, I lost all awareness of my own world, becoming completely absorbed in theirs. Such trances sometimes happened spontaneously, but I was learning to make them happen at will. Like what I hoped to do now.

Knowing that my husband and my dear friend had my back, I closed my eyes and began the process of letting go, which involved disconnecting from my physical body so I could enter Dawn's plane of existence. To accomplish this, I went through the exercises that Shay had taught me.

"Your mind must let go of the body and allow your consciousness to take control," she'd said. "This is done through focus and intention. Basically, you are doing a very deep meditation but with a set purpose."

Shay's psychic abilities were nothing short of amazing, and I was very fortunate to have her take me under her tutelage. Delighted though she was to help me, back when I first became aware of my gift, she didn't want to influence me with her techniques. She explained that we each must develop our own way of experiencing the spirit world. She didn't want me fussing and worrying about trying to memorize her ways because it would interfere with the process. Much like spell casting and not worrying about how others did it. And now, here I am, practically doing this at will and with far more ease than I ever thought possible.

It didn't take me long to start feeling like I was separating from my physical body, becoming light as air, drifting free from gravity and experiencing the sensation of floating through cobwebs.

In the vast expanse of my consciousness, I began to see a light, appearing as if distant, though it had nothing to do with space but rather my level of consciousness. All I needed to do was allow it to envelop me within its ever-expanding sphere. The more my awareness of it became, the

354

more it expanded, becoming brighter and brighter. It wasn't easy to not rush the process, for impatience could end any hope of delving deeper into an altered state of consciousness. And I was determined for this to be a success.

Minutes later, the light nearly blinded me in its brilliance and then I saw the Wheeler house as it used to be many ages past.

I heard crackling behind me and turned to see a fire flickering in the fireplace. A large, braided rug covered a good portion of the floor in front of it and all the furniture filling the room looked like what I would see in an antique shop. The smell of baking bread permeated the air.

I circled the room, taking note of everything and committing it all to memory. A noise behind me made me turn, and I saw a woman—clearly pregnant—standing in the open doorway to the kitchen, which was now separated from the living room by a wall.

The woman wore a long, pale blue dress with a white apron covering a good deal of it. Her light brown hair was pulled up into a loose bun at the top of her head. There was a calm air about her, one that immediately put me at ease. Though she was looking my way, I wasn't sure she could see me. And then she spoke.

"Who are you?"

So, she could see me. But she didn't seem startled or concerned, as one might be when seeing a stranger in their house. "Hello, my name is Tess Sinclair."

"I am Beth Wheeler, or did you know that already?"

Her complete acceptance of me was amazing. Did she think I was a ghost? If I didn't already understand that time … the past, the present and the future … all existed simultaneously, I'd be flabbergasted that I could be talking to someone who could potentially be one of Janice's great grandparents. "I see you are about to have a baby."

Beth's face softened with love, and she bent her head to look at her belly, cupping it with her hands. "Yes. It is either Grace or Jeremiah."

I wished I knew Janice's family lineage and made a mental note to look into it in the near future.

My silence must have encouraged her to come closer, for she stepped forward a few feet. "So where did you come from?"

"This house, in my time, belongs to Janice, one of your future descendants."

Beth's expression turned thoughtful. "I see. And why are you here?"

"I'm not sure. I came here, to this house, to try and connect with someone who crossed into spirit while on this property."

"A family member?"

"No."

"I don't want to know too much." She held up a hand to emphasize her desire for me to not say more than necessary. "What can I do to help you?"

That was a good question. Why was I here, at this point in time? I glanced over at the window and became curious as to what I'd see beyond it. "Do you mind if I look outside?"

Beth gestured for me to go ahead and have a look, so I crossed to the windows that looked out at the front yard. Some of the trees, which in my time were present, were not there, and the tree line was further away. The driveway was a dirt road, as it still was, but was more like wheel ruts on a well-traveled path than a road. I moved to the window that overlooked the pasture, where the well was located, and I was surprised to see it was all intact, looking relatively new, like it was recently built. The barn wasn't as big, but I did see horses and cows milling about the pasture, which was bigger than it currently was.

After ensuring I had everything committed to memory, I turned back to Beth. "May I ask you … do you know why this land is considered sacred?"

"Some of the energy currents that flow about this land, around everything in this world, converge here, making the whole area a magnetic force within the spiritual realm." She studied my face to see if I understood, and when I nodded that I did, she smiled in return, acknowledging my openness to such things. "It is a doorway of sorts, between perceived realities."

"Like a portal you mean?"

"Yes, like that. The portal is neutral, as doors are, allowing anyone to enter or depart at will, and so we entrust gatekeepers to control it. My family are gatekeepers, but we also use the energy field to perform good things, for the people and for the earth." She nodded toward the window facing the well. "I noticed you took more time to look out that window, may I ask why?"

"I was trying to memorize everything I saw. The well is new?"

"My husband dug it himself and just finished the rock wall around it. The water from that well is as sacred as the land from which it flows."

How sad it was all dried up and that Charlie thought to toss Dawn's body into it.

"It is no longer in use," I told her. "And the knowledge of what you've just shared has not passed down to our time."

"I see," Beth lapsed into thought. "Something must have happened to break the exchange of information."

"What could make so many people withhold knowledge like that, to the point that no one in my time knows why the land is sacred?"

"Ah, but then, not so many know. Such knowledge must stay with the few and not the many, or it becomes abused."

"Then why are you telling me?"

"Because you are here, though you ought not to be. We speak across the bounds of time, and such a matter demands plain truth."

I had so many questions but wasn't sure what to ask. Sheila's advice, telling me that one must learn to ask the right questions, told me this moment, this meeting, was no accident and I was being given a very special, and rare, opportunity to learn something new. But what to ask? "Do you know anything about the surrounding properties, like the one that borders the marsh?" I was very curious to know if she knew anything about my property and held my breath as I waited for her reply.

"The Abenaki used to have seasonal settlements all over this area. They honored the sacredness of the land and fought hard to keep it safe. At one time, there was a small, deep pool of water near the marsh. It was fed by an underground spring, and they used its waters for healing and for spiritual cleansing. Over time, the water stopped flowing. When the white settlers came, the pond dried up, leaving an empty cavern. To keep the cavern a secret, they built a house above it and one of my dearest friends now lives there."

My heart pounded in excitement over this bit of news. I had a room in my basement that we'd discovered recently, which had the feel of a cave. The energy was so strong that we decided to stay out of it until we understood what it was and why it was there. I couldn't help but wonder if it was all that remained of the little pond Beth just spoke of.

"I can see from your expression that you know of its location."

358

"I think it is in the basement of my house."

Beth nodded and looked away, her expression sad.

She was probably worried about the fate of her friend, but I didn't want to say much more about it, especially as I didn't know who exactly her friend was. What I could do, though, was reassure her a bit. "The property has been looked after and is now in my care, and I promise you that we honor how special it is."

Beth smiled her thanks for that bit of news, looking relieved. "That is good then."

"Will this portal as you call it remain here always?"

"Yes."

That concerned me, and Beth picked up on it. "Why do you look that way?"

"The property is in the process of being sold. We hope that whoever is buying it will take care of it. We will do our best to convey how special the property is to the new owners."

The concern was back in her expression. "I see. Guardian Spirits must be stirred, upset that the property is to change hands. If the right people take possession of it, then all will be well."

As Beth began to fade, along with everything else, I felt compelled to give her something good to hold onto. "Thank you for all your information. All is going to be well for your family!"

Beth looked very pleased, and I was glad she heard me.

And then I was plunged into the darkest of dark, and I wondered what would happen next.

Though I heard nothing and saw nothing, I felt someone approaching, and it made me nervous that I couldn't see who or what was coming towards me. I put out my hand and someone grasped it, the hand cold and the grip firm but not threatening. The moment my hand closed around it, accepting the contact, I could instantly see again.

This time I was in the farmhouse in present time, though I could not see Kade or Tara. Even so, I knew they were with my physical body.

The person holding my hand was Dawn.

She gave me a tug, letting me know that she wanted me to follow her. I went with her, all the way out the front door to the side of the house, where I saw Charlie and Dawn, who was no longer holding my hand but merged with the vision I was now watching.

"Charlie, we are going back to the house and calling the police. You need to let Tess and Dean go. This has gone far enough."

"Who is Tess?"

"She's the girl you are holding down in the basement."

"That's Lindsay…"

"No, it isn't! Lindsay is not here, Charlie."

"You don't know what you are talking about." Charlie turned from Dawn and started to walk away from her, but she called out to him, a determined note in the tone of her voice.

"I'm going to call the police."

Charlie turned to look at her, just as she pulled my cell phone from her pocket, bringing Lindsay's green scarf with it. She stared at it in surprise, not seeing that Charlie was charging back to her. "Where did you get that? Give it to me!"

I could see the fright that flared in Dawn's eyes as she back away, holding both the cellphone and the scarf from his reach. "Back off, old man! Don't you see what you are doing is crazy? You can't keep taking people and holding them hostage."

A crazed look was in Charlie's eyes, his gaze locked on the scarf. "Where did you get that? It's Lindsay's scarf and you had better give it to me."

Dawn stared at it and shook her head. Clearly, she had no clue where it had come from. "I got this jacket out of one of Lindsay's boxes, so she must have left it in there." She saw him advancing on her and backed away. "Don't come near me, Charlie, I mean it."

Charlie stopped, but his mouth was working in the effort not to say more, his hands moving restlessly at his sides. "Give me the scarf and the cellphone and then we'll talk about it."

"No! We need to call the police. There are too many people involved now, Charlie. And Tess is about to have a baby!"

"Why do you keep using her fake name? I don't care what you do about that man or Dean, I only want for Lindsay to stay with me."

"That girl isn't Lindsay

"Fine, whatever you say. Just give me that scarf. Lindsay's mother made it for her just before she died, and Lindsay cherishes it."

"Charlie, let's go back to the house and we'll talk…"

"No! You are a liar." Charlie lunged forward again, grabbing the scarf and yanking it from her grasp.

Dawn let out a scream and jumped at him, pummeling him with her fist and my cellphone. "You stupid old man! No wonder she left you! Give that to me."

Charlie tried to shove her away and she began screaming at him, telling him the things Charlie had told me she'd said. He tried to block her pummeling hands, then finally shoved at her again, telling her to leave him alone, and that's when she tripped over a protruding rock and fell hard against the boards lying on the ground. Her eyes went wide, and her screams went instantly silent, though her mouth stayed open.

Charlie frowned at her in the dimming light, moving closer to better see her. "What's wrong with you?" His expression became more concerned. "Dawn, are you okay?" He knelt down next to her and as he reached forward, she rolled away from his touch.

While mumbling unintelligible sounds, Dawn managed to get to her feet and then she slumbered away, heading towards the field, her gate jerky, her head slumped forward.

Charlie followed after her at a cautious pace. "Dawn, let me help you." The moment he touched her arm, she jerked from him and mumbled what sounded like a scream that got stuck in her throat. She was nearly to the well when she stopped, swayed on her feet, then fell backward. Charlie winced right along with me when we heard her head connect with the rock. She didn't move again.

Charlie stared at her for several long seconds, uncertain what to do, then covered his face and groaned. "My God what do I do?" He dropped his hands and inched forward. "Dawn?" When she didn't respond, he edged closer, until he was close enough to drop to his knees beside her. "Dawn?" He grasped her shoulders and shook her gently. "Dawn? Can you hear me?" He put his hand behind her head then jerked away. Blood covered his hand, and he stared at it with horror. "Oh my God." He looked at her face, saw the vacant stare of her eyes and realization struck, his face going pale. "No, oh no! Oh my God, Dawn!" His head dropped as he gave in to his tears then after a few moments of grief, he wiped his face on the sleeve of his coat and stood up. After a quick glance around, his eyes rested on the well. Minutes later, he was removing the cover and dragging

362

Dawn's body the short distance over to it. He bent and kissed her forehead then after closing her eyes, he closed his own and pushed her into the well.

After that he worked quickly, tossing hay and a few rocks into the gaping dark hole. Once he'd replaced the lid, he turned away, saw my cellphone lying on the ground and picked it up as he hightailed it back to the house.

I stood next to Dawn and watched him go.

"It was an accident, but it shouldn't have happened." Dawn spoke next to me, her tone subdued. "If I hadn't fought with him, I wouldn't have fallen."

"I am so sorry, Dawn."

"Nothing ever worked out for me."

"Dawn, if you see a light, you need to go into it. Move on from this…"

"I see a light, it follows me everywhere, but I don't deserve to enter it."

"Yes, you do, Dawn. You most definitely deserve it, and the light thinks so too, that's why it's following you."

"I've done bad things, and I've had terrible things happen to me. If I deserved that light, then I would be a better person, and people wouldn't have done the things they've done to me."

"Dawn…"

"It's true! I've been abused, used, lied to, tossed aside and unloved my whole life!" Her beautiful eyes glistened as they stared back at mine.

"It's over now, Dawn. You've suffered through so much and now it's time to rest from it, learn from it and move on." I wanted only to embrace her, but she wasn't ready for that. "Dawn, I care about you very much, and I am telling you that you deserve to go into that light. Love awaits you there. More love than you've ever known as Dawn. It's from where you came and to where you need to go!"

Dawn's gaze held mine and I could see how badly she wanted to believe me.

"Go into the light, Dawn. Please. You will review your life and evaluate the lessons learned from it, which is why we have the experiences we have in this life. As Dawn, you may not like what you have done or the things that happened to you, but in the Light, you are pure spirit, you are more than Dawn, you are the sum total of your soul and the many experiences it has had over the millennia. Your soul has existed for a very, very long time."

She stared at me with longing and hope, and I knew I was making headway. The last thing I wanted was for her to wander the earth plane as a lost soul. "I love you, Dawn, and that has to mean something, right? You are loveable, and in that light, you will encounter even more love. It's going to be okay. Please trust me on this, I wouldn't steer you wrong."

Dawn lifted her face, and I saw the light shining upon it, brightening her aura, filling her spirit, and a wondrous expression crossed over her face. "I feel it, Tess!"

"That's wonderful, Dawn. You are in for the most wonderful experience, but before you go ... do you know where Lindsay is?"

Dawn's gaze dropped to mine and regret clouded the joy in her eyes. "No, I don't. But she is safe." Her voice sounded hollow, more of an echo in my mind, and I knew she would soon be gone. "She never knew that Dean was faithful to her." Tears fell from her eyes, and they glistened in the bright light, their radiance reflecting a rainbow of color. It was quite fascinating to see. "I never told her."

"It's okay. We'll straighten it out." An idea about Lindsay was forming in the back of my mind, an idea that was taking hold and giving me hope. "You take care of you, and we'll take care of her."

The light grew brighter, encompassing Dawn's body and I took a step back. "Embrace the light, Dawn. Go and be at peace."

"Are you sure, Tess?" She looked frightened of rejection but hopeful of acceptance.

"I am positive."

The light grew to such brilliance that I could no longer see Dawn, and though it should have blinded me, it didn't hurt my eyes or even make me squint. All I could feel was love radiating from it, and I closed my eyes to better enjoy it.

"I think she's coming around," Kade said.

I opened my eyes and saw that I was standing out by the well with Tara on one side of me and Kade on the other. "I'm no longer in the vision."

Kade pulled me into his arms and held me tightly, rocking me in his loving embrace. We'd come to learn that this was the quickest way to ground me back into the reality of my physical world.

"Is everything okay, Sweetness?"

I nodded against his chest, loving the rumble of his voice, the firmness of his hold and the love he had for me. "It's all going to be okay."

Tara put her arms around both of us. "That's great news, Tess."

I enjoyed our closeness for a few seconds then pulled away. "We've lots to talk about." I glanced briefly at the well then turned from it and looked at my husband and my friend, focusing on them and their love for me. "It's just as Charlie said. Dawn fell against the board with the nails in it, and though badly injured, she managed to get up and run here, where she fell and hit her head on a rock." Though I knew she was in a wondrous place and was happier than she ever had been as Dawn, I was sad that her life here had to end that way. "I wonder why we didn't notice any blood."

"It rained that night, remember? It must have washed it all away," Kade said.

"And then we had some freezing temps after that, so everything froze," Tara added. "It's why you and Kade couldn't get the lid off the well when you first found it. You've nothing to feel guilty about."

"I know. We had no idea Dawn was down there, but I feel I should have sensed it." I let out a long sigh, wondering if I would ever develop my gift enough to sense things like that. And then I wondered if I wanted to sense things like that. "She's in a better place now." I looked at Kade and Tara, seeing they were pleased by this announcement, and that made me happy as well. "She went into the light."

Kade held out a hand and I took it gratefully, knowing he would always be at my side, always helping to lift me up, to give me a hand and to offer his support whenever I needed it. And I would do the same for him.

He slipped an arm across my shoulders, and we started walking toward the house. "Let's get inside where it's warm and you can tell us all about it."

"The house is warm?"

Tara laughed. "It started warming up a few minutes after you went into trance."

"That's a good sign!" Relief washed through me. We were getting it all straightened out. The truth was coming out and centuries' worth of knowledge lost was now known again.

366

"It's a great sign," Tara agreed. "I take it your trance was a good one!" When we reached the house, Tara sprinted ahead to open the door. "Do you want to talk here or back at your place? I'm sure Robin, Mary and Anya are going to want to hear about it."

"Yes, and we need to call Janice and ask her to come over as well."

"Okay then, let's straighten up the house, put the chairs back, and head to your place. I'll call Janice, though, right now."

Tara walked away to make her call while Kade and I picked up the few things we'd brought with us and checked the doors. I couldn't wait to share everything I'd learned about the Wheeler place, our property, Dawn and maybe even Lindsay.

We were soon headed home, and I could barely contain my eagerness to get there. I just loved it when things worked out, though I was still sad about Dawn. Then again, she was now in a very good place, and she needed the rest. Her life here had been far too challenging.

Kade gave me a quick sideways glance as we turned onto the private road leading to our house. "I can tell from the way you are acting and the energy exuding from you that you've a lot to tell us."

"I do, but what I am happiest about is that I think I know where to find Lindsay!" Though I'd never met her, I found myself most eager to make her acquaintance and prayed my hunches were right.

"Oh, Tess, I can't wait to hear what happened," Tara said.

As we pulled into my driveway, I was relieved to see that Janice was already there. Good. We had a lot to cover, and I didn't want to wait a second more than I had to.

Chapter 30

I didn't have to wait long before everyone was ready to hear what happened during my trance. Janice was excited to hear that I'd met and talked with one of her ancestors. It was interesting to hear that the earth's energy currents were what made our properties—mine, Tara's, Janice's and some of Charlie's land—so special. Kade loved that we finally knew how that strange room in our basement came to exist, though we weren't sure what we were supposed to do with it.

As for Tara, she was eager to do some dousing and find another underground spring from which a new pond might be fed, and since we all had artesian wells on our properties, the water had to be as sacred as the land from which it sprung, meaning it could be used for various ceremonies, rituals and healing.

When I mentioned that the woman I met in my vision was named Beth Wheeler, Janice went through her ancestry paperwork she'd brought with her. "Ok then! I have a great-great grandmother named Beth Wheeler. She had a son named Jeremiah and several daughters, but Jeremiah was my great grandfather!"

We marveled over that then discussed the revelation that our land was watched over by its own guardian spirits. As I remembered how much spirit trouble had occurred at my house before we cleansed it and eliminated the bad energy, it all made sense to me as to why Charlie might have succumbed to his mental degradation. He'd been soaking up the negative energy running rampant at his home.

As much as I was grateful for the new revelations, I was happiest knowing my contact with Dawn had helped her find peace. It gave me peace of mind knowing she was moving on with her spiritual journey. Though I could still talk to her if we desired to communicate, it would be from a whole new perspective. But honestly, I wasn't sure I wanted to continue our connection. I needed to let Dawn go and move on with my own life. Dawn's transition to a higher realm of consciousness would open new doors of understanding for her, and I couldn't see us talking again unless it was in the capacity of maybe a spirit guide.

"I'm sorry, Tess, about giving off that negative vibe by telling you that I didn't trust her," Tara said. "I guess I was focused on the negative aspects of her life, and I should know better."

"You were being protective of me," I said, totally understanding why she'd become so distrustful of Dawn. "Plus, you were picking up a vibe that something wasn't right about her, and it wasn't. She was a spirit, and I couldn't see that for some reason."

"You weren't ready to see her that way," Tara said softly. "And because you weren't ready, we saw her as you did."

"Well, I for one, think you are being very generous with her, which is what makes you so special, Tess," Robin said, her voice warm with affection. "I mean, despite knowing everything she'd done, you did not waver as her champion."

"She did things she wasn't proud of but merging with her spiritually like I did, I could feel all her history." I found it most fascinating that while in spirit, connected as we were via our energy imprint, I had access to all of

370

Dawn's life in an instant. "She was abused physically and sexually at a very young age. She learned early on that people couldn't be trusted and the pattern of her life was always the same as she aged. People deceived her for their own means, using her and then discarding her. Dean treated her with respect. Even after knowing she wanted a relationship with him, he didn't abandon her but tried to maintain a friendship with her. When she met Lindsay and began chumming with her, she actually came to like her as much as she admired Dean."

I felt it all while talking to Dawn in those last moments together, feeling all the pain and disappointment, the heartbreak and sorrows she'd endured over and over again. She'd been looking for someone to love her and she was so sure that Dean was that man, and then she thought of Charlie as the sort of father she'd always wanted.

"So, you mentioned that you think you know how to find Lindsay," Kade reminded me. "Does that mean she's still alive?"

"I think she is!" This part made me very excited. "Janice, when is the closing on your house?"

"In two days, why?"

"Is the person buying the house going to be present or will it be through lawyers?"

"He's coming to the closing."

"He?" That threw me a bit and I felt temporarily deflated. "You know who is buying the house then?"

"No, I haven't met him, but his lawyer said he'd be at the closing." Janice put a comforting hand on my shoulder, seeing that her replies did not meet with much happiness on my part. "Why?"

"I thought maybe it was Lindsay who was buying the house."

"But what kind of sense does that make?" Tara asked, her tone gentle, taking care not to sound reproachful of the idea. "If she is in hiding, which obviously she is, buying the Wheeler farm would mean she'd have to come out of hiding."

"Yes, I think she is finally in a place, you know, emotionally, where she feels it is safe to do that."

"Let's be there at the closing," Kade said. "We'll wait outside and when he comes out of the office, we'll introduce ourselves and go from there."

Janice nodded agreeably. "It's a good idea. I'm very curious about him myself."

Chapter 31

Two days later, Kade, Tara and I sat waiting outside the lawyer's office for the new owner of the Wheeler house to come out. Janice said she'd try to get him to meet us by telling him we were his new neighbors.

She did just that when they finally emerged, Janice coming out first and turning to speak to a tall man who looked to be in his early thirties. An older man and a younger woman also came out with them, but considering they had briefcases and said their goodbyes before hurrying away, I was guessing they were the lawyers or realtors handling the sale. Janice glanced in our direction then said something to the man who looked over at us.

The three of us waved, and he gave a friendly nod back, then accompanied Janice as she walked towards us.

"Hi Tess, Kade, Tara, this is Gary McIntosh. He just bought my grandparents' property. Gary, Tess and Kade's property abuts yours, and on the other side of their property is Tara's."

"It's very nice to meet you," he said, holding out his hand in greeting.

As I placed mine in his and felt his warm, firm grip, I knew at once we would indeed become friends. And then he said the words that made my heart skip.

"My … wife and I are very excited to be moving here."

I wondered at his hesitation and hoped I would discover the reason for it in our ensuing conversation. What was exciting was the fact he had a wife! "She didn't come with you?" My heart was pounding so hard I could feel its pulse in the veins of my neck. *Ok, Tess, you need to ask the right questions.* "What's her name?"

Gary's friendly expression closed right up. "Well, she isn't quite ready to meet anyone just yet…"

"Is it Lindsay?" I knew from the widening of his brown eyes that I had guessed it right. Thank God! "It's Lindsay."

Gary took a step back. "I really need to be going…"

"You've nothing to fear from us, Gary," Kade assured him. "We are relieved to know she is okay, and we hope that when she is ready to meet us, that both of you will become good friends and know you can trust us."

He looked undecided on what more he should say and then after glancing between us, meeting our gazes in turn, his stance relaxed. "She had to drop out of sight, or he wouldn't have left her alone."

"You mean, Charlie?" It had to be her father she'd run from. Dean was a good man.

"Yes, he was trying to get her to move back to the house with him and Lin knew that would be the worst thing she could do. Charlie is very difficult for her to deal with, and she just didn't have the heart to continue to defy him on a constant basis, so she left."

"But why do it the way she did?" I queried, genuinely curious. "I mean, it wasn't just Charlie she disappeared from?" I didn't want to come across as accusing, and hoped my tone didn't suggest any animosity. Obviously, she'd taken desperate measures, feeling it was necessary, and I only wanted to understand. After all, her disappearance set in motion a series of very difficult events.

"Please understand, we are not upset with her, it's just that we've been praying for her safety and looking for her ever since we learned of her," Tara said.

"There's more to the story than what you know." Gary glanced around. "Is there somewhere we can go to talk?"

"There's a small park down near the water," Janice suggested. "Let's walk there."

The five of us made our way to the park and found an empty picnic table where we could sit and talk. Once we were settled, Gary explained the part of the story we'd all been waiting to hear.

"Lin realized quite a way in, after being friends with her a while, that Denise, whom we now know is Dawn, was the one who was seeing Dean…" He lifted a hand when he saw me opening my mouth in protest, asking me to hold off and let him finish. "She knows now that Denise, I mean Dawn, and Dean were not having an affair behind her back, but she did think it at the time of her disappearance, which Denise helped to orchestrate by the way."

"What?" Now that caught me by surprise.

"When Dawn realized that Lindsay had figured it out, she convinced Lin that Dean was in love with her, but Den…Dawn, didn't feel the same way about him. She told Lin that despite his feelings for her, you know, Dawn, Dean wanted to be faithful to Lin because of the baby. Lin didn't want him to stay with her for that reason alone. I must add here that Lin was no longer in love with Dean by this point anyway."

"I'm sorry," I began, interrupting him despite his request that I wait. "But I feel it is important for you to know that Dean was never in love with Dawn."

"I know … we know. At least, now we do, since talking to Janice, who has been filling us in (he shot a grateful look to Janice). When Lin found out that Dawn was staying at her father's place…"

Another surprise I wasn't expecting. "How did she find out about that?"

"Lin maintained some contact with Dawn. She checked in with her from time to time to hear news of how Dean was doing, and she wanted to stay on top of what was happening with the police, which Dawn told her was no longer an issue."

"So, they spoke while Dawn was staying at Charlie's?" I was rather disappointed that Dawn hadn't shared that with me.

"Yes, but only once. During that conversation, Dawn told Lin she was staying at her father's house, and she said he was a little crazy and she understood why Lin wanted to keep him in the dark as to her whereabouts."

"But Dawn didn't know where Lindsay was?" It was important for me to know this because the last words she spoke to me were denial of knowing Lindsey's whereabouts.

"No, Lin never told her, and Dawn didn't want to know. But she did admit that Dean no longer wanted a relationship with her … with Dawn that is."

"Not that he ever did," I reiterated. "Did Lindsay know that Dawn was making Dean out to be the bad guy with her father?" His answer would tell me a lot about Charlie's daughter.

"She didn't, but I can tell you this … if Dean was ever officially blamed for her disappearance, Lin would have come out of hiding to clear his name." He let out a sigh, telling me he was tired of all the subterfuge.

"Honestly, she's been planning on coming out of hiding anyway, which is why we bought the house next door to her father."

"You do know what's happened to Dawn?" I asked gently. If Janice was keeping him up to date with information, then he must know, but it was a way to introduce the subject.

He gave a grave nod. "Yes, and Lin is very saddened by the news. Despite everything, she did like the girl."

We engaged in a moment of silence, then Kade spoke up, getting the conversation going again. "So, it was Dawn who told Lindsay the property was up for sale?"

"Yes. She said it in passing, telling Lin that she wished she had the money to buy the property next door because she loved it so much." He gave us a sideways look, as if considering something then gave a little chuckle. "Dawn admitted to having some fun with the construction crew. She knew a secret way into the house and about the secret rooms inside, and I guess she enjoyed messing with the construction crew, making them think the house was haunted."

That took all of us by surprise, and then we were all laughing. So that was why I never felt anything that day I'd pulled into the yard. There was nothing to connect with, other than Dawn next door.

"So anyway, when Lindsay hung up from that call, which disturbed her quite a bit, for certain things Dawn said indicated that Charlie was losing it mentally, she told me about all her happy memories at the Wheeler farm and how much she'd always loved it." He gave us a satisfied smile. "I looked into purchasing it soon after, figuring a cash offer would ensure I wouldn't have to wait for it to go officially on the market and risk losing it." He looked at us then let out another sigh, his shoulders relaxing as he did so. "I'm going to be honest and tell you that we are only engaged.

The only reason she isn't my wife yet is because we couldn't get married while Lin was hiding."

"Why did she feel it necessary to hide?" Tara asked him.

"Charlie's attempts to control her were increasing to an impossible degree. Lin was completely stressed out about it, and she even admitted that she wouldn't put it past her father to kidnap her." He looked at me with an apologetic expression. "She feels very bad about what he did to you, and Dawn and Dean."

I gestured that there was nothing for anyone to be sorry about. "It wasn't a pleasant experience, but we got through it." I thought about Dawn and a spear of sadness went through my heart. "I am sad about Dawn though."

Gary nodded. "Yeah, it's really tragic that it ended that way." An uncomfortable silence settled over us for a moment, then Gary cleared his throat and gave us all a pained smile. "Lin feels terrible about what she did to Dean—disappearing on him, having his son, and keeping him out of his life."

"So, she had a boy." I was glad that the baby was safe as well.

"Yes, his name is Jasper." Gary's expression was as tender as the tone of his voice, and I knew that he loved the boy. "Lin gave him Dean's last name and she plans to let him, Dean that is, be as much a part of Jasper's life as he wants to be. She finally feels secure enough to do that." His expression hardened into one of disapproval. "Dawn really messed with her head when it came to Dean." His lips compressed for a moment, his disapproval of Dawn quite evident. "She messed with her head in a lot of ways, telling Lin stuff that she claimed to be getting psychically. Lin was a mess when I met her."

378

"So where did Lindsay go?" It fascinated me that someone could just disappear like that, remaining unfound, even when the police were actively looking for her, though as to that, I don't think they were looking too awfully hard.

"Lin told Dawn that she wanted to remove herself from Dean's life, especially as she believed that he was in love with Dawn, and Dawn was all over the idea, telling Lin that she'd help her relocate somewhere that Dean and her father couldn't bother her. But then Lin found out she was pregnant and didn't think that Dean would let her go. Then her father showed up at her apartment and started pressuring her to go home with him. She told him she was pregnant, thinking that would make him abandon that idea, but it only made him more determined. So, Lindsay left the apartment, on the pretext of getting them some lunch, and called Dawn, who showed up and whisked her away to a friend's place. She convinced Lin that disappearing was the best plan to get both men to leave her in peace." Gary spread his hands to indicate he thought Lindsay had no other easy options. "Lin decided to go with it."

"So, where's she been this past year?" It wasn't vital to know that, but I was curious anyway.

He held up a hand that he would get to that. "Lin was actually planning to leave Dean long before she found out she was pregnant, so she'd been regularly drawing her cash out of the bank and stashing it, thinking it would be on hand when she finally decided to go. When she and Dawn came up with the idea of getting her out of town, Dawn picked up a couple suitcases Lin had packed the day before her "disappearance" and took them to that friend's house where she eventually took Lin." He seemed determined that we know the truth and not think badly of the woman he loved. "Lin hadn't planned to leave the day she did, but her father showing up sort of made the decision for her. She didn't mean for it to look like something had happened to her. The precautions she took—running off with Dawn, saying nothing to either of the men, and maintaining silence, were so Dean and Charlie would just let her go and not know where to find her. She was actually quite shocked to find out the police became involved."

"Did she really think Dean and Charlie would not alert the police of her disappearance?" Janice asked curiously.

Gary shrugged. "Lin thought for sure they would both think she did exactly what she did ... which was run away, of her own free will."

"I would think the police would have picked up on the fact that she'd been drawing her money out of the bank," Kade said. "That would have suggested to them that her disappearance was planned."

"Lin thought that too, but she didn't plan on Charlie saying that Dean had taken her. She was about to come out of hiding when Dawn told her the police didn't buy in to Charlie's accusations and believed that Lin left on her own."

"So why cash her checks and keep all her money on hand?" Kade asked.

We were being very nosy, but after all this time wondering about her, we were curious as to how it all went down.

"She didn't want Dean catching on that she was about done with their relationship, in case he tried to talk her out of it. She doesn't handle confrontation very well. In fact, she gets major anxiety just thinking about it. And I don't mind telling you, I think that's because of her father." He heaved a sigh of sympathy for Lin, then shook it off and continued. "It was also why she had to leave most all her things, so it would look like a last-minute decision and not something she'd been planning for quite a while.

380

She thought it wouldn't hurt him as bad that way." He shook a finger as he thought up an important point. "Speaking of her leaving behind her things, we managed to get most of her stuff when Dean finally packed it all up with the intention of sending it to Charlie. Dawn told him she'd take it to him, but she let Lin know about it and we arranged for her to drop off what Lin wanted at a storage unit, and we picked it up later."

"How did you two meet?" Janice asked, completely enthralled with the whole tale.

"Lin has a friend who lives in northeast Vermont, near the Canadian border, and she went to stay with her there. It's a small town and everyone knows Audra, Lin's friend, so no one thought anything of it when Audra told everyone her cousin was coming to stay with her after becoming a widow and with a baby on the way. I own a house right next door, and I fell in love with her the moment I set eyes on her."

"So, she's been living in Vermont this whole time?"

"Yes, and she's been feeling very guilty about running away. Our engagement, the birth of Jasper and just coming into her own has given her the courage she's needed to come out of hiding."

"What does Lindsay plan to do about her father?" Charlie was mentally ill, and he was right where he needed to be to get the help he needed, but I hoped that Lindsay and Gary wouldn't abandon him, not that I really believed they would. "I mean ... once he's free again, if they ever consider him mentally stable and not a danger to society, he will probably want to move back to his house, and then he'll be right next door to you."

"We'll deal with that if or when it happens. But I have assured Lin that I will not let her father try to run her life. But she does feel that she should be here for him because he obviously is not well and rest assured, we will be supportive and ensure Charlie gets the help he needs."

"Tell her to come meet us," I implored him. "We will be good and loyal friends, and everyone needs those in their lives. And tell her that she should go see her father. It's all going to be okay. Dean isn't happy about her hiding from him and keeping him from his son, but he's very glad she's alive. He's a good man and will not be a problem."

Gary looked at his watch then held up a finger. "Give me a minute and I'll give her a quick call. She's not far from here. We got a room at the Bayview Inn."

"Oh wow!" Janice said, glancing at me. "Did you know that it used to be haunted?"

Gary nodded. "Yes, but the owners said the ghosts that were there have been put to rest."

"Well, yes, thanks to Tess and Kade," Janice informed him.

I motioned for Gary to go ahead and make his call. "See if she'll come meet us."

Twenty minutes later, we watched Gary and a lovely young woman make their way toward us. She was pushing a stroller and looking a little apprehensive as she neared our group. Gary was speaking low and earnestly, and she kept nodding her head though she didn't take her eyes off us. When she was just a few feet away, I marveled at the accuracy of the picture that Kade drew of her. Not to mention the accuracy of my vision because I could see a little dark mole not far from her mouth, as I'd seen in the picture Kade had drawn, when the angle of her head had changed.

Wanting to put her at ease, I went right to her and gave her a hug. "You don't know how happy I am to finally meet you!"

Before she could respond, Janice was giving her an enthusiastic hug as well. "It's so great to see you again, Lindsay! I am so very happy you are the ones who bought my grandparents' property." Her eyes widened as she thought of something then she gave an amused chuckle. "And now we must call it the McIntosh Farm! I just love that, and you do have some nice apple trees on the property as I am sure you remember!"

Lindsay was smiling that she too was quite happy about it, and after greeting Kade and Tara, giving them both a hug, she turned back to Janice. "I promise we'll take good care of it."

"I know you will!" The two girls hugged again then drew apart and smiled at each other. Their friendship, I knew, would only grow over the years ahead.

With introductions out of the way, we took a peek at Jasper, who was sleeping soundly, then we sat down to catch her and Gary up on all that had happened in the past couple days.

Lindsay was at once contrite as she listened to me explain about her father holding me and Dawn captive, and I brushed off her concern. "It's fine. I had my baby with my husband and friends present and that's what mattered most to me." I paused for a moment, considering something I wanted to share, knowing it was the right thing to do. "I got help from spirit, actually, from someone who was very concerned about what was happening." I looked at Lindsay, seeing her interest, and also a touch of hope. "It was your mother."

Lindsay's eyes widened and then began to glisten with tears. "Really?"

"Yes. She loves you and your father, and she's been so worried about both of you."

"I want to believe that…"

"She was wearing a set of dolphin earrings…"

Lindsay gasped, then moved her hair out of the way. She was wearing the earrings that I'd seen her mother wearing. "She loved dolphins. We even went to Florida before she died so she could swim with them."

"She also showed me her rings ... they were yellow gold with braided bands. The engagement ring was a teardrop diamond."

Lindsay began to cry softly. "Yes, I have them in my jewelry box."

"She was very helpful in assisting me and Dean's escape," I told her gently. "As to that, Dean was very helpful as well, and he was very considerate of my condition."

Lindsay's tears for her mother were replaced with sorrow for her actions. "I handled everything so badly. I don't know how Dean will ever forgive me."

"Dean is happy you are safe, Lindsay." I put my hand on hers and gave it a squeeze. "He'll be very excited to see his son."

"I hope he won't try to take Jasper away from us."

The fear in her eyes made me wish I knew the right thing to say to help her feel better. "I don't think he'll be like that. As understanding as he's been about Dawn, who really played you both badly, I think he will be very understanding about why you did what you did. He learned firsthand how ... um ... your father's skewered thinking has made him do things that he shouldn't be doing. Your father wouldn't have let up on you, Lindsay, and Dean knows that, especially now." I didn't doubt that Charlie would have made Lindsay a captive in her home, thinking he was doing right by her, of course. Hopefully his mental health was not so deteriorated that they couldn't help him get better. I honestly felt that once he saw Lindsay, and had her back in his life on a regular basis, he was going to get well.

"We've spoken with the police and with the people overseeing Charlie's care," Gary said. "And we are quite certain that Charlie won't be charged with anything. He mental instability was to blame for his actions, and his testimony about what happened to Dawn are consistent with what you said happened, Tess, and with the findings on Dawn's autopsy. But he will remain in custody while he receives treatment and will only get released if he is deemed safe and is mentally cleared."

"My father's mother had mental health problems too," Lindsay told us. "She eventually killed herself, while my father was still a young boy, leaving him with his father who was a very controlling, very unpleasant man from what I've heard. He died when my father was in high school. He got into a fight in a bar, and someone killed him. My father got some money from that, and he bought the property he now owns. He's lived there since graduating high school." She heaved a sympathetic sigh. "I should have taken all that into consideration, before running off on him like I did, but I was a young girl looking to escape the oppression that seemed to control that house."

"It has lots of negative spirit energy," Tara said. "Dark spirits are active there, but don't you worry, my Coven is going to drive them out and clear that place right up. Your father fell victim to that energy and given what you've just shared, he was an easy target."

Lindsay gave her a grateful smile. "Gary and I are going to do all we can to see he gets the help he needs." Her expression firmed. "No more running away."

Tara and I reached over to cover her hands. "And you have a lot of new friends who are going to be here to support you all."

Her eyes glistening with tears, Lindsay nodded wordlessly, unable to speak, then cleared her throat and threw Janice a smile. "I'm excited to be living in Bucksport again and in the house that I've always loved." She and Janice hugged again, then looked at each other in such a way that I could tell the bond they'd forge would be as great as the one I had with Tara. Lindsay shook her head in wonder and glanced around at each of us. "I can't believe how things are turning out! Though I am very sad about what happened to Dawn."

A grave pall settled on our group, but I was quick to dispel it. "Dawn is in the light and she's right where she needs to be."

Tara nodded to lend emphasis to that statement. "She is in a great place and now, so you are!"

Lindsay's smile returned. "I was so happy to learn about the farm going up for sale and ecstatic when Gary told me he made an offer on it. The one good thing we got out of this was learning about that through Dawn."

"And we are all going to help you however we can," I assured her. "I even know a teenage girl who is an excellent babysitter!"

We chatted for a while longer and then Jasper woke up. We all fussed and fawned over him until Lindsay said it was feeding time, and they needed to get back to the hotel. We agreed to have dinner together within the next couple of days, exchanged phone numbers then said our goodbyes.

As we watched them walk away, their heads bent toward each other, perhaps talking about the future, which was going to be far better than anything they imagined, I turned to my friends and my husband, his hand clasping mine the moment he saw me looking.

"I love you, Kade, and you too, Tara, and you Janice. I love my life here. I don't think anything gets better than this."

Later, as Kade and I made our way home, I looked out at the passing scenery and thought about how much I truly loved my life. It was good to have a special gift that helped people in so many ways. I loved my spiritual connections and the fact that I talked regularly with my Spirit Guide, Sheila. And more than anything, I was grateful for my loving husband, our beautiful daughter, a dog and cat we adored, the best circle of friends, a wonderful family and a very special property that I called home. Life was good. Just like the State of Maine's sign on the interstate, this really is "the way life should be".

The End ... for now

Other Books by Deborah J Hughes

Tess Schafer/Sinclair-Medium Series

Be Still, My Love – book 1

Hidden Voices – book 2

Vanquishing Ghosts – book 3

Rosemary's Ghosts – book 4

Ghost Trouble – book 5

Haunting Ground – book 6

Distracting Ghosts – book 7

Paranormal Encounters – book 8

Spirit Matters – book 9

Haunted Illusions – book 10

Romance

Tangled Up Hearts

Moments in the Moonlight (special appearance by Tess Sinclair)

Paranormal Thriller

No Matter What

About the Author

I'm often asked why I choose to write the books I do and whether I actually believe in the things I write about. One of the most frequent questions I get is, "Has any of it ever really happened?"

Now that this is the end (maybe, who knows for sure) of a ten-book series about a medium and her experiences, I figured I'd share a bit more than the usual bio. All of this is on the "about me" portion of my blog, which you can visit on www.deborahjhughes.blog. I also share some suggested posts that cover a lot of what I have experienced and believe in and why.

Aside from the Tess Schafer/Sinclair-Medium series, I have written a few others: one in the paranormal/romance genre (Moments in the Moonlight), one in the romance genre (Tangled Up Hearts), which contains no paranormal elements (it is more in keeping with the Harlequin type stories of the 70s – I was a voracious reader of Harlequin books in my early teen years), and one paranormal thriller (No Matter What) based on the theme of reincarnation (the first book I ever actually finished).

My interests are quite varied. For one, I've been a palm reader since I was sixteen years old. At first, I dabbled with it for fun and then began to realize it was much, much more than a form of amusement for friends and family. I came to respect this age-old art of "fortune telling" and have found it to be accurate, helpful and very insightful. Eventually my interests led me to numerology (which I've dabbled in), astrology (which I love but can't do myself) and then many years later I became involved with Tarot cards.

I have participated in and practice different forms of spirit communication to include the Ouija board (yes, it CAN be dangerous but when handled PROPERLY it's a very easy form of spirit communication ... and I am happy to report that I have never encountered anything bad in any of my communications), channeling (through a spirit guide), table tipping (a fun, non-threatening form of spirit communication that still must be done properly) and automatic writing (takes more preparation but the information coming through is similar to channeling).

I have a deep respect for all forms of communication with the spirit world. Our loved ones, when they cross over, truly continue to care and love us, and they really do visit us often! Their biggest challenge is getting us (loved ones here in the physical world) to realize they are "alive", well and thriving. There are so many (over there) who are eager to come through and show their love, give a message of support and encouragement, and there just are too few opportunities for them to do it. Yes, I am saying we need more mediums in the world! Ideally, however, it would be better if people learned how to communicate with their loved ones themselves!

As for how this interest was formed ... well it began at the age of seven when our family (my parents, three brothers and a sister) moved into a haunted old farmhouse. What took place during the seven years we lived in that house has influenced the things I believe about God, religion and all matters spiritual. Seriously, one cannot live for seven years with very active dead people (ghosts!) and not see life from a whole different perspective. Our life experiences influence our views, opinions and beliefs and though I lived in fear for most of those years, I am grateful for the experience.

Young as I was and having no understanding about the workings of the paranormal world, I was often terrified, sometimes curious and never dismissive about such things. It helped to have a mother who was not afraid of ghosts and actually rather enjoyed sharing our home with them. Her fearlessness did help lessen some of my own fears, especially as I grew older. An avid reader, I was forever checking books out of the library (we didn't have the internet back then, darn it) that helped to explain paranormal phenomenon and I even got to a point of making contact with our spectral residents.

The more I read, the more I learned, and the more eager I became to learn more! Thus began my never-ending interest in all things spiritual/paranormal. The material I read exposed me to all manners of subjects involving the paranormal and spiritual aspects of existence. Later, when I began channeling and automatic writing, I learned even more.

Reading, however, wasn't my only passion. I started writing about the same time I started reading, and it was hard to divide my time between the two. I felt driven to write and I can honestly say it was almost an obsession. I couldn't stand having a blank piece of paper in front of me, I just HAD to write a story. To this day, I still have most of those notebooks and pages of partially written stories (before I could finish one story, another was begging to be told!). As I got older, I knew what I wanted to do with my life ... I wanted to be an author. To my way of thinking, there was nothing better to do in life than write stories. I still feel that way, but life keeps pulling me in many directions, capturing my time and attention.

After graduating high school, the reality of the "real" world kicked in. I had to figure out a way to support myself for I wanted to be out on my own, making my own way through life. All that reading had exposed me to the world at large and I wanted to see it. So, I went to travel school in Pittsburg, PA, thinking the best way to see the world was to work in the industry that helped take us there. But after graduating from their course, I ended up back home, where I remained jobless because I had no car, thus no way to get to work. It was a dismal situation because I saw few prospects open to me. And that is how I ended up in the United States military.

At the age of 20, I raised my hand and pledged four years of my life to the United States Air Force. Although my plan was to serve those four years and separate, I ended up staying for 20 years, five months and seventeen days (yes, folks, every single day counts!). Those years led me through the experiences of so many things. The days were challenging, amazing, exciting, boring and oftentimes darn right frustrating, but wow what a ride! The toughest thing I did was go through family separations, the first one happening just after serving a little over a year. I was sent to Korea six months after my son was born and since he couldn't go with me, I didn't see him again until he was eighteen months old! Oh my, was that hard. And the challenges continued. I endured considerable strife with difficult bosses and colleagues (I was often a lone female in the company of many men), the horrors of war, marital messes, financial hardships, family stresses, life messes ... the list goes on! But to be fair, I also got to meet many people (good and not so good), see a lot of places (good and not so good), experience other cultures (mostly good!) and be exposed to many interesting situations and circumstances. My career ended well, with a great husband (he served 28 years in the Air Force), great kids (we are a blended family with 7 kids, and they have given us 15 amazing grandkids), great friends and a great last assignment.

Inevitably, being the writer that I am, all the stuff mentioned above, a good deal of it anyway, has ended up (or will eventually end up) in a blog post. Some of it has, or will, find ways into my stories.

As for my current beliefs, well there's so much more than my childhood experiences that have influenced the things I hold as my truth.

The bible, which I read often during my teen years, is full of supernatural elements: angels, demons, prophetic dreams, omens, etc. I was most fascinated with the story of Jesus and his teachings (so, yes, I hold Christian beliefs close to my heart). The one utterance of his teachings that most captured my attention (paraphrasing here) is: "These things I do, you can do AND MORE!" Wow, what a thought!! Religion is a very broad, fascinating study on its own, and I wish I had more time to study them all, but I don't! As for my standing in that department, I hold many Christian beliefs as part of my truth, but I do not restrict myself to just Christian dogma. For the most part, Spiritualist ideals also align quite strongly with my beliefs.

My life experiences, the things I've been exposed to in one way or another, have inspired stories and once my stint with the Air Force was done in 2003, I finally became an author in 2011 (it took me a few years!) Honestly, it would be impossible for me NOT to write! Sometimes I am so motivated to get a story written that it drives me crazy. I find no peace until it's written. This, I believe, is a good sign that writing is my calling.

Stories come to me so fast sometimes that I barely can keep up. I often feel as if my brain is dictating (or something is dictating to my brain) and my only role is to record it! When I am in the throes of writing a story, there's a thought in the back of my head that wonders where it's all coming from. The fact is, I don't outline or plan the plot, it just comes to me, flowing from my brain to my fingers to the keyboard. I'm the first reader of my story and I find that to be quite a privilege.

So, that's just a little bit "About me". Hey, it could have been longer … I AM a writer after all! (smile)

Reviews are incredibly important for every writer, as they play a big role in helping books reach more readers. If you feel inspired to leave a review, I'd be deeply grateful—it truly makes a difference. Thank you so much for considering it! And even if reviews aren't your thing, I still want to thank you from the bottom of my heart for reading my book. Your support means the world to me!

Feel free to check out my blog/website at www.deborahjhughes.blog

Or send me an email Deborah.hughes@rocketmail.com.

I am active on Facebook and would love for you to join me there at www.facebook.com/AuthorDeborahJHughes/

Wishing you all a life filled with blessings!

www.ingramcontent.com/pod-product-compliance
Lightning Source LLC
Chambersburg PA
CBHW070904260626
47162CB00007B/2563